Every Little Step She Takes

Carolyn Steele Agosta

Published by
Carolyn Steele Agosta
North Carolina
Visit my website at http://www.carolynagosta.com

First paperback edition: September 2010
First Kindle edition: July 2010

Agosta, Carolyn Steele, 1952—
Every Little Step She Takes / by Carolyn Steele Agosta, 1st ed.

Summary: Amanda Long, an eighteen-year-old ballet student begins a dark affair with Richard Gessler, well-known businessman and supporter of the arts. When their affair is discovered, following an attempted murder and a suicide, the resultant publicity causes Amanda to disappear for six years. When she resurfaces, she must reconcile with her family, and finally face Richard on her own two feet.

ISBN 098295610X
Fiction

Printed in the United States of America

This book is dedicated to my husband, Matt, who has always believed in me.

Part One

Chapter One

The first time Richard Gessler gave me a bath, I was still a virgin. He was fifty-two and famous, and I was an unknown eighteen-year-old dance student. The tabloids would later claim that he targeted me from the start, but it's not as simple as that. We had a mutual need and if it was seduction—if it was seduction—then by God, it was sweet.

For everything else that came after, I hold my share of the blame.

A bird in flight, that's how Mom always described me. Vivid, alert, nothing could hold me down. And that's exactly what I was on that afternoon in May—a cygnet, dancing across the floor in Act II of Swan Lake. In less than a week, the opening ceremony for the Gessler Center for the Performing Arts would take place, and our rehearsals were beginning to reflect the pressure.

The dance hall smelled of dust and sweat. Sunlight poured in at an angle from the clerestory windows, revealing swirls of dust motes stirred up by our actions. Julie, the pianist, gave us two bars to catch the beat, and then Heather, Beth, Moira and I linked hands and began again, dancing combinations that moved us across the floor in a series of arcs and diagonals. Our toe shoes provided a muffled clop-clop on the wooden floor, counterpoint to Tchaikovsky's timeless melody.

The combinations were part of me, absorbed through weeks of practice, months of effort. Pointe work, grapevines, *pas de bourré* and *sissones fermé*—all were as natural to me as breathing. Mme. Trohatchev's critical eye caught any mistakes and she called out instructions. "Amanda, your arm should be higher. More arc, girls, more arc, you should be further upstage. Beth, you're late on the *relevé*." Her rebukes didn't matter. We were dancing. Instinctively, I took note of position and angle and spacing, but my heart and soul lifted me through the dance, the music carried me on its back.

For days, he'd been watching from the sidelines. I'd almost forgotten he was there, although Mme. Trohatchev made a point of reminding us before we began. Richard Gessler, Burgess College's most famous alumnus, honored benefactor and patron of the arts. He sat on the edge of a folding chair, elbows on knees, hands lightly clasped. A crisp white curl at the very front and center of his black hair shone as distinctively as a blaze mark on a shiny black stallion. He had the look of a racehorse, too, sleek and well-fed, with a vigor and energy barely contained. He was a man who looked like he was fully alive.

A film crew taped the rehearsal, running to shoot us from different angles, scuttling sideways like crabs to avoid capturing themselves in the mirror. Their movement drew my gaze and I missed my count. The director's voice cut through the music, calling out instructions, invading my senses. There were too many distractions, too many eyes watching. This wasn't like recitals where the audience was at a comfortable distance.

Mme. Trohatchev called a halt for a minute and Heather, to my left, whispered "For an older man, he's pretty good-looking." She nodded in Mr. Gessler's direction. "Rich as hell. I wouldn't mind grabbing a piece of that." I stole a look at him, wondering if he had ever been a dancer, and decided probably not. He was built more like a football player, big and solid. Our gazes met and he smiled, little crinkles appearing at the corners of his eyes.

"Amanda, what are you doing?" Mme. Trohatchev's voice brought me back to attention. I blushed, aware of people watching. "Pay attention," she commanded. "What step are we on?"

Mr. Gessler watched. Everyone watched. I could hear a tiny whir as the cameras honed in on me, the director almost spastic with gestures. He looked so thrilled to finally see a bit of drama. I couldn't speak, flooded with embarrassment and standing there like an idiot, twisting one foot back and forth. The longer Madame waited, the more foolish I felt. *Sissone fermé, entrechat quatre*, my brain told me, but somewhere between my thoughts and my lips the connection broke. I began to sweat. Little curls formed at my temples, those giveaway knots that would forever ban me from being a liar or even a really good poker player.

"Answer me, Amanda. We're waiting." Rather than speak, I did the step, a sideways leap with one foot extended. Madame accepted this with a dour look and indicated we should start again. Pressing my hair back with both hands, I took another surreptitious peek at Mr. Gessler. He continued to watch, and as I placed the back of my hand against my hot cheek, he winked.

"You were embarrassed in there. I'm sorry." Mr. Gessler stood at the foot of the steps of Langley Hall, hands in his pockets, rocking back on his heels as if he were waiting for someone. "I didn't want the filming to discompose anyone, but . . ." I shook my head and gave him a little smile, hurrying down the path with my dance bag slung over my shoulder. He walked alongside, glancing around campus and then at me. "Or maybe you're just shy. Too shy to speak to me?"

I started to shake my head again and caught myself. "It wasn't the cameras. Just my own stupid self. I should have been paying attention."

"You're a good dancer. I can tell. You stand out among the others."

"Oh, I hope not. In the corps de ballet, we're supposed to all look the same. Not draw attention, not pull the eye. It would be like a wrong note in an orchestra." I hurried, wondering why he didn't have something better to do than talk to me. He kept pace, shortening his long stride to match mine. We waited for traffic on College Street and he turned to look down at me, his eyes crinkling at the corners again.

"And how do you like that? Being in the *corps de ballet*, I mean. Seems like it would be frustrating, having to be just like all the rest. Anonymous. Or is that simply part of the dues you pay before becoming a prima ballerina?" His voice, deep and melodious, held only a trace of Southern drawl.

4

"I don't mind." Shrugging, I looked down and away, flexing my foot against the curb. "It's a challenge. Sometimes I think being in the corps is harder than the solo positions. You have to be able to concentrate. You know? Make sure you're doing exactly the same as all the other girls, stay in position, have your timing right and all without having any special attention on you. It's—oh, I can't explain—but you're part of something and you have to give the others strength too, by holding up your end." I could feel myself blushing again. "I guess I'm not saying it very well."

"On the contrary. You just gave me a glimpse into a dancer's life." The light changed and we crossed the road. He kept to my side as we passed cafés and bookstores, discount video places and a shabby second-run movie theater. "Let's stop for coffee."

I looked up at him. "Why?" Then, feeling even more embarrassed, stammered something about having to do homework. He smiled at me, unperturbed and I apologized, feeling more and more foolish. "It's just—I figured the trustees or Chancellor or somebody would be looking all over for you. Why have coffee with me?"

He chuckled. "I enjoy staying in touch with the students. Besides, I'm tired of talking business. Come on, humor an old man. Have coffee." He pushed open the door of Woodbine's and we went in. The narrow diner was only half full at that time of day, but I saw a few heads turn. A grill and counter ran along the left side of the room, booths along the right. We took a seat about halfway back and he ordered coffee for himself. I asked for lemonade "Tell me about yourself," he said.

There wasn't much to say. I was a freshman, three months away from my nineteenth birthday. I'd been dancing since I was five, *en pointe* since age twelve. I hoped to someday dance in New York.

"That's where I live." He sat back, his hands palm-down on the table. "I work in Manhattan and live in Connecticut, but my office maintains an apartment for me on the upper west side, near Lincoln Center. Opera, ballet, theater, concerts, it's all there." He nodded to the waitress who refilled his cup, then fixed his gaze on me again. "And your family? Where do they live?"

I fiddled with the paper wrapper that had covered my straw. "Painter's Creek. Near Charlotte. My mom teaches history at the high school and Dad sells insurance."

"No siblings? Brothers? Sisters? Do you have a boyfriend?" I shook my head and began folding the wrapper into accordion pleats. He watched me for a minute. "When I first saw you, I wondered what you were doing in that class. You look like you're only fifteen, maybe even younger." His voice got deeper, sounding amused, and he put one hand on mine. "And I can see you're very shy."

I dropped the paper wrapper and grabbed my duffel bag. "I really have to go. Term paper due. Thanks for the lemonade, Mr. Gessler." I did not want to embarrass myself further. If I kept babbling, he'd think I was a total idiot.

"Call me Richard. Wait a minute." His hand shot out and grabbed my wrist, gently but without letting go. He looked me up and down, speculatively, as if he were deciding about something. "I want to ask you a question. Do you have someone, a mentor? Is anyone helping you, guiding your career?"

His fingers were still wrapped around my wrist. Tentatively, I pulled back. Mentors were for prima ballerinas, for stars. He wasn't, like, *coming on* to me, was he? "I don't know what you mean. I'm assigned to a faculty advisor, like everyone else at school."

"No, more than that." He stood and I was freshly aware what a big man he was, over six feet tall and wide through the shoulders and chest. "I mean, has anyone taken you under their wing? Helped you to plan ahead, figure out what you'll do beyond Burgess?" His other hand came up and rested on my shoulder. "You remind me of my daughters. I have two, you know, wonderful girls but grown now."

I stepped back, wondering if everyone in the place was looking at us. His hands were still on me, and I thought, this is getting weird. If he didn't watch out, people would think he had a thing for me. Jeez, a middle-aged man like that. Give me a break. "I have to go now."

"Stay in touch." He tipped my chin up so I had to look at him. "Think about it. You have a special gift. A good mentor could make all the difference. With a little assistance, you might be famous someday."

Heat rose through my body and I pulled my hand loose. "I'll think about it." I hurried out of the coffee shop and nearly got blinded by the sun. And a bit dazzled by the turn of conversation. I could still feel his hand on my shoulder. What did he mean? Was he suggesting himself as a mentor? Was he hitting on me? No, that was ridiculous. The poor man would probably be shocked to know I even considered it. But what *was* that conversation all about then?

I felt so different in my costume. The stiff bodice form-fit to my ribs and small breasts and the short white tutu swayed with every movement, and added its own rhythm and weight to each dance step. With my hair pulled back in a knot, my heavy stage make-up, and the smooth feathered hairpiece, I didn't look at all like myself. I appeared older, more confident. Pretty.

We lined up backstage for the dress rehearsal, bouncing up and down on our toes to keep our muscles warm, trying to corral our nervous energy so that it worked *for* us and not against. The stage lights were on, the auditorium dark, just as it would be during the actual performance. When the music came up, we moved out onto the stage in a serpentine line, three running steps and then an arabesque, repeated over and over.

We formed two lines and the Prince walked through, looking for the Swan Queen. Odette appeared, gliding up through the ranks to the front edge of the stage. Although we were posed with our eyes downcast, I couldn't resist taking a peek. Mary Kelley, the finest ballerina in our school, danced Odette's role. North Carolina Dance Theater Two, in Charlotte, had already accepted Mary and she would start with them in just a few weeks. I envied her for having a roadmap, a plan for her career.

Then all other thoughts disappeared as I lost myself in the joy of the dance. Every step, every move seemed to be right, coming from somewhere deep within me. My senses were alert to each nuance, the slightest variation of stance or position or tempo. At the end of Act Two, the swans encircled Odette and the Prince and filed out, leaving them alone onstage for their sad duet. I felt like crying from the beauty of it all. The music reached its final phase, those familiar grieving notes, and Mary Kelley exited the stage in a beautiful *pas de bourré* position, full up on her toes and making tiny sideways steps while her arms moved in graceful wing-like arcs. One final *adieu* to the Prince and the curtain came down. We swans gathered again and moved onstage to take our bows, and then the other dancers and principals did theirs.

Of course, we had no audience to applaud us, but a few of the stagehands, dressers and technicians paused long enough to clap.

The rehearsal was over. Immediately the footlights dimmed and house lights came up. Members of the orchestra gathered their things, the crew yelled to each other about spotlights and curtains and backdrops. Mme. Trohatchev came onto the stage, called us together, and asked us to remain until M. Beloit could speak to us. After-performance jitters claimed me as the adrenaline in my system rushed around with nowhere to go and my muscles, so warm and limber, began to cool down.

"Girls, that was sloppy." M. Beloit, the advanced classical ballet instructor, strode onstage, a sheaf of notes in his hand. "All the endings on the *adagio* were late; people were out of position, and my god, look at you. Your powder is coming off in streaks; you all look like a bunch of zebras." His voice rose. "If you don't give a damn, why should I?"

He turned to Mary Kelley. "What's the matter with you? Don't you even listen to the music?"

She burst into tears. "The tempo was too fast, way faster than in practice. . ." M. Beloit pivoted on one heel and strode off in disgust, leaving the rest of us in silence, glancing furtively at each other. *Monsieur Bellyache*, somebody hissed. I headed for the dressing room where the mood was subdued, girls muttering quietly as they removed make-up and changed into their street clothes. Had we really been that terrible? I hurried to dress, fighting tears all the way.

When I stepped out into the rainy afternoon, someone called my name. Richard Gessler waved at me from inside his car, parked near the curb. "Need a ride?" When I hesitated, he added, "Come on, it's not good for you to walk in the rain after being heated up. You'll get stiff and maybe catch a cold." He leaned over, unlatched the passenger door and swung it open.

The car was an import, some kind of low-slung sporty convertible. I debated for an instant but then, as cold rain swept in a sudden gust, dropped down into the shelter of that warm enclosed space. "Did you see the rehearsal?" I asked. He nodded. "Were we that bad?"

"The man's crazy. Plus a fool to get his principal dancer upset like that." He patted my knee. "You were just beautiful. I could pick you out of the crowd, even with all that make-up.

You're so tiny and your hair is so dark." His hand moved back to the gearshift and we drove off.

"But were we really sloppy?" It was silly, I knew, to keep asking. My voice shook a bit. "It *felt* right. I thought we were okay. I thought we were really good. If I can't tell the difference, then how am I supposed to get any better?"

He looked directly at me. "Oh, Amanda. You're devastated, aren't you? That bastard. He's just a little man with a little power who only knows how to abuse it. Don't let him get to you."

"He's not. Not really." I dug in my pocket for a tissue and blew my nose. "He tries to give us some discipline. We have to do our best. Ballet is very competitive, you know. For every position that opens up in a dance company, there are hundreds of dancers trying out for it."

"You defend his method?"

"No, but I understand why he drives us so hard. Most dancers never get into a professional company at all, and those who do never get beyond the *corps de ballet*. So we have to push ourselves, have to reach for perfection. Being good isn't enough."

My little speech exhausted me and I sat quietly, watching the scenery slide by. Mr. Gessler drove in silence for several minutes, glancing at me from time to time. "I like the way you see things. You're not afraid of a challenge. How do you know when you've given your best?"

I managed a smile. "I don't. Ever. I always think I'm doing my best, while I'm in the middle of it, but afterward there's a part of me inside that says *you could have done better.*"

Rain pelted the window and I thought about all those frustrating times I'd tried to explain things to my dad. "You see, I'm not sure if I can do it. Make a career of dancing. There are so many girls trying to succeed, maybe it's an impractical dream."

"Nonsense. A dream is always worth pursuing." He pulled up in front of my dorm building and turned to me. "If I want something, Amanda, I go after it." Chuckling, he reached out and brushed his fingers against my cheek. "And there haven't been too many times I haven't gotten what I wanted. Go after your dreams, little girl, they're the only things that give life its zest. Don't settle for 'could have been'."

He promised he'd see me at the performance and I ran up to my room, full of thoughts about my future. Could I really make it? Mr. Gessler was so nice. I wished my dad was the kind who doted on his daughter. Instead, we bumped heads over everything and it looked as though our relationship would only get worse.

A month ago, I'd made the mistake of coming home for a surprise visit, only to walk in on an argument between my parents. Mom was in tears, and Dad was red-faced and shouting. When I asked what was going on, they both yelled at me to stay out of it, but eventually I learned the truth. Dad had gotten involved with another woman, Janine Somebody, and Mom had found out.

Since then, they kept saying everything was better, the affair was over, and they'd patched things up, but it sure didn't feel that way to me when I phoned home and heard Mom's depressed voice, and Dad's change-the-subject breezy remarks. They'd both be at the performance, driving the three hours from Painter's Creek just to see me dance. I'd be glad to see Mom but as for Dad, I almost wished he wouldn't come.

The morning of the recital, I woke early. Exams were over, the semester had ended, and students were moving out of the dorms. Already my roommate had departed, leaving behind dog-eared posters and an overflowing wastebasket. I prepared my shoes, sewing on the ribbons, and breaking in the box of the toe with a little mallet. Always, new shoes for a performance. Some girls burnt off the fabric at the tip, to give greater purchase on the floor, but I didn't like to destroy my shoes that way. I'd dreamed of beautiful pink satin toe shoes since I was a little girl and it seemed a sacrilege to make them ugly before a performance even began. Instead, I stitched dozens of tiny crisscrosses to give traction. By the end of the evening, the shoes would have black streaks of rosin and floor wax, but at least they'd be pristine to start.

A knock sounded at my door and a young man from a delivery service handed me a package. Heavy, flat, wrapped in gold-striped paper, it contained a biography of Maria Tallchief, former prima ballerina with the New York City Ballet and George Balanchine's fourth wife. I leafed through the pages, admiring the beautiful photographs. Tucked into the book, a note. *She was his muse, his inspiration to great things. And I look forward to great things from you. Best wishes for the recital tonight, Richard Gessler.*

A flush rose through me, flaming into my cheeks. He was so nice. Why had he singled me out? I was nobody.

Insignificant. Not especially pretty or talented. Sometimes Mme. Trohatchev couldn't even remember my name, but Mr. Gessler made it a point to speak to me several times in the past few days, every time we saw each other at rehearsals. I ran my fingers lightly over his signature. Somebody saw me as special. Somebody *believed* in me. I would remember that.

The recital had ended. Post-performance hubbub filled the lobby and reception area. We milled around, dancers and musicians and stage technicians, pumped with adrenaline and the pride of doing well. Some parents smiled awkwardly, knowing they were only peripheral to the excitement. Others were on the alert for any opportunity to push their child into the spotlight. I could see Mr. Gessler surrounded by administrative types and pointed him out to Mom.

"So that's the famous man." She handed me a cup of punch and some cookies. "Eat these. You look so thin. Don't they feed you here?"

"Looks to me like you've lost a pound or ten yourself."

Mom smiled and shook her head, but her cheeks turned pink. "Not really. Oh, maybe a bit. I've been working in the yard a lot, wait till you see." She turned to Dad. "Won't Amanda be amazed at all the changes out back?"

Dad stood with his arms folded over his chest, leaning against the wall. His gaze had been ranging over the crowd but at this, he looked at Mom. "I guess." Turning to me, he added, "I've had your car serviced—oil change, tune-up. We might need to get the tires rotated though. Call over at Tony's on Monday and see about it." I promised I would and he went back to staring at the crowd, looking like he couldn't wait to leave.

Mom pressed her napkin to her lips. She straightened her shoulders and smiled at me. "Are you glad the semester's over? Or do you feel a letdown now, after all the big build-up? I'm glad you're coming home," she added, the smile running down like a wind-up toy. "I've missed you a lot."

"Oh Mom. . ."

We were interrupted as Mr. Gessler joined us, and I introduced him. "It's a pleasure to meet you," Dad said, shaking hands with vigor. "This is a fine facility you've got here."

"Thank you." Mr. Gessler's had a friendly expression on his face, but his eyes twinkled with mirth as he glanced at me. "This is a fine daughter you've got here."

"Oh. . . yes, of course." Dad patted my shoulder. "We're very proud of her." A photographer from the college, working the crowd, stopped and snapped a picture of the four of us.

Mr. Gessler turned to Mom and asked what I would do that summer to keep in shape. She opened her mouth to answer and Dad said, "I understand you're thinking of expanding. You know, Charlotte offers many fine opportunities for business ventures. It's the banking capital of the south. I have a lot of contacts in the business community." I stared at Dad, my face flooding with embarrassment. The crowd began to shift as the school chancellor stepped to the podium and Mr. Gessler winked at me.

Turning to my parents, he said, "Grace, Steve, I'm glad we met. Hope to see you again." Giving me another wink, he added, "And I look forward to seeing Amanda when she returns in the fall. Have a good summer." He nodded at us and joined the chancellor at the podium.

All the exultation of performance drained away. I'd had enough of family time for one night. Mom followed Dad out of the hall and she kept asking if I was all right. "I'm *fine*, can't you see that?" I snapped, and immediately felt ashamed when I saw the hurt on her face.

After an awkward pause, Mom reached out to stroke my arm, tilting her head a bit to look at me. "We'll pick you up in the morning then. You're all packed, right?" I pressed my lips tightly together, shrugged, and gave her a hug.

Dad had his hands in his pockets, jingling his car keys. "Good night," I said. "Hope you enjoyed the show." We thumped each other on the back as though testing for ripeness, and they turned to head for their hotel. I started to walk to my dorm, but something in Mom's face as she waved good-bye, made me stop. "Hang on," I said. "I'll walk you to the car."

Mom shook her head. "No. I don't want you out in that parking lot all alone after we leave." A reasonable statement, but then why did she look so sad, like she was about to burst into tears? Why did she keep looking away from me?

"What's wrong?" I asked. Mom turned her back, wiping her eyes.

Dad frowned and cleared his throat. "We might as well tell her now," he said to Mom. Mom shook her head violently, and dug in her purse for something—a tissue. "What difference does it make? Give her some time to absorb it tonight, before we drive home tomorrow."

Mom slowly nodded and turned to face me. Her face composed, she squared her shoulders. "Amanda, we have some news."

"Janine's pregnant," Dad said abruptly. "She's pregnant, okay? I didn't expect this. Didn't plan it, but there it is. She's due in October."

Oh. My. God.

I walked into my room, dumped my dance bag on the floor and threw myself on the bed. Janine was pregnant. The thought drove everything else out of my mind. How could this happen? When the phone rang, I half-expected it to be Mom but, instead, I heard Richard Gessler's voice. "We never got a chance to talk," he said. "May I come up?"

I looked at the clock. Nearly midnight. "This isn't a good time. It's really late."

"I'll only stay a minute. Please, I have to leave tomorrow and I seriously would like to talk with you."

Oh, why the hell not? My life was screwed anyway. I pressed the button that unlocked the lobby door and glanced around my room. Labeled cartons were lined up on my roommate's bed, an open suitcase sat on my desk. I whisked a pile of sweaty leotards out of sight, checked myself in the mirror, and opened the door to let him in.

Chapter Two

"Thanks for the book. You were nice to think of me."

"My pleasure." He looked around and smiled. "These dorm rooms are so small. I'd forgotten. At least you have a private bathroom. In my day, we had to share with the entire hall." His glance fell on the book he'd sent. He picked it up and leafed through the pages. "Interesting, meeting your folks. I like your mother, she seems very nice."

"Thanks." We were both silent for a moment as I waited for him to say something about Dad. He didn't. I stood there, an idiot in a daze, as he smiled down at me. I remembered his hand on my shoulder, that day at the coffee shop. "How did you like the recital?"

"You were perfect." He raised his eyebrows as I smiled and shook my head. "Hey, I said perfect. Listen to me. Have you given any more thought to what I said the other day? About you needing a mentor?" He grabbed the straight-backed chair to my desk and placed it facing the bed. He sat, taking my hands in his, and pulled me to sit on the edge of the bed. "I know we didn't really get a chance to discuss it, but I've thought about it a lot. You have so much talent but, if you don't mind my saying it, not much self-confidence. Isn't that true?"

"Well, I . . ." A flush rose up my neck and flooded my cheeks. I couldn't think about that right now. "I'm just a freshman, after all. I don't expect anyone to make a fuss over me."

"Ah, but you should. People should definitely make a fuss over you." His voice dropped a bit. "I certainly would, if you were my daughter."

Yeah, well, I'm not, I wanted to say. I'm the daughter of a man who got his damned secretary pregnant. What a joke, what a situation comedy. Such an old cliché. I could feel depression flooding through me like cold rainwater. And following right behind, a burning anger. My diaphragm rose and I swallowed hard.

"Nothing improper," he added, his voice taking on an amused lilt. "I'd be your guide. Introduce you to new ideas, new experiences. Take you to see some of the best ballets, arrange for you to meet people. There's another world out there, far beyond Burgess College's boundaries. You need to think about where you want to be in five years, in ten."

"Oh, Mr. Gessler—Richard—I can hardly think past this summer."

The thought of going home descended on me like a dark mantle, bringing me back to reality. I pulled my hands out of his grip and balled them into little fists. He watched me for a moment and then asked softly, "What's wrong?"

"It's nothing." I rose and went to the window. Only a few lights showed in the dorm across the road. "I just . . . it's so hard to see into the future. I have a hard time looking ahead. There's no guarantee what tomorrow will bring, no matter

19

how hard you work. I just try to get through one thing at a time." Turning back to him, I placed my hands behind me and leaned against the window ledge. "Maybe you should wait until the fall, see if you're still interested when the new semester begins."

His eyes narrowed a bit as he regarded me. "Why? Why waste a whole summer? Is there something you haven't told me?" I shook my head. "Something between you and your father? I sensed some weird vibes."

I looked away. What good would it do to tell him? Might as well keep our dirty laundry to ourselves. I'd been holding the awareness of Dad's affair for the past month, I could hold the additional bad news, too, couldn't I? "No. Nothing."

"Amanda." His voice made my name sound so different. He rose and put his hands on my shoulders. Little shivers ran down to my elbows. "You can tell me anything. I want to help you. Talk to me, sweetheart. What is it?"

"Accidents happen. They happen all the time, and plans get changed. I don't know if I'll be back in the fall. So many things can change between now and then."

I could hear my voice scaling up in the quiet room. I should shut up, shut up right then, not go on in that shaky pre-hysteria but Mr. Gessler stood there, so close, asking what I meant. His dark gaze bent on me in sympathy. Things change, I wanted to tell him. They change and they're never the same. To my horror, tears welled up and I tried to turn away. He put his arms around me and held me close, and I couldn't help thinking how long it had been since someone had done that. Weeks, months of holding back, keeping my

20

emotions under control, reached their limit and I found myself sobbing into his jacket lapel.

Mr. Gessler didn't say anything, just rocked me back and forth in his arms as I cried, choking and shuddering. He handed me a handkerchief as I began to regain control of myself and I wiped my eyes, backing away from him to sit on the edge of the bed again. I felt exhausted, limp. Self-conscious but not embarrassed. He stood, waiting, until I calmed myself.

"I'm sorry," I finally said. "You don't need to hear my troubles, there's nothing you can do about them anyway."

"Try me." His voice and face were bland, impossible to read, but he clearly expected some kind of explanation.

Why shouldn't I tell him? Why not tell him the *whole* thing? I would be leaving tomorrow. We'd probably never see each other again. Maybe telling a virtual stranger would give me a better perspective, a different viewpoint. Jeez, I had to talk to *somebody* about it. I drew in a deep breath, focused on his silver tie bar, and began.

"I had a brother, Mark. He was twenty. We—oh, we weren't like some TV show brother and sister, you know. Fighting and making up, fighting and making up. We were just—I don't know. Okay. We were okay with each other. He let me play in his band sometimes. He taught me how to whistle. He was always up, always in a good mood. Everyone liked him." I paused for a moment, remembering. "You know, the kind the teachers like, even when he joked around in class." Mr. Gessler regarded me levelly and said nothing, but his gaze bright on mine. "Anyway, last year he was . . . killed . .

21

. in a car crash. A lot of people blamed my Dad, 'cause they had a big argument beforehand. I don't know. Mom says we can't be sure, not to judge. Mark could have fallen asleep behind the wheel, we don't know. He never did stay angry about stuff." I stared down at the handkerchief, twisted in my hands. "And then a couple of months later, Dad . . . he had an affair with his secretary. She's pregnant. They're having a baby next October. I just found out tonight." My voice began to shake again. "So you see, I'm not sure of anything. I might not be able to leave my mom next fall. She's been so strong until now, I can't stand it for her."

"You'd give up your career for her? You must love your mother very much." He sat next to me and took my hand in his. Stroking it, warming it with his own, he murmured, "No wonder you're so upset. You've had a lot to deal with. Poor baby."

His lips pressed for a second against my hair. He was so nice and I was acting like a child. "Sorry I broke down like that. I didn't mean to." I pushed my hair back, sat up straighter, and handed him his handkerchief. "But you can see, maybe I'm not the best candidate to be your protégé. Who even knows if I have what it takes anyway?"

"I think you do. You're overwrought right now. Who could blame you?" He pulled a silver flask from his jacket pocket and looked around for a glass. I smelled the liquor as he poured it into a paper cup, and shook my head. "Drink," he said, holding it to my lips. "It'll settle you down."

I choked on the fiery stuff. Richard crossed his left ankle over his right knee. I sipped at the scotch until it was gone and he poured me a second shot. "What you need," he said, "is to relax. You're all keyed up from the recital still. Take a hot bath. Wouldn't that make you feel better right now?" I nodded, holding the cup with both hands. "I'll run some warm water for you. It'll be good, relax your muscles and help you sleep. When my daughters were little, I used to give them a bath every night before they went to bed. We had a whole ritual. You know, bedtime story, all that. Did your father ever do that for you?"

"No," I whispered. "Dad? Hardly. Not the cozy type. Mom was the one . . ."

"I'll be right back," Richard said, getting to his feet again. "I'll run you a tub right now." He smiled fondly down at me. "And maybe afterward I'll read you a bedtime story. One with a happy ending."

The bath water was very warm. I slid into it slowly as if I were old and fragile, sinking down until the suds rose over my shoulders. My knees came up, making knobby islands in a sea of foam. I closed my eyes and briefly considered falling asleep. When Richard knocked at the door, I barely answered, just mumbled in his direction.

He pushed the door open an inch or two. I could see his reflection in the mirror. He'd removed his coat and tie, unbuttoned his collar and rolled up his sleeves. "How is it? Warm enough? May I come in?"

I nodded. Somehow I had known he would ask. Despite all my earlier doubts, he definitely was interested in me in *that way*. Under the warm water, my nipples tightened. I was naked, in a room with a man older than my father, and I was very slightly drunk. If someone were to walk in at that moment, the situation would be hard to explain. My dad would blow a gasket and I pictured him, face red, mouth screaming, and the top of his head exploding like a cartoon rocket. The image gave me great pleasure. In fact, It gave me *extreme* pleasure.

Richard sat on the closed lid of the toilet, watching me. He had brought another cupful of scotch with him and held it out. It began to taste not so bad. When he spoke, his voice echoed off the bathroom tile. "Amanda, would you like me to wash your hair? I used to do that for my daughters when they were little."

No one had done that for me since I was a child, back when everything was right and I felt cherished. I lay back with my knees up, tightly together, and my arms crossed over my breasts like a nun. He worked his fingers through the thick mop and slowly massaged my scalp, making little circles that became larger circles, and spreading the sweet almond-scented shampoo. I grew dizzy as his fingers smoothed and tugged and slid.

"Black as sin," he murmured. "Where did you get such black hair?"

"My Grandma Connor. Everyone says I look just like her." My mouth felt strange, loose and uncoordinated. I could barely form words. I just wanted to sleep, there in the water. Close my eyes and never wake up. His fingers continued their delicate massage, working over my temples, behind my ears, along my nape. I couldn't help imagining his lips on mine.

"Okay, let's rinse."

I sat up and tilted my head back while he used the sprayer to rinse my hair, separating the strands, and pulling straight the tangled curls. My arms were wrapped around my knees, drawn up against my chest.

"I know you're a good girl," he said softly. "A virgin, right?" I nodded. "And you don't want to do anything wrong. I understand this and think it's great." He picked up the soap, rubbing it between his thick, square palms. "I know your parents love you. They're just in a difficult place right now. You have to give them some space." He began to wash my back, running over the tense muscles, kneading the knots in my shoulders. I cradled one cheek against my knee while he felt every knob in my vertebrae, ran his fingers along each scimitar curve of rib.

Tears of fatigue welled up in my eyes. "We used to be happy," I sniffled. "I think we were, anyway. I don't know . . ."

"Yes, you do." Richard picked up a sponge and squeezed it out over my shoulders, letting the warm water stream down my sides. "Don't keep saying you don't know. I'm sure you know quite a lot. What you want. Why you let me come up here tonight."

"Not really." *Liar, liar, pants on fire.* I knew the reasons, but there were too many, and they were too jumbled together, for me to sort them out. I didn't even want to. I didn't want to think at all.

"I care about you." His voice was quiet, gentle. I gulped, looking at him through more tears. He ran his fingertip along the curve of my jaw and smiled. "And you need me. Don't deny it, sweetheart. There's something between us, we both feel it, and after what you've told me, I can see more than ever that I should help you." Leaning forward, he kissed my cheek. "And it's all going to be fine."

Richard's shirt got splotched with water and he paused to remove it. I looked, curious, at his bare skin. A thick mat of black and white curls covered his chest, tanned a deep brown, matching his face and arms. He lathered his hands again and washed my arms, encircling me with his own as his soapy fingers ran down from shoulder to biceps to elbows, along forearms to wrists, palms and fingers. I felt my knees go soft, let my legs stretch out before me in the tub, and as he brought his hands back up the insides of my arms, my breath stopped for a second. I felt an ache inside, more intense than anything I'd ever experienced. With a shuddering gulp, I sat up straighter and closed my eyes again as he began to wash my breasts. They were small, a mere suggestion of roundness. My nipples, though, were stiff, their usual pale pink aroused to a dark magenta.

"Your skin is so soft," he whispered. "White as milk. You're a little baby, all perfect and new. Flawless. Stand up, sweetheart."

I stood. Bracing my hands on his shoulders, I quivered as he ran his soapy hands down my legs. Gently, he placed my left foot on the edge of the tub. Around and under and over my foot, he slid his hand, brushing against the sensitive arch, knuckling into the ball, slipping between the toes. I was almost delirious by then, drifting along on a stream of languor and desire. His hands moved higher, flexing my calf, caressing my knee, molding my thigh. By the time the back of his hand brushed against my pubic hair, I ached for more. He leaned forward and pressed a gentle kiss to my belly and my knees began to buckle.

"Not yet," he whispered and I briefly considered begging. I began to whimper as he washed his way leisurely up the other leg, over the high round curves of my ass and then between my legs. His fingers paused, then probed, slipping inside me to send my blood in a rush through all my extremities. Each of my fingers, each toe, felt a separate little jolt. And inside, an insistent throbbing. "Please. . ."

Using a sponge, Richard rinsed the soap away and pulled loose the stopper of the tub. The sprayer dangled from the shower head and he turned it on, adjusting the stream to a stinging volley. I gripped both his shoulders again, clinging to him as he scoured my skin with the hot spray. I was in agony, I was in heat, all my senses were fraught with a desire I couldn't even name.

As he wrapped me in a towel and carried me to the bed, my only thought was *Don't stop. Tell me what to do.*

He laid me on the bed, still wrapped in the towel. "You okay?" he asked, stroking my hair as he lay beside me. I nodded, too overcome to speak. Richard put his arm over me and pressed close to my side. "I'm a good father," he said, his breath warming my cheek. "My daughters and I, we're very close. We can talk about anything. You don't have that, do you. You don't have anyone to talk to."

"No," I choked out. "No."

"I'm sorry for you then. A girl should be able to turn to her father for anything."

I closed my eyes but tears seeped out between the lashes. "Can we talk about something else?" My voice sounded ragged and hoarse.

Richard cuddled up even closer. "I'm sorry. I don't mean to worry you. You're such a little thing. I hate to think there's no one to take care of you."

"I can take care of myself." I covered my eyes with my arm. I'd cried in front of him too much already. He pulled my arm down, leaned over, and kissed my eyelids.

"Amanda, I told you I'm a married man. I have a wonderful wife, and I wouldn't ever do a thing to hurt her. Do you understand that?" I nodded. "But there's a part of me—a good part, I hope—that has so much love to give. I don't want to waste it." He leaned up on an elbow so he could look down on me. "Let me hold you, make you my little baby for a while."

He didn't wait for an answer. His arms encircled me; one under my head, the other over my waist, his hand stroking my bare shoulder. "You're so sweet," he murmured as his lips pressed against my forehead. "So sweet." His mouth moved lower, brushing against my eyelid, my cheek. My heart beat so hard I could scarcely breathe. He traced my jaw line with his lips and followed the curve of my throat to where the pulse raced madly beneath my skin. His fingers drew back the damp towel so that my breasts were bared, and my nipples sprang up, feeling incredibly sensitive. Using the flat of his palm, he skimmed their surface, making me moan. I thought I'd die as his mouth closed on the budding tips.

"You *are* my baby," he said. "My innocent Amanda." Gradually he peeled back the rest of the towel and the last of my reserve. "Give yourself to me," he whispered. "Let me be the one to awaken you." His hand, warm and solid, slid down my ribs to my belly, caressed it for one delicious moment, and then explored further, pulling my thighs open, playing with the curly thatch between my legs, probing, seeking. I arched in desire, aching where those warm fingers touched me.

Richard knelt between my legs. "This is mine," he whispered. He pressed his lips against me, making my body rise, making the blood roar in my ears. I moaned and gripped the bedspread with both hands. He wrapped his arms around my thighs, pulling them further apart and pinning me to the bed. "This is for nobody but me." His tongue, warm and wet, traced a path from my knee to my groin, causing me to arch and writhe with pleasure, with desire.

"Richard," I breathed.

"Yes." His delicate assault continued. I twisted and moaned.

"Please. . ." His mouth did indescribable things to me, sensation upon sensation, shock after shock. "*Please,* Richard. . ."

"You're my baby."

"Yes."

"Only mine."

"*Yes.*"

"Say it."

29

"I'm your baby, Richard. I'm yours." My voice sounded thick and guttural, I was burning alive.

He took me then, with just his mouth and lips and tongue and teeth. I cried out, jerking and straining against his hold, feeling something building within me until I shrieked and began sobbing. He held me, wrapping his big arms around me, pressing himself to me as I shook with my first true orgasm. I cried helplessly, with emotional and physical release and Richard climbed on top of me, warming me with his body. "Shhh," he whispered. "It's all right. It's okay, Baby. Daddy's here."

I wasn't sure how long I lay in his arms. It seemed a long time. The air began to grow cooler and he helped me climb under the covers and tuck them up to my waist. Leaning forward, he gently kissed my breasts.

"Damn, I hate to go," he said. "Look at me." With difficulty, I opened my eyes, looked at him up close. I felt suddenly afraid at what I might see, but his eyes, his quirky brows, now seemed familiar. "Kiss me."

I lifted my mouth obediently. Smoothly, gently, his tongue barely flickering against mine, his kiss touched me more deeply than anything else we'd done. I clung to him for the merest instant and then he stood and began getting ready to go. I watched as he fixed his tie, adjusted his jacket, examined his hair in the mirror.

Technically, I was still a virgin. Or was I? It didn't matter; chastity had become a burden to me. At almost 19, I felt a freak, an anachronism. I'd been a virgin on the verge for a long while and only my lack of a boyfriend had kept me pure. Now, what was I? A virgin whore?

"Are you a good letter-writer?" His voice interrupted my thoughts. I tugged the blanket up to my shoulders and nodded. "Here's my private address. Write to me. I want to know how you're doing." I looked at the scrawl on the back of his business card—a post office box number, with the name Richard Smith.

"What are you, a spy or something?" I asked, flipping the card over and back.

He chuckled, and then grew serious. "I mean it. It'll be hard for us to stay in touch while you're home over the summer but I truly want to hear from you." I nodded, feeling diffident, unsure. He was such an important man and I was nobody. Richard sat on the bed and leaned over, one hand on each side of me. "Amanda, it's been a special night. I don't want you to think I make a practice of seducing young girls. Every word I said about this connection between us was sincere. What we just did, that was all for you. I think you needed it, to relax and get all the sad stuff out of your head. Maybe I'm flattering myself, but . . ."

I blushed and shook my head. "You don't have to apologize." I couldn't say anything more. I'd let it happen, after all. I felt shocked at myself but—shame on me—no regret. I just kinda wished he'd leave.

He stood up, slipping his flask back into his pocket, turning off the bathroom light. "I hate to go. I feel like I'm deserting you." Richard opened the door and turned to me. "Remember, now. Write me. Even if I don't answer right

31

away, write to me every day. I want to know everything." He walked swiftly back to the bed and kissed me—tenderly, lovingly. "You're my baby now, okay?"

"Okay." I was his baby. What did it matter anyway? As simply as that, I handed over my life to him like I was loaning an umbrella. I never thought to ask if I would get it back.

Chapter Three

June 3

Richard,

Well, I'm home now and you said to write, so I am. I don't really know what to write about. My summer dance classes don't start till nearly the end of June. I work out every day, keeping in shape. My old dance teacher lets me use her studio for two hours in the morning in return for helping her with clogging classes—little six-to-ten-year-old girls all learning how to double-toe-step.

I also work at Garrick's. You know, the store that sells CDs and DVDs and video games and stuff. What else can I tell you? Have you ever been to Painter's Creek? Probably not. There's not much to say, pretty boring. There's no painter and no creek. I mean there once was a guy named Painter, but he was really a farmer and the creek got so polluted with dye from a textile mill they forced it underground through big culverts. So actually the town is a bunch of farmers with their heads in the dirt. The town started during the Revolutionary War and I think some of the same people still live here. Certainly the same attitudes.

I miss school. Hope you are well and happy.

Amanda

On the first night home, Mom and Dad took me to Whatta-Burger where we always celebrated when I was in high school. Without Mark there to tease and joke, dinner seemed awfully quiet, the only sounds being us chewing and swallowing and asking politely for someone to pass the ketchup.

The next night, Dad sat in the dining room and finished some paperwork and Mom took me to the mall. She told me all about her students and the Color Guard and what the neighbors were up to. She bought me shorts and sandals and shirts and a bathing suit. "We're going to have a great summer," she said. "Why don't I teach you to cook?"

"I went up to Mark's room today. His stuff is all still there."

"Yes, I know." She held my hand a moment and then picked a bit of lint off my shirt. "What would you like for dinner tomorrow? Pasta? I think I have some manicotti noodles. We should have an international food festival this summer. Try recipes from different countries."

The night after that, Dad watched TV and Mom worked in the garden and I went up to Mark's room again. His wrestling trophies and guitar and CD collection all sat there. All clean; Mom apparently dusted and vacuumed each week

34

and I wondered what comfort she found in doing so. I lay on the bed and watched out the window as the sky went from coral to purple to black. If Mark had been there, he'd tell me to get the heck off his bed before I stunk it up, but he'd also crack terrible jokes and sing songs with lyrics from MAD magazine. I wondered if he still existed somewhere besides my memory. Somehow I couldn't picture him in heaven, plucking at a lyre. More likely poking holes in the clouds and dropping hail on unsuspecting mortals. I wondered if Dad ever came up to Mark's room.

Dad's new secretary was a fat, middle-aged, lady named Mrs. Monroe. Janine had been packed off to Gastonia or Shelby or wherever she'd come from and her name never got mentioned. According to my calculations, her pregnancy had begun to show. Maybe the baby already kicked inside her. Dad's baby. *My half-brother or sister.* Jeez.

Hardly any of my old friends were around. They were scattered or working long hours or paired up with someone. And Sissy was busy.

I went to visit her one day. She sat on the rickety wooden steps going up to the trailer, and kept an eye on the two toddlers she babysat, and held Teri on her lap. She looked like hell, with big circles under her eyes and no make-up. I suspected she hadn't even taken a shower that day.

"How's it going?" I asked, trying to act as if the answer wasn't obvious.

"Not too bad." Sissy avoided my gaze. "Dad's been pretty decent to Dave. Considering the ten kinds of holy hell he threw when we told him I was pregnant, that's not bad.

35

Momzilla's still ticked off. She loves to come over and say 'I told you so.' Dave's going to night school, taking accounting and marketing classes and soon as he gets his associate's degree, Dad says he'll give him a big raise. Then maybe we can get a house. Here, hold Teri a minute." She plopped the baby in my lap and ran over to stop the two other kids from fighting over a tricycle.

I looked down at Teri. She chewed on her sun suit strap, slobbering all over herself. It felt bizarre, looking down at her and seeing Sissy's eyes. Maybe a little of Dave, too, around the chin and mouth. What would it be like to have a baby inside of you? And go through all that pain, delivering it? I gave Teri a little hug and looked at Sissy. "You guys don't want to move away from this dead zone?"

She took the baby from me and sat on the steps again. "Not really. I know, I know," she said, looking at the expression on my face. "Painter's Creek is a hole above ground. But it's not a bad place to raise kids." After pulling up her t-shirt, she unhooked the cup of her bra and let the baby nurse. I couldn't help but look. God, it was so weird! Sissy had such a good figure in high school, curvy as a ripe peach and now she barely fit into her jeans and had milk in her breasts, where blue veins showed. "Remember the time we went to Myrtle Beach with the band and those boys jumped from one balcony to another? And one kid threw up into his tuba?" She smiled, relaxing as the baby curled up against her, one small pink foot waving in the air. "I'll never forget the look in Mr. Hartman's face. And remember the bus rides, coming home from competitions, when we were all trying to change out of our uniforms and the guys were trying to get an eyeful?"

"I remember Donna Claymore always *let* the guys get an eyeful."

We both laughed but a little sizzle ran right up over my scalp. Sissy and I had been best friends since we were seven years old. She just turned nineteen last month and already into the 'let's remember' thing, like her life was over, as though all the good stuff had already passed her by. Old people did that. I wanted to jump up from the rickety lawn chair and run straight back to Burgess and start dancing again. No one could tell what my life might hold, but I sure hoped the good things were all *ahead* for me, not already passed up.

June 10

Richard,

Well, I'm still bored. I think about you in New York City, able to go to the Met and the Guggenheim, to see ballet at the State (I hear the Mark Trophé Ensemble is appearing there right now—bright green envy!). But things are not so bad here. After all, McDonald's has come out with an exciting new burger. Ha ha.

I'm not sure what to write you about. The store is okay. Sometimes I'm amazed at how much people spend on this stuff. I bought a DVD of the Royal Ballet performing *Swan Lake*. I've already watched it at least twelve times. Natalia

Makarova dances the lead role. She's wonderful and the corps de ballet is <u>awesome</u>. I've doubled my dance time at the studio, which means I have to get up at 5 am. But I'm willing to suffer for my art!

Hope you are well and happy.

Amanda

PS Are you even getting these letters?

I had too much time on my hands. One day I went down to the basement and practiced piano. Mom came down, smiling all over, and sat next to me on the bench. "Remember this?" she asked, and picked out the tune to *You've Got a Friend.* "First song you learned all the way through."

"Yeah. You blighted my youth, making me learn all those moldy oldies." We ran through our repertoire of duets—*Happy Together, We Can Work It Out, Bye Bye Love.* I blundered into the opening bars of *Bridge over Troubled Waters* before I remembered it had been played at Mark's funeral. Mom put her hand on mine, stilling the keys, and then I shifted to *Baby Grand* and she was okay.

"I've been thinking about this fall, Mom. Maybe I should transfer to UNC-Charlotte, maybe live at home and commute."

"Don't be silly. You love Burgess."

"I know. But . . ."

Mom smoothed my hair back and forced me to look at her. "No. We won't have any of that. I'll be fine. You finish your education as planned and then we'll see. Mollie Taylor always said you were the best assistant she ever had. She might be ready to hire a full-time teacher by the time you graduate." She smiled at me. "How about some lemonade?"

I followed her upstairs, wondering if I'd just made things worse for myself. She didn't want to hold me down but she didn't want to let me go either. Teach? No way! I was between a rock and a hard place. How could I bring up the idea of a mentor and the New York stage now, while she mentally planned a Painter's Creek life for me?

Dad stayed gone a lot. When I thought about it, I remembered he had always been away a lot in the evenings, returning to the office to work or seeing clients, but now every time he left the house I wondered if he went to see Janine. Did Mom wonder about that too? Whenever she wasn't at work in the garden, trying new recipes, or preparing school materials for next fall, she went down the street to the Carrikers' house. Anne's little girl was dying of leukemia. Mom would go down and do whatever was needed; shop for groceries, clean the house, watch the other kids while Anne stayed at the hospital. They had a bond. Anne was losing a child, Mom had lost one. The only difference? Anne had to sit and watch death happen, while Mom hadn't known it was coming at all.

June 18

Dear Amanda,

Yes, I'm getting and reading your letters. Forgive me if I don't answer right away, I've been traveling this summer.

I enjoy your letters very much, but I wonder—don't you date at all? Surely there must be some men in your town who want to ask you out, they can't all be pimply teenagers. Have you ever dated much? I'm so curious about everything. Tell me about your boyfriends.

I'm glad to hear you're keeping up with your training. Never take your eyes off the prize, don't let anything keep you from concentrating on your dancing. Discipline is the key. I'll be back in North Carolina in the fall, look forward to seeing you then.

Best,

Richard

*

Toward the end of June I went to Sissy's for dinner. She cooked hamburgers on the grill and I set the picnic table with paper plates and plastic silverware. The two daycare kids had gone home and Teri slept in a wind-up baby swing in the shade.

"Set four places," Sissy warned, "Travis is coming too."

"Travis?" I hadn't seen Sissy's oldest brother since Mark's funeral when he'd been one of the pallbearers. "I thought he moved to Chapel Hill."

"He did, he's just back for this week. He bought Chris Mauney's '67 Corvette and he came home to trailer it back. Oops, dammit." She swore as a hamburger slithered off her spatula and landed on the grass. Gingerly, she picked it up and

40

blew on it. "What they don't know won't hurt them." She grinned at me and set the burger back on the grill. "Here come the guys now."

Dave and Travis pulled up in Dave's pick-up truck. The late afternoon sun gleamed off Travis' blonde hair. *Golden Boy.* That's what they used to call him, back when he quarterbacked the high school football team. The Golden Boy, dressed in the school colors of green and gold, taking the team to the state championships. I remembered sitting in the stands with Sissy and her parents and brothers, cheering him on. We were in seventh grade and more interested in boys closer to our own age, but I noticed how his arms and hands looked, muscular and capable, as he handled the football. And then after the game, he came up to his folks, tipped off his helmet and the sun glinted on his short blonde curls. He grinned down at me and tousled my hair and my mouth went dry.

As he climbed out of the truck now and walked toward me, I began to have the same feeling. Tongue-tied, awestruck. A kid looking at a king.

"Amanda! How are you?" Travis hugged my shoulders and pecked my cheek. "How was school?"

"Um," I said, eloquent as ever. "Okay, I guess."

He turned and went into the kitchen. I could hear him and Dave wash their hands at the sink, and get a couple of beers from the fridge.

"He leaves tomorrow." Sissy gave me one of her looks. She put the finished burgers on the table and went inside for the potato salad and tea.

Everyone fell on the food like a pack of hyenas. Teri woke up and Travis put her on his lap while he ate. He seemed a natural as an uncle, talking to Teri in some unintelligible language, smooching her soft, chubby cheek. He looked good. I tried not to stare. He'd filled out some since high school and his hair was sun-bleached practically white while his sideburns were strawberry blonde. I felt a flush rise up in my face when I looked at his blue eyes and saw how his red-gold skin stretched tight across his cheekbones.

He looked at me and grinned, strong white teeth showing. "How are your folks?" I almost choked before I remembered he'd been out of town and probably hadn't heard about Dad. "What?" he said to Sissy who must have kicked him under the table.

"They're okay," I finally managed. "Busy. You know."

Giving Sissy a mystified look, he let the subject drop and Sissy began an animated discussion of the new restaurant on Main Street. After dinner, she took the baby indoors to change her diaper and Dave cleared the table. Travis sat on the wooden swing at the edge of the tiny patio and patted the seat next to him. "What's up?" he said as I sat down.

"Nothing."

He looked at me, and then set the swing going with one push of his foot. After a few minutes, he began speaking of a variety of things—his job, people we both knew from school, the high school athletes he coached on the side. "Mostly guys who've been sidelined by injuries," he said, rubbing his knee, "helping them get back up to speed." He talked about his brothers, Mack and Johnny, one going to college in Colorado, the other stationed at Camp LeJeune. "We're getting scattered all over. I'm glad Sissy and Dave are staying near the folks. Dad's health isn't the best." He laid his arm across the back of the swing and rubbed my shoulder. "You still play guitar?"

"Not much. I can't seem to get into it."

"You were good, you shouldn't stop." The swing went back and forth some more. I pulled my feet up and wrapped my arms around my knees. "Remember the time Mark's band played for the street festival in Lincolnton?"

I smiled. "Oh jeez. Up on that flatbed truck?"

Travis chuckled. "And Mark tried to make like Lenny Kravitz or something, picked up the mike, swung it back—"

"And fell off the truck! Shoot, yes." I started to laugh. "In the middle of singing *American Woman,* down he went, mike, guitar, everything. Nearly took the amp with him. He got a standing ovation."

"Yeah. And he bowed, like he'd planned the whole thing. Remember what he always would say? Re-e-l-a-a-x-x. Everything's—"

"—co-pathetic." I finished the phrase for him. "Yeah. Mark didn't get riled over much." My smile coasted to a stop. "I really miss him."

"Me too. He used to watch me work on my car and tell terrible jokes."

"Mark-jokes, oh man, they were awful! What was that one about the three-armed Tilt-a-Wheel operator? And remember the country song titles? Like *I Swore to Love Her Truly, but Her Falsies Let Me Down.*"

"And those games he made up. Spoonsies. ElbowFight."

43

"Liar's Baseball."

"And the stuff he ate. Peanut butter and mayonnaise sandwiches with potato chips in the middle."

"Ranch dressing on his pizza."

"Milk in his ginger ale."

"Underwear on his head."

Travis hugged me and I damned near started bawling but Sissy came out of the trailer crabbing about the faulty air-conditioner and saved the day. We sat and talked and played with the baby until the sun went down. As I hugged Sissy and got in my car to go home, Travis said, "Tell your folks hey for me." I drove off knowing Sissy would fill him in about my parents. She wasn't a gossip but Travis was family, he had a right to know.

Instead of going straight back to Mom's, I headed out into the countryside north of town. When I got to the old closed-down gas station, I parked the car and got out.

The moon shone like a big silver plate in the sky, leaving everything on the ground in shades of grape. A too-familiar walk; across the road, up past the house with the white fence, and then around the curve. My shoes on the pavement sounded loud compared to crickets and the whoosh of traffic half a mile away. I followed the sharp curve of the road where it was badly designed, slanting down where the turn banked, instead of up. Mark had been familiar with it. Driven it a million times. Maybe that was the problem, he didn't pay enough attention. Or his mind had been on other things. No skid marks, suggesting he'd either been distracted or had fallen asleep behind the wheel.

We would never know what caused the accident; that was one of the worst parts. Could I hold Dad to blame, not knowing the truth? I was *mad* at him, for sure, angry that Mark's last night alive had to be messed up by a stupid argument, but hold him accountable? He and Mark argued a lot; they were both bull-headed. They still got along all right the rest of the time. But, oh, Dad's behavior since then made it so easy to stay mad at him.

I sat on the bank where morning glories climbed a telephone pole, right where his car left the road and flipped over twice. The area was lush with kudzu. Mark died instantly, they told us. Wasn't wearing his seatbelt. Hit the roof of the car, broke his neck and died immediately, no pain. Maybe they thought we'd feel better, believing that. No one was quite sure how long he'd been there, how much time elapsed before another car came along and saw the headlights gleaming through the green leaves of the kudzu vines.

I sat for a while, thinking about him. Remembering his freckles, and the little notch in his ear, and the way everyone had to leave the room when he took off his socks. The afternoon before his argument with Dad, Mark had been practicing a riff he'd just learned off a Clemency CD. I got my guitar out and tried it too. Mom called us to dinner and he said, "Don't worry. We'll work on it later." During dinner, an argument started between Dad and Mark. He'd been skipping out on his classes at the community college. If I'd known that afternoon would be the last I'd spend with Mark, oh god, all the things I'd have said and done. But it was too late. I couldn't change the ending.

45

There had to be a way to put my family back together. I drove home, parked in the driveway and walked into the house. Dad sat in the living room, reading his paper. Mom sat in the bedroom, stitching away on some embroidery. Televisions on in both rooms; the same show, same sitcom with over-the-top acting and canned laughter. I clicked off Mom's TV and sat on the footstool, taking her slippered feet into my lap. "Remember when I used to rub your feet and scratch your back?"

She smiled. "Your grandma always said I'm half-cat." I began stroking her soles, the high arches, but she tensed and pulled back. "I think I'm too tired tonight, hon." The smile faded from her face and she set aside her cross-stitch. "How about some lemonade?"

Mom hurried to the kitchen, passing Dad in his chair, and I lingered to ask him if he would like something to drink. "Maybe we can talk her into cutting us a slice of cake, too," I said, leaning over his shoulder. "What are you reading? Stock reports? Bor-r-r-ing." I grinned down at him but he avoided my eyes and turned the page.

"Please, Amanda, you're in my light."

"Is there anything good on TV later? I could make popcorn." I perched myself on the footstool, giving him my most winning smile.

He just rustled the paper and muttered, "There's never anything good on during the summer. Only reruns."

I waited a few seconds longer, but he didn't lower the newspaper by an inch, so I went into the kitchen, slumping down in my seat and frowning at the frost-beaded glass of lemonade my mother had poured. "He's such a crab."

Mom set a slice of pound cake in front of me. "He's got a lot on his mind."

"I'll bet."

"Please, honey, don't make this harder. We're under a little financial pressure right now. Nothing terrible, but-"

"Do you have enough for my tuition? If you don't, I could pitch in. I've got Mark's insurance money." It had never occurred to me to worry. "Is business bad? Dad's not going to get laid off or anything, is he?"

"No, no. Don't worry. You save the insurance money, keep it for a nest egg after you graduate. Dad feels he has to make some provisions for the baby. Which is only fair." Her eyebrows raised in emphasis. "He's trying to do the right thing."

"A little late."

"What would you have him do? Janine will have to raise that baby alone; the least he can do is provide some financial support. Or should he compound one error with a worse one?" Her eyes met mine levelly. "We're all doing our best, Amanda. Some things might be hard for you to accept, but I wish you'd try. Have some compassion on our mistakes." She kept her voice low, yet I could almost feel Dad's ears strain to hear us from the other room.

The damned tears were gathering again, so I crammed cake into my mouth. It tasted like sponge rubber and I had to force myself to swallow. "I don't see where you've made any mistakes, Mom, but Dad—he could bend a little. He hasn't said one nice word to me since I've been home."

"Have you said any to him? What do you expect? He knows you blame him."

"For the mess with Janine? Duh. Who else should I blame? For gosh sakes, Mom, how can you be so accepting? Don't you get angry? Don't you want to just slap him?"

Mom took my hand in hers and spoke again, her voice lower and even gentler than before. "Honey, there are two sides to everything. I'm not perfect either. Try to understand. He's the only dad you've got and I don't want to see you two go through the whole summer at odds with each other. Maybe he doesn't understand what you need. Please—"

"Preach to him, Mom." I pulled loose and allowed my voice to rise. "Let him admit it, then, if he's so sorry. Let him start showing you and me one atom of kindness and maybe then I'll believe. *Maybe.*" I stormed out of the kitchen and went to my room, ignoring Dad as I passed by and slamming my door. It had always been this way, always. Mom being the placating soul in the midst of the uncivil war of Dad's and my so-called relationship. It was as though someone had assigned us roles long ago and we could never change character. It made me sick.

July 1

Richard,

Sorry I haven't written in a while. Classes started at the summer workshop and I'm trying hard, concentrating. Keeping my eye on the prize, like you said. Still work at the music store, too, so pretty busy.

You asked me about dating. I'm not. Haven't met anyone I would even want to. Never did date much. In high school, we did a lot of group things. I was in the Color Guard for the marching band (I know, cheesy) and a competition dance troupe, so that took up most of my weekends and sometimes my brother would let me sit in with his band. He had a guitarist who got drunk a lot so whenever he didn't show up, Mark would let me play rhythm guitar and sing back-up. It was pretty cool, we used to play for school dances and backyard parties and sometimes we even got paid.

So I didn't date a lot, except my senior year I had a boyfriend named Buzzy, a great boyfriend until he got into X-treme moto-cross and always ended up in the hospital or hopping around on crutches. At Burgess, nobody dates much. Half the guys are gay and the others have lines of girls fighting over them. Plus nobody has any money so we just hang around in a group and do cheap freebie things. I really miss school.

Hope you are well and happy,

Amanda

Anne's daughter died on a Wednesday night. Mom spent the last hours at the hospital waiting room with the Carrickers' other two children asleep on a couch, while Anne and her husband sat vigil with their little girl. In the morning, Mom was pale but calm, giving me instructions about Dad's dinner while she prepared to pick up Anne's relatives from the airport and help with the details for the funeral.

"Do you think you can broil some chicken for him?" she asked, looking in the fridge. "And there are some salad fixings, and maybe you could . . ."

"For crying out loud, Mom, hasn't he heard of Burger King? Let him eat out, it's not that big a deal."

She frowned at me. "Amanda Connor Long, what's the matter with you? I'm asking for a little help. For heaven's sake, Anne's daughter has died and I'm trying to—"

"I know, Mom. I just think Dad could live without a hot meal for once. I mean, Jesus! Is he incapable of fending for himself?"

Mom took one step toward me, her eyes narrowing. I flinched and she turned away. "Don't use the Lord's name," she said, her voice shaking. "You know I hate that. Go clean your room."

I stomped off to my room, slamming the door behind me. It was a slamming kind of summer. A few minutes later, I could smell chicken cooking in the pan.

The day of the funeral, we all dressed up in our darkest, hottest clothes and went to church. Strange, to be in church again after so long. I'd stopped going after Mark died, didn't want anything to do with a God who let something like that happen. The place was packed. Everyone looked mournful,

50

taking furtive peeks at Anne and her husband. Anne appeared to be sleep-walking through it all. The coffin was so small, I couldn't stand it. I finally had to sneak out the side aisle and go outdoors so I could breathe.

After that, at the cemetery, I didn't feel like talking with anyone. Mark's grave wasn't far away; I could see a spray of flowers on it. Roses from our garden, it looked like. I peeked at Mom. She stood quietly, wearing her navy crepe dress with the collar like a little cape over her shoulders. Dad stood next to her in his good gray suit. His hands were in his pockets and Mom held her purse. They didn't touch. They didn't look at each other or at Mark's grave. They might as well have been strangers. I turned and walked away.

*

July 23

My Dear Amanda,

I enjoy your letters so much and am proud of your hard work. You haven't mentioned your parents so I guess things are going better.

I find it hard to believe you've done so little dating. From what I remember of the girls in the arts program when I was in college, they were pretty wild and adventurous. And you played in a band, too! Come on, you must have plenty of stories to share. What about you and your boyfriend? What did you do together? I'm amazed you're still a virgin, so many kids start sleeping together in high school now. Did you and your boyfriend go part of the way? Did you let him touch you? Did

51

you ever let him do to you what I did? Did you touch him? Be my good girl and tell me.
With affection,
Richard

July 26
Dear Richard,

I think we might as well stop writing each other. I don't have any juicy stories for you, sorry. Remember, I'm just this stupid kid who lives in a stupid poky town and you know what? I'm pretty much sick of grown-ups and parents and other advice-givers right at this moment so why don't we forget the whole thing? Have a nice life. Goodbye.
Amanda

Chapter Four

I began sleeping up in Mark's room. I don't know what I thought would happen. Maybe that Mom would yell at me or Dad would complain. I busted for a fight but nobody would stand up to me. Whenever I made an outrageous remark, they'd just walk away, as though they were in a conspiracy to ignore my behavior. I couldn't wrestle with fog. That was what it felt like, bullying my way through a cloud of fog that didn't respond in the slightest, didn't change or fade or go away. It just sat there, blanketing my world, muffling noises, obliterating landmarks, covering everything with a benign gray.

The Summer Olympics started. I moved a portable TV to my room and watched, lying on the bed stomach-down, my face a couple of feet from the TV screen. The athletes fascinated me. What was it like to spend your whole life preparing for the Olympics and have everything rest on a three-minute gymnastics routine or maybe a dive that ended before the audience could even take a deep breath? I envied their passion and drive. I pondered their futures. Even if they won, how did a person go through the rest of his or her life after the intensity of such an event? And, jeez, what if they lost? How could they go home to face the disappointment of their friends and family?

One evening Mom called up the stairs that I had a phone call. I turned the sound down on the TV and picked up the cordless phone.

"Amanda?"

Oh, that voice. "Richard?" I gasped. He chuckled and the sound sent a little shiver of something all over me. "I can't believe you called."

"I thought I'd better after that last letter you sent. Sounds like things aren't going so well. How are you?"

I swallowed hard. "Okay, I guess."

"Really? I figured you were pretty angry with me."

"I don't know. Not angry, but . . ."

His voice was warm, deep. I could picture him smiling into the phone. "I wouldn't blame you if you were. I was out of line. It's simply that I want to know everything about you."

"Why did you call, Richard? Doesn't seem like there's any point."

"I was worried. You sounded pretty down. How are things going at home?"

I sat up on the edge of my bed. "Oh, you know. Longs spells of drought-like conditions interspersed with sudden electrical storms." My attempt at humor ended suddenly as my voice broke. "Occasional light hail," I managed between tears. "Acid rain."

"Oh sweetheart, I was afraid of that." His voice grew even softer, even more tender. "I wish I was there right now. I'd take you in my lap and let you cry as long as you need to. Tell me what's wrong; what sparked that letter of yours. Did you have a fight with your dad?"

"Oh, he . . . I told a friend of mine about how, you know, Mom and Dad never talk. And he said I should try to get them to go to counseling. So I got all excited about the idea and even found a family counselor and talked Mom into going and then Dad wouldn't."

"Who's this friend?"

"Oh, this guy I know, Travis, he lives down the street. Anyway, Dad said—"

"How old is this Travis? Do you like him?"

"Richard, he's just a guy I know. Would you listen? Dad said no way to the counseling idea. They already tried that after Mark died and it didn't help and besides, he wasn't the one who moped around acting all tragic. Well, that made me mad, because Mom hasn't done that, she's stayed busy. So I jumped to her defense and then Dad goes 'and you need to stay out of this, I can just imagine what you'd tell a counselor and besides aren't you too busy with your fabulous classes anyway?' Unbelievable! He's such a schmuck. So I told him to bite me."

Richard roared. "Did you really tell him that? Oh my god, that's so funny." After a few minutes he said, "No wonder you were upset. I apologize for bothering you with foolish questions while you were dealing with such serious problems at home. Forgive me?"

That was a new one on me. An apology from a grown man. "I guess. But don't ask me any more creepy questions, okay? I mean, those really scored high on the *ick* factor."

"I promise. Listen, I want to talk with you again. When's a good time to catch you when nobody else is home?" We

55

arranged a time for him to phone and I hung up. Later when I went downstairs, Mom asked me who called.

"Someone from school," I told her, pouring myself a glass of juice. "Checking up, making sure I'm doing okay over the summer."

"Isn't that nice? I hope you told them how hard you've been working, how much effort you've been making."

"Yeah, Mom. I did."

August came, bringing a lot of rain and thunderstorms. I kept my schedule tight, getting up early to exercise before class, working after class, and generally staying away from home as much as possible. The store stayed open until ten most nights. I liked working there, I enjoyed straightening stock or running the cash register. A lot of guys shopped there, from middle-schoolers rancid with acne to middle-agers with bald spots and gray ponytails. I thought about Richard's question—asking why I didn't date—and I had to admit, the answer remained the same: nobody I saw interested me. Yes, some of the guys were cute, but whenever I talked to them, they seemed so shallow. Immature. Caught up in their pick-up trucks and video games and action movies. I couldn't imagine any of them watching *Swan Lake* or being the slightest bit interested in ballet.

So after store hours were over, I went home and spent my evenings up in Mark's room, practicing the guitar and playing along to his old CD's. I wasn't terribly good, but I played real loud and felt some satisfaction in knowing I made it hard for Dad to hear his news programs. Nice to know I could do my bit for family disharmony.

One morning Dad asked me to follow him to the auto dealership so he could leave his car to have the transmission worked on. Afterward, I drove him to the office and decided to make one more try. Be nice, I told myself. Keep my temper. Give him a chance. "Dad, I know we've been on the outs all summer and I'm sorry about that. Dealing with all this is hard for me. What's going to happen after the baby's born?"

I could hear an angry little puff of breath. He looked out the side window. "Nothing will change, Amanda. I'll still be married to your Mom; I'll still be your Dad. Everything will continue just as it is."

"Just as it is?" We were already at his office. I pulled into a parking place and looked at him. "Do you think that's good enough? Dad, we hardly speak. You and Mom hardly speak. How can you go on like this?"

"I'm not sure I can." He looked away, his eyes cold and bleak. "But I don't think there's any other choice. Sometimes that's the way life is." I watched him, open-mouthed, as he got out of the car and pulled his briefcase from the back seat. He leaned down and looked at me through the open car door. "Amanda, I'm not going to hash it out here and now, in the middle of Main Street, but suffice to say there's a lot you don't understand. This whole thing really isn't any of your business—it's your mother's and mine." He took a deep breath and let it out slowly, then flashed me a thin smile. "I know you're upset, but for now you'll have to butt out." Then he closed the door and was gone.

I went down to the basement where Mom ironed shirts and pillowcases and nightgowns. I sat on a little stool she'd made for me when I was four, embroidered with a picture of a Raggedy Ann doll and my name in chain-stitch. "Mom, I've tried to talk to you and Dad all summer. I'm worried. What will you two do when I go back to school? You guys seem so distant from each other; in fact, Dad seems actually angry, although what *he's* got a right to be angry about, I don't know."

"Now, hon, you've got to understand. This isn't easy on your dad either." She hung up one shirt and reached for another. "I think your idea about the counseling is a good one, though, and Steve has finally agreed to go with me. A marriage counselor, not a family counselor, but it's a start. We begin sessions next month. So you see? You've helped." They were pleasant words, but as she said them, she kept her head bent, eyes on her work. She didn't meet my eyes, she didn't smile, her face remained taut and drawn.

"Mom. . ."

"Honey, don't. Please let me and Dad work this out on our own. Stop pushing on the bruise." She put the iron down and looked at me, her eyes filled with tears. "You need to back off. This constant picking doesn't help. I love you, but I can't bear your sympathy. Please, Amanda. Give it a rest."

Summer workshop classes ended and I began packing to return to school. As a sophomore, I would be allowed to bring my car and, at Richard's suggestion, decided to get an apartment off-campus instead of staying in a dorm again. "You're going to be working so hard," he said, "I know what dorms are like, never quiet, nobody gets any rest." I argued my case with new-found courage until Dad gave in and arranged for me to rent a single room and bath in an old house out Merriman Road.

For my birthday, Mom and Dad gave me an electronic keyboard so I could play with headphones and not disturb anyone. I decided to bring my guitar to school as well, figuring I shouldn't lose what progress I'd made over the summer. I had a job lined up in town at another Garrick's, a fresh supply of dance clothes and shoes in my suitcase, everything set to go.

One evening, after going over packing lists yet again, Mom said she and Dad were going out for a walk. I was glad to see them go. Not only because it meant they might even talk, but because I wanted to think.

Mark's old bedroom was long and narrow, just a finished-off attic. The stairs came up at one end and in the middle, past the stair enclosure, was a big closet. Walk-in type, with shelves on one side and hanging space on the other. Most of the time, the door hung slightly ajar. I opened it all the way and snapped on the overhead light. The far wall, facing me, was blank and I knelt down to lift away the wooden strip of floor molding, held in place by a single tack. Setting it aside, I felt for the crack at the bottom of the painted plywood wall. For a moment, nothing moved and I thought perhaps we'd been found out after all, but then the section gave and I opened the secret door.

Under the eaves some additional attic space existed, that the builder never used. I got on my hands and knees and crawled in, sniffing the familiar scent of musty wood. There wasn't much light, only what came through the small opening. I could see Mark's old stash of girlie magazines, thick with dust. A battered tin ashtray and disgustingly moldy pack of Marlboros were next to the cushion I'd rescued from a discarded sofa when I was ten.

It seemed bigger then, our secret hideaway. Mark and I would play up there on rainy days, hidden from Mom, safe from prying adult eyes. There, Mark taught me to smoke a cigarette, the cool way, with chin tilted up and eyes half-closed. There, we played interminable games of Star Wars, where he was Han Solo or Luke Skywalker, and I always had to be Boba Fett. I remembered lying on that cushion, reading *Adam of the Road* with a flashlight while Mark made designs in the wooden rafters with his penknife and Mom and Dad argued downstairs. *Ree-laxxx*, he'd say whenever their voices got louder and I'd look up in concern. *Everything's co-pathetic.*

I sat hunkered down, arms wrapped around my legs, and thought about Richard. He had phoned earlier and our conversation still ran in my head. "Do you ever think about the night we had together?" he asked. "I do, all the time."

"I don't know. Sometimes."

"Does it make you excited?"

"I don't know." Even as I said it, a little buzz ran through my veins.

"Amanda, you do know. Tell me what you think about it."

I hadn't been able to answer. Suffocated with emotion, I could barely speak and Richard went on to tell me what he thought. "You're nineteen now, becoming a woman, with a woman's feelings and desires. Maybe you don't desire *me*, but probably one day soon you'll find someone you will. Are you ready for that? I love thinking of you as a little girl, but it's also time to grow up, make decisions. I hope you'll feel like you can talk it over with me."

"But Richard, you're married. We shouldn't be together like that."

"Does that mean you've thought about it? You've imagined being with me?"

That was what worried me most. I *had* thought about it. Some nights in dreams, Richard lay right there in bed with me, holding me in his arms, making me come alive. It was wrong to think of him that way, to pretend in my mind he was free. What drew me to him? He was so much older, middle-aged. *Married, with daughters even older than me.* And yet, he turned me on. No one else had even come close, and every time I thought about the night in my room, a little electric charge zinged deep inside.

So I sat in the attic room and prayed for Mark's advice. "If you're anywhere in the cosmos right now, I could sure use a word." Not that I really expected it. If Mark did exist somewhere, he was probably hot-rodding down a highway, listening to Aerosmith at full volume and making up new words to the songs.

61

Nothing. Not a word, not a whisper. Not even a terrible Mark-joke. If he was anywhere around, he kept mum. With no one else to turn to for advice, I would have to rely on myself. As Richard had said, I needed to make some decisions.

"Phooey," I muttered as I climbed out of the crawlspace and fastened the 'door' shut again. "Where's a good Jedi master when I need one?"

My 'last supper' was breakfast. Mom made waffles for a special treat. She even had boysenberry syrup. All my stuff was in my case and ready to go. It was like a scene from *The Wonder Years*, or maybe a Hallmark Hall of Fame special. The three of us in the sunny kitchen, eating together for the last time until Thanksgiving break. A big pitcher of orange juice sat on the table, I could smell coffee, and Mom's china plates gleamed. We sat there, scarfing up waffles and sausage, making little clinking sounds with our silverware. In the background, the radio played softly. The oldies channel, Seals and Crofts singing *Summer Breeze*. Perfect.

I found my moment, finished the last sweet bite of waffle, swallowed some juice, and began.

"Mom, Dad, I have something to say."

They both looked at me, surprised, maybe a bit wary.

"Mark."

They stared at me.

"Mark. You remember him? That guy who used to live here? I've been thinking about this all summer and I'm pretty sure he would hate what's been happening here."

Mom looked at Dad and cleared her throat. "Amanda, I know you must have some reason..."

"You bet I have a reason. *Mark*, Mom. Your son. The one whose bedroom is still practically a shrine. The one whose grave you sneak out to and leave flowers on. He died and ever since, we've all been falling apart, letting this family implode like some used-up old building no one wants anymore."

"I don't know why you need to bring this up right now." Mom fiddled with her coffee spoon. "It's your last morning home."

"And I can't pretend any more. I'm not that good an actress. You, on the other hand, make Meryl Streep look like a rank amateur."

"Hey." Dad set his coffee cup down. "Drop the sarcasm and apologize to your mother."

"I will if you will. Have you, yet? Or are you going to keep calling her a martyr?"

"You forget who you are, young lady," he said, his face reddening. "We're the parents, you're the child, and you have no right to talk to us like this."

"Then act like parents. I swear, you two are worse than little kids, hiding from the facts like they're a boogey-man. I've tried all summer to get you guys to talk about this like grown-ups, but you won't talk! We're a family, you're married, doesn't that mean *anything*?"

"Listen, young lady. If you think you can get away with—"

"Oh, why don't you—"

"Stop it!" Mom gripped my hand. "The two of you, just stop it! Can't we have one day without all this bickering?" She put her hands to her temples. "After all we've been through, is a little peace and harmony too much to ask? Hasn't this kind of arguing cost our family enough already?" Dad's head whipped around. He stared at her and started to speak but Mom turned to me and begged, "Please, let's drop the whole thing."

I saw red. "Drop it, Mom? Okay, suuuuure, I'll drop it." I picked up my plate and threw it to the floor. "How's that?" I threw my glass against the wall, where it left a satisfying blotch of juice. Mom stared at it, her mouth hanging open. I shocked myself a little, as well, but these were drastic times. "This is my family, too. You can't keep shutting me out! For God's sake, what's the matter with you people? We could talk about stuff if you'd only try. But no, you won't talk, you won't listen. Jeez, if Mark had known we'd end up at each other's throats like this, maybe he wouldn't have had his accident. Maybe he'd have just shot himself instead."

My dad reached over and his hand met my cheek with a resounding smack. The chair and I toppled sideways, landing on broken china. A shard bit into my shoulder and my cheekbone hit the floor. "Way to go, Dad," I mumbled, tasting blood inside my mouth. "Two points."

The color drained from his face. I saw it, saw his skin turn greenish-white before Mom pushed him out of the kitchen. She helped me up, hissing between her teeth when she saw the blood on my lips and arm. I got dizzy then and she pulled me over to the sink where I threw up all the waffles and sausage and especially the boysenberry syrup.

"Oh, Amanda, why did you do that?" she whispered. Mom pressed a wet cloth to my mouth. "It won't help anything."

"Just wanted to end the summer with a bang," I slurred, gagging on blood and bile. "Break up some of the damned silence around here. But hey, don't worry. At least we're not bickering now."

Chapter Five

The first week of classes, temperatures hovered at the hundred mark. I awoke sweating, went to sleep sweating and in-between drank gallons of water. My deodorant worked double overtime and I bought the giant economy-sized container of talc.

In each new class, I endured the stares at my bruised cheek and split lip. I learned to introduce myself as Amanda Long, holder of the Klutz Award in Advanced Facial Contact with Runaway Basketballs. My lie was not only accepted, people seemed to go out of their way to make friends. Sometimes, I decided, a falsehood was worth the guilt trip.

On the second Monday of the semester, I attended a class in ballet technique, a class in pointe, and a music perspectives course. Afterward I worked at the store, ate low fat ricotta cheese on celery for dinner, and went back to the campus media center to watch a Minkus ballet on DVD. By ten o'clock, when I got back to my apartment, I was sweaty, itchy, and the blister on my left foot stung. The rickety exterior staircase that led up to my second-floor room smelled like pigeon poop. After a shower, I slipped naked under a single sheet. The air conditioning was a joke, but an oscillating fan ran back and forth, sending puffs of air that at least moved, even if they weren't actually cooling.

Too jazzed to sleep, with thoughts about class that morning dancing through my head, I jumped when the phone rang.

"Hey, sweetheart. How's my girl?"

"Richard! You got my letter."

"And you've started classes. How are they going?"

"Good. Tough. M. Beloit is a lot stricter than Mme. Trohatchev, but I like Merle Berry, the pointe teacher. She's fantastic, used to dance with the Toronto Ballet and she's so nice."

Richard chuckled. "I can see you're happy. It's a nice change." His voice deepened and got softer. "Did I wake you?"

"I wish. It's too hot to sleep. I'm lying here thinking up horrible tortures for this stupid housefly that keeps buzzing around. Do you think that death by hairspray would be considered cruel and unusual punishment?"

Richard chuckled again. "Tell me, have you thought any more about my proposal? About being your mentor?"

I rolled over to a cooler spot on the sheet, laying on my back and pointing my toes in the air. "Yes. I'd like having someone I can go to for advice. Mom has always been enthusiastic but she doesn't realize . . . she reacts like a mom, not a coach. Instead of being tough, she's protective." I could hear a rustling sound at the other end of the phone. "What are you doing?"

"Getting comfortable. Taking off my shoes, sitting in bed. It's been a long day." More rustling. "Okay. Good, then it's settled. Be prepared for me to be very demanding on you." I heard him swallow something, probably scotch. "Now and then, I'll be coming to North Carolina and we'll have dinner, you can catch me up on what you're doing. How does that sound?"

"Good." The answer came out of me quickly but then my worry-genes kicked in. "I mean, that'd be nice." I flexed my ankles, watching my calf muscles stretch and round up. "The thing is . . . I don't want people to misunderstand."

"No, of course not." He swallowed again. "That might be a bit of a problem, I grant you, but we'll work around it. What classes do you have tomorrow?"

I slid down in my bed, curling up on my side and tucking the phone between my shoulder and chin. "Ballet Partnering and Foundations of Western Thought. They don't want us to graduate as complete dance dummies. You should see the textbook for the Western Thought class. Weighs more than I do."

"Well, cheer up. Maybe you'll meet some handsome young man in the partnering class."

"Nah. I'm too busy for romance."

"Oh Amanda, never say that. Romance lifts the heart, makes you feel alive. No, you'll probably meet some lusty hotshot who'll drive all thoughts of me right out of your head. I'll be the only one cherishing memories of a very special night."

His words brought a warmth to my face and my next words were a whisper. "I haven't forgotten."

His voice got very soft. "And when you think about it, what do you do?"

"Do? I . . . just think about it."

"You don't touch yourself? Why not?"

"I don't know." I huddled even lower in the bed.

"You don't know, you don't know. Ah, sweetheart, some day you'll realize you can't go through life not knowing. You have to decide what you want and go after it. Shall I tell you what I'm doing, Amanda? Have you guessed? I'm thinking of a shy young girl, with milk-white skin and beautiful black hair, who gave me a wonderful gift not so long ago. Do you know what that gift was?"

". . . no . . ."

"Trust. You trusted me. Would you trust me now?" After a moment's silence, he asked, "What are you wearing, sweetheart? A nightie? A t-shirt?"

"I . . . I'm not wearing anything. I'm naked."

An even longer pause followed, and a sigh. "Well, that's a fine coincidence, Amanda, because I'm naked too."

"*Richard.*" I couldn't help it, a little thrill of desire ran through me. My nipples tightened and goose bumps rose.

"I want you to touch yourself." His voice came over the phone line in barely a whisper. "Will you trust me? Let me help you relax. Run your fingers up over the fronts of your thighs." My skin grew warm as he told me what to stroke and tug and caress, first my arms and legs and belly, then ever more intimate places. "I want to hear you," he said and I moaned and breathed his name as the exquisite pain rose and exploded. Through his own hoarse grunts and heavy breathing, I knew he was equally turned on and when he climaxed, a surge of empowerment went through me that excited me even more than my own orgasm.

"Oh god, that was fantastic," he said and I cradled the phone against my cheek and kissed the receiver in lieu of his face. The air felt colder now and I pulled the sheet up over me and cuddled against the pillows.

It was almost like real sex. Even though hundreds of miles apart, I felt as though we'd shared something special, something more than just masturbation. Imagining him stroking himself while thinking about me made me quiver.

"Sweetheart, I hope you don't think I make a practice of this." He seemed to be able to read my mind, answer my concerns before I could even raise them. "I feel so close to you right now. I think what we did strengthens our bond. Is that okay? I wouldn't want to do anything you don't like."

"It's okay," I said, rolling into a ball and huddling under the sheet. "I just . . . it makes me feel kinda funny. I mean, you're Richard Gessler and I'm just . . ."

"You're my baby. Someone I very much care about. Got that?" I could hear him moving about at the other end of the phone. "Getting myself decent," he said. "I might even be able to sleep now. How about you?"

"I think so."

"Then here's a kiss good-night for you. Hope you have a wonderful day tomorrow."

"You too."

"I'll call you soon. Be my good girl till then."

I hung up the phone. Rubbing my face against the pillow, I wondered what I had just done. Crossed a line? Started an affair? Did it count as cheating on his wife if he never actually touched me? I didn't know, but as I wrapped the sheet more tightly around me, I felt as though I had stepped out on a stage without knowing the dance. What was my role? Maybe I could fake it. Or perhaps this ballet was mine, to choreograph with the steps that I wanted to do. I just didn't know.

In mid-September, Mom phoned to say she'd be coming to Raleigh for the day to see a special exhibit at the art museum and wondered if I could have lunch with her.

"You're taking time off in the middle of a school week? What's up?"

"Nothing. Can't I come see my daughter?" she asked. "I miss you."

We arranged to meet at Café Margaretta. The steam-bath temperatures had finally given way and the weather was actually pleasant. I sat outdoors on the terrace, watching other diners who were mostly business types and older women dressed for shopping. I recognized a few faculty members but the only other student besides me was a girl waiting tables. Mom arrived on time, all Liz-Claiborned and Cliniqued, a tribute to Belk and its fine ladies' department.

"Why don't you skip class this afternoon and we could go to a matinee?" She picked through her salad, a colorful creation with orange slices, almonds and curling bits of lettuce. "What do you think, shall we be naughty?" I could catch a faint thread of her cologne—White Linen—above the stronger aroma of vinegar and oil. My ears felt full, like when we drove up into the mountains and I had to swallow hard to pop them.

"Naughty, Mom? You? I wouldn't want to be guilty of corrupting a grown-up." My stomach was too knotted for me to be able to eat. "Why don't you just say what you're here for?" A disconcerted expression crossed her face and I felt a shiver of exhilaration at my boldness.

She set her fork down and pushed back her plate. I watched her hands, carefully folded, neatly manicured. Mom's voice was always beautifully modulated. She never had to speak loudly to command attention in the classroom and her face betrayed nothing, but her fingers were pressed together so tightly they were white at the tips.

"Did I ever tell you I once wanted to be a concert pianist?" She smiled at me and I noticed, as if for the first time, how green her eyes were. "Bet you didn't know that." Mom stared off into the distance. "We've been talking about a lot of things during this marriage counseling. It's made me remember. . ." She sighed and covered my hand with her own. "Then your dad's folks tried to separate us and we ran away to get married."

I knew all about this part. Thought it was romantic. Dad's parents didn't approve of Mom; everyone knew her father drank, big time. They tried to force Dad to go away to college, some place out of state, and he'd fought back. He and Mom drove to Indiana where there was no waiting period, got married by a justice of the peace. Old news.

"I even kept up with my piano lessons for a while," Mom continued, "but once Mark was on the way, well, things changed. I turned my concentration to being a wife and mother." She smiled again at me, almost shyly. "I was your age. Everything seemed so dramatic." The suspense I felt must have shown on my face, because she sat up a little straighter and began speaking more quickly. "What I'm trying to say is . . ."

She took a deep breath. "Amanda, I didn't honestly know what I was doing. Your dad and I dated all through high school. He was my hero. Popular, gifted, I thought he would *save* me. He made me feel special, not just the daughter of the town drunk, not an outsider, for once. And I guess dating me made him feel like a rebel. Our needs drove us together; desperation and rebellion hurried us into a wedding before we were really ready. The next thing I knew, there I was, standing in front of the clerk in that tacky little office, promising to love and honor. It all happened so fast. Mark came along and you were born and I made this family the center of my life."

"So are you sorry you got married? That you had kids?"

She laughed a little and shook her head, putting her fingertips to her forehead for a second. Then she reached out and clasped my hands in hers again and met my eyes. "No, Amanda. What I'm trying to say, and apparently botching it badly, is that your dad and I . . . we haven't been happy for a long time. A long time."

My ears felt like they were filling up again.

"Even before Mark di. . . was in his accident, we had been living together like two polite strangers. We both had so many dreams when we were young. I tried to create a bright picture

73

of happy family life, but it wasn't real. And your dad's been so unhappy in his work, so frustrated."

"Maybe if you talked more."

"We've tried. But the more we talk, the less we understand."

I kept looking at our hands. Hers, so capable, long-fingered, slender. Perfectly trimmed fingernails, neatly polished in a shade of mauve that matched her lipstick and the little flowers in her blouse. My hands were small, knuckly, the nails bitten off and ragged. A wristwatch, heavy and too big, weighed down my wrist like an anchor.

"Amanda, I'm sorry to put more burdens on you, to cause you any pain, but I can't help it. Your dad and I are going to divorce."

The waitress came by to refill our iced tea, but Mom waved her off. I pulled my hands loose and picked up a piece of bread from the basket. A nice piece of bread, crusty and warm. The butter melted into it with satisfying grace. Grace. I always thought Mom's name suited her perfectly, which was more than I could say about my own. All my life, she'd handled everything with grace and style. At school, she'd always been one of the most popular teachers, everyone's favorite. In the neighborhood, Mom was the one that people leaned on in times of trouble and turned to for advice or aid. All my girlfriends envied me and Sissy had practically lived at our house for years. "You don't know how lucky you are," she always said. Everyone loved Mom.

Everyone, apparently, except Dad.

"I hate him." The words, murmured so low as to be almost inaudible, came out before I even realized how I felt. I dropped the bread.

"Amanda! Don't say that, he's your father."

"I don't care. I hate him." I could feel a flush rise as my heart hardened in my chest. I stared at Mom. "You're just doing this for him. You don't want the divorce, but you're going along with it rather than fight. God, don't you get sick of being so damned nice?"

I started to rise from the table, shaking and dizzy. Mom grabbed my hand and pulled me back down. With a quick glance that took in the interested gaze of our fellow diners, she murmured, "Wait a minute, don't run off!" She pulled some money from her purse, tucked it under her plate, and took me by the elbow. We walked in noisy silence. Mom's heels clicked on the brick sidewalk, my sandals shuffle-slapped in syncopated time.

"I didn't want to tell you this way, in public," she said after we turned onto the shaded walkways of the Arboretum. "I had planned to wait until later when we could be alone. I'm sorry." Vines ran crazily over the arched trellis, forming a dim green tunnel with a sandy floor and treacherous roots. "Please don't hate your father. Believe it or not, he's a good man. And don't think he's the only one at fault. We're both to blame." She sighed at my pointed look. "I'm so sorry, Amanda. I know this is a lot for you to deal with."

"I'd say it's a lot for *you* to deal with." Dad would probably marry stupid Janine and raise his new and improved version of a family. And Mom would live alone in that house, and keep teaching school and working in her garden, and never change in a million, zillion years. She'd continue to forgive anybody anything. And I'd be a damned orphan, alone, unable to put my shattered family back together.

We walked and Mom talked. I was the village idiot, mute and anguished. Her soft voice murmured on and on, endless shit about how even though they were divorcing, they still respected each other, they'd still be friends, they'd still be my parents. All I could think was *crap*. Crappola, crappalooza, crappinentlies. I wanted to go home, but home had become a whole different thing. It would be foreign, now, and strange.

"Amanda, please. I know everything looks awful right now, but I promise you, it'll get better. Tell me you'll try to understand. Of all the things in the world, I never wanted to have my family break up, but it's happened now and we have to make the best of it."

Mom tripped on one of the roots and fell, sprawling, to her knees. I couldn't believe it, one minute she was fine and the next, she'd gone down on the dirt, palms scraped, pantyhose torn, hair hanging in her eyes. I helped her to a bench. "I'm fine," she insisted, attempting to laugh, her hands shaking as she dug in her purse for tissues. "How ridiculous, I never trip like that." A trickle of blood seeped down her leg, trapped between skin and stocking. I'd never seen my mother hurt before and I wanted to put my arms around her and rock us both back to younger, safer days.

"This is silly," she said, sitting up straighter and pushing her hair back with both hands. "I'm perfectly fine. Let's find a restroom where I can wash up." With that, she stood, back straight, chin up, and reached her hand out to me. "Come on, Amanda. Stop looking so shocked. It was simply a tumble, no big deal."

I had to admire her but at the same time, I thought, *we're too close. When she hurts, I bleed.* And her pain was more than I could take.

"I have a surprise for you." Richard's voice, deep and silky, purred into my ear. God bless AT&T. "How'd you like a little visit?"

"Really? When?"

"I have some business to handle. Probably could do it over the phone, but this gives me an excuse to come to Raleigh. How does your weekend look?"

I rolled on my back in the bed and raised my feet, resting them against the flowered wallpaper and letting my head and shoulders hang off the side of the mattress. "I have about a ton of homework, but I don't care about that."

"You should care; I don't want your grades to fall. Anyway, you can do it while I'm in meetings. I'm more interested in how your evenings are planned."

"I don't know. Richard, I'm not sure about this. It's one thing to talk on the phone, but. . ." I rolled again and sat up. "Things have been kind of bad lately. My folks are divorcing."

A moment of silence fell, and then, "I thought you said they were seeing a counselor."

"Well, apparently Dad wants to quit. So that's it. Mom's out on her ass. Out with the old and in with the new."

"You mean she's going to give up? Not fight for her marriage? I think that's wrong. I wouldn't quit that easy. She should give him a piece of her mind."

"She should, but Mom wouldn't say shit if she had a mouthful." Richard's attitude surprised me. "I didn't realize you felt this strongly about marriage."

"No? Well, I'll tell you right now, I'd never divorce my wife. We've been together for too long, I owe it to her. Those guys who dump their wives for some little trophy tramp make me sick."

"But you—"

"But what? I've been up front with you all along, Amanda. You've known I was married from the start. But that doesn't mean we can't have something special."

I got out of bed and began pacing the room, walking from one patch of sunlight on the floor to the next. "Richard, you confuse me."

"Well then it's a good thing we'll see each other soon. I want everything to be open between us, sweetheart. I'll see you on Friday, okay? We'll have dinner."

Thursday night, I cleaned my place—did all the laundry, dusted and vacuumed. It was kinda fun. I put some music on the CD player and danced while I cleaned. Very Mrs. Doubtfire. Did the old room some good. By the time I'd cleared off the top of my dresser, straightened up the contents of the stacked milk crates that stored my books, CD's, and kitchen supplies, and draped a scarf over the bedside lamp, the place actually looked cozy. I shoved the raggedy old armchair over the stain on the rug and arranged a throw casually over the back of the chair. It took three tries to get it to look just right.

I ironed the outfit I planned to wear for Richard and did my nails. Not until the middle of the night did I begin obsessing about things. Had I misread Richard's intentions all along? Did he just see me as a fling, perhaps? A little tootsie stashed on the side for when he happened to be in town?

He didn't seem that way. All along, I'd felt his kindness and concern. He really liked me. But how did that jibe with his attitude about marriage? I didn't want him to be unfaithful to his wife, but where did that leave me? We couldn't possibly develop this into a full relationship, so what did I want? To my shame, I knew I wanted to see him again, come what may.

Sleep was impossible. I couldn't find any position that seemed comfortable. As soon as I curled up on one side, I felt compelled to go to the other. My legs were restless and my neck cramped and it was totally beyond me where I'd put my arms in bed all my life. I was too hot, then too cold. I got up and checked my appearance in the mirror. Lucky for me, I had Grandma's fine white skin, not prone to pimples unless I had my period, but then they were red shinies that glared like Rudolph's nose. My period wasn't due for ten more days; perhaps I'd be all right.

Thoughts about my period led to thoughts about contraceptives. Not that Richard and I were going to sleep together. . . but what if we did? I was already on the Pill as a way to regulate my periods, but that was no protection against—

"Oh *stop*," I said aloud. I would not have sex with him. He was a married man. Once again I turned over and mashed my face into the pillow. If I didn't get some sleep soon, none of it would matter anyway because I'd be dead. And maybe better off.

We arranged to meet away from campus. I parked my car and waited, fussing with my hair in the rear view mirror. First I tried pulling it back, then I set it loose, then I pulled it back again, then I set it loose. Finally, I could see Richard pull up in a rental car and park about a dozen spaces away. I got out and walked toward him, smiling and feeling a little shy.

"Amanda?"

A voice sounded to my right as some guy sprinted across the road. Oh my god.

"Travis? What are you doing here?" From the corner of my eye, I could see Richard get out of his car and stare at us. I turned slightly, facing Travis, hoping Richard would get the message and wait a minute.

"I was passing through." He looked me up and down and tousled my carefully arranged curls. "Saw you combing that mop of hair. Got a hot date or something?"

"Hey, stop that." I pulled back out of his reach. "Passing through from where?"

"Wilmington. Had to stop for gas." He jerked his head backward, indicating the gas station/convenience store across the street. "Bought a new car."

"Another car? You just bought that Corvette in July."

Travis grinned. "Yep. And fixed it up and sold it. So now I'll do the same with this one." He turned and pointed, and I realized that his Blazer had a trailer hooked to it, carrying a small sports car. "Corvair. '66 Supersport."

Which meant nothing to me, but I could see he was pleased about it. "You're really into that, huh?"

He shrugged. "I like taking something that's broken and getting it running again. So, how you doing?" His eyes searched mine carefully, and I looked away, down at my feet and then a quick glance at Richard who still watched.

"I'm fine. Not a problem in the world."

"Sissy told me your folks split up. I'm sorry to hear it."

"These things happen." I took a tighter grip on my purse. "Listen, I have to go. Nice seeing you." I took another peek at Richard.

"Who's that guy?" Travis asked. "Is he waiting on you?"

"Um, no. Not really. I just wanted to speak with him a minute, he's somebody from the school."

"He looks pissed that I stopped you."

"No, no. He's just a guy. I don't even know him that well. Well, take care." I turned to go and Travis grabbed my arm.

"Wait a minute. I'm glad I ran into you, I've wanted to say something." I looked up at him. The street lamp made a halo of his golden hair and I remembered again, for a minute, how he looked that day at the football game. "I always liked your family. Your mom was the only teacher who ever made History interesting to me." He released my arm and shoved his hands in his jacket pockets. Cars swished by us and I could smell frying onions from the diner next door. "Your dad's not a bad guy either."

I began to wish he'd leave. "Yes, they're both the salt of the earth." I pulled a scrunchie from my pocket and began to tie up my hair again.

Travis reached over and took it away from me, keeping one of my hands in his. "Look, I know it's tough," he said, running his thumb over my knuckles. "You ever want to talk, give me a buzz. Okay? I know the history; you might feel better talking to someone who remembers what your family was like before. I always envied you, in fact." He smiled and laughed. "You know our house—always noisy and full of arguments. Sounds foolish, I know, but you guys were something special to me, like a benchmark of what a family should be. It slays me that this is happening. Mark was the hub that held you all together; the clown, the happy guy. You and your mom were the heart and soul. I hate to think your family might fall apart now. Chapel Hill's not so far away. I could come over, we could hang out."

My eyes filled up and he stared down at me, stroking my hand. God, he was so nice. For a minute, I almost forgot about Richard. I almost made a complete ass of myself, but a woman walked out of the convenience store with a bag in her hand and called, "Travis? Did you want coffee or Coke?"

She was pretty, in a conventional cheerleader's sort of way. Curvy, blonde, sweet-faced and I wished with all my heart that she'd drop dead. I looked up at Travis and he shrugged a little, not smiling. "That's Stacy. I have to go but, listen, I mean it. Let's get together. Call me." He dug in his wallet and pulled out a business card. *Travis Pennell, UNC Athletics Foundation.* It had two phone numbers and a UNC logo. "I'm on the run a lot. Use the cell number. We're having a great season," he added. " Beat the hell out of Duke." There was the blinding flash of his grin. "I love my job."

"Travis?" Stacy called again. "What'll it be?"

"You better go," I told him. "I'll be fine. I'm not letting this divorce stuff tear me up." I met his eyes squarely. "You're busy. Don't worry about me; I have someone I can talk to."

Travis looked a bit perturbed, and then his face smoothed out. "Okay," he said. "Well, be good. Say hey to your folks for me." He turned and walked to the diner, throwing an arm around Stacy's shoulder as they went in the door. I caught one backward glance from him, and then I went to Richard.

Chapter Six

"Who was that guy?" Richard asked as we got into his car. "Someone from school?"

"No, just a guy. My girlfriend's brother. I don't really know him that well." I looked at Richard's profile, at his strong hands on the steering wheel. "He's nobody."

We dined at a place in Durham, off the expressway. The odds were less that he'd run into somebody he knew. Even if he did, we were just having dinner. I felt funny though, sitting adjacent to him in the corner booth. After those things we'd done on the phone, we knew each other intimately, but we didn't truly know each other at all.

The waiter took our order. Steak for Richard, salad with vinegar and oil, and single malt scotch.

"And for your daughter?" the waiter asked. Richard winked at me.

"My daughter will have the salmon. Honey, you want milk with that?"

No, I told him, ginger ale would do. "Come on," I whispered after the waiter left. "I'm not five years old. Give me a break."

"I'll give you something," Richard grinned, and a little shiver ran through me. "Nervous?"

I shook my head no.

"Liar." He took my napkin and spread it across my lap, brushing my bare thigh with his hand as he did so. He turned slightly, facing me and resting his arm across the back of the seat. "Don't feel bad if you are. I'm nervous, too."

"Now who's lying?" I asked lightly, but my voice wobbled.

The restaurant was busy, a typical Friday night crowd. Silver clinked on china, voices talked, waiters passed back and forth. A sappy Sinatra tune played in the background. Each table had its own little lamp, like one of those movie restaurants from the forties. The kitchen was across the room, viewable from the dining area. The chefs had tall white hats and occasionally flames would flare up over the grill. Through the window, I could see dusk falling, with the late-day sun reflecting off parked cars.

"Amanda?"

Richard pulled the edge of my sleeve so that my hand slid off the table and he covered it with his own warm hand. At his touch, it all came back to me—the bath, his caresses, myself splayed on the bed. I felt suffocatingly shy, unable to breathe, unable to look at him.

"Honey, you don't have to be afraid of me," he whispered. "I won't do anything that you don't want." He laced his fingers through mine and gave them a little squeeze. "We can just talk. All weekend, I don't care."

Before I could answer, the waiter returned with our salads. He hovered about us forever; it seemed, solicitous about fresh ground pepper, butter for our rolls, and topping up our water glasses while we waited in silence. Finally he left.

"I just feel a bit shy," I told Richard. "I'll be fine." I managed a smile. "Did you take care of your business?"

He relaxed and sat back, took a sip of his drink and settled down to eat. "Well, it's the kind of thing that's never finished, but it went pretty well." He described plans for a new wing at the Alumni Center. I listened, but mostly I watched. He seemed different in this setting. With his tweed sports coat and tailored shirt, he looked like any successful businessman. Middle-aged. Graying. Inclined to portliness. I watched his hands as he cut up his steak and his wedding ring flashed in the lamplight. Up close, I could see the little crinkles around his eyes and the many silver threads in his hair. That one pure-white lock curled over his forehead, a mix of maturity and boyishness.

"So I told them it didn't matter to me, but what they need to do—hey, you're not eating." He stopped talking and pointed with his fork at my salad. "Not hungry?"

"Oh, starved, I forgot for a minute." I picked at the lettuce. It occurred to me that he was an important man, busy with all kinds of things, a man with a great deal of power and money, yet he had set aside the rest of this weekend just for me. For us. "Don't you worry? About whether I might turn out to be a troublemaker or something?"

Richard signaled to the waiter for another drink. "No, I don't." He wiped his lips on his napkin and smiled at me. "I've spent my life studying other people, figuring out what they're really like, judging their probable actions. That's the real secret in business, you see. Understanding people. And I know you would never do anything to hurt me. As I would never hurt you."

The waiter brought Richard's scotch, clearing away our salads and returning with our main course. I asked for more ginger ale. Richard held my hand under the table. As soon as we had a bit of privacy again, he turned to me. "Why did you ask me that?"

"You said you were nervous, too. Are you afraid your wife will find out you're seeing me?"

He hesitated before answering, seeming to turn over various replies in his mind. "I wouldn't want her to worry. She's a good woman and I don't want to upset her. The truth is, our relationship is unique. We love and respect each other but we don't spend much time together. She has her interests, I have mine. Nevertheless, we're still a family and nothing will ever change that." He stared out the window. "Maybe this will be hard for someone your age to understand, but I value the longevity of my relationship with Diane. We've been through a lot together and we know where we stand."

He smiled ruefully down at his plate and then looked at me. "Trouble is, even though we have an emotional attachment, we don't have a physical one. Somewhere along the way, Diane decided she wasn't interested in sex. Not with me, at least. It hurts, I can tell you. Hurts a lot." He sighed and took another sip of his drink. "I don't know what she does with that need. Maybe I don't want to know. It sure leaves a big hole inside of me." His hand tightened on mine. "I suppose I could go the more traditional route. Prostitutes. A mistress. The idea doesn't appeal to me. I want to be needed, Amanda. I *need* to be needed. And that's why I'm nervous. Afraid I'll be overanxious. Afraid I'll scare you off. I'm fifty-two years old, more than twice your age. Why would you ever be interested in me?" His eyes were serious, with pain behind them. I wanted to lean forward and place a kiss on his lips but it wouldn't have been seemly there in the restaurant. I had never thought that *he* might need *me*.

The poor waiter looked very disappointed at the amount of food we left on our plates. Richard tipped generously to cheer him up, and we left. The evening was beautiful—not cold, not hot—and I suggested we walk back to my place. Richard strolled quietly, his head down and his hands in his pockets. I wanted to reassure him that I found him interesting, that his age wasn't an issue for me, but I couldn't find the words. All of a sudden, I felt very protective of him. He'd shown me his vulnerability, trusted me with that sensitive sore spot, and I wanted to make him whole.

The outdoor staircase that led to my second-floor entrance looked even shabbier and more paint-worn than ever. I hoped he wouldn't find it tawdry. Once upstairs, I turned on the lamp and lowered the shades. Richard prowled the room, looking at my books and posters and photographs.

"Would you like something cold to drink?" I asked him.

"What have you got?"

I checked the contents of my little fridge. "Diet Coke, orange juice, and milk. Er, no, forget about the milk."

He chuckled. "Nothing stronger?"

"Sorry, no. They check I.D.'s at the grocery stores, so I can't buy anything."

"No problem. Is this you?" He pointed at a photo tacked to the wall.

"Yeah. That's me with my brother's band. But don't look at it, I'm a troll."

He smiled and shook his head, looking around the room. "You keep things very neat, no clutter. I thought girls your age were into make-up and stuffed animals and posters of boy bands." I thought about the mess I'd cleaned up the night before and just smiled. "Great chair," he said, noticing it and sitting down.

It *was* a great chair. I bought it at a yard sale. Big, overstuffed with well-padded arms, the teal green leather chair was perfect. Except the previous owner's dog had chewed up the seat cushion. At another yard sale, I found a cushion that fit, and although it didn't match, it made the chair perfect for me. Oversized, squishy, a chair to curl up in. I even took naps there sometimes.

"Come here." Richard patted his thigh. "I've dreamt of this."

I had, too. Awkwardly, I climbed into his lap, dangling my legs over the arm of the chair. At first it was uncomfortable. I felt stiff and clumsy, until Richard spread his knees wider and my fanny slid down between his thighs. Suddenly, we were a perfect fit. I lay my head against his chest and he rested his chin on my hair, with his arms around me.

"I can hear your heart." I said. "Lub-dub, lub-dub'."

"No, it's saying 'Amanda, Amanda'. Do you know I love your name?"

I smiled at that. "I always hated it, myself. 'Amanda' seems like a name for a girl who shops at The Gap and majors in education or nursing. The kind of daughter my mom should have had. A girl who always has her homework done. You know what I mean?"

"You better have your homework done, too, or I'll spank your little backside." His stomach went up and down when he chuckled. "No, from now on, for me, Amanda will always mean a little wild child with amazing black hair all untamed and rowdy, and a body that's charged like a lightning bolt. And the sweetest blue eyes," he added, his voice growing deeper, "and delicious, soft pink lips." His mouth came down on mine, causing a pulse to start up in my lips and our breath mingled while our tongues touched. A lovely kiss—gentle, tentative, filled with hope and longing. "Oh, Amanda," he whispered. "What am I going to do with you?"

I could only tuck my head under his chin. "I want to be with you, but I don't want to hurt anyone."

He lifted my chin so I had to look at him. "Who would you be hurting? My wife? I told you, she doesn't want that part of me. I don't know what she thinks I do about that side of my life, but she doesn't really care as long as I don't embarrass her."

"But you'd be unfaithful."

Richard snorted and sat up straighter. "Faithful? Has she been faithful? To me, fidelity means staying true. And I do stay true to her. I'm her husband, I meet her needs. Has she met mine? Women seem to think men can get along without sex, but they're wrong." His voice rose and I began to feel alarmed. When he saw me drawing back, Richard stopped and took a deep breath. "Sorry. I'm scaring you, aren't I?" He put his arms around me again and held me close. "All I want to do is take care of you, Amanda. Lord knows someone needs to. You're struggling all alone and no one is even paying attention." He kissed me again. "But the question is—will you let me?"

I felt like crying. Someone cared, really cared about me, someone who needed me to care about him too. I twined my arms around Richard's neck and kissed him. "Yes," I whispered. "I will. I want to. We'll take care of each other."

His hand slid up under my top, across my ribs and over my naked breasts. The minute he touched my nipples, a little surge of excitement ran from my breasts to my vagina, as though a closed circuit had been opened. We kissed, more greedily now, murmuring and moaning as his hands thrilled me more and more. I raised my arms and Richard pulled my top off, pressing kisses to my throat, the space between my breasts and finally, after agonies of waiting, kissing and sucking on the pointed pink tips. "Oh God, Amanda, I don't think I can wait," he groaned. I slid off his lap and stood in front of him, unzipping my skirt and letting it fall to the floor. Richard's eyes traveled over me and he moved forward, sitting on the edge of the seat. "You're so beautiful," he breathed. His hands caressed my hips and bottom, then he pulled my panties down and I stepped out of them.

He buried his face against my stomach for a moment. I pulled loose and moved to my bed, jerking the blankets free and climbing in.

Richard stood above me, frowning a little, looking shocked. "Are you sure, Baby? Are you really sure?"

I nodded, unable to speak. After a minute, Richard undressed and set his clothes on the chair. I couldn't look, I put my arm across my face. I wanted him so badly, but I felt shy at the same time

He slid into the bed beside me. The mattress gave beneath his weight and I rolled toward his warm skin, his solid body. The hair on his chest and thighs made a pleasurable friction against mine, and he was fully aroused, no doubt about it. We kissed again, and I reached out to turn off the lamp, but he stopped me. "I want to look at you." His fingers slid lower, over my belly, and between my legs, and then he rolled over on top of me. I gasped as his legs nudged mine open and I could feel the heat from his body. "This might cause you a little pain, the first time. Are you sure you're ready?"

I closed my eyes tightly and nodded. Hurry up, I thought. Get it over with.

He began slowly, guiding himself in, making me realize how different real life was from talking on the phone. I moaned and he pressed his face against my hair. It didn't hurt, but I couldn't help backing away as he entered me more fully. "It's okay, Baby," he whispered and kissed me, a deep, urgent kiss that filled my mind and senses. As he rocked against me, I whimpered. This was so different! So real, so full of sensation, so overwhelming. I tasted scotch in his kiss, smelled his after-shave and the scent of his skin.

His breathing sped up, grew heavier, and I heard my own breathing grow ragged. I felt him, not only between my legs, but his weight on top of me, the slight roughness of his chest hair against my breasts. He grunted and I realized how much pleasure I gave him. The clock ticked and traffic rumbled out on the road. I kept my eyes shut tight. Richard moved faster and harder. The bed creaked as we rocked, as I wrapped my legs around his hips and pulled him even more deeply into my body. This was really happening. He was in me—hard, urgent, bigger than I expected. I felt on fire, burning up as Richard drove into me again and again.

I couldn't stop the noises in my throat, the animalistic grunts and cries. Richard gripped my hair with both hands, pulling back slightly so my throat arched. He growled and buried his face in my neck. As he made his final plunges, I felt something warm running between my legs and knew I was bleeding, smelled the metallic tang. I was no longer a virgin. Richard cried out, raising his head like a lion, and then collapsed on me.

"Oh god," he sighed. For a moment, all was still. I wrapped my arms and legs around him, holding him in. I hadn't climaxed, but that was okay so long as he had. Maybe my first time was too fraught with nerves; nevertheless, I felt wonderful. Alive, and relaxed, and spent. But even more than that, I felt wonderful about myself. I was a woman now, and I'd made my man happy. It was enough.

"I'm sorry," he said later. "I didn't last very long." We lay in bed, his head and shoulders propped up on pillows, my head on his chest. He fanned my hair out and played with it—brushing a lock across his own cheek, tickling the tip of my nose, running his fingers through it over and over. "It seems like I've been waiting for you forever. Usually I can hold off for a long while before I climax, one of the few advantages of old age."

"I wish you wouldn't talk of yourself as old," I murmured. "Every time you go on about how ancient you are, it makes me feel even younger in comparison."

"You are young. You're my little baby."

"And what's with this Daddy/Baby thing?" I asked, rising up on one elbow to look at him. "At the restaurant, you let that waiter think I'm your daughter."

Richard's eyes grew serious. "Did that bother you?" He sat up in bed, pushing the pillows further behind himself and resting his elbows on his upturned knees. "Would it upset you to call me Daddy?"

"But why would you want me to?" It didn't make any sense to me. "You didn't . . . you're not this way with your daughters, are you?" I glanced down at myself, naked where the sheet gapped away.

"Lord, no! Never!" He pulled me close. "Understand this, Amanda. I never, *ever*, had any kind of sexual feelings for my daughters. That would be really disgusting." He shook his head. "Believe me, I have no interest in that at all. It's just. . .you're so young. I like it that you're so innocent and inexperienced and new to everything. In some ways, I do have

94

fatherly feelings toward you. I love the idea of guiding you in your career, helping you along. God knows your own father's not doing it." His voice was angry and I felt a thrill, realizing he felt upset on my behalf. Richard cuddled me to his chest. "But if it bothers you, I won't insist."

"You have to admit, it's kind of freaky."

He looked wounded. "Well, I don't think so. I thought it would be sweet, but if you don't want to. . ." He kissed me and I pushed him away, murmuring that I needed to clean up. Richard threw back the sheets, revealing the bloody smears, the red spatters on my thighs. "Look at that," he whispered and I tried to cover myself but he held back my hand. "No, don't hide. It's beautiful. You've given me something no one else can ever have." Dampening his fingertips in the blood, he marked his own chest. "I'm your first and for that alone, you'll never forget me. I'll always be a part of you." Richard kissed me then, possessively, his mouth leaving me no ability or desire to protest. Perhaps it was ignorance, but I was in bliss.

The second time Richard Gessler gave me a bath, it was in a spacious tub in a lovely old bed-and-breakfast. There wasn't much of a break to fall break, only one day off actually, Columbus Day, but we managed to turn it into a long weekend and Richard took me to the coast.

I'd been to Myrtle Beach many times, and Wilmington once, but we headed for the Outer Banks and the historical towns preserved like fine old china around the Albemarle and Pamlico Sounds. Elizabeth City, New Bern, Manteo. We played tourist, traipsing through houses and graveyards, visiting the English-style gardens and a reproduction of a seventeenth-century sailing ship.

God, it was fun. Richard made the perfect companion—witty, knowledgeable, able to deal with any emergency but not too sophisticated to act a little goofy sometimes. We rode the Cedar Island ferry to Ocracoke. I had never ridden a ferry before and Richard seemed to enjoy my excitement. "Didn't your family do things together?" he asked as we stood at the railing. The wind was cold and most other people were huddled in the cabin but Richard and I went as far forward as we could get, watching the gulls and listening to waves splashing as the ferry cut through the water. My hair lifted on the breeze, cork-screwing in the salty air until Richard gathered and bunched it in his fist. He opened his jacket and I squirmed inside, wrapping my arms around his waist.

"We never traveled much, but we used to do other things." I tilted my face up for his kiss. "When I was a kid. Mom liked to organize family outings—crafts festivals and museums and concerts, stuff like that. I saw *The Mikado* when I was only five years old. And *Giselle* when I was six. That's what started me on dance lessons."

"What about your dad? Did he go too?"

"He's more of a sports guy. He and Mark used to go to all the high school football games, and to UNC-Charlotte to see 49ers basketball."

"But not you?"

"No. I'm a *girl*. So, in my dad's view. . ."

"I see." Richard held me a little closer and kissed my forehead. An old couple came out on deck, the man's white

96

hair pulled straight back by the wind while the woman's blue-gray curls hardly budged. Richard nodded to them and they stared back, frowning. Then he picked me up, threw me over his shoulder and whirled in a circle, laughing and making me squeal. "Come on, sweetie," Richard said loudly. "Let's get some hot chocolate."

"Okay, *Daddy*," I laughed. As we walked past the old lady, I smiled and she smiled back. I bet she thought it was great to see a father and daughter getting along so well. I bet she thought we were just cute as the dickens.

We had three nights together. They each started the same. Richard bathed me, in an old claw-footed tub at the B&B, and later a whirlpool bath in a modern hotel in New Bern, lathering my hair with almond-scented shampoo, bringing all my senses alive as he ran the soap over my wet body. Then he carried me to bed and the magic began. He acted the part of movie director, controlling the lighting, setting, wardrobe, the pace of action. He determined when and how and what, and through it all, he loved to watch me. Loved to push me to my limits and beyond, loved to listen to me cry out with desire or fulfillment, loved to be my master.

"Mmm, you wear me out, Baby," he murmured, on our last night. "I feel completely exhausted, and relaxed. Come give me a kiss."

Although I could barely move myself, I obliged. Richard was a great kisser. I was the one worn out, sated with physical effort and emotional release. "I hate knowing we go back home tomorrow," I said, playing with the curly hairs on his chest. "You'll be so far away and all."

"Not so far. We'll talk on the phone."

"It won't be the same. Not after this, you've spoiled me." I snuggled up against him and mushed my nose into his shoulder. "When do you think you'll be able to come again?"

"Not for hours," he said, laughing and making the bed shake.

"I don't mean that. Seriously."

"Seriously, I'd say maybe a month. My schedule is pretty heavy. Besides, my older daughter is coming for a visit, along with her husband—oh, that reminds me. . ." He climbed abruptly out of bed and pulled on his boxers. "I meant to call her."

I tried not to sulk as I eavesdropped on their conversation. I knew he was close to his daughters, there was no good reason for me to feel jealous, but I did. They sounded so damned chummy on the phone. He teased her about the new dog she had (*and I'm not that mutt's Grandpa, you hear me? I'm his very good friend.*), he asked about her new job at some art gallery in Tribeca, they bantered about football teams. They had a history of closeness, that's what I envied. A lifetime of communication.

"Hey, what's this long face?" he chided me after he hung up.

"Nothing." I swung my feet over the edge of the bed and stood up. "I guess I better get dressed."

Richard didn't buy it. He grabbed my wrist and pulled me to face him. "What's the matter now?" When I didn't answer, he took both my arms and shook me a little. "Don't be like that, tell Daddy what's wrong." I made a face and he mockingly pulled me across his lap and administered two sharp smacks to my butt. "Tell me, or you get more."

I wriggled off, falling on my ass on the floor and then, abandoning my mutiny, climbed into his lap. With his arms around me and my face tucked down so he couldn't see it, I admitted my shameful jealousy. "I only get you for a few days here and there, or a couple of phone calls. Seems like you could wait to call her when I'm not around. This is *my* time, I don't want to share you during it."

Richard hugged me and held me close for a long minute. Then he pushed my hair out of my face and tenderly kissed my cheek. "That's the nicest compliment anyone ever paid me." He kissed me again and then pinched my bottom, making me jump. "However, you need to get over that. My family will always have claims on my time. Tell you what, I'll make you a deal. Call me Daddy, and let me think of you as my third daughter, and that will mean you have claims on my time, too."

It still seemed gross to me. Kind of yuck, like those little-girl flowered panties he liked me to wear. "Why is it so important to you?" I asked, stalling so I could think more how I felt about it.

"It just is. Anyone could call me Richard, only you can call me Daddy. Even my own daughters say 'Dad'. They're too grown-up and involved with their own lives to have time for me. Don't you see how special this makes you?" He rubbed his forehead against mine. "I don't ask much," he whispered. "Can't you do it to please me?"

"I guess," I said, and then kissed him to get the bad taste out of my mouth. "Daddy." A little shiver ran over me, as though someone had run a finger down my spine. He hugged me tight. "That reminds me of another thing." Richard lifted me off his lap and set me in the big chair while he got some papers out of his briefcase. "I've given this a lot of thought, even more after I saw your videos from dance class." In his hand were brochures from various dance schools in New York. "I want you to read these over and think about maybe transferring next semester. It would do you a lot of good to study with better teachers, the best. You said you were behind in training. This way you could catch up . . . hell, leapfrog over the others."

"You've got to be kidding!" How in the world did he think I would explain that to my folks? They'd no more let me go to New York than they would give me permission to jump from an airplane without a parachute. It was unthinkable. And besides, I was in the elite dance troupe at school and it had taken so much effort to get there. Did he really think I should give it up now? "Richard, I mean Daddy, maybe you overestimate my skill."

"No, I don't. I've watched you very carefully, ever since that first day. You've got something, Amanda. Underneath all that shyness and diffidence, you have a drive, a flame. When you dance, there's this blaze in your eyes, single-mindedness. I think you have what it takes to succeed."

I felt heat rise in my face and I couldn't look at him. Did he mean it? Could he really see the light that turned on inside me whenever I danced? "I'm too intense," I mumbled. "Nowhere near as graceful as Mary Kelley. You remember her? From Swan Lake? I'll never be in her league."

Richard sat on the foot of the bed and, leaning forward, framed my face in his hands. "Yes, I remember her. And you're right, she's lovely. She was perfect as the Swan Queen, but you, you're unique. You stand out among all those other dancers like a diamond among pearls. You draw the eye. Yeah, you're sharp-edged and different, not smooth and round and bland, like them. Maybe you won't ever dance the role of Odette. But you could sure the hell dance Odile. Or *The Firebird. La Bayadere.* Don't sell yourself short."

"I'm not," I whispered, although my heart did a little clog dance all its own. "I just think it's good to know the truth about yourself."

"The truth is I'm crazy about you and I want to help you any way I can. All I ask is for you to think about it. You could get far superior training. And think about this. We could see each other whenever we wanted. I'd get you an apartment, you'd be completely free to come and go as you like. Independent, but we'd be able to be together." He held me close. "I don't want to let you go," he whispered. "I just found you, I can't let you go. I won't."

Chapter Seven

A few days after my trip with Richard ended, autumn announced itself. Like a relative who has moved into the house, the new season arrived loaded with baggage. Leaves changed, temperatures plunged, the entire campus broke out in sweaters and corduroys and a new vitality filled the air. With our batteries recharged, the tempo in class accelerated, bringing with it extra homework and greater amounts of rehearsal time. My cold-weather clothes were back at home, so one Saturday I loaded my car with summer gear and drove to Painter's Creek for a visit.

Dad had moved out. The house seemed so different, yet so much the same. There were holes—books missing from the bookcase, empty spots on shelves, more space in the front closet. Things felt disjointed, strange, like a *corps de ballet* with gaps in the line. It made my teeth ache.

Mom delighted in my sudden appearance. With great gusto, she sorted clothes on my bed and helped me decide which things to take back to school, which to pack up until next summer, and which to send to Christian Ministries.

"There's lots of wear in this yet," she said, holding up a shirt I'd never liked. "Someone will be glad to get it." She counted the clothes that were deemed acceptable to keep.

"Why don't we go to the mall? You need a new winter coat and some other things." A faint blush crept across her cheeks. "We could go out for dinner, too. Or maybe you'd rather go visit Sissy?" Her voice was so wistful that I didn't have the heart to admit how much I would have liked to do just that, go see Sissy and not spend time with Mom.

I felt like a shit. I *was* a shit. She was so nice and life had treated her bad. I ached inside, watching her work at being cheerful and upbeat. If only she'd complain and bitch, I'd feel she was strong enough to get through the rough times. Instead, Mom seemed like fragile and brittle spun glass, one false move and she'd shatter.

We did the mall thing, bought shoes and jeans and earrings. I let her talk me into a trim at the beauty parlor. "Not too much off," I warned the hairdresser. "Trim it but don't let it look like it's been trimmed." Richard would have had a fit if I cut it short.

I tried to make it fun. Pretended like I bought Mom's lighthearted act, clowned around myself. We teased each other about our widely different taste in clothes, I convinced her she looked dashing and mysterious in a cobalt-blue wool cape, we even indulged ourselves with ice-cream sundaes. I almost hated to bring up the divorce, but since it was clear she wasn't going to, I felt I needed to have at least a clue about what would happen next.

"Mason Kennedy is handling the divorce," she confessed. "At least, my side of it. Steve has a guy from Charlotte taking care of his side. We're being very decent," she said, emphasizing 'decent' with a look to tell me not to worry.

"Neither of us wants to beggar the other. Rather than sell the house, I'm going to refinance and buy Steve out. That way, he has some funds for himself and I won't have to move. It'll be all right, I can manage the mortgage payments."

Weird. She called him 'Steve' twice, instead of saying 'your Dad', the way she always used to. I drew designs in the ice cream. "I thought Mason Kennedy was Dad's friend. Didn't they used to play golf?"

"Yes, but he's my friend, too. We used to go out together, the four of us, before Mason's divorce. Since then, he's kept to himself a lot. Anyway, I trust him."

"Where's Dad living?"

Mom stirred her ice cream. It was melting any way, neither of us seemed to have much appetite. She pressed her lips together for a second and then said quietly, "In Gastonia. With Janine." At my frown, she added, "Well, he wants to help her. The baby is due almost any day now. They're not getting married or anything, but he'd like to be there when the baby comes."

"It doesn't matter." Like hell it didn't. I pushed my ice cream away and stood up. "How about a movie?" Sometimes life just totally sucked.

I went to see Sissy the next day, before I headed back to Raleigh.

"Dave's not here," she apologized, "that's why everything is such a mess." The small living room was strewn with baby toys, laundry in various stages of being folded, plates with dried food, and scattered newspapers. "I haven't been feeling very well lately."

"Don't worry about it, for gosh sakes. You think I come over here to see your housekeeping?"

Teri wailed from the next room. "Get her, would you?" Sissy said. "I'll go fix her bottle."

The baby stood in her crib, holding onto the rail. Baby paraphernalia filled the small dark room, which reeked of diaper. The phone rang in the kitchen and I decided I'd better just go ahead and change the baby's smelly pants. Sissy might be tied up for a while.

It wasn't my idea of fun. I'd never done much babysitting and wasn't used to changing poopy diapers. Teri stared gravely at me while I fumbled with snaps and wipes and diaper tapes. She'd grown a lot since summer. She had little pearly teeth and could stand if she held onto something. Soon she'd probably be walking.

A year from now, Dad's baby would be this size. I couldn't stand to think about it. Like so many other things, I walled it off in my mind. Pretty soon, I'd have to rent warehouse space for all the things I tried to keep out of my thoughts.

Teri reached out her arms to be picked up. Trusting soul. I hooched her onto one hip and she immediately twined her legs around my waist like a little monkey. Without that dirty diaper, she smelled nice. We stared eye-to-eye and she suddenly put her hands on my cheeks. "Mbock! Mbock-mbock!"

"Easy for you to say," I whispered. "Don't try to charm me, Stinker-Butt. I'm wise to you." I carried her out to the kitchen where Sissy was winding up her phone call. She handed me the baby's bottle so I took Teri into the living room and settled in the rocking chair. Teri latched onto the bottle with determination but her gaze never left my face. After a while, it became disconcerting.

"That was Dave," Sissy said from the kitchen doorway. She leaned against the doorjamb and I couldn't help noticing she had put on more weight. "He's going to stay late at the store, to go over the books with Dad. Sales are down and they're worried." She slumped in the corner of the couch. "Dad'll pay him for the overtime, and we can use the money, but all these long hours couldn't have come at a worse time."

I broke my staring contest with Teri. "Why? What's worse about this time than any other?"

"I'm pregnant again."

"Sissy! Teri's only—"

"I know how old she is! You think I haven't been counting on my fingers, too? They'll only be seventeen months apart. What am I going to do, Amanda?" She burst into tears. I tried to get out of the seat. It wasn't easy with twenty pounds of Teri on top of me, but Sissy waved me off. She dug a tired Kleenex out of her jeans pocket and blew her nose. "Oh, shoot, I'm sorry. Didn't mean to be dumping this on you with everything your family is going through. It's just. . . . I'm tired, Amanda. I'm so tired. Teri doesn't always sleep through the night, I'm still babysitting those two little brats, and I feel so sick half the time. I feel like an old lady! My life is over! I'm nineteen years old and I might as well be sixty. If I'd known things were going to turn out like this. . ."

Teri finished her bottle and threw it on the floor. I set her down and she immediately crawled over to Sissy and stood up, holding the edge of the couch for support. "She's getting to be Speedy Gonzales," Sissy said, managing a smile. "One day she was just barely sitting up, and now, soon, she'll be walking." The smile left Sissy's face. "What are you going to do when your Dad's baby is born? Are you going to go see it?" I'm sure my face spoke volumes, because Sissy chose her next words carefully. "You should think about it, Amanda. Like it or not, that baby is going to be kin to you. Your half-brother or half-sister. It's not the baby's fault how things happened."

I sighed. "I know. But then I'd have to see Janine, too. Don't know if I'm up to that. I swear, Sissy, if this is growing up, I don't want it. I'd rather stay a kid."

She shook her head and began folding laundry. "It wouldn't matter. Trouble comes to everyone, sooner or later. Deserve it or not. It doesn't matter how careful you are, whether you wear seat belts or check your smoke alarms or pray on your knees five times a day. Sometimes you wonder why you get up in the morning, how you're going to drag yourself from one day to the next, but hey, what else you gonna do?"

I thought about my mother, dragging herself through her daily routine, trying to fill in the empty corners of her life with flowers and beauty and acts of kindness for her neighbors and it seemed to me God had a pretty piss-poor way of rewarding virtue.

"Well, enough about troubles," Sissy said, in a more upbeat tone of voice. "So. How do you like college boys? Meet anyone special?"

I shrugged. "You know, college boys are highly over-rated. I'm thinking of going for older men, they're much more reliable."

She laughed and kept right on folding laundry.

I had a lot to think about as I drove back to college. I was still mulling it over when Richard phoned.

He was glad to hear I'd gone home for a visit. "Did you tell them about moving to New York?"

I couldn't, I told him. "They've got so many troubles right now. I just don't want to add to their problems. My poor Mom, she's so sad."

"And partly to blame, maybe. She should have fought harder."

"I don't know. I can't judge her. Everything isn't black and white, you know. Good guy, bad guy."

"So you're just going to put everything on hold while they sort themselves out? You have a right to your own life."

"I know. I just don't want to worry them right now. When I think of all the things Mom did for me over the years, seems kind of ungrateful if I pack up and take off. She's going to be so lonely once Dad's baby arrives. I hate to make her feel deserted."

"Oh. I see." His voice went calm and icy. "Everyone's feelings count more than mine."

"No, Richard! How can you think that? I just don't want to hurt anyone."

"Richard? I'm Richard to you now? Fine, Amanda. Don't hurt anyone's feelings. Good night." He hung up on me. I sat there, stunned, the phone still in my hand. Oh, Richard, I didn't mean it that way. Damn, damn, damn! Shit!

All my fine swearing didn't make me feel one bit better. Dammit.

Richard didn't call back, and I wasn't allowed to phone him. I paced around the apartment, did some stretches, but there wasn't room to dance and I needed to *move*. The college had a few small rehearsal rooms that stayed open late; I threw some things in my dance bag and headed over there.

In the half-empty building, sounds echoed. Someone played piano in one of the other rooms and I heard music, voices and thuds as a large contemporary dance class practiced in the big hall. It didn't take me long to change into my dance shoes, turn on my portable CD player, and begin dancing.

The music was Celtic, *Jimmy Mó Mhíle Stór*. My senior year in high school, I used it for the dance recital and did my own choreography. The song still gave me the greatest pleasure, moving to the sad strains of piano and guitar and three women's voices interwoven in a lament for a sailor long gone from shore. The melody began slowly, then gradually built in speed and force. More instruments joined in—flute, fiddle, bodhran and pipes, adding layers and intensity. Like my life. A lot of intricate elements all acting together to form a single song. Richard wanted me to move to New York, which made alarms go off inside my head, big time. We had already gone way beyond the mentor-protégé relationship. I was beginning

109

to lean on him, need him, and I believed he needed me but where did that leave us? He was still married. I still had my parents to think about.

My dance moves grew in intensity. I did a series of leaps—*jetés, cabriolets*—that Mark used to call 'show-off' dancing. How could I possibly go to New York? It would mean leaving school, dropping out in the middle of term. People would wonder why I left.

The instrumental part of the music dropped away and only the three women's voices were left, twining around each other's. I began a series of adagio movements even more difficult than the glitzy stuff. Control and coordination were required. Balance. I couldn't cut corners. Whatever decision I made, it should be for all the right reasons.

The song came to a close and I stood still for a minute, catching my breath. A slight movement near the door spooked me and a man's figure came into view, M. Beloit. "What are you doing?" he asked.

I gestured at the CD player behind me. "Just practicing."

"What was that dance? Show me those closing moves again." I did the adagio steps—*grand fouetté, relevé, renversé.* "Where did you learn that? Are you one of my students?"

I could feel the familiar blush rising in my cheeks. "Yes, I'm in the Partnering class, 232."

M. Beloit nodded, his eyes half-shut. "I see. Very nice. It's late, you should get going." He shut off half the lights and I scurried to change shoes and gather my things. As I passed through the door, he said, "Increase the bend of your body at the end of the *renversé.* You're not extending enough."

"Yes, sir," I murmured and hurried home. Very nice, he said *very nice*! From M. Beloit, that was almost the equivalent of a third curtain call. I had to tell Richard.

No. I couldn't tell Richard. Until he phoned me, we would be out of touch. I tried calling Mom but she was out. Probably at Color Guard practice. I left a message and debated phoning Dad. Would he even care to know? Ever since he moved out of the house, we had communicated through his office voice mail. I dialed the number and extension. A man answered, not Dad. "Is Steve Long there?" I asked.

"Mr. Long doesn't work here anymore," I was informed. "Can I help you?"

"No." Dad had moved on and not told me. Well, at least I knew where I stood.

Richard didn't call. For three days he didn't call, so finally I wrote him a letter.

October 18

Daddy,

I'm so sorry to have upset you. You know I want to please you, I'm just very mixed up right now. This isn't easy for me. Please call. I just know we can work everything out if only you'll call. Remember, you always say that communication is crucial. Don't let what we have die out over one argument.

Call me. PLEASE.

Class work reached critical mass. I spent hours at the library, listening to tapes and CDs, preparing a research paper/performance project on O'Carolan, a Baroque composer. In Foundations of Western Thought, we were studying the history of art patronage, people like the Medicis, Vanderbilts, Andrew Carnegie. Richard's name even came up once, as an example of someone who used his support of the arts as a way of raising himself socially. "The man grew up blue collar but married money," the instructor said. "His wife is very wealthy, inherited a real estate fortune, but Gessler also has an ability to judge people quickly and figure out who will produce results. He understands human psychology. Once he made his money, he began to sponsor a number of arts projects, here and in New York. He could have put his money into buying a sports team or another Planet Hollywood-type restaurant but instead he invested it in the arts."

Another student asked whether it wasn't more likely that corporate sponsors would be the major impetus in the twenty-first century and the teacher veered off the topic of Richard Gessler. I sat thinking about what he'd said. What in the world was I doing, getting involved with someone as well known as Richard? Who the hell did I think I was?

I poured more energy into my studies, working late at night in my room. Another week went by without hearing from Richard, then one night I got a call.

"Amanda?"

"Daddy? Oh, Daddy, I'm so glad to hear from you!"

"Well, thanks, honey. You haven't called me 'Daddy' since you were a little girl. And I'm glad you're glad. I've been worried that maybe you didn't want to talk to me anymore."

"Oh, um, *Dad*. Well, how are you? I tried to call your office."

"I've moved up. Working with Hughes-Neely now, in Charlotte. But that's not why I called. I've got some news. You have a little brother."

I caught my breath. "Janine had her baby?"

"Yes. He's eight pounds, seven ounces. A big boy! We're naming him Joshua."

"Oh. Congratulations." I had to sit down. It shouldn't have caught me by surprise but it did. "Is he okay? Is Janine okay?"

"He's great! They both are. He's beautiful. Listen, do you think you could tell your mother for me? I don't want her hearing about it from strangers."

My breath caught and it took me a minute to answer. "Don't make me, Dad. I can't bear it."

After a moment's silence, he said, "Okay. I'll do it myself. I just thought it would be easier for her coming from you." His voice sounded sulky, resentful. "Amanda, I know this is probably not great news for you, but please, can't you be a little happy for me? I don't ask you to forgive, but can't you try at least a little understanding? It's not that I didn't care for your mother, you know. Our marriage wasn't terrible. I have a lot of affection and respect for her. But we don't love each other anymore. Not the way a man and wife should. I'm forty-five years old, Amanda. I don't want to go through the rest of my life only half-alive."

"Seems to me like everything was just fine until Mark died. Then you guys grew apart instead of closer. Why didn't you try harder?" I dropped down into my big chair and pulled my knees up tight. "Why did you turn to someone else instead of Mom?"

"Oh, Amanda, don't let's go into all that right now, I just wanted to tell you about the baby."

"Now is the only time I've got, Dad. Every other time I ask, you skip around it."

"Well, Amanda, I only know this. Strong relationships grow when there are problems. Weak ones fall apart. What happened to us proves it."

"That's lame, Dad, that's so lame! You could have done differently, you could have made better choices. You chose to be selfish, to only think about yourself and too bad for Mom and me." My voice wobbled and I got a tighter grip on myself. "You don't care about us!"

"I didn't choose to hurt your mom."

"You didn't choose not to!"

"That's quite enough, young lady." His voice lowered into precisely modulated tones. "I'm sorry you feel this way. I only called to tell you about your brother, and I don't—"

"He's not my brother! *Mark* was my brother! This kid is just your bastard and he'll always be your bastard to me." I slammed the phone down, shaking, pulling my hair with both hands, stamping my feet against the cushion. Damn him! I hated him! He was so selfish, so self-centered, he didn't care how much he damaged others! How could he do this to me, how could he do it to Mom? I didn't want to speak to him ever again.

Richard still didn't call. He didn't call and he didn't write. I went through my days in a dingy fog of depression. The weather was sunny and beautiful, mocking me. I kept the shades pulled down in my bedroom, sought remote carrels at the library to work, busied myself in the back room of the music store. I didn't want to talk to anyone, and nobody bothered to talk to me.

Even dance class failed to lighten my mood. M. Beloit didn't make any further mention of the night he found me dancing. Instead, he hounded and browbeat his students and as I watched him throwing his melodramatic little tantrums, I brooded over the fact that I could have had real training, real professionals teaching me, if only I'd listened to Richard.

My solace was music. Night after night, when I couldn't sleep, I'd mess with my new keyboard. I began working on coming up with my own variations on basic arrangements. It seemed natural to play some of Mark's favorites—U2, Counting Crows, System of a Down, even some old Lynyrd Skynyrd. I felt like I would die of loneliness, and the worst part was I only had myself to blame.

Completely by accident, I found out Richard was on campus. I had needed some toe wraps and moleskin, so I ran over to the campus drugstore before class. A big crowd gathered in front of Jetton Hall, with a speaker at a podium, a banner saying

Anniversary Day, and rows of folding chairs for dignitaries. Then I saw him. He sat in the front row, his arms folded, the white streak in his hair drawing my eyes like a beacon

Slowly, I eased my way to the edge of the crowd. Students crossing campus between classes stopped to see what the fuss was about. Loaded down with book bags, they talked and laughed with their friends. I edged between a low brick wall and some juniper bushes until I got to the very corner of the open space around the speaker's podium. *Look at me, Richard.* I sent thought waves as hard as I could. *Look at me.*

It seemed to work. His eyes traveled away from the speaker, now introducing the student body president, and roamed over the crowd. I held my breath as his gaze swept past me and then back again.

"Hi, Daddy," I mouthed.

The vertical line between his brows deepened and his chin came up. His eyes narrowed. After a minute, he looked away.

There had to be a way to convey a message to him, to let him know how very sorry I was, how much I needed him. I couldn't let this opportunity slip away.

Slowly I let my book bag straps slide off my shoulders. I lowered the heavy pack to the ground in front of me and knelt down on one knee, pretending to search inside it. Nobody paid any attention. I brought my other knee down and sat on my heels. My hair was pinned up that day; I reached back and undid the clip so the curls and waves slid loosely past my shoulders. Richard's gaze traveled back to me. I kept my eyes steadily on his as I bent forward for a moment in a pose of supplication, my hands flat on the ground. Please, I said silently, hoping he would lip-read my prayer. Then I lowered my head to my knees, kowtowing to him.

When I looked up, Richard had shifted in his seat, bringing his left foot up to rest on his right knee. He still watched me, his face unreadable. I rose again to my feet, my hands clasped in front of me. All my senses were so intensely trained on him that it was as if a tunnel of pure vision existed between us and everything else was in a haze.

The student body president, a well-known kiss-ass in a suit and crew neck sweater, finished his spiel and was lightly applauded. The crowd shifted and broke up as the ceremony ended. Students headed on to their classes, the dignitaries came down from the platform, several people circled around Richard. I walked over, head down, eyes on the ground, until I got within a couple of feet from him and then I managed to stumble on the leg of one of the folding chairs. Strong hands grabbed my arms before I could fall.

"Are you all right?" Richard steadied me and I nodded, searching his face mutely for some sign. He took a quick glance around, leaned down and whispered in my ear. "Go home. Wait." Then he let go of me, patted my arm with a kind expression on his face, and walked off to join the rest.

It was late when he arrived. The package had been delivered hours before, along with his note of instructions. I heard footsteps coming up the stairs, the turn of the unlocked doorknob as he came in. There was a rustle as he removed his clothes, then he slid under the blankets, cuddling up to me.

His hand, warm and solid, curved over my naked behind, his breath tickled my ear. My eyes remained shut. I could hear and feel him next to me, but I was too groggy to move, too lethargic to respond. He began to kiss me—my neck, shoulder, arm. Then he rolled me over on my back and pulled up my nightie, covering my breasts with passionate kisses, helping himself to every part of my body. I wanted to kiss him back, to hold him, to tell him all the words of love that I knew, but the pills he'd sent were too powerful. They kept me from opening my eyes or uttering a sound, they made my legs and arms limp and pliable. My mind could recognize what Richard was doing, but the strong sedatives had erased my will.

He was very thorough that night. His lovemaking seemed to last for hours, he explored every inch of my body and acted pleased when a moan or cry escaped me. Toward morning he stopped, wrapped his arms around me, and went to sleep. I woke when the sun was already high, streaming through the gaps in my curtains, promising a nice day.

I still felt groggy. My head pounded and I was stiff and a little sick. I crawled out of bed and went to the bathroom. There were hickeys on my throat and breasts and tummy, and my mouth felt tender and sensitive, as if Richard had been too rough. I couldn't remember for sure, there were times I'd slipped in and out of awareness.

Richard was awake when I came out of the bathroom wrapped in a towel. He pushed the pillows against the headboard and sat up in bed, waiting for me. "Come here," he said. "Come to Daddy."

I walked to him slowly. On the floor lay my new nightie. Silky, short, white with little purple flowers, it matched the ribbon on the neck of the teddy bear. They had arrived in the same package as the pills and Richard's note. It took me a long time to decide to follow his instructions.

Richard took my hand and pulled me down next to him on the bed. He opened my towel and looked lovingly at his handiwork, placing a soft kiss on each of my bruises.

I curled down against his side, "Why did you want me to be knocked out? Don't you like for me to be *with* you when we make love?"

He kissed my forehead and cuddled me closer. "Of course, I do, Baby, have I ever acted like I don't?"

"Then, why?"

"Tell me this first. Why did you go ahead and take the pills if you were unsure?"

My cheeks flushed and I buried my head into his chest. "To please you, I guess."

"You guess?"

"To please you, Daddy."

Richard heaved a sigh and slipped his hand under my chin, bringing my face up to his for a kiss. His lips were soft and warm and gentle. A sweet kiss, a delicate kiss, just on the corner of my mouth. The kind of kiss anyone could give a baby. "Well, Amanda, I think you know the reason."

I looked at him. His mouth, his cheeks with morning stubble, his eyes. The brown was so dark, I almost couldn't see his pupils, but I could see the warmth of his expression.

"You wanted me to show how much I trust you. That I would leave myself completely unguarded and defenseless. Is that it?"

He nodded. "And do you? Trust me? Enough to come to New York? Now, not next semester."

That was it. Yes or no. If I said yes, it meant dropping out of my classes, losing my place in the dance troupe, leaving North Carolina. Lying like hell to my mother.

Or I could say no. Entirely my choice.

Richard waited patiently for my answer. My gaze traveled across his chest where the gold crucifix lay half-covered by the mat of curly hair. Lying against him, I could feel the rise and fall of his breathing, could hear the quiet thud of his heart. His left arm was around me, keeping me warm but not holding me down.

"My biggest worry is Mom. I don't like hiding things from her."

"I don't like it either. Tell me something, does she support your career? Would she be happy if you got a scholarship to study at the Joffrey or ABA?"

I rose up on one elbow. "I don't know, but that's not the issue, is it? What would upset her is me living with you."

"But you won't. You'll have your own place. All I'm doing is providing financial support." Richard smoothed my hair back with his hand. "Amanda, your mom loves you and you love her. I don't want to destroy that, all I'm suggesting is you don't force her to see something she'd rather not. Most parents aren't ready to face the fact that their children have grown up and become sexual beings. What would happen if

120

she found out about you and me? Would she stop loving you?"

"No, of course not. But she'd be upset."

"So don't upset her." He kissed me again, tiny little kisses all over my face. "Amanda, this is your decision. I won't try to influence you. The only thing is, if you don't come to New York, our relationship will have to end. It's killing me doing this half-and-half thing. Make your decision, my darling, and follow your heart."

There were tears in his eyes, actual tears. He needed me. I was special to him in a way I was to no one else. With one movement, I rolled over, straddling his lap and wrapping my arms around his neck. I kissed him, a long, deep kiss, a woman's kiss. "I'll go," I whispered. "If you really want me."

Richard held me close, stroking my hair. "Want you? My god, Amanda, I want you more than ever." His tongue thrust deep into my mouth and he rose up, rolling me back against the mattress, covering me with his big body. He entered me, quickly, forcefully, driving all doubts from my mind. "I want you all right," he whispered, "and I will have you. From now on, you're truly mine. And darling, I'm going to make you so happy."

Chapter Eight

When Richard decided to do something, he did it. While I showered, dressed, and ate a Pop-Tart for breakfast, he booked our flight, set up hotel reservations, packed his own things and arranged for my landlady to hold the room for me and forward my mail.

I didn't like leaving all my personal possessions behind. Richard gave me permission to bring only what would fit in my emptied book bag. I put in a few items of clothing, my purse, and my dance shoes. Richard added the teddy bear, leaving no room for anything else.

"Don't worry about the rest," he insisted, urging me out the door. "I'll buy anything you need when we get to New York."

He had instructed me to wear a little schoolgirl outfit he'd bought, sweater and plaid skirt with knee socks. "I feel like an ass," I complained. "And I look like one too."

My mutinous expression only tickled him and he threw an arm around my shoulders. "Now don't be mad. You look adorable. It's only for this flight, honey, I had to tell them you were under age. I didn't want to use your driver's license. We're traveling incognito, my pet."

"Why? Maybe your name means something to people, but mine doesn't."

"Oh, for crying out loud, Amanda! If you keep quibbling, we'll miss our flight!" He regained his composure and hurried me out to the car. All the way to the airport, my stomach got tighter and tighter; worse than exams, worse than those final moments before a stage performance. I wasn't ready. I had thought he would give me a few days, a little time to adjust my thinking. Now it was like standing at the open door of a plane, being told to jump and not knowing if my parachute had been secured.

"You keep frowning," Richard warned as we walked through the terminal, "and I'm going to turn you over my knee." He looked at me, speculation in his eye. "In fact, it wouldn't bother me at all to flip that little skirt up and—"

"Never mind," I said hastily. "I'll be good. It's just . . .oh, this stupid teddy bear. Don't you think it's a bit much? Dressing younger is one thing, but at this rate, I'll be back in the womb."

He chuckled and gave me a discreet pat on the butt. "Be my sweet girl a little longer. We'll have such a great time, exploring New York together. I can't wait to show you Manhattan."

We had seats in First Class. "Hope you enjoy your flight, Mr. Smith," the attendant said.

"Smith?" I mouthed at Richard. He nodded. I cupped my hand over his ear and whispered, "What do you have, a fake I.D.? Show me." Richard dug in his pocket and handed over a New Jersey driver's license for Richard Smith. It looked perfectly legal. I handed it back and whispered, "I'm beginning to think you *are* some kind of spy. How did you get hold of this?"

He leaned back in his seat, rubbing his shoulders against the upholstery and sipping appreciatively at his scotch on the rocks. "Darling," he said softly, "when you have money, anything is possible."

He dozed for a while on the flight. I mostly watched out the window, brooding on the fact that I would have to call my mother and find some kind of explanation for my actions. I felt sick, physically sick, at the thought of telling her I'd left school.

Richard snored softly and I turned to look at him. His empty glass dangled from his hand. I moved it to the tray table. With his mouth slightly open and his reading glasses sliding down his nose, he looked older. Less vibrant, more tired. He looked like any middle-aged businessman. I curled up in my seat, wrapping my arms around my legs. Images of the previous night kept coming back to me, unbidden. They were confused, a shifting montage, and I didn't know which were accurate and which were shaded by my doped-up state.

I could remember Richard leaning over me; kissing me, licking me, stroking my body while he murmured indistinguishable things against my skin. His touch had been gentle, delicate, but two images remained in my mind, images that disturbed me. In one, he posed me, arranging my semiconscious body into different positions, followed by the click and flash of a camera. In the other image, even more unnerving, he cradled me in his arms, pressing kisses on my unresponsive lips and sobbing like a child into my hair. What kind of man was he really? He seemed so strong and in control most of the time. Powerful, magnetic. Why, then, did he want someone like me? He could have his pick of almost any woman. What had his tears meant? Joy? Pain?

Thinking made my stomach twist. With an effort, I turned my mind to other things. Dance lessons, rehearsals, the Lincoln Center. I pictured that perfect toe shoe. Spotless, elegant, beauty defined. It was the single pure image I understood. All my other confusions and doubts would be resolved in time.

The entire ride from the airport into the city, I pressed my nose to the window. Richard pointed out various landmarks along our route but I kept finding my attention drawn to little things—pigeons in a park, trash and grit clinging to surfaces, intense sunshine wiped out by the shadows of buildings. Our hotel was off Central Park, a dignified old building clad in heavy stone. Richard must have already made arrangements; we and our luggage were whisked immediately to a suite on the twelfth floor. I could see the skating rink and a huge L-shaped pond from the windows.

The rooms were more luxurious than any I'd ever been in. Rich satin draperies at the windows, thick carpets, a bed as big as a swimming pool and piled high with pillows. There were televisions and phones in every room, including the bathroom, fresh flowers, thick terry-cloth robes in the mirrored closets, a refrigerator stocked with soft drinks, liquor, fruit and snacks. Richard watched as I explored, chuckling at each exclamation I made.

"I can't believe it." I whirled around and dropped down on the bed. "Is this really where I'm going to live? Or is it just temporary until you find me an apartment?"

"This is it." He walked over and took my face in his hands. "You're going to love it here." The hotel was residential style. "Most of the residents have been living here since the Jimmy Carter administration, I'm afraid. You won't have much in common with them, but that's okay. I intend to monopolize your time." We kissed and I pushed all doubts and worries to the back of my mind. He was right, I would love it there. We'd be together and everything would be fine.

"Are you tired?" he asked. "Do you need to rest? Because if not, I want to show you something." We went down to the street and Richard hailed a cab. Within minutes, we were cruising along Central Park South. "I'm showing you this because it's the safest route to go and besides, I know it'll be drawing you like Mecca, even though it's west, not east."

I didn't know what he was talking about until we pulled up to the curb and I looked out the window to realize I was staring at the Lincoln Center. On the left, the New York State Theater, home of the New York City Ballet. Straight ahead, the arches of the Metropolitan Opera House, and hallowed halls of the American Ballet Theatre. Back in a corner, the Julliard Dance School. "I can't believe I'm here," I whispered, my breath fogging the window glass.

We got out of the taxi and walked hand-in-hand through the plaza. I felt like I was visiting a holy shrine. "We'll see all the shows," Richard promised. "You'll be able to completely immerse yourself in dance. There's so much here, sweetheart, and I'm going to give it all to you."

I watched people swarming in and out of the buildings. Some were obviously tourists, but there were others, slim-legged young people in groups of two or three, whom I was sure were dancers. They were easy to recognize—the lightness in their steps, the energy with which they walked, the dead-giveaway gym bags they carried over their shoulders. Soon I might be one of those fortunate people, taking classes, preparing for performances. My hand tightened on Richard's and I rubbed my face against his sleeve.

From there, we went to the Ballet Shop. Richard bought me new workout clothes and shoes, a portable *barre*, even a fold-up dance floor to place over the carpet in the hotel suite. "I want you to be able to keep up your workouts until we can get the classes arranged. Besides, I'd love to watch you go through your routine." He added dance and workout DVDs, and ordered everything delivered to the hotel.

Next door was a music store. Richard spied some guitars in the window as we walked by and pulled me inside. Before I knew it, he had bought a beautiful Ovation acoustic, black with a spruce top and multiple sound holes. "There'll be times I can't be with you and this will keep you from getting too lonely." I brushed my fingers lightly across the strings before the clerk boxed up the guitar to go. Richard knew me better than I thought.

At our final stop, a clothing store, Richard loaded me down with jeans and sweaters, skirts and tops. His deliberations over underwear and nighties embarrassed me in front of the middle-aged clerk, so I stood by the window and watched traffic go by. "We'll deliver this right away," I heard her say as we left. "Thank you, Mr. Smith."

I began to feel concern over all this money he'd spent. "How are you going to explain these bills? Won't your wife see them?"

"Let me worry about that. Now look, here's the park. I'm going to show you the quickest route back to the hotel."

The day was overcast and damp. A strong scent of wet earth pervaded as we walked along the rain-darkened sidewalks. "The park's pretty safe these days," Richard observed as we stepped aside to avoid a boy on roller blades. "As long as you stick to the main paths and daylight hours. But keep your guard up. Don't talk to strangers and don't carry cash. I'll get you a credit card." He threw an arm around my shoulders. "You could stay within a two-mile radius of the hotel and still see about twenty of the finest museums in the world. And the food! The food here is unbelievable. The variety. If you decide in the middle of the night that you want some Moroccan tajine, you can get Moroccan tajine. If you want kebab or black bean soup or couscous with lamb, you can get it. Not to mention," he grinned as we stopped at a hot dog vendor's cart, "the finest Coney Islands available to man or beast." He ordered two with everything and we sat down on a bench to eat.

"Ah, this is what I mean," he said, throwing back his head and taking in a big lungful of air. "This is it, this is life. Knowing what you want to do and doing it with all your heart." He grinned and winked at me. "So what are you thinking, Amanda?"

I took a bite of my hot dog, keeping my eyes down although I could feel a blush rise to my cheeks. All my worries still bubbled under the surface. Worries about my mom, about his wife, about leaving school. Self-doubts about my ability to fit in at a New York City dance school, concerns that I'd sold my soul for a shiny gift-wrapped dream. Yet I couldn't deny the excitement I felt. Everything was so alive there. Opportunities abounded. I could almost feel the energy rising from the sidewalks. And Richard. He seemed so happy, so fulfilled. My heart melted in gratitude and, speechless, all I could do was swallow hard, curl up next to him on the bench and rest my head on his shoulder. He held me close and seemed to think that was enough. I hoped it was.

*

New York City in the autumn was a wonderful place. The weather was cold but sunny, the trees in Central Park put out a final burst of color before they went bare, and every day had an exhilarating surge of possibility. Richard managed to spend most of his time with me, taking me to the theatre, museums, and the ballet. We saw *Rodeo* and *Allegro Brillante*, choreographed by Balanchine. When I asked if he worried about being seen, Richard shook his head. "Diane hates the city. Besides, she's too busy with her horsey friends in Connecticut."

"What about other people? Couldn't somebody recognize you and maybe make trouble?"

"I'd like to see them try." He looked so ferocious for a minute that I pulled back, but then he winked and grinned. "You let me worry about that, Baby."

Every morning I did my workouts and danced for hours, preparing for the audition Richard promised to arrange. Come mid-afternoon, I jogged in Central Park or practiced guitar, learning some of Richard's favorite songs. A couple of blocks away I found a deli where I could buy fresh fruit and vegetables, yogurt and cheese, homemade soup to carry home in a container. Sometimes I helped Mr. D'Angelo, my neighbor on the twelfth floor, to walk his dogs—two pomeranians and a suluki that had ambitions of being a bloodhound. Twice a week, I used my cell phone to call my mother.

"When am I going to see you?" she asked one Wednesday evening in early November. "Did you get the message I left on your machine? The Color Guard has their contest in Northville coming up, why don't you come home for the weekend and see it? They're really doing great this year. You'd love the choreography."

"Gee, I'd like to, Mom, but I can't. I'm working every spare minute at the store, and besides, I have homework up the wazoo. I have that history paper due, remember I told you?" I still hadn't told her I wasn't in Raleigh. The lies were getting easier, even though the guilt kept getting worse. "Why don't you see if Sissy would like to go? I bet she doesn't get out much, she might really enjoy the chance."

"Oh. Well, maybe I will." Her voice took on that bright, anxious note I knew so well. "Anyway, I'll see you soon for Thanksgiving break."

"Uh, yeah. Mom, how's it going with Dad? He left me a message with his new office number but we seem to keep missing each other, playing phone tag. We haven't actually talked in weeks. Is he okay? Does he like his new job?"

"Yes. I think so. We haven't talked much lately. He's been pretty busy, I suppose." She gave me his apartment phone number. "I'm sure he'd love to hear from you. Why don't you call him right now? He should be home from the office."

I told her I would, and hung up. I didn't want to call his new apartment. Janine would be there. Dad might be busy, changing his new son's diapers, talking baby talk, doing raspberries on the baby's round little tummy. No. Much better if I called when he was at work and we could have a quick, business-like conversation.

I'd wait.

One Sunday afternoon, Richard and I went to the Lincoln Center to see *Sleeping Beauty*. The theater was full of blue-haired ladies and little girls, all of whom, I had no doubt, would go home dreaming they were Aurora, a beautiful vision *en pointe*.

For this special occasion, Richard asked me to wear one of his chosen outfits, a demure little-girl dress with blue flowers and a high waist. Along with a pair of Mary Janes and some high white stockings, the look was innocent and made

131

me feel creepy. I wasn't old enough to enjoy looking so young. Richard and I walked into the theater hand-in-hand and sat in the dark watching the ballet. Soon, his fingers stroked my thigh, sliding above the stocking and searching in a way that left me squirming.

"Don't, Richard. Not here." I pulled my skirt down, pushed at his hand.

"What did you call me?" His breath tickled my ear but he didn't sound amused.

"I'm sorry, Daddy. But don't do that now."

The ballet unfolded but I couldn't enjoy it with Richard teasing me every so often by putting his hand in my lap, or even surreptitiously pinching my breast. I watched as Carabosse arrived at Aurora's christening, enraged and insulted that she hadn't been invited. The prelude ended, so did the entr'acte, and in Act One I finally got to see the ballerina who would play the grown Aurora. She was lovely. Megan Cristoforri, I'd seen her picture many times in *Pointe* magazine. I watched intently as she got to the dance of the roses, holding my breath each time she held her position balanced on one toe, knowing how difficult those moments of stillness were, how much control they took. Richard's hand again slid up between my legs. I squeezed my thighs together and pushed him away. "*Stop*," I whispered. "In a few minutes they'll have the *danse vertigo*. I want to watch."

"Oh come on, Amanda. You know you like it." He became more insistent, pinning my arm down with his and forcing his fingers even higher under my skirt. An old lady sat on my other side, emanating a slight scent of cinnamon gum and hogging the armrest. I reared back a bit in my seat, trying to avoid notice. "Show Daddy how much you love him," Richard whispered. He managed to hook the leg opening of my panties. Aurora took the spindle from Carabosse, laughing at her parents who kept trying to warn her. Then, in a moment, all was lost as she pricked her finger and Carabosse's power overcame her, forcing her to dance under the witch's spell, forcing her to spin the very web that entangled her.

Aurora dropped to the floor in a dead faint, Tchaikovsky's music rose in Carabosse's moment of triumph, and Richard had his triumph too as I opened my thighs a bit and his fingers probed. When intermission arrived and the house lights came back up, my skirt was modestly in place and Richard had a satisfied smile on his face. As I climbed over him to go to the Ladies' Room, he licked his fingertips and murmured, "Told you you'd like it."

I got to the bathroom ahead of the crowd and snagged the last stall in the row. The metal walls of the toilet cubicles seemed to amplify every sound. I huddled on the closed lid of the seat, blowing air out through my pursed lips, almost whistling, forcing my breathing to slow and my heart to settle down. All around me I could hear women's voices, little girls chattering, the sounds of faucets running, toilets flushing. I knew that backstage at that moment, dancers would be checking their make-up, changing costumes, doing stretches and limbering-up exercises to keep their muscles warm and elastic between acts.

My chest felt tight and constricted, my mouth was full of tears. I wanted to please him, I did, but not like that. Not in

133

semi-public, not so sleazily, not at the ballet. Richard could be so warm and loving, but sometimes a tiny cruel streak appeared and I hated myself for submitting to him. Was our relationship only about sex? Nothing more? I wasn't a fool. He liked to control me, and there was even a part of me that enjoyed submitting to him, but not when he went too far.

All dancers had to deal with suspension of will. I was accustomed to following orders—dance the ordained steps, hold the required technique, force my body into unnatural positions. I'd been trained to drive myself past my own limitations. I dealt with that part of my chosen career, I even embraced it, but *this.* . . .

Voices rose and fell. I could hear speculation about how long my cubicle had been occupied. I lifted the lid of the toilet and pulled down my panties. In a moment of shame, I remembered what Richard had said. *You know you like it.* The panties had a damp spot. Richard had made me wet.

The audition at the School of American Ballet went with suspicious ease, almost perfunctorily on the part of the instructors. They informed me that I could join the school in January, when the new workshops would begin. I felt relieved but apprehensive too. "Did you bribe them or something?" I asked Richard upon returning to the apartment. Taking off my coat, I stood in front of the dresser, facing the mirror and speaking to his reflection. "This isn't Burgess, it should have been much more difficult to get in." Richard came up behind me and put his hands on my waist, nuzzling my hair and I squirmed away. "Did you do something?"

Richard just smiled. He took my wrists in his hands and raised one, then the other, to his lips for a kiss. Then he stretched both my arms out wide. "Come on, Amanda. Get real." My arms were winged out, pulled back slightly so that my back was arched, and Richard rested his chin on top of my head. "My sweet little girl. My tiny dancer." I could see him outlined behind me, as though I were a picture and he was the frame. His fingers gripped my wrists, encircling them easily, and I felt the latent power emanating from his body. "Did you really think anyone would accept you now? A dancer who dropped out of a prestigious dance program with no warning?" he crooned against my hair. "Of course I did something. I had to."

"Richard! I wanted to earn a place on my own merits! It's not right to bribe—"

"It was that or nothing," His gaze met mine in the mirror, his expression darkening. "And I've told you not to call me Richard."

I pulled loose and put the width of the room between us. "Oh, for pity's sake. None of this Daddy stuff right now. I want to talk." Folding my arms across my chest, I straightened up to my full height.

Richard frowned and a flush rose in his face. "I give you everything and you still refuse to do the one thing I ask? Fine, Amanda. I suppose you don't feel you owe me a daughter's obedience. Maybe you don't care if you break my heart. But if your conscience doesn't accuse you of *ingratitude*—" He turned and head to the door, grabbing his briefcase and overcoat.

"Daddy, no, I didn't mean it that way." I raced after him, catching hold of his arm. "Please, I'm not ungrateful, I just—"

"You just want to have it your own way." His face was tired-looking, old. Weariness seemed to settle on him and his eyes held no hint of a smile. "I guess we all do. But I thought your way was mine, too." Richard shook me loose and left the apartment, slamming the door behind him.

I burst into tears, sliding to the floor and knuckling my eyes like a child. "Oh *Daddy*." I couldn't bear that cold look in his eyes. I hadn't meant to be accusatory; I simply wanted to be treated like an adult. To stand on my own two feet. Instead, I'd blown whatever chance I had back in North Carolina and, if Richard was right, the only way I could make it in New York was with his help. Then, on top of everything else, I hurt his feelings and behaved like a selfish two-year-old. Damn. Damn, damn, damn. I couldn't do anything right.

Richard came back later that night. I flew to him with my apology and he held me close, cuddling me on his lap as I promised it would never happen again.

"It's my fault, too, darling. I've been too busy at work, and it's not going to get better." He pushed my hair off my face and kissed me on the forehead. "We'll simply have to be more understanding of each other than ever. I promise, I won't bring any further pressure to bear at the school. I've gotten you in, but whether you remain will be entirely up to you and how well you dance. You'll still earn your way."

I twined my arms around his neck and covered his face with kisses. "It doesn't matter, so long as I know you forgive

136

me. I hate having squabbles." He smiled and I rested my head against his shoulder. "I do love you, you know. You mean everything to me."

"Do I?"

"Yes."

"Yes, what?"

"Yes, Daddy."

Thanksgiving was going to be a problem. Mom kept asking when I would come home. "Maybe I should go for a short visit," I suggested to Richard one morning after I thought he'd been all mellowed with a round of lovemaking. "After all, your wife will be expecting you to be with your family that day. I could fly to Raleigh on Wednesday, drive my car to Mom's, stay over till Saturday, and then drive and fly back. No one the wiser."

"I don't want you to go. Tell her you have rehearsals." At school, I knew, they would be getting ready for a performance of *The Nutcracker*.

"That's no good. She'd want to come see me in the show."

"Well, make some kind of excuse. I need you here." He swung his legs over the edge of the bed, sitting there in his black silk boxers and peering over his reading glasses. "Call your mother," he said. "Let's get this settled right now."

"But—"

"Now, Amanda." He handed me the phone. I looked around for a robe, but Richard had begun tapping his foot, so instead I went ahead and dialed Mom's number.

"Hi, honey! How are you?"

"I'm good. Uh, Mom. . ."

"We came in first in the competition! Superior rating, and first place Color Guard. You should have seen, the girls really put their hearts into it."

"That's great! Congratulations. But, I have some bad news. I can't come home for Thanksgiving after all." She didn't respond. "Sorry, it's just that we're having a big sale starting early Friday morning and my boss says he really needs me here."

"Well . . . what will you do on Thanksgiving Day? I hate to think of you being all alone." Her voice had lost its enthusiasm and I felt like shit.

"A girlfriend invited me to come over. Remember Jennifer? So I'll be okay, but I don't want you to be alone either."

"Oh, me, don't worry about me. I'll . . . I can invite someone over. Maybe Anne's family, she might not feel up to cooking a big . . . ." Her voice trailed off.

"Mom?"

"Yes, I'm here. Well, do what you need to do, and if you change your mind, just come ahead. You don't even need to call, I'll be here."

"Sorry, Mom. I'm really sorry."

"Don't be silly. If you have to work, you have to work. I understand."

Richard watched me, his eyes narrowed. I hurried to finish. "Okay. Good-bye. Hope you can find someone to come over. Maybe Sissy's family. And, you know, maybe if I

138

explained to my—" Richard shook his head. "Well, anyway, talk to you soon." I hung up the phone, folded my arms in front of my waist and excused myself, and went into the bathroom.

The overhead lights were harsh, unforgiving. I blew my nose hard on some tissue and pushed my hair out of my eyes. My reflection stared back at me from the mirror. The cotton panties and little girl's undershirt made me look about twelve years old and that was how I felt. Stupid girl. Stupid, skinny, ugly little girl.

Chapter Nine

Thanksgiving dawned bright and clear. Richard spent Wednesday night with me and talked again about renting a hotel room for Thursday right on Broadway, the route of the Macy's Parade, but I stopped him. "Don't bother. The parade will be on TV and I'll be more comfortable here. Since I'm going to be alone."

"All right. You've made your point." After all the hassle, it turned out Richard had to be with his family that day. "I should have known," he said. "My daughters are both in town, plus Emily's husband and Theresa's fiancé. I simply can't get out of it. I promise to make it up to you."

"Doesn't matter." I shrugged and faced the window. "I'll be fine. I'll watch the parades on TV, and order room service, and maybe later in the day, you can sneak off to your den and give me a phone call. No big deal." Richard looked dismayed for a moment, and then he laughed, gave me a bear hug and slapped my behind. He let himself out, keys jingling, after admonishing me not to eat too much turkey and I stuck out my tongue as the door closed behind him.

Around noon, I phoned Mom. She sounded flustered and happy. "I'm so sorry you can't be here, honey," she said, "but your idea was great. Sissy and her family will be here around one-thirty. I'm so looking forward to having a big gathering; it's been years since I've done that. And Sissy's mom sent beautiful flowers and candles. We'll have fun. Thanks for the suggestion."

I swallowed hard and smiled, so she'd hear it in my voice. "That's great, Mom. Well, I'm heading off in a while to eat with Jennifer's family. Thanks for being so understanding about my not coming home. My boss said to tell you how much he appreciates it."

The lies left a bad taste in my mouth. My guilt was less, knowing Mom would enjoy a big family party, even if it wasn't her family, but I suddenly felt a pang of envy. Sissy would have the pleasure of my mom's turkey and dressing, her creamy mashed potatoes with bits of chive in them, deep-dish apple pie, the works. I'd been with Sissy's family on holidays before; Mom's house would be noisy and crowded but the rooms would also be full of laughter and camaraderie. No matter how much Sissy argued with her mother the rest of the time, holidays were always fun.

"All three of Sissy's brothers are coming too," Mom added. "They seemed real pleased with the invitation. Travis said to tell you hi. Oh, and Mason Kennedy sends his regards. He's in the kitchen right now, peeling potatoes."

"Why's *he* there? He's your lawyer."

"He's a friend, too. I found out he would be alone and invited him over. Holidays aren't easy for the divorced. We have to help each other out."

I felt a momentary sting of discomfort. Did Mom have a boyfriend already? She was very vulnerable, maybe it was too soon. I wasn't ready for her to start dating.

"Well, I better go now," I said. "Need to shower, get cleaned up, all that. You have a great day!" And tell Mason Kennedy he could just mash his potatoes somewhere else.

The hours stretched ahead of me, blank and empty. I had no appetite for solitary turkey and all the trimmings. Richard's defection burned in my heart and Mom's news left me too disquieted to sit still. I dressed warmly and went for a walk.

The parade had ended. Crossing the road, I headed into the park where sidewalks were crowded with people in family groups, going back to their homes and apartments on the Upper East Side. Everyone seemed to be in good humor. Adults chatted loudly, children chased each other or the birds, and babies slept in strollers or nodded weary heads on their daddy's shoulder. I strode along, taking in deep draughts of cold air, grateful to be able to stretch my legs. Walked for hours, up to North Meadow and back. The sunlight began to fade and a cold wind whipped up. Richard had warned me not to be in the park after dark, but then Richard was off in Connecticut somewhere, having a cozy old time with his family.

I couldn't help seeing the irony. Richard was a married man. He had a wife; a wife he professed to respect and care for, even if they didn't love each other anymore. He was still married to her, and I? I was the Other Woman. Or maybe the Other Girl. No better than Janine. All the things I accused my dad of doing, Richard was doing, too. With me. I was in love with a married man and I paid the penalty with days like this, when I was shut out, on the wrong side of a glass door. I lived a kind of half-life, waiting for him to come over, accepting all the rules he set down, always teetering on the edge of self-respect.

How long could we go on like this? Already Sissy asked a lot of questions, unwilling to accept my excuses. "I don't care," she said, when I gave my reasons for not coming home. "You should be here anyway. This will be hard for your mom and just because I'll be there, that doesn't let you off the hook." I could tell I'd fallen in her estimation. I was an ungrateful, uncaring daughter who didn't appreciate the warm, loving mother I had.

"Loan me a ten?"

A voice at my ear took me by surprise, and the tall young man's hand on my elbow, propelling me toward the Dairy House, spooked me. Early dusk had begun to fall and fewer people were in the park. He had curly dark hair and green eyes, and anyone seeing us from a distance would have thought, from the way he smiled at me, that he was my boyfriend.

Too shocked to yell, I tried to pull away. He put his other arm around my waist and half-lifted, half-dragged me up the steps and under the Victorian gable of the deserted Visitor's Center.

"No!" I kicked and flailed but only a squeak came out of my throat. I couldn't breathe. His hands felt under my jacket, brushing against my breasts, hard on my ribs. Wheezing gasps ripped through my lungs and then he found the shoulder strap of my purse, angled across my chest. With a sudden movement, he pulled out a knife, the blade flashing at me before he cut the strap and was gone. I fell to my knees, scared and stunned, dizzy with the surge of adrenaline that arrived too late. He was out of sight by the time I stumbled to the path, gaping at people walking by who were totally unaware of what had happened.

I'd been robbed but I was okay. That's what I told myself as my wobbly knees took me home. I was okay. He'd gotten a few dollars, my hotel key, an old comb and a half-gone pack of gum, but nothing more. I could feel dampness where I'd started to wet my pants. I pressed my gloved hands to my mouth to keep from whimpering.

The hotel lobby was too warm after the cold air outside. I had to get another key at the desk and the clerk stared at me as he handed it over. Maybe he could smell urine on me; maybe it was just the whiteness in my face that I could see reflected in the shiny brass tiles behind him that caught his attention. Either way, I hurried to get into the elevator and out of sight.

The apartment was cold and dark. I snapped on all the lights in every room and turned on the TVs. Checked behind every curtain, looked in each closet. I was scared to wash with the bathroom door closed, but scared to leave it open too. Finally I managed to take the world's fastest shower, pulled on my warmest clothes and curled up in the corner of the big armchair. After a minute, I took a couple of little bottles of Bailey's Irish Cream from the mini-bar, found some packages of nuts, and sat there alternating between the two until my shivering stopped. I could have been killed. What if the guy had knifed me? I didn't carry any identification, they would have labeled me a Jane Doe and I'd have disappeared from the face of the earth.

Or worse. What if they *had* identified my mutilated body? For a moment, I imagined my mother's horror if the police had phoned and told her I was murdered. Jeez, I'd be dead *and* caught in my lies. That thought was enough to persuade me to have another Bailey's. By the time Richard phoned, I'd moved right past calm and was well into giddy.

"I'm fine, Daddy, I'm great. Except for being mugged. But don't worry; it was just a little mugging. A mug-ette. A mini-mug. Practically a—"

"You got mugged? I'm coming over."

"You don't have to. I'm fine. I'm more than fine. Did you know there's eighteen peanuts in each package of peanuts but only twelve cashews in the cashews?" The phone went dead. The room began to feel too hot and I peeled off my sweater.

By the time Richard arrived, I was sitting on the edge of the bed in my underwear, feeling dizzy. My skin was clammy and my mouth kept filling up with saliva. He burst in, his overcoat swinging open as he rushed across the room to me. "Are you alright? Oh honey, when I think of what could have—"

"Daddy, I'm fine," I said, reaching up for his hug, "You didn't have to come all this way." I could feel cold air coming off his coat.

"Never do that again, do you hear me?" Richard held me at arm's length for a moment as if to assess any damage and then bundled me into his arms again, rubbing his cheek against my hair. "Damned park, they should have closed it down years ago. Full of crack heads and worse."

He sat down and cradled me in his lap, rocking back and forth. "Poor Baby, it's all my fault. If you ever go off alone again, I'm going to blister your ass," he said, but his voice was tender. I looked at him woozily and then ran for the bathroom. A few minutes later, my stomach emptied of the nuts and liquor, I sat exhausted on the tile floor while Richard held a cold, wet cloth to my forehead.

"Sorry," I muttered. I managed to brush my teeth and rinse out my mouth, then Richard tucked me into bed and everything hit me at once. "Oh Daddy, I was so scared! Hold me please." He climbed in next to me and I clung in desperation. "I was all alone and it was getting dark."

"I can't stand this," he said, looking down at me. "Leaving you here, knowing you're alone. It's torture, Amanda. I hate it more every time." I lay huddled in his arms, wrapped inside his overcoat. The shakes were beginning to fade, but I kept making little hiccups. "Something's got to give," he said, rubbing my arms. "There's got to be a way."

He kissed me one more time and eased out of the bed, promising he'd be back early in the morning. I felt sick the rest of the night, waking frequently at the slightest sound and dry-heaving into the sink. My legs shook, and no matter how many blankets I piled over myself, I still felt cold. I was totally dependent on Richard. Couldn't get by without my old man.

After that, Richard checked in on me more frequently. The business still gobbled up his time, but he called me by phone several times a day and came over whenever he could. He liked to stop on his way to the office, and wake me with a kiss and early morning cuddle. Afterward, he'd go over my plans for the day, making sure he approved, and then go to work.

He found me a tutor to work with until the semester began. Her name was Mme. Dumont and she had once been a dancer with the New York City Ballet, possibly back in the Ice Age. Over sixty years old, angular and wizened with wrinkled rouged cheeks that looked like dried Carolina mud, she ran a studio in Chelsea and took me on as a private student.

She didn't like me much. Perhaps she saw me as beneath her notice, too raw and immature, under-trained. At any rate, she apparently needed the money which Richard provided, so she agreed to teach me. I was grateful. I wanted to dance again, I needed to dance again, and this I did. Endlessly. Occasionally I even did a dance the whole way through, but mostly I only managed about twelve or sixteen bars before she stopped the music and made me start over.

No problem. I was happy to go to her little studio upstairs over a flower shop, work my heart out for a while, and come home all sweaty and tired. Richard enjoyed meeting me at the apartment afterward and giving me a bath and massage. I liked it, too. My energy level zoomed.

"You have color in your cheeks," Richard observed one day. "You needed this, I guess. Without dancing, you droop like a flower that hasn't been watered. Now you look more like that fiery little sprite I met. I think you'd wither and die if you couldn't dance."

I did a couple of quick clogging steps and jumped in his lap. "What can we do to get color back in your cheeks? You've been looking droopy, too. Oh, wait. I know how to fix that." I grinned at him and squirmed back and forth.

Richard laughed and gave my rump a slap. "Ooh, I'd like to let you, but I've got to go." He got up, setting me back on my feet. "There's a lot happening at work right now. We're trying to buy out a particular corporation and they're playing hard to get." He put on his overcoat. "Not to worry, though. There isn't a thing I've ever put my mind to that I haven't gotten." He stopped at the door to give me a final kiss. "I won't be back tonight. The wife is giving me hell about working too many hours, so I'll see you tomorrow." He gave me a rib-crushing hug and a final slap on the butt and was gone.

I spent a lot of my free time watching DVDs. Dance DVDs, especially *Swan Lake*. I remembered what Richard had said, that someday I might dance the role of Odile, the evil temptress who convinced Sigfried she was really Odette, the Swan. Natalia Makarova danced both roles in the video, but I knew of other ballet companies who used different dancers. Odile appealed to me. Her strong legs, her balance. The *pas de deux* with Sigfried showed her caprice and cruelty, but it was still a beautiful dance, one that would require a lot of strength and control. Odile got what she wanted with tricks and subterfuge. Odette suffered. She died for love. Odette was the heroine, but it Odile's dance that I watched again and again and again.

Christmas approached. I ran out of excuses to give my mom. I'd have to go home for at least part of the holiday and Richard was not happy about it.

"I don't see why," he kept saying. "You're an adult; just tell her you're not going home."

"I can't. It's Christmas, she'll never understand if I'm not there. Believe me, she won't take no for an answer and if I don't show up, she'd drive to Raleigh and start investigating. It's better if I go."

"But I'll miss you," he grunted. "Damn it, this is the last holiday where we'll be separated like this, I mean it."

There was a kind of devious happiness in my heart, though. I was going home. I'd be able to check on my apartment, see some friends, and be independent. It would be glorious.

It *was* glorious, driving my own car again, tooling along I-85 on a beautiful day with the sun shining and the sky a famous Carolina blue. I'd forgotten how blue it could be. New York's sky was mostly gray-white, not terribly heartening. And the temperatures in North Carolina were so much nicer! I was able to get by with only a cotton button-down shirt and a sweatshirt. No heavy coat, no gloves, it was great.

On Christmas Eve, Mom and I went to midnight Mass. The scent of incense wafted through the church, crowded with people in holiday finery. Little girls in white dresses and silvery tissue angel wings sang *Silent Night*. I peeked at Mom out of the corner of my eye, caught by the rapt expression on her face. She loved that kind of stuff. How could she? Church only made me mad. I glared at tall young men, home from college, or showing off new fiancées. Mark should have been there, making faces at me when Mom wasn't looking, trying his best to crack me up so I'd embarrass myself. I watched families like the McCanns, three generations squeezed together in one pew. Mr. and Mrs. Leatherman, seventy years old at least, still holding hands. They were adorable and I was jealous. Why couldn't Mom and Dad end up like that? It wasn't fair, it wasn't right. Maybe I was a sinner, but Mom deserved better.

Afterward we went home and had cocoa. Mom sat in Grandma Connor's old rocking chair, wrapped in her green velvet robe, and talked of the things she'd been doing. Helping with the Operation Christmas Child program, packing shoeboxes with gifts for the needy. Going down to old Mrs. Huber's house and addressing Christmas cards for her. Attending a performance of *The Messiah* at Spirit Square.

"Mason's never been to Spirit Square before. I told him he should be ashamed to admit it."

"Mason? You went to *The Messiah* with Mason Kennedy?"

Mom blushed. I couldn't believe it. Her cheeks got pink and this little glow came into her eyes. "We see each other now and then. No big deal."

I had been lying on the floor at her feet, but at this news I sat up, hooking my arms around my upturned knees. "Is he coming over tomorrow?"

At the tone of my voice, Mom's face became serious. "No. He's spending Christmas with his daughter in Atlanta. I don't want you to become upset over this, Amanda. As I said, we just go out occasionally, it's nothing really."

The room was dark except for the glow of the tiny white Christmas tree lights.

"It doesn't matter," I said. "I'm . . . I'm glad if you're having a good time. He's a nice guy." She smiled and I got up to give her a hug. Her scent was so sweet, so familiar as I pressed my face against her hair. I held her close and could feel the sharp angles of her shoulder blades in back. *Angel bones*, we used to call them. "I think I'll go to bed now. Merry Christmas." I kissed her cheek and hurried off to my room. A soft 'I love you, honey' followed me down the hall. I changed into pajamas and got under the blankets, listening as Mom went about switching off lights and locking doors. The radio played in her bedroom for a while, something by Corelli. Finally, everything was silent. I waited until I was sure she was asleep, and then I sneaked upstairs.

The moon was full, throwing a blue-white light onto everything in Mark's room, so that it looked like the set of an old fifties-era TV show. The daybed had been pushed against a side wall, away from the window, and all Mark's posters were gone. Everything of his was gone—the trophies, the books, his guitar case and amp. I opened the closet and pulled the light cord. Against the back wall were stacked cartons, each neatly labeled. Mark's Clothes. Mark's Music. Photo Albums. Mom had finally packed away Mark's stuff.

She had to do it. I knew that. It was only right for her to deal with the realities of life and hadn't I been complaining about that all along? But, oh. *He was gone.* I kept seeing something out the corner of my eye, but when I turned to look, there was nothing there. Nothing. An empty room. Like

151

no one had ever lived there. I shivered and folded my arms across my chest, tucking my fingertips into the hollows of my underarms. Mom was coming to grips with things. She was strong, she didn't need me. That was good, wasn't it? So why was I crying? Mark was just so *gone*, like he'd been ripped out of a family picture. Him and his fedora and those stupid high-top sneakers he used to wear to every music gig, and I would never, *ever* see him again. I snapped off the closet light and hurried down the stairs, slipping near the bottom so that I had to grab the banister. Once in bed, huddled under the blankets and trying to sleep, I remembered it was already Christmas morning and soon Mom and I would be wishing each other a joyous Noël. Joyous. Joy-Us. But there was no joy and I wasn't really sure about the Us.

Mom was thrilled with her gifts. Thanks to Richard's generosity, I was able to buy her a number of the small luxuries she loved. Godiva chocolates, a small bottle of White Linen perfume, a new leather wallet and a beautifully bound copy of *Gone with the Wind,* her all-time favorite book.

"It's too much, darling, you shouldn't have spent all that money," she said, although her eyes were sparkling.

"All that overtime I worked, I could afford it." Lie, lie, lie. I was probably going to hell. Straight to hell, do not pass Go, do not collect two hundred dollars. I opened the gifts she'd given me—sweaters, CD's, a big coffee-table book of famous choreographers. Under my turtleneck, I wore Richard's gift. He'd given it to me just before I left, and asked that I wear it the entire time I was gone.

"It's a symbol," he whispered as he adjusted the black silk ribbon around my throat. "This is my collar and, although the leash is invisible, it still connects you to me." He touched the diamond drop pendant and set it swinging. "We're soul-mates, you and I. We can never be separated, and although I'm letting you go for now, remember you're tied to me and when I call, you must come."

I felt unnerved, knowing I was wearing a diamond worth thousands of dollars. From time to time, I touched the ribbon. The symbolism could be read two ways. Lots of women wore rings to proclaim their allegiance to one man. Couldn't the necklace be viewed in the same light? I wondered what it said about Richard's intentions toward me. After a while, I had to force myself to stop touching it.

*

We had Christmas dinner with Sissy and her family. Loretta, Sissy's mom, was so grateful about Thanksgiving, she wanted to repay the favor. We all got together at their house, three doors down from Mom's.

Being there again was fun. Once upon a time, Sissy and I had been in and out of each other's house on a regular basis. I knew the crack in the bathroom light switch plate, and the feel of the banister, and how the furnace made a sort of rumble before it turned on. Sissy, dressed in a red accordion-pleated maternity top that made her look bigger than she was, scolded her father, brothers and husband in a way that was eerily reminiscent of her mother's bossiness, and we soon arranged ourselves around the big table. Mom looked flushed and excited. She had always wanted a big family, she told me once. I guessed this was the closest she'd ever come.

Loretta fixed a huge meal—ham, sweet potato casserole, corn bread, green beans, collard greens, 'nanner pudding, pecan pie, and gallons of sweet iced tea to wash it down. I sat next to Mr. Pennell, Sissy's dad. His first name was Calvin, but I'd never been able to bring myself to call him by that, it seemed too informal. A sweet old guy, older than my day, he liked to tease us girls with little puns and corny jokes. I was accustomed to thinking of him as almost elderly. It came as a shock to realize he was only a year or two older than Richard.

He said the blessing and we all began the serious business of eating. Conversation came to a halt for a while but near the end of the meal, Mr. Pennell started things back up. "How's school treating you?" he asked, helping himself to more green beans. They were fixed with cream, parmesan cheese, and tiny fried onion rings, and he put a big helping on my plate without asking.

"About as well as I deserve," I said, blushing. "I've been pretty busy."

"So I hear." He gave me one of his lopsided grins. "Sissy says you're never home anymore."

"Um, no, working a lot. You know how it is."

"Now Cal, don't you be monopolizing 'Manda," Loretta called from the other end of the table. "I want to hear all about her dance stuff. I bet someday we'll say 'we knew her when'. She'll be famous, you wait and see."

"Well, I wouldn't hold my breath if I were you," I warned, blushing some more.

Travis sat across from me at the table, pinned between my mom and his brother. He grinned at me now, a more youthful version of his dad's smile. "She'll probably be off to New York one of these days. Have her name up in lights."

I caught my breath. "Well, New York is where it's at for dancers. In fact, I might have a chance to study there next semester."

"What?" Mom stopped with her fork halfway to her mouth. "Why didn't you tell me?"

"It's not for certain. Just a possibility."

"But New York is so far away." Her anguish was plain.

The hubbub around the table suddenly silenced and I felt my cheeks grow red. "I know, but it'd be a great opportunity. I can't stay in Painter's Creek forever. You didn't expect me to, did you?" Everyone's face turned toward me as if on a swivel and I could feel all the warning signs to stop. "I have to move on with my life, Mom, same as you do. After all, I'm nineteen. Almost grown. I know what I want, and I have to go after it with all my heart. And for me, that means moving away from here. And you know, some day it might mean that for you."

Mom stared down at her plate, her own face turning pink. She smoothed the napkin on her lap.

Travis cleared his throat and started to speak but Loretta interrupted. "Oh, 'Manda, you just haven't learned to appreciate all the good things in Painter's Creek. Why, of course, your Mom has to stay here, the high school couldn't get by without her. Besides, *some* people even *choose* to move back here. We have good news for Christmas," she added, raising her eyebrows for emphasis. "Travis is coming home for a while. He's going to help out at the store."

This brought forks down all over the place. Only little Teri kept eating, shoving green beans into her mouth at machine-gun pace. "What do you mean?" Sissy asked faintly. "Nobody told me."

"Well, we just decided." Loretta said, in a no-nonsense voice. "Cal needs the extra help and neither Mack or Johnny can come home right now."

"I've been trying to help." Dave's ears were red and he stared at his plate. "I realize I'm not very experienced yet, but Travis shouldn't have to give up his career."

"I'm not." Travis turned to speak directly to Dave. "I'm sorry Ma announced it this way, I was going to speak to you first. You're a big help to Dad, of course you are. I'm not trying to take your place. You're working your ass off going to night school, and raising a family. I'm simply trying to give you and Dad both a break."

Sissy snorted and stabbed a piece of ham with her fork. "Well, let's all hail the conquering hero. Golden Boy to the rescue. By all means, bring him back and lock the mules in the barn." She threw down her napkin and left the table.

"Now, Sissy," Mr. Pennell began. "Honey, don't be like that, nobody wants to shut you in the barn."

"Damn it, Ma, I told you to wait." Travis got up from the table, put his hand on Dave's shoulder for a minute, and then went off to find Sissy.

"Sit down," Loretta insisted. "Eat your dinner! Let her go sulk if she wants to." Travis ignored her, and the rest of us sat in stunned silence. After a minute, Dave excused himself and left the room.

Mom and I sat, embarrassed and uncomfortable, until Mr. Pennell reached over and touched Mom's hand. "I sure didn't want everyone to get riled up. Truth is, there's a big chain hardware store gonna go up out by the highway. Things don't look so good and we thought maybe Travis, with all his PR experience. . . Dave's a good boy, he's just young." Mom murmured her understanding and I excused myself, carrying my plate out to the kitchen to scrape and rinse it.

Through the window over the kitchen sink, I could see Travis and Sissy arguing in the back yard. I didn't want to return to the dining room where Mack and Johnny were giving long involved explanations of why they couldn't come back to work in the family business, so I went out the side door and around to the front porch. The sunshine felt reasonably warm, and I sat on the front steps. It seemed the only thing to do.

After a while, Travis came around and sat next to me. "Sorry about that. Sometimes Ma has her own way of doing things. You know. Anyway, really sorry you and Grace had to see it." He sighed and looked up at the sky. "Feels like rain coming. Maybe even snow."

What an optimist. The temperatures hovered in the upper 40's. "Don't worry about us," I said. "We're not exactly shocked by family hassles. Besides, it was my fault the conversation went that direction anyway. Sometimes I can feel these big toads drop out of my mouth but I can't stop them."

157

Travis nodded sympathetically. He stretched out his left leg, massaging the knee with one palm. The action made his arm bump against mine and I thought maybe I should move over and give him more room. But I didn't. "I'm still surprised you're coming home to work at the store. I thought you loved your job."

"I do. Did." He narrowed his eyes, focusing on the rooftops of the houses across the street. "I'll miss it. But what the hell," he added, rising and offering me his hand. "I'm young, I'll get other jobs." Travis pulled me to my feet and I found myself face to face, standing close. "You know how it is. Family. Be it ever so insanity-inducing, there's no place like home." He glanced up at the house. "No matter what I do, the business still might not survive, but I'd kick myself later if I didn't try to help."

He smiled down at me but I couldn't smile back. He would sacrifice himself, just the way Mom did, and it made me feel small-hearted. Richard said I should look out for myself, Mom and Travis believed in looking out for others. I could choose to do right or I could choose to be happy, but it didn't look like there was any way to choose both.

Chapter Ten

The rain became, not snow, but a sleety drizzle. Sissy called to complain about her mother's high-handedness. "Oh, it's not Travis I blame. What burns my butt is Ma didn't bother to tell us. She still treats Dave like he's twelve years old. And Dad lets her walk all over him. I am fit to bust." After about twenty minutes, she finally calmed down enough to invite me to a New Year's Eve party. "Ma's even giving me hassle about that, saying I shouldn't spend money on entertaining, like it's any business of hers."

After the phone call, I went down to the basement to find Mom doing the laundry, humming as she folded clothes fresh out of the dryer. I sat on the little stool at her feet. "Have I ever thanked you for not being Loretta Pennell? If not, I do so now. That woman still orders her kids around as if they were, well, kids. When will she realize they've grown up?"

Mom smiled ruefully. "It's not easy," she admitted, taking a shirt out of the dryer and shaking out the wrinkles. "Sometimes our children give us serious cause for worry." She pursed her lips and set the shirt on the ironing board. "In fact, that brings me to something I want to say." She plugged in the iron and set it on end to heat. Her gaze came up to meet mine. "Amanda, I'm a little worried about you. You've been so busy this fall. I can hardly ever get you on the phone. You haven't been in contact with your dad; he can never reach you either. Now you mention an opportunity to study in New York. Why didn't you tell me before?"

"It's not definite yet. Oh, Mom, would it be so terrible if I went? I have to think about my career. I'd call you all the time; maybe you could even come visit me." Reckless of possible complications, I plunged on. "And I meant what I said about you needing an open mind. Why should you stay in Painter's Creek? Doesn't it have bad memories for you now? I think about you all alone here and it makes me sad."

Mom looked down and began ironing the shirt. I watched, as I had watched her iron many a shirt. Always in the same order; collar, back yoke, sleeves. Button placket, left front, back, right front. In and out between the buttons, each movement neat and orderly. "Sometimes I think about moving," she admitted. "Your grandparents are getting up there in age. I probably should live nearer to them. Except we'd probably drive each other nuts." She finished the shirt, put it on a hanger. Her gaze was far away for a moment, and then she set the iron back on the stand and looked at me. "Amanda, if New York means that much to you, then go. Live your dream. Don't let your worries about me keep you from doing what you want." She smiled and pulled me up from the Raggedy Ann stool, giving me a hug. "You have your whole life ahead of you and I hope it's filled with wonderful things. Take a few risks now and then. I wish I had." She laughed and rubbed her forehead against mine. "I guess I'm saying be bold

160

with your life, but be careful, too. You're very precious to me."

On the twenty-seventh, I drove to Charlotte to visit Dad. His apartment was off Wendover, not far from the Mint Museum. The buildings were new with fancy security gates at the entrance. Dad opened the door before I could even finish knocking and ushered me in with a big grin on his face. He didn't look like the same old Dad. The man in front of me looked five years younger, with a different haircut and no eyeglasses and a turtleneck sweater instead of shirt and tie. "Jeez, Dad, did you get a makeover?" He laughed and took my coat, showing me into his living room where an elaborate Christmas tree shared space with a bassinet and baby swing.

"Things have changed a bit," he admitted, his eyes gleaming. He patted my shoulder and turned to look at Janine who had just entered the room.

I hadn't seen her in a long time. Over a year. She still wore her little Mona Lisa smile. What caught my eye, though, was the baby.

He snuggled up on her shoulder, a round little sack in pajamas, his head covered with downy black hair. He was asleep and as she turned so I could see his face, he yawned. Little fists opened and spread, the fingers like a starfish, and his mouth crumpled in on itself, making sucking motions before he settled down again.

Tears filled my eyes. I remembered calling him a little bastard and knew I could never do that again. Dad put his arm around my shoulders. "Isn't he beautiful? He's the most beautiful baby in the world." Dad took him from Janine, cradled the baby in his arms for a moment and held him out to me.

I backed away. Didn't mean to, just wasn't quite ready for the way Dad looked, so filled with joy, so eager to share it with me. "I'd probably drop him or something," I muttered, but Dad insisted and I found myself looking down at the baby in my arms. I felt unable to move or speak a word. His ear had a little notch, the same as Mark's.

Janine broke the spell by going into the kitchen and coming out again with a tray full of tea things and some cookies. Dad said, "Here, give Joshie to me," and I watched as he laid the baby in the bassinet. He covered Josh with a blanket and put his hand over the baby's hair for a moment before he sat down next to Janine on the couch.

They had gifts for me—a jacket and scarf, perfume, a silver bracelet with moon and star charms. I felt embarrassed. The shirt and tie I'd selected for Dad didn't seem to suit him now, and I had nothing for Janine. Her smile didn't waver and she poured a cup of tea. As she handed me the cup and saucer, I noticed the ring she wore. White-gold band, large diamond, third finger of her left hand. I glanced at Dad and he nodded, sitting back and putting an arm around her. "We're getting married. Soon as the divorce is final."

I should have been expecting it. Without warning, tears gushed from my eyes and my nose began to run. I set down the teacup and grabbed a napkin, blowing my nose and realizing too late that the napkin was cloth and not paper. "I'm sorry, I should be congratulating you. It's just . . . "

Dad frowned and leaned forward to touch my knee. "Josh deserves a family, don't you think? And it doesn't change my relationship with you."

Maybe not, but didn't our relationship *need* to change? Oh, god, what difference did it make anyway? Lots of my friends had lived through their parents' divorces and remarriages. We were supposed to just deal with it, not feel abandoned, not feel as though the solid earth beneath us had dropped away. "I understand," I said. But I didn't. Intellectually, yeah, okay. Emotionally, though, it felt like Dad had climbed on a ship and sailed out of sight.

Somehow I got through the rest of the visit. I avoided looking at Janine's self-satisfied simper and the baby never did wake up. I was glad for that. It would have been tough to see his open eyes, to watch him moving and snuggling up to Dad. Janine made a point of saying that she breast-fed and I sure didn't want to see that.

I came home to find Mom on the phone, laughing, her face all lit up. I stood in the back doorway and looked at her perched on the kitchen stool, her hair falling away from her face in graceful waves. When I set my keys down on the counter, she looked at me and her expression changed instantly from smiling to serious. "I have to go, Mason," she said into the phone. "Talk to you later." Then she walked up to me and gave me a hug.

I stood there stiffly, unable to relax my nerves. Mom took my hand and pulled me over to the kitchen table, making me sit on a chair. She sat down next to me, still holding my hand. "Tough day?" she asked.

In slow motion. I turned to face her, noting things that crossed my vision on the way. The shelf full of antique figurines, the floral wallpaper, the cookie jar we'd had since I was five. "He's getting married," I said. "Did you know?"

Mom rubbed my hand between hers. "I think it's a good thing. I do. The baby should have both parents and Steve seems happy." She leaned forward and kissed my cheek. "And you should be happy for him."

I wrenched myself loose and stood up. Breathing hard, I backed away from her until I stood in the doorway to the living room. "Happy for him? It's not enough that I have to accept all this, but I have to be *happy* for him too? I don't understand you! You guys got married and you promised to love each other forever. I thought the vows meant something. Mom, you go to church all the time and you buy into that whole Catholic thing about no divorce and now you're saying I should be happy for Dad that he's marrying the woman he cheated with? Has everyone gone crazy? Are you really happy? Or are you just pretending because there's nothing else you can do? I don't get it, Mom. It's like every value you ever taught me is meaningless."

Mom stood and lifted her hand toward me and I jerked away again. "Amanda, I know it's hard. When we're young, we see things in black and white. But when we get older, it becomes clear that there are a million shades of gray."

"So? There are no rules? Everything is decided on a case-by-case basis? Like, if I decide there's a good reason to do something wrong, it's okay? Is that what you're saying?" I whirled away from her and ran to my room, locking the door shut behind me. My bed skidded a couple of inches as I threw myself on it, and Mom's voice came through the door.

"Amanda, please. Let's talk about this."

"No! I wanted to talk all last summer and you guys were too busy." I sat up and looked at my reflection in the mirror. My face was red and my hair tumbled every which way. The crescent moon charm on my new bracelet caught on a thread from the quilt and I jerked it loose. The bracelet broke off and flew across the room, landing on the floor near my dresser. Good. I looked at my bedroom door. The light seeping through the crack underneath was broken by the shadows of Mom's feet. I took a deep breath and bit out, "I'll be polite and all, and I'll try to wish them well. But don't ask me to be happy, damn it. Just don't ask for that."

That night I packed my things. In the morning, I told Mom I wanted to go back to my apartment early, before New Year's Eve. "There's going to be some parties at school." I avoided her eyes and carried my suitcase out to the car. When I came back in, she blocked my passage through the kitchen until I looked at her.

"Amanda, let's not fight about this. You have the right to your feelings and I'm sorry if I made things worse." There were tears in her eyes, which only brought about the same in mine.

We hugged. I rubbed my face against her shoulder. "I don't want to fight either. I just need a little time alone, okay? Time to adjust to this."

She patted me. "Okay. But listen . . . you know how it was with my father and me. Please don't let that happen with you and Steve. He's the only dad you've got." We both wiped our eyes. "When will you hear about the New York thing?"

"Probably as soon as I get back. I'll call you." Somehow I would get a few things arranged with Richard, set some boundaries, regain control of my life. I'd start my classes and Mom would come for a visit and everything would be good. Somehow.

"So who's this Travis guy again?" Richard lay on his side, lazily tracing circles on my backside. We'd finished making love and the buttering-up had begun.

"At the Christmas dinner? I told you, he's Sissy's older brother. They used to call him 'Golden Boy' when he was in high school." I propped up on one elbow and looked at him. "Remember the guy I talked to in the parking lot that time? That was him."

"You like him? You think he's good-looking?"

"He's nice. I had a major crush on him when I was about twelve. Way out of *my* league, though." I started to get up but Richard grabbed my hips and held me down.

"I see. He's out of your league. What does that make him, some kind of a god or something?" His voice was silky, deep. He rolled over so that his leg crossed the backs of my thighs, forcing me to stay face down on the bed. "What does this guy do for a living?"

"He works for the Athletic Foundation at UNC. Well, used to. Now he's going to run Sissy's dad's hardware store. Don't do that, it hurts."

Richard pressed harder with his leg. "This paint-pusher, you like him, do you? Did you get wet when you were talking to him?"

"Oh, Daddy, for crying out loud. Let me go." I tried to roll sideways and Richard pushed my shoulders to the mattress, bringing his mouth close to my ear.

"Good-looking, young, athletic, I bet you want him, don't you. I bet you'd like to screw the shit out of him."

"Stop it!" The pillow muffled my voice and Richard's knee pressed into my back. "He's nothing to me! Now stop, I don't like this!"

Richard's big body loomed over mine and then his hand came down with a smack on my bottom. "You don't? You don't like this?" He smacked me again and I yelped and writhed. "Maybe you don't like any of this, huh?" His hand came down on me a third time, and he dug his fingers between my legs. "Maybe you're tired of the old man, maybe what you really want is that Golden Boy. Huh? *Huh?*" He began spanking me hard, his hand coming down on my rump in a volley of slaps. It hurt, but it scared me even more than it hurt. What was wrong with him? I hollered and tried to get away, twisting and squirming against his hold. All the time, he continued, his soft, deep voice shaking with anger. "Mine, don't you forget. I found you; shit, *I made you*. Don't think you can get away now. You're mine, you belong to *me*."

I finally broke free, rolling off the bed and landing on my knees. I turned, evading his reach, and scrambled across the carpet to the bathroom, hurling myself inside and locking the door.

167

"Open this door!" He pounded on it with his fist. I could see the door quiver in its frame.

"No!"

"Amanda, I'm telling you, open this door!"

"*No!* You're scaring me!"

He hit the door one more time, and then stopped. I backed away from it, fearful of what he'd do next. I grabbed one of the terrycloth robes and put it on. It was Richard's, too big for me, and the hem reached to the floor, but that didn't matter.

"Amanda." His voice got quieter. "I'm sorry. I didn't mean to scare you. Now come out." I waited. "Please, darling. I'm sorry."

I crept close to the door again and put my ear against it. I could hear him breathing heavily. "Go into the other room," I said. "Call me when you're in there." Footsteps crossed the bedroom. I could hear the door to the sitting room open.

"Okay. I'm way over here. Now please come out."

I opened the door and peeked out. Richard stood in the doorway to the sitting room. He wore a pair of boxers, black silk with silver checks. His hair stuck up in back. At my doubtful look, he sighed and sat down in the big armchair, patting his thigh with a rueful expression on his face.

Wrapping the robe more tightly around myself, I moved across the room and stood facing him, hesitant to climb into his lap. Richard had to coax me back into his arms. "I'm sorry, Baby. Sometimes I worry that you'll get tired of this old man and leave me for a young guy."

I burrowed my head against his chest. "You scared me," I said in a tiny little voice. "You've never done that before. I don't like it."

Richard hugged and rocked me. "I'm sorry. I've had a lot on my mind lately. Things at work, things at home. It's been a hell of a couple of weeks." He ran his hand over his hair, and shook his head. "That doesn't excuse my taking it out on you. Did I hurt you?" Carefully, he peeled back my robe and examined my behind. Twisting my hip up, I could see palm prints on my backside, red against my white skin. "Man, I am really sorry." He kissed his fingertips and rubbed them softly against my bottom. "Want me to kiss and make it all better?" he smiled.

I tried to smile, too. "What's going wrong at home?"

Something flickered momentarily in his eyes. He toyed with the belt of my robe. "It's nothing. Almost nothing. I'm sure we'll get it all settled soon."

"Richard, tell me."

That was a mistake. His eyes went cold at my inadvertent use of his name. "Your *Daddy*," he enunciated precisely, "will tell you what you need to know when you need to know it. No more, no less." He set me on my feet with an unnecessary thump and walked away, into the bedroom.

I thought about following him and apologizing, but then decided what the hell. He'd hurt me, I wasn't sure I trusted him. If he continued to keep me in the dark, why should I ask forgiveness? I went over to the refrigerator and poured myself some juice.

He came out of the bedroom dressed in one of his business suits. "I have to go to the office. Meanwhile, be thinking about what you'd like to do on New Year's Eve."

"Won't you be with your wife?"

"No." His eyes came up to focus on mine, challenging me to ask questions, so I didn't.

"Okay. I'll think about it. Can I choose my own outfit for once?"

Richard hesitated a minute, then "Of course. I know you'll want to please your Daddy." He dropped a kiss on my forehead, patted my rump—making me flinch—and left.

After he was gone, I sat for a long time by the window, watching people in the park. Richard's temper scared me. I'd seen signs before, his implacable resentment when I said or did something he didn't like. The way he could turn on his employees or business associates, shouting over the phone, reaming them some new butt holes. But physical blows, I hadn't expected that. That spanking wasn't discipline, it was jealous rage. I didn't like it one bit.

If Richard and I were going to work things out, he had to start accepting my true age. The father-child thing didn't work. I'd never liked it any way, maybe New Year's Eve could be a new start. I knew exactly what I wanted to wear. I saw it every day in a shop window on the way to Mme. Dumont's—a long, flowing skirt in cobalt blue silk that would swing and ripple with every step, and a deeper blue short-sleeved pullover in the softest cashmere. I modeled it for Mr. D'Angelo in the apartment next door, pirouetting in the satiny high-heeled sandals that I bought to match.

"What do you think?" I asked, "Will he like it?"

Mr. D'Angelo, a dapper little man with scant silver hair and wiry black eyebrows that pointed in all directions, walked around in a circle and studied me from different angles. "It's a little long," he said. "You'll be tripping on the hem. Ask Mrs. Meyer on the tenth floor for the name of her seamstress." He crouched down, lifted the hem an inch to look at its finishing, and stood up again. "I have to say. . . Miss Amanda, if you don't mind my asking, but . . . how old are you?"

"Nineteen." I blushed. He'd never even hinted a bit of curiosity before.

"Ah, nineteen. That's a great age. I remember being nineteen." He smiled, a rare event, and then seemed to remember his dignity again. "Yes, well, I have to take Cyrus and Mitzi and Jackson for their walks. If you'd like to go with me, I'll wait till you change. It's a beautiful day out."

As I removed my new outfit and put on my jeans, I couldn't help thinking how it almost seemed odd to admit my age. What did a nineteen-year-old feel like, anyway? What were they *supposed* to feel like? Sissy was nineteen. My mom was nineteen when she got married. Half the time, I acted younger, playing a child's role when I was out with Richard, and half the time, I was older, living a woman's life in bed with him. Never his equal, never his peer.

New Year's Eve would be the test. The end of one thing, and the beginning of something else. I hoped the beginning of a better situation for Richard and me, based on mutual strengths, not weaknesses. I wanted to grab hold of my life with both hands and take control. I needed to believe I was capable of that.

Chapter Eleven

Richard showed up on New Year's Eve with two heavily loaded suitcases and a big grin. "Guess what, sweetheart, I'm moving in!" He tossed one of the bags on the bed. "No more leaving you all alone at night, no more holidays apart. From here on, it's strictly you and me." He heaved the other suitcase onto the bench at the foot of the bed. Then he stopped and took a good look at me. "What are you wearing?"

"It's my dress for tonight," I replied, "I, um, well, do you like it?" His gaze ran over me and he indicated that I should turn around for him.

"No." He grinned again, "But what the hell, it's New Year's Eve, we are going to the ball." He rubbed his hands together briskly, opened up one of the suitcases and took out some things. "Give me five minutes."

I wandered into the sitting room. What had happened? He'd moved out of his home? Had he told his wife about us? I thought he said he'd never consider breaking up his marriage. Oh god, what did this mean for us? I fiddled with my hair, paced up and down. Richard came out, freshly shaved and dressed in a tuxedo.

"Help me with this tie, baby," he said, handing me the bit of black silk. I had no clue how to fix it, so after a few useless minutes, Richard swore to himself and stuffed the thing into his pocket. "The hell with it. I'll get the chauffeur to do it." He called down for his car to be sent around. "Let's go."

When we got to the lobby, there was no the limo in front of the hotel and the doorman hurried over to see if he could help. After checking with the garage, he turned back hesitantly and whispered a few words into Richard's ear.

"What? I'll be damned," Richard growled. "Well, get us a cab."

Too many mysteries for me. As soon as we got into the taxi and Richard had given the driver instructions, I asked what was up.

"Don't you worry, little girl," he chuckled, throwing an arm around my shoulders. "I had to set someone straight, but now things are just dandy." He leaned back, giving a big, gusty sigh of satisfaction, and smiled at me. "You let Daddy take care of everything." He chucked my chin, set the diamond pendant swinging and whistled a couple of bars of *Another Opening, Another Show*.

The restaurant overflowed with glitterati. Two soap opera stars, the new soprano from the Met, Dixon Phillips of The New Yorker. This wasn't one of our hole-in-the-wall places, but rather a restaurant so exclusive it didn't even have a sign out front. Richard looked around with a smile of appreciation, nodded to a couple of people he knew, and squeezed my hand. The maitre d', a dapper little man with a goatee, spoke softly to him and Richard responded with a grunt.

I could barely hear the reply. ". . . so very sorry, but the reservation was cancelled about an hour ago. I can try to get you another table if you care to wait. . ."

A dark flush covered Richard's face and he shook his head. "Never mind." He grabbed my arm and propelled me out. Once in the cab, he couldn't make up his mind where to go. "All the damn restaurants will be full. The clubs, too. We might as well go home." The cabbie rolled his eyes, waiting for instructions. "God *damn* her," Richard burst out. "Of all the petty things. No! I'm not going to let New Year's Eve be ruined. Where would you like to go, Amanda?" he asked, turning to me suddenly. "Paris? Rome? We could be in London by—"

"Daddy, wait. Don't let's get crazy. Tell you what, Mme. Dumont's having a party at her studio. Let's go there, she invited me."

He stared a minute and then began laughing. "What the hell, why not? We'll go slumming." He gave instructions to the cabbie, leaned back in his seat and gathered me to himself for a big hug. "Mmm, sweetheart, what would I do without you?" He ran his hand slowly up my silk-covered leg and under my top. "Oh, honey, Daddy's little girl feels so good." His lips covered mine and he gradually forced me backward on the seat, half-lying on me.

"Daddy, stop! The cabbie—" I whispered.

"Let him get his own date, you're all mine," he smiled, reaching under my skirt. "What's this? Silk panties? Garters? Why, Amanda, you're all dressed up under there. . . ."

175

Mme. Dumont's party was in full swing. She had been a fixture in the New York dance world for years and I recognized dancers from present and past as well as an eclectic mix of musicians, dressers, sponsors, students and hangers-on. She had never warmed up to me much, but I guessed she knew a good thing when she saw one in Richard.

"Mr. Gessler, what an honor!" She swept through the crowd like a ship in full sail, her draperies flaring back and the traditional obsequious admirer at her elbow. "Allow me to introduce you to some of my friends."

She steered Richard off toward the bar and I stood awkwardly, not knowing what to do or with whom to talk. I recognized one of Madame's other students from passing him on the stairs and we were chatting when Richard returned, holding a glass of champagne and a scotch on the rocks.

"Great party," Richard said. "Do you know, she once danced with Nureyev? Here, Amanda, drink up." He pushed the champagne into my hand, and extended his own hand toward the other student. "Richard Gessler, how do you do?"

It threw me, his willingness to 'come out', all of a sudden. Richard put his arm around my waist and chatted in a friendly way. In fact, he was quite convivial all night; outgoing, friendly, eager to talk with one and all. He kept his arm around me most of the time, making it quite clear that we were a couple. I don't know why I didn't like it. For once, I was being treated as an adult, and I should have been happy, but something too bright in his smile and too outspoken in the way he repeatedly introduced his name into the conversation, made me distrust this sudden change. If he had, indeed, told his wife the truth, what would that mean? Was he going to separate from her? What would he expect of me?

Now I was the one eager to go home, I was the one wishing for anonymity. There were several people at the party who had some social standing in New York, people who were not only patrons of the ballet, but also deeply involved in businesses and charities, who would be familiar with Richard and with his wife.

Richard inhaled one drink after another. He became louder, more amorous, running his hand down my backside or pressing kisses to my neck. "Let's go," I urged, "I'm tired."

"Does baby need her early bedtime?" Richard asked, not bothering to lower his voice. "Shall Daddy tuck you in?" My face flamed and I turned away. Richard grabbed my arm and pulled me back. "It's almost midnight," he said, his voice suddenly sober. "Wait."

More champagne was handed round as the crowd got ready to count down the final seconds. I didn't care for any and shook my head, but Richard grabbed a glass for me. "You have to drink in the New Year, honey. It's bad luck if you don't." He held the glass to my mouth, forcing me to drink if I didn't want it to dribble down my chin. "We don't want any bad luck, do we? I don't deal well with disappointments."

I forced it down, and a second glass as well, as the partygoers chanted "four, three, two, one, *Happy New Year!*" Everyone shouted and the kiss-fest began. Richard drew me into his arms for a deep kiss, his tongue thrusting into my mouth, his hands pressing my hips against his sudden erection. I turned my face away from the overpowering fumes of scotch and he bent me back further, putting one hand on my breast, over my top, and kissing my throat. He caught the diamond pendant in his teeth and worried it, like a dog. Then he made a devilish grin and pulled his black silk tie, crumpled and forgotten, from his coat pocket.

"Here, baby, baby, baby," he said, sliding it under the silk ribbon around my throat. He pulled on it, like a leash. "Come to Papa." Richard drew my face up close to his own, his fist tight under my chin, holding the tie. "Kiss me," he demanded. His mouth came down hard, insistently, bruising my lips against my teeth. My pulse roared in my ears, and anger burned inside. I couldn't push away as long as he had hold of my collar, so I reached up and snapped it loose in the back, breaking away from him as I did so. He was left holding bits of fabric and a dangling prize; I was left holding the scraps of my dignity.

"I'm going home," I said, and stalked out of the studio, my coat thrown over one shoulder. What the hell was wrong with him?

There were no taxis to be seen. I trudged along the damp sidewalk, struggling into the inadequate jacket and tripping on my skirts. Damn him. *Damn* him. The subway station up ahead was probably closed and I had no money anyway. If I could find an open restaurant or store, I would telephone the hotel to send a car.

"Amanda, stop." Richard's voice at my shoulder made me jump. How had he caught up so quickly, without my hearing him? He pulled me around to face him and, without speaking, wrapped me in his arms and held me tight.

I pushed back for a moment, and then succumbed, pressing my face to his shirt front. Heedless of lipstick stains or mascara, I sobbed quietly into his chest.

"I'm sorry," he murmured, "I'm such a shit, I really am." As if by magic, a taxi rounded the corner and Richard snagged it with a toss of his head. Life would always be like that for him, I guessed; whatever he needed, it would show up.

It was a quiet ride home. As he climbed out of the taxi, Richard accidentally stepped on my skirt and tore part of it loose from the waistband. "Oh, damn, have I wrecked it?" he asked.

"Don't worry," I replied, holding my torn finery to my side. "This caps a perfect evening."

Later, in bed, in the dark, my face muffled against my pillow, I asked Richard what had happened. "Your wife, did she. . .?"

Richard sighed and folded his arms behind his head. "Let's say she is not amused. Apparently, she's had someone checking up on me. I told her the truth; that I don't want a divorce but do want to live separately, but she's being ugly about it. I'll give Diane credit; she sure knows how to work fast. She managed to find out where we were going and cancelled the restaurant and limo. God knows what else she'll do. But it doesn't matter." He rolled over on his side and began stroking my hair. "Everything's out in the open at last and eventually she'll have to deal with it. She's no fool, she'll realize that it'd be better in the end to keep her dignity and her social standing and just let me do my own thing."

He moved closer, running his hand down the length of my back. "Now, the bigger question is, where does that leave us? What do you say to an extended tour of Europe? I know you'd love London, and we could. . ."

I stopped listening after a while. His words went on and on, painting a picture, but I didn't want to look. The very thing that I never wanted had happened. People would be hurt. My mother would find out the truth, Richard's daughters would be shocked and heartsick, his wife had already shown that she was not immune to pangs of jealousy, and all because of me. I thought he said she didn't care! That she was quite happy with the status quo, that she had her own lovers. Now a completely different picture emerged.

I never wanted to hurt anybody. A little tenderness was all I ever looked for or wanted, and now people would brand me a slut and a whore. They'd assume I was just a gold digger who played Richard like a trout on a line. I only hoped, for my mother's sake, that we could keep it fairly quiet.

My grandma once said, "Better watch what you ask for, you just might get it." I had once wanted a special world for Richard and me. Now that I had it, I wasn't so sure we could live there.

He hung around all the time; every minute, every day. I couldn't take a step without him at my side. Richard came down to the gym while I worked out, he went with me to my dance lessons, he made his business phone calls in the sitting room while I did my daily stretches. The harder I exercised, the louder he seemed to get. There were an awful lot of arguments, him yelling at someone to take care of something, then slamming the receiver down or throwing his cell phone across the room. It didn't seem to make him mad; in fact, he was always in an excessively good mood after one of these calls. Half the time, he'd sling me over his shoulder and carry me to bed, use me soundly, and go off whistling for a shave and shower. Whenever I tried to find out what was up, he waved away my questions and changed the subject.

One day when Richard had gone to work, I sneaked off to the public library and did a little online research on Diane Gessler. Wasn't difficult, there were plenty of references to her charity work with animal rights, Special Olympics, and The Equus Society. Her photo popped up with regularity and I studied one that showed her in riding clothes, presenting a cup at the Quarter Horse Invitational. Perhaps my view was slanted, but she looked pretty formidable. I wouldn't want to lock horns with that lady. Richard's continued silence on the subject wore me out. My stomach twisted like an old dishrag and I had had enough.

I figured the best time and place to bring up the subject was after lovemaking and in bed. Richard had propped himself up on several pillows, watching TV, and I cuddled next to him, my head on his chest. He lay there, stroking my hair, and I played with the silky curls on his chest, twining them around my fingers.

"Daddy?"

"Hmm?

"What's going to happen? You've been making all kinds of arrangements. When are you going to tell me what's going on?"

"When you need to know."

"I need to know now. Come on, Daddy, I'm not a child. Keeping me in suspense like this, it's not fair."

He looked down at me. "Do you trust me?"

I nodded, but looked at my hand on his chest. He put his finger under my chin and made me look up again.

"*Do* you?"

"Yes, Daddy, I trust you. But—" I couldn't help it, I had to know. "But why won't you tell me? Is your wife making trouble? What's going on with all these arguments with your office? Why—"

Richard pulled my head back down to his chest and began stroking my hair again. "You know," he said dreamily, "I really liked that time you took the pills. Let's do that again. That showed trust." His voice got very quiet. "I promise you, Amanda, there's nothing to worry about. Think about all the things I've given up for you, and please behave. Now, go to sleep." He pulled his pillows lower on the bed and rolled on his side, facing me. Obediently, I turned over so we could sleep spoon-fashion.

"Daddy," I whispered. "Did you take pictures of me that time?"

He nodded, drowsily.

"What did you do with them?"

I only received a soft snore in reply.

The last time Richard Gessler gave me a bath was the night before classes would begin at The School of American Ballet. The bathtub was huge and Richard climbed in with me, admitting that bending over the tub hurt his back. I sat between his legs, facing away from him while he massaged shampoo into my hair. All day Richard had been sweet to me, undermining my resolve. We were going to be so happy, he kept promising. "You're going to love your classes. I can't wait till you start. And maybe in the spring we can travel. Go to Europe. Wait till you see the Royal Ballet in London." All day he had stayed by my side, smiling, teasing me, being the charming and magnetic man I'd seen when we met.

In the bedroom, on the nightstand, stood the little bottle of pills he'd brought home that afternoon. "You'll be uptight tonight," Richard said. "These will help you sleep." I felt half-willing to take them. The long tether of lies was strung out and about to snap. Every day I combed the papers for any mention of Richard or his wife. Sometimes I fantasized about picking up the phone and calling Diane, but then realized I had no idea what to say. What could I say to the woman whose marriage I'd ruined? And then there was the whole situation with Mom, who left messages for me on my cell phone, wanting to know about the dance workshop I'd fabricated. And asking why she hadn't received a tuition bill from Burgess. I wouldn't have minded sleeping for quite a long while, if it meant I could forget about these worries.

A cold shiver ran through me as if a draft had entered the room. Richard kneaded the muscles in my shoulders. "Don't be so tense," he said. "Relax." I tried. Tried to lean back in his arms and enjoy the warm water, but nervous tremors made me pull my legs up and cross my arms over my chest. "Our troubles are behind us," he said, rinsing my hair with the sprayer. "I finally settled everything today."

I was about to ask him what he meant when the bathroom door opened. A woman—tall, blonde, quite attractive in a fashion-shark kind of way—stood in the doorway, regarding us with disfavor. One corner of her mouth curled down, her eyes narrowed. Even without the riding clothes, I knew who she was.

"Diane!" Richard stood up, sudsy bath water running down his body, making the dark hair cling to his legs. "How did you get in here?" She looked pointedly at his groin and brought up her right hand. Casually, lightly, she held a gun aimed directly at me.

"Hello, darling. So, this is the little ragamuffin, hmm? She seems awfully young, Richard, even by your standards." I got to my knees, my arms crossed over myself.

"Put it down," Richard said, ignoring his naked state and stepping out of the tub. "Don't be an ass."

She laughed and lolled against the door frame. "Now, Richard, I thought you were quite fond of ass." Her eyebrow went up and a muscle in her jaw flexed. "Did you really think I'd let you get away with it? I told you I'd do whatever it took to stop you, you just didn't believe me. For once, darling, you've misjudged."

Richard lunged for the gun, but she was quicker. The first bullet hit him in the gut, slamming him backwards so that he fell back in the tub, knocking us both against the wall. She fired a second shot, the report deafening in the tiled room, and the sudden weight of his body pinned me down as blood began spurting into the water. I screamed, churning my legs in an effort to get out from underneath. Richard's face turned toward me, white, staring, and he started to slide sideways. I tried to hold onto him, terrified that he'd slide under the water, but all of a sudden, I couldn't breathe. In slow motion I looked down and saw blood all over my chest. Richard's? Mine? I didn't even know.

Diane Gessler stood in the doorway, lazily watching as I floundered beneath her husband. "Too bad you didn't know what a bastard he is," she said, looking down and admiring the little pistol in her hand. She gave me a half smile and then put the gun to her chest and fired.

Chapter Twelve

Diane Gessler was dead. That was the only thing I knew for sure. I lay like a sandbag in the hospital bed, surrounded by apparatus and equipment, hooked to tubes and monitors, my eyes closed and wanting to stay that way.

I could hear things. Whispered voices, tiny beeps, distant phones ringing, and the *fwee-whomp* of the ventilator. The acrid smell of hospital disinfectant fought with scratchy sheets for invasion of my senses. My right side felt heavy, achy.

Mom entered the room. A faint whiff of her perfume announced her presence even before she bent over me, her hand brushing back my hair. "Amanda?" she whispered. I opened my eyes to see her anxious face. "Oh, Amanda, you're going to be all right." She squeezed my fingers, careful not to dislodge the I.V. needle taped to my hand. "Honey, that was a close one, but you'll be fine."

"What—" My tongue felt sticky, thick.

"Your lung partially collapsed. Don't try to talk."

"Richard?"

Her face closed down for a second, and then she said in a low voice, "He's in Intensive Care. I understand they've removed his spleen, but he's expected to recover. They'll know more in a day or two." She tried to smile and I saw tears in her eyes. "Don't think about it, honey."

How could I not? How could I forget the sight of Diane Gessler as the light went out of her eyes, as blood gurgled from the hole in her chest, as she slid down the door frame into a loose-jointed pile on the floor?

What had we done? I never meant to hurt anyone. Richard had always assured me she didn't care, yet she tried to kill us. And succeeded in killing herself. Nothing was what I'd thought. She was dead, and I was to blame.

"It's not your fault," Mom said, reading my mind. "You got mixed up in more than you could handle. You're so young. You didn't know what you were doing."

I should have. Regret deeper than anything I'd ever felt settled into my heart and I strained to turn away from Mom, only to be thwarted by the IV tube taped to my hand and my own weakness. I knew he was married, had known all along, but I refused to face the facts. It was easier to pretend she didn't care than seriously think about what pain I might be causing. She would never open her eyes again and it was time for me to wake up, to stop sleepwalking through life.

Covering my face with my free hand, I told Mom to get out. "I don't want you here. Things are going to get ugly. Go home."

"Don't be ridiculous. You're my daughter and you're hurt. Of course I'm staying here." She tucked the blanket more firmly across my waist. "It's a great big world. This will all blow over in a few days."

"Oh please, Mom. Just go." Tears seeped from my eyelids but I didn't have the energy even to sob. Her presence was agony. I couldn't bear for her to touch me or comfort me or be strong for me. I only wanted to sleep and sleep and sleep.

Mom was wrong about the scandal blowing over. Things got worse every day. Even shut away in my hospital room, I knew. I saw it in the faces of the nurses when they cared for me, their furtive glances and whispered conferences with each other outside my door. I saw it in the security guard posted to forestall any unwanted visitors. I could figure things out by the fact that my phone had been removed and my TV kept turned off.

The police came and questioned me, making me relive every second of that horrible night. The questions they asked were embarrassing enough, but little flicks of interest showed in their eyes, making me cringe. One of the officers kept nodding as he took down notes, as if it were an old familiar story. Mom sat next to me, holding my hand, her cheeks flaming at my responses. Bad enough she had to hear everything; even worse, each morning she had to ran the gamut of reporters laying siege to the hospital and her hotel.

"Don't keep me in the dark," I begged. "I might as well know the worst."

She fussed with the flowers on my table, trimming the stems, adding an aspirin to the water. "It's not so bad," she said, her back to me. "Of course, he's pretty famous so you have to expect some press coverage." She turned and folded her arms across her chest. "Why don't I ask the doctor if we can wash your hair today? Your scalp must feel awfully itchy and dirty by now."

"The heck with my hair, Mom! What are they saying about Richard and me?"

Pursing her lips, Mom sat down in the chair next to my bed and took my hand in hers. With her eyes on the blanket over my legs, she told me about the New York Times article in that morning's paper. "They say she might have been temporarily insane. Apparently she and Mr. Gessler had been quarreling a lot, and there's talk that she discontinued her lithium. Also, he . . ." She stopped and looked at me. "Amanda, did you know that he—The papers say he intended to adopt you, or make himself your guardian. At least his lawyer said something like that." She hurried on. "Of course, that's ridiculous. There must be some kind of misunderstanding. I'm sure it will all be cleared up soon. How could he adopt you? You *have* parents. You have parents who love you very much." She looked at me pleadingly. "You didn't know anything about an adoption, did you?"

I just lay there, mouth gaping like a fish on land. *Adopt me?* Oh, my god, no wonder Diane Gessler went after him. She could have survived a divorce—she had money of her own, and looks and a glamorous lifestyle. But adoption would have meant their daughters would be affected. If Richard planned to adopt me, it could only be so he could legally take care of me, be my guardian, leave me something in his will. Which meant taking something away from his real daughters, and surely, Diane Gessler wouldn't stand for that. All her maternal instincts would be aroused and she'd fight like a mother tiger for her young. No wonder. "I didn't know. I promise you."

Mom heaved a sigh of relief. "I knew it. I knew you couldn't have okayed something like that. That man—" She bit off the rest and busied herself with smoothing my hospital gown and picking imaginary lint off the blanket. "We'll get everything straightened out and take you home. The doctor says you're making good progress and can go home in a few days."

Did she really think we could all return to some kind of normalcy? I wanted to grab her by the arms and shake her. What kind of la-la land did she live in? "Where were you, Mom? What were you doing when they reached you? How did you feel when you found out your daughter wasn't at school like you thought, but hundreds of miles away living in sin with a man older than Dad?"

"Don't talk like that," Mom snapped. "There's nothing to be gained. You made a mistake, you've paid a terrible price, and now it's over."

"Over? Oh my god, Mom, it's just starting. People will tear me apart. And you. And Dad. They'll drag up every bit of dirty laundry they can find. I've brought shame on you all. I'll never be thought of as anything but a slut."

"Don't say that!"

"Why not? It's true."

"You're not! Don't say that!" My mother's hand whipped out and slapped me across the face. She gasped, and then put both hands over her own face and whirled away from me. Her shoulders shook.

190

I was tired. Tired to death. "Go home, Mom," I said, closing my eyes. "Just please go home."

On the fifth day, they let me move around. I tottered into the bathroom like an old lady. My legs shook, my body felt unfamiliar. Still hooked to the IV, I had to push the pole with me into the bathroom and was glad to have something to hang onto. My right lung felt floppy and heavy as a sodden sponge, which I suppose it was, despite the tight wrappings around my ribs. I finally got a glimpse of myself in the mirror and realized why my mother was so anxious to wash my hair. Not only was it greasy and flat, but tiny bits of blood and gore were still visible. I had a sudden vision of Richard's face as he lay on top of me in that tub, his eyes gazing in dull surprise, his mouth hanging open.

Bandages crisscrossed my chest, high up between my collarbone and breast. The second bullet from Diana's gun had buried itself in my chest, causing my lung to collapse. I'd have two lovely mementos of the event; a scar from the bullet and one from the emergency chest tube. Marked for life.

Basically, I looked like shit. My skin was pasty and pale, I had circles under my eyes down to my knees, Betadine stains darkened my skin and, to add insult to injury, my period had begun.

The nurse sat me on a chair in the shower and began to wash me. It took all my strength just to keep from tipping over when she raised one arm to wash underneath.

"Sorry about this," I said. "Not very pleasant for you."

"Don't worry. I do this all the time." She carefully lathered my hair and I thought about the last time it was shampooed. Oh god, Richard. She rinsed with a sprayer. "How are you feeling?"

"Like I've been beaten and dragged. When do they release me?"

"Probably tomorrow if you keep doing well. Although I don't know how we'll sneak you out of here. Those reporters and photographers are wild to see you, ever since the photos came out." A stricken look spread over her face.

"What photos?" I asked.

"Nothing. It's nothing." She whipped through the rest of my bath and dried me off, wrapping my ribs afresh. "You get back in bed, now."

I bided my time, waiting till the nurses were busy with a new patient. Mom was late in arriving; maybe the crush of reporters had worsened, maybe she couldn't even get to the hospital. I eased out of bed, carefully holding the back of my hospital gown closed, and opened the door to my room. The security guard, a young guy with a scraggly goatee, looked startled to see me there.

"Could you please find my mother for me?" I asked in my sweetest voice. "I think she went to the drink machine." He nodded, looking eager to be doing something, and I stepped back into the room. The minute he was out of sight, I glanced around and slunk over to the nurse's desk, hanging onto the IV pole. One nurse, with her hair wound in a big bun, talked on the phone, her back to me. The other was nowhere in sight, but her copy of one of the tabloids laid on the edge of the desk. I snagged it and moved as silently as possible back to my room.

The magazine was disgusting. I sat hunched on the toilet, hiding out in the bathroom for privacy, and pored over the pictures and text. There was the photo of my family and Richard taken at the recital, a grainy picture of Dad carrying Josh out to the car, and the photos Richard took of me when I was drugged.

In a way, the pictures were completely harmless. I wasn't nude, not entirely, and nothing private showed. Still, the erotic nature was undeniable. Richard had done a good job, if I looked at it from simply a photographic viewpoint. Soft lighting gleamed on my skin, making me look like a very young child. Some pictures were full-length; me on the bed in nightgown or panties, partially concealed by blankets or my hair. Some were close-ups, centered on my face. One that disturbed me the most showed me naked from the waist up. In it, I was laying on my stomach so my breasts were hidden and one arm curled around that stinking teddy bear. My hand lay next to my face, near my open mouth, and I looked like I was about to suck my thumb.

Dear god, it was revolting. My face burned, my stomach twisted. It made us look so awful, so disgusting. Our relationship wasn't like that, I wanted to tell people. We loved each other, we weren't sick and perverted, but there was no way to explain. No way to make it look less grotesque, no way to diminish the shocking image. Pornography would almost have been better. That damned picture would be branded on the memory of every person I ever knew. Sissy would see it,

Mme. Trohatchev would and my friends at college, my friends at home. My kindergarten teacher, for chrissake. What would they think? What would anyone meeting me for the first time think?

I wanted to die.

There was more. On another page were pictures of Diane Gessler and a list of the many charities she supported. One photo showed the daughters, taken at their mother's funeral two days ago. Black suits, tasteful black hats, sunglasses to protect them from the stares of the vulgar crowd. His older daughter, Emily, made a statement to the press. "We want to emphasize, my sister and I, that we love both our parents. Their marriage had a few problems lately, but we'd hoped they'd all be worked out. This action of my mother's was completely out of character and I can only guess she felt driven to it by grief and despair." Of me, she said nothing, for which I was grateful. The damage I'd done was implied well enough.

"Amanda?" Mom knocked on the door of the bathroom. "Are you okay?"

I came out, newspaper in hand. She stood by the door in her neat Alfred Dunner pantsuit and Mia loafers, her hair smooth and gleaming, looking so wholesome and all-American that I could have cried. "I guess you've seen these," I said, tossing the paper on the bed.

"Yes." She bit her lip. "We'll simply have to deal with it."

"I didn't know, Mom. I promise you, I didn't know he took them. I didn't pose for him. I was asleep."

"Of course you were." She put her arms around me, gingerly, cautious of my injury. "I know you would never . . ."

Crying hurt too much. It was an emotional release I didn't deserve. I stood stock still in her arms, keeping my grief inside, locking it down in a small metal box, burying it beneath mountains of guilt. Mom smoothed my hair.

I eased into bed. "Did you read the article? It's terrible. Insinuates all kinds of things. They make us seem—oh, it's so awful." I turned on my side, gasping at the unaccustomed exertion, and then I curled up into a question mark, asking, "What happened this morning? You're so late. Did you have trouble?"

"Well, yes. Quite a crowd downstairs today. I don't know why they haven't better things to do. Plus, I talked to Mason Kennedy this morning. We've been trying to figure out how to get you home."

"Mason! Why involve him?"

"Hush, Amanda, keep your voice down." Mom pushed back on her hair, a sure sign she was distracted. "I think he and Travis are going to fly up here and drive us back. Travis will loan us his cottage for a while and—"

Travis! Worse and worse. "I hate to bother them. Can't we manage on our own?"

Mom sighed and sat down next to me, taking my hand in hers. "I wish we could, Amanda. I wish I could simply take you home and have everything get back to normal, but now I can see it will take a few weeks. I thought about going up to Michigan, maybe stay with Grandma and Grandpa, but I'm afraid we'd only bring the thundering hordes down on them. I admit, I'm out of ideas." She patted my hand and made an obvious attempt to brighten up. "Your dad plans to phone this afternoon. I talk to him every day, letting him know how you are, and he's real anxious to see you. Of course, all this publicity's been hard on him, too. The reporters have been going on and on about his . . . his relationship with Janine, and saying terrible things about . . ." Her voice trailed away.

I regarded her mournfully. "Hasn't been easy for you, has it? I'm sorry, Mom. So, so sorry."

She pressed my hand to her cheek and smiled at me. "We'll live through this. You'll see. It'll be old news by next week." She rose and went to the window. "The weather's quite cold here, isn't it? We'll have to get you some clothes to travel home in, and a coat." She whirled around, more color in her cheeks. "I'll call Sissy, have her stop by the house and get a few of your things to send with Travis." Filled with purpose and a plan, Mom excused herself to go make a few phone calls and left me alone.

I tried to rest. My very bones were exhausted, but sleep eluded me. The usual daily hospital noises—phones, voices, apparatus being wheeled about, the *ping* of the elevator doors—all conspired to keep me awake. I wanted to sleep. Get unconscious and forget all my troubles.

How could I go home, back to North Carolina? I would be shunned and stared at everywhere I went. I certainly couldn't re-enroll at the university, not after making shame for them, causing their major benefactor to be disgraced. I didn't want to go back to Painter's Creek, no way in hell. I wished I could disappear.

I was finally beginning to drift off when my door opened. "Oh, what now?" I wailed.

"You must feel better, you're crabby," Richard said from the doorway, sitting in a wheelchair with an attendant behind him. At my stunned expression, he smiled and rolled himself further into the room. The attendant left, closing the door behind him. "Surprised?"

"My god, how are you?"

Richard chuckled. "For an old guy who's lost half his innards, not too bad. How are you?" He did look pretty good. His skin seemed paler than usual, almost yellow, but he sat up straight in the chair, dressed in a silk robe over pajamas, as vital as ever.

The newspaper lay across the foot of my bed. I glanced at it and stiffened my spine. "I'm not good. I feel like crap, I've broken my mother's heart, and now all this." I indicated the damning photos. "Everyone's going to think we were freaks, into all kinds of disgusting stuff. Why didn't you tell me about these pictures?"

Richard picked up the paper and eyed it appraisingly. "You look so sweet," he said. "I love you like this." Then, after deliberating a minute, he turned to me. "I don't think they're disgusting at all. Why should I? Lots of men like their women to dress up. Some like high heels and garter belts, some like thongs. I happen to like baby-doll nighties. What's wrong with that? You're not *really* a child."

"But they make me look—oh, nobody will understand. And what about this adoption stuff?"

197

He placed the newspaper on his lap and folded his hands. "I'm sorry. I should have told you what I was doing. I planned to, after everything was done, like a wonderful surprise. We would be having an elegant dinner at some place special and I'd kiss you and tell you."

"Richard! Wake up! I'm not a child, you can't adopt me! You sit and spin this fantastic story and all the time—" My voice began to wobble, so I stopped and calmed myself. "Richard."

"Daddy," he corrected me.

"*Richard*. Your wife is dead! It's our fault!"

His face grew dark. "The hell it is. She did it herself. I never, *ever*, harmed her in my life. That's why I didn't want to divorce, just live separately. And I never intended to rob my daughters of anything. I wouldn't do that, don't you know by now? All I did, all I ever wanted to do, was love you. Is that so terrible? Yes, I planned to adopt you. Adoption seemed the best way to provide for you, to make sure you had health insurance and an education. I could have paid for these things anyway, but I thought a legal relationship would be best. Are you mad because I didn't talk marriage instead? Would that have changed your mind?" He shifted restlessly in his wheelchair. I could see he wished to stride about the room, as he used to during those business arguments on the phone.

The situation was all too much for me. "I don't care about being married. I don't give a damn about that. What bothers me is always being kept in the dark. Like you said, I'm not really a child. To me, that part of our relationship was just a game, a form of affection, but in truth I'm a grown woman. I can take care of myself."

He smiled a little and shook his head. "Oh, Amanda, I don't know anyone less capable of that than you. You need me. Whether you want to admit it or not, you need me. I would never have been able to talk you into anything you've done, if you hadn't run to meet me halfway."

A soft light glowed in his eyes. I felt myself weaken, falling as always under the charm of his gentleness and affection. How tempting it could be to crawl into his arms and shut the rest of the world away. "We're connected, you and I," he said. He reached into his pocket and pulled out the diamond pendant, swinging from its satin band. "Even without this, a cord goes from my heart to yours. Pull it tight if you must, snap it free if you can, but it will always exist." His hand reached out and caught the sleeve of my gown. "Amanda," he whispered, "I need you, too. I'll always need you." Slowly, he tugged on my sleeve, drawing me closer, putting the necklace into my hand. "Kiss me."

I sat like an idiot, the diamond pendant warm in my hand, my mouth open and Richard leaned forward, a little smile on his face and a light in his eyes.

"Amanda!" My mother stood in the doorway, her eyes emerald green in shock. She strode to the bed, putting herself between Richard and me, glaring down at him. "Get out." When he made no move, she pushed on the arms of the chair, rolling it back a foot or two. "Haven't you done enough damage? I ought to—Get out!"

199

The security guard appeared, looking extremely ill at ease. "Take this man out of here," my mother ordered him. "If you were doing your job—"

"Amanda," Richard said, looking directly at me. "No one can protect you now like I can. Remember that. I'm the only one who can keep you safe. Any time you want to get hold of me, call my cell phone." He glanced up at my mother. "Mrs. Long, I love your daughter and I'd never hurt her."

"Get *out*!" my mom hollered, pushing the chair hard so that the unfortunate security guard got caught for a minute between wheel and door. "Don't you ever come near her again!"

Richard's attendant showed up at this opportune moment and grabbed the handles of the wheelchair, turning it to go through the door. Before he disappeared from sight, Richard turned to me and said, "Remember! Our situation has changed, but our love hasn't. Don't let anyone tell you different."

Mom slammed the door on his face and turned to me. She breathed hard, her eyes wild and bright, her hair fairly crackling around her head. "What a terrible man," she said, beginning to shake. "Terrible man. If that's what he calls love. . ." She dropped into a chair, putting her head in her hands for a minute before pulling herself together and facing me. "I've spoken to Travis. He and Mason will arrive this evening. And apparently not a moment too soon. Then we can get out of this godforsaken place and get you home. Get you safe."

"Mom, I . . . he's not entirely to blame. I have to admit. . ."

"Don't talk about it now, Honey. We're both upset. We'll discuss it another time." She patted me on the shoulder, looking distractedly around the room. "My goodness, these flowers are drooping. I'll go get some water for them." With another push at her hair, Mom left the room.

And me? I was left to sit on the edge of the bed, thinking, the diamond pendant burning into my palm like a brand.

Chapter Thirteen

The doctors sent me home with taped ribs, prescriptions for antibiotics and painkillers, and a list of instructions—no lifting, no driving, keep an eye on the wounds for any sign of infection. The medicine made me groggy at times and half the trip was a blur.

Travis's cottage sat off a quiet dirt road with few neighbors. I'd wondered how he could afford a place on the lake, but seeing it made me realize he had one of the old fishing cottages built when the lake first came into existence. Not 'high end' at all.

The aluminum-sided house was tiny, mainly one room which served as kitchen, dining room and living room combined. A bank of windows faced the lake and a brick fireplace took up one corner. The kitchen appliances were tacky, cheap wood paneling covered the walls, and he had the ugliest carpet I'd ever seen. Some kind of horrible sixties-era orange and avocado green, going bald in places. Nevertheless, it seemed comfortable with groaning bookshelves, a TV and stereo and a big round table with chairs. The bedroom was small and the bathroom miniscule—only a shower and no tub. Considering what happened the last time I had a tub bath, maybe just as well.

"Not much to look at," Travis acknowledged, "but the view is great." The sun had set and the moon rose over the lake, reflecting a silvery line in the water. "And it's quiet, especially this time of year. You won't be bothered. Groceries are stocked up and I'll stay here at night on the couch."

Mom bustled around the kitchen, getting her bearings and heating water for tea. "I can't thank you enough, but I sure hate infringing on your privacy."

Travis shucked his coat and hung it on a peg. He dug his hands into his pockets, fists balled up, and shrugged. "No problem. I only hope it'll be private enough and we don't end up with the whole town down here checking you out."

"Which could happen." Mason Kennedy had been pretty quiet the whole trip, offering only an occasional suggestion regarding route or precautions. "Amanda should think about a statement to the press."

"Oh no, she doesn't want to talk with them." Mom stepped out from behind the counter, putting herself between Mason and me. "What would she say? No, much better to stay quiet and wait for everything to die down."

"It won't, Grace. Not until they hear from her. Better if she can prepare a comment and put the right spin on it." He turned and spoke directly to me. "Tomorrow, I'll drop by and we'll talk. It's possible you might still face legal action. All depends on whether Diane Gessler's will is contested. I've heard she left everything to her girls, including her GBW stock. Gessler got cut out completely. Depending on what happens, he might want to argue she was insane at the time she changed her will, which could lead to a lot of ugly claims. I think it would be a good idea for us to hammer out a statement together."

"I don't want her talking to the press. Might only make things worse. They'll twist whatever she says and—"

"Maybe we should ask Amanda." Travis's voice was low. Everyone turned to look at me.

I had that horrible all-eyes feeling, just like in Mme. Trohatchev's class when they were filming the rehearsal. I waggled my foot and wished I were back there again, before all this happened.

"What do you want to do?" Travis prompted.

"I don't know." Ha. I could almost hear Richard tease me. *Yes you do know, Amanda. And if you don't, better figure it out.* "I'll think it over."

Lame. Man, I was so lame.

Mason turned to leave and Mom walked him out to his car. Travis and I were alone in the cottage for a moment. All day, I'd been aware of Travis's kindness. When he first arrived at the hospital that morning, he'd leaned down to kiss my cheek and throughout the long drive, he'd been unfailingly thoughtful of my comfort. Yet his eyes kept skimming away from mine whenever he spoke to me. "I know Mom has said 'thank you' about a zillion times," I began, "but I want say thanks too. I don't know what we would have done without you."

"Don't mention it." The kettle whistled and he got out three mugs and a box of teabags. "I'm glad to help. Your mom's a nice lady." He turned to the fridge. "You take cream? Sugar?"

"What are people saying?" He stood a moment longer, his back to me. "Travis, tell me the truth."

The room seemed suddenly quiet. Under his plaid flannel shirt, I could see Travis square his shoulders before he turned to face me. For the first time all day, he looked straight in my eyes, and what I saw there made my heart sink.

"It's pretty ugly. They're like wolves, snarling over a carcass, sniffing out blood. Not only you, but your dad and his kid, and any tiny, nasty thing their evil little minds can devise. You know how this place is. On the surface, all nicey-nice. But underneath, watch out. There's a lot of sympathy for your Mom, though. I mean—"

"You mean, people feel sorry for her. Poor woman, her son died, her husband fooled around, her daughter screwed up big time. Jeez, I can't stand it, all that sympathy. All that damned gleeful, gossipy sympathy."

"I know. Condescending, that's how they'll be. People are always secretly glad to know other people have problems. I guess somehow they think it makes everyone more equal. Nobody better than anyone else."

He walked over to the fireplace and hunkered down to adjust the logs and add kindling. Once the blaze started, he dusted off his hands and looked back at me. "Believe me, I know what I'm talking about. After I messed up my knee—"

Mom walked back into the cottage, huddled deep into her sweater. Her eyes were red, like she'd been crying, but now a bright cheerful expression flash-froze to her face. "Oh, the tea is all ready. Good." She wrapped her fingers around the mug.

"I'm tuckered. Anyone feel like watching a DVD? I brought a couple of favorites."

We spent the rest of the evening watching a comedy that didn't make any of us laugh and Mom fell asleep on the couch. I persuaded her to go to bed and made myself more comfortable in a sweatshirt and pair of long johns. My movements were stiff, with a lot of pain under my taped ribs, but I was beginning to feel a bit more human. Travis had fixed up the couch with blankets and sheets by the time I came back out.

"How long do you think it will take?" I asked, clicking off the DVD player and removing the disc. One of the late-night talk shows began and the audience laughed at the opening monologue. "I mean, for everything to die down?"

Travis shrugged. "Depends on if some new scandal eclipses this one. He's not a big movie star or something." He drew the drapes and kicked off his shoes. "Maybe you'll get lucky and—"

"What about that Gessler guy, huh?" The stand-up comedian addressed his audience. "Now there's a piece of work, don't you think? Have you seen those photos? I hear they're going to be published in one of those big coffee-table books. Should be out in time for Father's Day." I stared as the audience laughed their appreciation. Travis snapped off the TV.

Neither of us knew what to say. Travis shuffled his feet and threw out his hands. He started to speak but I just said good-night and walked away. I managed to go to the bathroom, undress, and crawl into bed before the tears started to come. Mom was curled on her side, a pleasant-smelling, slender form under the blankets. I lay on the very edge of the mattress, arms crossed over my chest, and silently wept for all the things I had done and all the things I now would never do.

By next morning, the weather had turned colder. My legs felt shaky, starved for exercise. I put on my heavy coat and went down to the pier. Little drifts of fog hovered over the water and fingers of frost pushed up through the clay soil. Old and weather-beaten, the pier shimmied and swayed as I walked to the end and sat on a built-in bench. The cold air hurt my lungs, especially the injured one. Each step jolted my ribs and I wrapped my arms around myself, trying to hold them steady. Despite the quiet, or perhaps because of it, every individual sound seemed amplified. Water lapped at the uprights, rollers creaked where the dock attached to the pier. Far across the lake, a single fishing boat sped, its motor a mosquito's drone. Smoke drifted from the chimney, smelling wonderful, and yellow streaks appeared in the pearl-grey sky. Behind me, the screen door slammed and pine needles crunched as Travis walked down the path to the pier.

"Brought you some coffee," he said, handing me a steaming mug. "Grace is making breakfast."

"She's like a quilt, isn't she? Wrapping her warmth around everyone, trying to bring comfort. I don't think scrambled eggs and biscuits will cut it this time, but I give her credit for trying."

"Doing her best, I guess." Travis sipped his coffee and looked out across the lake. "I'm sure she must feel pretty confused about what you did and why." He finished his coffee in a few gulps, swiped his hand across his mouth and squatted down to get face to face with me. "I guess that's another reason why people talk. They can't figure out why you'd get involved with a guy like him."

His eyelashes were golden. I never realized that before. The sun glinted off them now, making me aware of their length and how they curled. Tiny freckles stood out on the bridge of his nose, sprinkled over the taut lines of his cheekbones. He'd shaved and I could see a line of smooth skin low on his neck, above the white rim of his t-shirt. One of the buttons was missing from his coat.

"I was lonely. Richard was kind. He believed in me, in my dreams. Oh, I don't expect you to understand—" I added, when Travis suddenly stood up. "After all, you've always had friends, you've always had girls swarming around you, the big football hero."

"Oh, drop that." He leaned on the railing, looking away from me. "Did you really *like* him? How could you have anything in common?" His voice sounded tight, controlled, as he stared out over the water.

"Yes, I did. I was crazy about him." Even in profile, I could see Travis wince. "Look, that's the way it was! None of you will ever understand anything if you don't believe that. Yes, I loved him! Would it be better for you if you thought I didn't? Why? Seems to me, my actions would be even harder to forgive if I didn't do it for love." My anger suddenly dissipated and I felt cold and sick. "So now I suppose you think the worst of me."

Travis turned back to look at me, his gaze roving over my hair and face, just as mine had his. "I don't know. I'm beginning to realize I don't really know you at all. You were always just Sissy's friend. Mark's sister. And then . . ." He stopped, turning his mug around and around in his hands, and his voice dropped away. "Sometimes you think you know someone, but it's all an illusion. So I'm not sure what I think." He shifted his feet, holding out his hand to help me up. "Besides, doesn't matter what I think. Who the hell am I to make judgments?" He picked up my half-full mug, the coffee ice cold. He tossed the remains into the lake with one quick move and we walked back up to the cottage. The sun shone full on the face of the house by then, reflecting in the windows a promise of a beautiful day. I felt as though I'd stepped into a shadow, though, and shivered with the chill

"I can't get over there, hon, it's crazy here." Dad's voice sounded tense, clipped. "Reporters are everywhere, following me around, following Janine. Bastards."

I gripped the phone, staring out the window at the lake. "Dad, I'm really sorry about this. Please believe me."

"I know. I'm just worried about trying to see you. If I drive out there, someone's sure to figure out where you are. What a mess." There was a muffled sound as he spoke to someone at his end of the line, his hand covering the receiver. ". . . out of here. Amanda? Listen, I'm going to square Janine and Josh away first, maybe send them to her parents' for a while. Then I'll figure out a way to come see you, okay?"

God, what a hassle I was making for everyone. "It's all right, Dad. I'll see you soon." I hung up and folded my arms across my chest, rubbing the aching spot below my collarbone. It seemed like everything was going from bad to worse. Travis went to work and Sissy called to see how I was. She'd gone to Mom's house to check mail and phone messages and been besieged when she came out.

"Selena Hunt wants to interview you on her show, and so does Trevor Keith. Your mailbox was stuffed so full, things were falling out on the ground. I'd bring them by but Travis says don't, too big a chance someone might follow me. Geez, Amanda, I can't believe all this. It's a nightmare."

"No kidding." I sat in the rocker, gingerly stretching to relieve my aching side. "I can't stand it, I feel like a rat in a trap. What will I do? I mean, even after this blows over, I don't know what the hell to do. I sure can't go back to school."

After a moment of silence, she said, "I guess you have to go forward. I felt that way when I found out I was pregnant with Teri. Oh, I know, it's not the same, my problem didn't hit the headlines or anything, but I still had to go to class every day and face everyone, hear the whispers." Her voice trailed off. In the background, I could hear Teri blathering some kind of baby talk and banging on something. "Eventually I moved on. So will you. Hold your head up, do whatever you really want to do, laugh it off."

"A woman is dead. I can't laugh that off."

"I know." She sighed. "I don't have any other answers, though. Somehow you just go on. By the way, did Travis tell you? He found us a place to rent, Dave and me. It's not big but at least there's a yard for Teri to play in and we'll have more room than now."

I closed my eyes, listening to her describing the house, thinking about irony. Her life came together just as mine went to pot. A couple of months ago, I'd been judgmental about her carelessness, her lack of foresight, her bad choices. I was an idiot.

Mom did laundry. Travis had a small washing machine but no dryer, so she carried the basket of wet clothes out to the drying line by the side of the cottage and I followed.

"I haven't strung clothes on the line since I was a girl," Mom said, smiling. "We had a dryer, but my mother liked to hang things outside in the fresh air. You have no idea how nice it is, smelling sheets that have been dried in the sunshine."

I sat on a stump and watched her. A little breeze played with her hair. She wore it down these days, soft and loose on her shoulders. All my life, while I grew up, she kept it in a knot on the back of her head, smooth and neat. Now it swayed and dipped around her face, emphasizing the curve of her jaw and the little hollows under her cheekbones. Her cheeks were pink in the cold air and her green eyes held a soft light. I'd forgotten how pretty she was.

"I hope this nice weather keeps up," she said. "It's so beautiful here with the sun on the lake. Mason says—"

"You're in love with him," I said. Mom's blush confirmed it.

"Don't be silly." She picked up the empty clothesbasket and turned to go to the house. A sudden shy smile escaped and I had to grin. "We're just friends." She looked at me, half-laughing. "Amanda! Don't get romantic notions, I'm not—"

"Miss Long, could you answer a few questions, please?" A man, microphone in hand, ran down the path to us. Another man trotted behind him, a huge videocam on his shoulder. I heard the sound of car doors slamming above us, up the hill on the front side of the cabin.

Mom grabbed my arm and pulled me up the walkway, directly toward the man. "Keep going," she hissed in my ear. "Whatever happens, don't speak, just keep going." She put her arm around my waist and hunched her shoulders as though we were fighting a driving wind.

"She has nothing to say," Mom asserted. "Leave us alone."

The man didn't move until we were practically pressed right up against his shirt. My knees went soft. I couldn't trust my legs to make it up the slippery, pine-needle-covered trail. The guy with the videocam backed up, keeping us in his sight, until he tripped on a rock and sat down suddenly. With that, several more people appeared around the corner of the cottage, obstructing our way to the porch.

"Miss Long, please, just a few comments! Did you know he was married? Had you ever met Diane Gessler? Why did you let him take those pictures? Do you really suck your thumb? What are your plans now? Did you know about the other girls?"

Other girls?

We got to the stairs. Mom put her arm out, like a football player blocking a tackle, and forced our way through those bodies and onto the steps. I stumbled, falling to my knees and wheezing, as my breath seemed to stop in my throat. My chest burned. Mom bent over me, trying to get me up, her arms around my waist. "Come on, Amanda, come on. . .get up, sweetie. . . come on. . . ."

I focused on little things—a leaf caught in a crack of the railing, Mom's hands and the dent on her finger where her wedding ring used to be, the way the doormat curled up at the edges.

"Please, Miss Long! One statement is all we want!"

"She has nothing to say," Mom yelled. She pulled the screen door open, half dragging me toward it.

I finally managed to get on my feet and gave one agonized look at the reporters. They all seemed to pause a minute, their mouths open like Christmas carolers in mid-Noël, and I stammered, my voice thick and uneven, "I never meant to hurt anyone."

Mom put her arm around my waist and bodily lifted me inside, slamming the door shut behind us. I sank to the floor, unable to move, while Mom hurried to lock both front and back doors, pull the drapes shut, and phone Travis. The knocks and shouted questions continued and I just lay there, legs sprawled out in front of me, hands limp on the floor.

"Get up, Amanda," Mom said, grabbing my coat by the shoulders and hauling me toward the bedroom. I slid along the floor like a ragdoll and she pulled us both into the closet, where we huddled until things finally got quiet. Mom kept her arms around me, rocking me and humming, smoothing my hair.

I couldn't move. I couldn't do a thing. Shock reverberated through my body, miniature explosions that jarred and sizzled. My mind went on overload.

Other girls? Richard had other girls like me? Other girls before me? Memories flooded back, washing over me in waves that sent more shudders through my frame. *Do you think I make a practice of this*, he'd asked. *Write to me, c/o Richard Smith. I would never do anything to hurt my wife. You're unique, special. I will always love you.*

Had anything he'd said been the truth? Any of it? Had it all been lies? Or just Richard Gessler's *version* of the truth. And what was truth anyway? He told me his wife didn't care, she had someone else. And her eyes that night, when she glanced so dismissively at me. I didn't matter to either of them, except as a pawn in their own personal battle. I was nothing, I was nobody.

Mom rubbed my hands, murmuring my name. Louder and louder she said it, shaking me by the shoulders, getting to her knees to jerk me around and still I couldn't respond. "Amanda! Answer me!" Her eyes were wide, her hair tousled and falling over her face. "*Amanda!*" She slapped me across the face, the sound hanging in the air for moments afterward.

Slowly I came back. The ache in my chest rose and grew. My eyes locked on hers and I remembered I could move, breathe, speak. "Mom," I said.

"Oh God, Amanda." She threw her arms around me and burst into tears. Vaguely, I patted her on the back, nodding and saying her name again.

"Mom . . .Mom."

We climbed out of the closet. Out in the yard, horns honked and car doors slammed, following the brief wail of a squad car. Mom tiptoed to the front door and lifted a corner of the curtain.

"It's Travis. And Don Simmons from the Sherriff's department." She waited by the door, watching, and I could hear car engines starting up and wheels churning gravel.

Finally, Travis and Officer Simmons came in. I sat on the corner of the bed, limp and exhausted. Under my red sweater, I wore a white turtleneck shirt. I pulled it up over my mouth, pressing it to my face with my fingertips, taking in the texture and scent of the ribbed cotton. Clean. White. Spotless.

"I think she's in shock," Mom murmured as Travis came into the bedroom, kneeling in front of me and pulling my hands away from my face. I just looked at him, too dazed to move.

"Amanda, honey? You okay?" He rubbed my hands in his. They were warm, strong-fingered, capable. Travis threw a look back at my mother. "You think she needs to go to the hospital?" I started to shake then and Mom grabbed a quilt to place around my shoulders.

"Take her into the living room," she said. "Start the fire." Travis picked me up and I cried out as he carried me to the couch, pain shooting through my back. I smelled his after-shave, clean and fresh. Don Simmons stared down at me, his face expressionless. I knew him well, as a familiar sight at school events and public doings. Once he stopped me for failing to use my turn signal, letting me off with a brief warning. When Mark died, he drove the squad car at the front of the funeral procession, headlights flashing as we proceeded down Main Street, traffic parting to right and left in front of us. A whole town in mourning for one of its children, lost.

Mom brought my pain pill and a small glass of water, made me choke it down. Every breath hurt, I thought I might black out.

"I'll make sure they're gone," Don said, "and I'll stick around a while to see that they don't come back. Better think about moving her, though, now that they know."

He nodded to my mom and left. Travis had the fire going by then and he sat on the couch with me, looking worriedly at my mother. "He's right, Grace, and so were you. She's not up to dealing with the press. Maybe we should take her north, to your relatives."

"And bring all this down on them? I can't. My mother already has health problems and my dad, well . . . I don't know. I need to talk to Steve."

"I thought he was gone, Sissy said he took Janine somewhere."

"Oh, that's right." Mom lifted her hands helplessly and let them fall back in her lap. "I have no idea what to do. Maybe I should head west, out of state somewhere. But if Amanda's not up to it—"

"Please don't talk about me as if I'm not here," I said. They both turned to stare and I pushed the quilt off my lap and stood up. I swayed slightly, feeling unbalanced, and Travis grabbed my arm. Shaking him off, I said, "It doesn't matter. Just throw me to the sharks."

Mom sat on the edge of her chair, pressing her hands between her knees. "Honey, I promise you, we'll figure something out. Everything will be fine, you'll see."

"Oh, for god's sake, grow up, Mom! Nothing is going to be *fine*, ever again. Don't you see that? You might as well go home and let me deal with this myself." Taking care to walk very upright, I made my way back to the bedroom and closed the door, locking it behind me.

Of course, my words were all bullshit. I had no idea what to do. I didn't want to be the object of a feeding frenzy but my options were dwindling. If I could have gotten out of there on my own, I would have. However, with no money and most of my stuff still in my apartment in Raleigh, there seemed no way. All I had were my limited wits and a determination to stop being a problem for everyone.

The painkiller knocked me out and I slept for a couple of hours. When I woke, Travis was nowhere to be seen and Mom had fallen asleep on the couch. I didn't think it through, just wanted to be out of everyone's hair. Wanted to get away from everyone. I dug through Mom's purse and took her wallet and car keys. She'd understand. This wasn't theft, but a loan.

I stuffed some clothes into a pillowcase, threw in my medical supplies. Every movement caused twinges of pain, but I sucked it in. The medicine had taken the edge off. I changed out of the oversized red sweater I'd been wearing and pulled on an old high school sweatshirt and my varsity letter jacket from marching band. Ironically, when Sissy went to pack some clothes for me to come home, only these few memento items were left in my closet. A baseball cap of Travis's hung on a peg. I braided my hair and covered it with the cap.

Mom's lipstick was mauve, a rich satiny color. I used it to write a note on the mirror. *Don't worry, I'll be all right.* At the last minute, I grabbed the diamond pendant from Richard and stuck it in my pocket.

The grogginess had cleared, leaving my mind sharp and running hot. I checked to make sure nobody hung around outside and silently got into Mom's car. By the time anyone knew I was gone, I'd be far away.

Chapter Fourteen

I headed toward Raleigh, my apartment and my car. As I drove up I-85, my mind raced. My savings account was decently full, almost all of Mark's insurance money, plus what I'd earned over the summer. If I lived cheap, I could probably get by for nearly a year. I'd have to hide out for a while, keep a low profile, but the feeling was exhilarating. I was in charge of my own life again. Surely there would be jobs I could get. Waitress, factory worker, Wal-Mart clerk. I wasn't picky and I could live in the car for a while. Wash up in gas station bathrooms. Hang out in malls. Eat canned beans.

Well, maybe not canned beans.

I'd be a gypsy, traveling from place to place, a few months here, a few months there. By the time I came home again, I'd have seen the whole country from California to Maine. People would forget about the scandal and I'd have a brand new set of adventures to fill my mind.

I pulled off at a truck stop outside of High Point and did an inventory. In addition to my own wallet, which someone at the hotel in New York must have sent along with me in the ambulance, I had Mom's credit cards, about $200 in cash, several cents-off coupons, and even a packet of hand wipes. Bless her heart

The wonderful scent of hamburgers wafted from the diner. I jammed Travis's cap on my head, zipped up my jacket, and went in. While waiting for my carry-out order to be filled, I noticed the TV, mounted on an overhead bracket by the counter.

"I never meant to hurt anyone."

I saw myself, up there in living color, looking almost unfamiliar as I stared at those reporters. My eyes were huge, my skin paper-white. They did a close-up on my face and split the screen, adding the now-infamous thumb-sucking picture. There wasn't actually any news to go with the film, just the identification, "Amanda Long, witness to the Diane Gessler suicide and attempted murder. Mrs. Gessler, well-known contributor to many charities, was buried this week." The picture switched to a copy of the DVD that had been made at Burgess. I watched myself dance, watched as Mme. Trohatchev questioned me and saw Richard in the background, leaning forward from his chair.

All around me, people went on with their meals. A row of truckers sat on stools in front of the counter, watching the news and stuffing themselves with meatloaf, potatoes and gravy. The news program moved on to a story about a fire and then a commercial. I pulled the cap down a little lower over my face, paid the girl when she brought my bag, and left.

What a fool I was, what a dim-bulb. Shit for brains. Mom had been right, I should never have said anything. My lame comment only made me look even worse. A cry-baby, a whiner. I never meant to hurt anyone. Well, so? Did I think that lack of intent meant lack of responsibility?

220

I stopped for gas in Durham, running into the convenience store to grab a Coke. My stomach churned. By the checkout counter were half a dozen tabloids. Inquiring minds wanted to know. Ha! Sick minds. Ugly, nosy minds. I bought several different magazines, throwing the money down on the counter and speed-walking to the car. Pictures of me, Richard, and Diane Gessler were splashed everywhere. Inside, the articles concentrated on new information coming out. Two young women, identified as former lovers of Richard, discussed his inclination for little girls.

"He offered to pay me to dress up like a child," one of them said. "That's where I drew the line." Apparently, it wasn't the money but the wardrobe that offended her.

"Richard Gessler is a closet pedophile," the other one said. "He's sick and perverted." The newspaper mentioned that her affair with him lasted over six months.   One of the papers brought up questions about Richard's business dealings. The magnifying glass turned on Richard in general also trained on his corporation and their recent spate of buyouts. A sidebar talked about his daughters; now that they'd inherited their mother's stock, a considerable amount of power was in the hands of two women who might or might not be on good terms with Richard.

They had pictures of him at the opening of the Gessler Center for the Performing Arts. He looked so happy; smiling and relaxed, that white curly lock electrifying against his tanned face.

What was he doing now? Where was he? I wondered what I truly was to him. A toy? A challenge? Had I ever been a real person to him? Because he had been real to me.

It wasn't much further to Raleigh. I couldn't wait to get my own stuff. Mom's car was beautifully maintained and ran like a charm, but the only CD's she had in there were Bach and Handel. I wanted my own music, and my books and clothes and toe shoes. My pillow and the blue mug with the Degas dancer on it and my beat-up old Yamaha guitar. My special hairbrush that I bought with my own money when I was ten. It was *my* stuff, I wanted it.

I drove past my apartment twice, checking for reporters, before I finally pulled into the driveway. My landlady's car was there, next to my old Chevy, and I parked Mom's car along the curb where it would be out of the way. Mrs. Rudisill nearly freaked when she saw me and babbled as I waited for her to get the key.

". . .been here night and day, asking questions, asking to take pictures of your room. I didn't let them, of course, but some looked in the windows. I figured somebody would be here sooner or later to get your belongings. Here's the key, do you need any help?"

Someone had been through my room, either Mrs. Rudisill or somebody else. Things had been moved, shuffled through. I bit back my anger and concentrated on packing. There was no knowing how far behind me anyone was. If Mom had awakened shortly after I left, she could be on her way there already. Didn't matter, all I needed was fifteen minutes lead time.

I tossed clothes into suitcases, bags, laundry baskets. Whatever was handy. I grabbed my checkbook and car keys from my desk, even remembered to get my car insurance info out of the file drawer. I dragged stuff down the rickety stairs and dumped it all in the open trunk of my car. My chest ached something fierce and I had a bad wheezing spell that scared me. The last thing I needed was to injure myself further. I couldn't take another pain pill or I wouldn't be able to drive.

I packed my guitar and toe shoes and took a last look around the room. Seemed like some kind of symbolic gesture was due before I made my exit to the great big world. I didn't have the phone number at the cottage, so I called Sissy.

"Where are you?" she gasped. "Everyone's going berserk here! Travis threw an absolute *fit*."

"He did? What did he say?"

"I don't think you want to know. What will you do?"

I told her to let my mom know that I would leave her car at my apartment, along with her wallet and cash. "I'm going away for a while. I've got Mark's insurance money. I'll get by on that until I can get a job."

"Oh, you're crazy. Come home!"

"No. I can't do that. Not now. Maybe not for a long time. Tell my mom. . . tell her I'll call. Tell her not to follow me. I'll be fine."

I didn't want to stay on the line. I could feel urgency building up inside of me. I had a final few things to carry down but as I stepped outside onto the stairs, a news van,

223

Channel Six, pulled into the driveway and spewed out a camera man, a reporter and two guys who began cranking up a huge antenna thing. I backed into the apartment and slammed the door.

"Miss Long, please! We only have a few questions!"

Damn it! Mrs. Rudisill must have called them. What was wrong with that woman? Footsteps thundered up the wooden stairs and I shot the bolt on the door. The curtains were open and I dropped to the floor, gasping in pain and crawling over to pull the cord. I caught one glimpse of the camera lens pointed into my room before the curtains swung shut.

I had another wheezing spell, so bad I thought I'd never get any air into my lungs. My heart felt like it would explode, and my head pounded until I thought it would split wide open. The stupid reporters kept shouting outside my door. "Please, Miss Long, can you tell us anything about Richard Gessler's relationship with you? Is it true that he planned to adopt you? Did your parents receive any money from him? Are you pregnant?"

They hammered repeatedly. Those people had no soul. I sat on the floor in the corner of the room furthest from the windows, huddled up in a ball, my hands over my ears, sick and dizzy. Don't pass out, don't pass out, I kept telling myself. My phone began to ring.

I crawled over to the receiver. The reporter outside banged on my window and yelled, "Did you ever meet the Gessler daughters? What do you think of them? As their adopted sister, would you have joined them at family get-togethers?" I picked up the phone, pushed the button to sever the connection, and unplugged the damn thing. In addition to continued knocking at my door, I could also see the doorknob being tested and the door vibrating in its frame. Momentarily, I pictured the assembled press jamming together on that rickety porch and the stupid thing collapsing under them. Still on my knees, I backed up again into the corner of the room. My big leather chair was nearby. I dragged it over in front of me, remembering Richard sitting in it, with me on his lap. I'd felt so safe.

"What were Diane Gessler's last words?" the reporter shouted. "Did she appear to be sane?"

The knitted throw was still on the back of the chair. I pulled it down, wrapping myself in its thick folds. My whole body screamed in agony, I couldn't breathe, my headache was blinding. I covered my ears, trying to block out the sounds. Curled up in that little space, rolled into the smallest possible ball I could make, pressing my arms tight against my ribs. If I was ever to suck my thumb, this would have been the time. What a picture it would have made.

I concentrated on my breathing, trying to slow it down, to calm myself. Closed my eyes tight, tried to block out all the noises, the anger, the fears. In through the nose, out through the mouth. In . . . out . . . in . . . out. Long slow Lamaze breathing that Mom taught me years ago to calm down before a recital. Occasionally I still coughed—dry coughs, no mucus. I remembered what the doctor had said, that discolored sputum was a sign of infection.

An hour or more passed and gradually the outside noises died away. I wondered if the reporters had left or were just waiting for me silently, like those big black crows outside the school in that Hitchcock movie. Late afternoon sunshine slanted around the edges of the curtains, throwing odd patterns on the floor. I drew the blanket off my head and slowly stood up, still holding my side. Everything was quiet, peaceful, calm. The van was gone, the street had returned to normal.

Was it safe to go down? Did I want to risk it, or wait till nightfall? As I debated, a car came down the street and pulled into the driveway behind my car. Two men got out and, with a little shock that ran right through my body, I realized one was Richard. He glanced up at the window and I could feel him staring right at me. Mrs. Rudisill must have called him, too. Maybe she had even used the TV crew as a way to keep me from leaving before he could get here.

I didn't recognize the other man, some kind of flunky. He remained at the bottom of the stairs while Richard came up. He moved slowly. Probably felt as shitty as I did. Step by step he came up, his eyes on the window, watching me watching him. He didn't bother to knock, just spoke through the door. "Amanda. Let me in."

For a moment, I debated. Then an unquenchable desire to *know* made me slide the bolt. As the door swung open, I backed away, folding my arms at my waist.

"Hi, baby," he said softly, his hands in his jacket pockets, making no move to step inside. "I've missed you."

This, then, was the man I'd been reading about. The one with the string of young girlfriends, the one with some questionable business transactions, the one who disregarded

226

all barriers of difficulties or ethics, and simply went after what he wanted. I stood there, frowning, unable to form a single word.

The spell broke as he stepped over the threshold and I involuntarily backed up. "What do you want?" I demanded. "I'm not coming back to you."

"Yes, you are," he said, his voice soft and reasonable. "We belong together."

"You had other girlfriends." I swore I wasn't going to say that, but the words came out.

"Yes, but before I met you. Not after."

"You said you didn't make a practice of it. You said I was special. You lied to me, Richard. You're a *liar*! I saw that video. I wasn't anything special that day, all you saw was this stupid kid who couldn't even speak up for herself. Passive. Submissive."

"Exactly."

"Well, that's *not* what I want to be loved for!"

I turned away from him, pulling my purse strap up over my shoulder, and picked up my guitar. He grabbed my upper arm and turned me to face him. Shaking me a little, he said, "Don't you see? You needed me. You weren't like the others, you weren't into the money, you didn't have to pretend to be a little girl. You *are* a little girl, a child, and you need your Daddy." His voice became lower, crooning. "We can be happy together. I know you, Amanda, I'm the only one who knows the real you, who loves the fire inside you and the passion you're capable of. I'm the only one who can help you now, who can protect you from being chased and hounded. We'll go away, no one will bother us, we'll—"

There was shouting down below. Richard was at the door in two steps, still holding me by the arm. At the foot of the stairs, Travis argued with Richard's assistant. My mother was there, too, remonstrating with Mrs. Rudisill. It was a big, horrible circus.

"Well, if it isn't the Golden Boy," Richard said loudly, a smile on his face and a cold light in his eyes. "How's the paint and wallpaper business? I bet you're the plywood king, eh? Lord of the lumberyard, toolbox tycoon?"

Travis's eyes blazed. He watched as Richard came down, a big hand wrapped around my arm, my guitar case banging against the railing at every step. They faced off at the bottom of the stairs, practically toe to toe. I could almost hear snorting and the pawing of hooves. Mom hurried over and pulled me away from Richard. His eyes flickered over at her for a moment, as though assessing her potential as a foe, and then he concentrated on Travis.

"What can you possibly offer her?" he asked Travis. His voice was low, controlled. He might have been at the negotiation table, calm and confident. "She has great potential as a dancer, why stand in her way?"

"Oh, yes, I'm sure that's all you want, to guide her career," Travis hissed. "You're disgusting, you make me sick. Anyone who could do what you've done—"

"Oh? And what have I done?" Richard circled slightly to the right. He was taller than Travis, bigger in build. He used that height to his advantage, leaning forward so that Travis

228

had to back up. Despite age and injury, Richard was still a formidable presence. "Sleep with her? Oh yes, I've done that. Quite a lot." He smiled when Travis flushed. He kept circling, forcing Travis to do the same. "But she *wanted* it. Don't believe me? Ask her."

Neither man looked at me. I stood there, swaying with dizziness, fighting the impulse to start wheezing again. They didn't even look at me—I hardly mattered. They were dueling for position, for superiority, that damn competitive bullshit men have. Richard thrust his head forward again. "You want to drag her home. For what? Painter's Crap offers her nothing, *you* offer her nothing. You're just a two-bit football hero in a two-bit town. She deserves more."

"You randy old bastard," Travis said, his fists doubled. He thrust his head forward, making Richard take a step back. "All you care about is yourself. You think you can get away with anything, simply because you're rich? Pathetic old goat."

"Yeah, I'm old. And ten times the man you'll ever be. Go play with your caulk guns, I'm bored with this." He turned toward me, totally ignoring Travis and holding out his hand. "Come on, Amanda, let's go." His smile was confident. When I backed away, he added, "Come on. Where's the girl I know? Where's my wild child? You don't need them," he added, nodding his head at Mom and Travis.

Mom's arms tightened around my waist and she screamed at him. "Get away from her. Haven't you done enough already? Haven't you hurt her enough? You should be locked up." She pulled me backwards, stumbling over Mrs. Rudisill's crooked paving stones.

Richard stopped, putting his hands in his pockets and giving my mother a rueful smile. "I won't argue with you, Mrs. Long. I've learned too well not to get between a mother bear and her cub. Amanda, honey, come here."

They all stared at me. Mom tried to steer me toward her car, but I pulled loose, wheezing a little, shivering, looking at each of them in turn.

Mom shook her head a little, saying "You don't want him. You couldn't."

I looked at Richard. His eyes were warm, crinkling at the corners. I thought about all the wonderful times. I thought about all the hurtful and confusing times. "I love you, sweetheart," he murmured.

"Daddy, I . . ."

"Daddy?" Travis's voice was harsh in the cold air. "You call him *Daddy*?" He stood in the driveway, his hands clenching and unclenching, breathing hard. His eyes met mine and then he took a step back.

I looked at the ground. My face flooded with embarrassment as my mother gasped. Oh god, what had I done? Calling him that must have hit her like a slap in the face. I couldn't look at any of them. I walked right past Richard, evading his hand, and got into my car, eyes blurred with tears. His car was parked behind me, so I drove forward, right over Mrs. Rudisill's flower bed, cut through the yard, and bumped down over the curb with a jolt that made me yelp.

I had no choice, no other choice. As I drove away, I caught one last glimpse of them in my rearview mirror. Mom, running after me, shrieking my name, Richard with his hands in his pockets and his head raised, and Travis, standing apart and alone.

I was halfway to the interstate before I realized it and then had to circle back to town and get some money from the bank. Pulled over behind the Tasty-Freeze, I counted the cash. My hands shook so badly, I kept dropping bills. Before I hit the road and left everything behind for good, there were two things I wanted to do. I dialed Richard's cell phone. He picked it up on the first ring.

"Richard, I need to talk to you."

"I knew you'd come around. Where do you want to meet?"

I told him how to find the Botanical Gardens, to wait for me at the entrance on Davidson Street. I'd meet him there in twenty minutes.

Then the second thing. I dug through the stuff piled on my back seat and found a large envelope and the scissors. Adjusting my rearview mirror so I could see myself, I grabbed my braid, took a deep breath, and sliced.

For three days I hid out in a motel room, too depressed to move. I hated Richard. Oh God, how I hated him. Even more, I hated myself. I'd seen that look in Mom's eyes. I'd seen the expression on Travis's face. I knew they were shocked and repulsed. I disgusted them, a sleazy piece of trash. That one word, Daddy, had probably confirmed all their worst fears. I had not only become that man's mistress, but I'd also engaged in a sickening form of charade. Seeing it through their eyes, I finally realized just how sick it had been.

What would I do with the rest of my life? I couldn't return to school, not with everyone staring at me and whispering. Nobody in their right mind would hire me for a job. And worst of all, I couldn't dance. Who would admit a ballet student to their program when she'd brought so much shame down on her previous school? Who would ever hire Amanda Long for a dance company after those screaming headlines of "Tiny Dancer" and "Pretty Ballerina". And if I couldn't dance, I didn't want to live.

Not that I had to.

The thought nearly made my heart stop. I didn't have to go on. No one could make me. I could slash my wrists or take pills, or hang myself from the light fixture and be done with this pain. Hell, I could just continue to lay there like a slug, let my lungs fill up with fluid and die. There would be an obituary, more magazine and newspaper articles, maybe a sentence or two on the evening news and it would be over. People would forget that Amanda Long ever existed. Another blow for poor Mom. Then again, maybe for the best. People would have sympathy for her, would rally around, but she'd pull through. It might even be easier for her in the long run, she'd never have to see me again. She'd probably be glad.

Whatever I did, it would have to be soon. I couldn't go on with this weight in my heart and no place to go. I thought about Mark, jerked from his life by a twist of fate, no choice, no decision. God took him and left me, what a joke. What a hell of a joke. Oh God, how could You have made such a terrible, stupid mistake?

Richard phoned me that night. I should have known not to pick up the motel phone, but the pain pill made me groggy. I had the damn receiver to my ear before I fully woke up.

"Bitch."

"Richard? How did you find me?"

"You're using your mother's credit card, you ignorant bitch. How hard was that to figure out? You think I can't find you if I want to? Cunt. Whore. Think you're pretty smart, I bet. Wanted to make a damn fool of me, huh? Made me stand for two fucking hours at that garden. In the freezing cold, I might add. How could you do that to me?"

His voice shook with fury. Cunt? Whore? He'd never used words like those before. "Richard, I—"

"I was *worried*, damn it. I thought maybe you had trouble with reporters or got in a car accident or something. God damn it, Amanda, I thought you cared about me more than that! After all the things I've done for you, the things I've given up for you. And then I go back to my car and find that package. Oh, yeah, your fucking message, that was real cute. Do you have any idea how I felt when I looked inside that envelope and saw your hair? Your beautiful hair, all cut off? I cried like a fucking baby. And the pendant. Did you have to throw that back in my face?"

"Yes, I did! It's over, that's the message. I don't want your gift and I'm not your little girl anymore."

"Bitch! You could have been straight with me, you could have met with me and said things were over. Dealt with me face to face."

233

I sat up in bed, having finally found the light switch. I had to pee. I kept rocking back and forth on the lumpy bed, a bedraggled quilted bedspread wrapped around me. "No. You would have tried to talk me into staying."

"So? Is that so terrible? Damn it, Amanda, I thought we had something special. I was your Daddy. It wasn't just about the sex." His voice lost some of its anger and deepened into those affectionate tones I knew so well. "You love me. I know you do. It's not too late. We can still work it out."

"*No*. For God's sake, your wife is *dead*. I feel so guilty about that."

"Bullshit! That is pure nothing but bullshit! What will you do, hide out the rest of your life? Slink from one dive motel to another? Turn into the fucking *Fugitive*, is that what you want to do? Stupid little lying cunt whore."

"Stop saying that! God, Richard, don't you feel guilty about Diane?"

"You've got somebody else, don't you? That's what this is all about. You're humping that lumber jockey. Checking out his roto-tiller. Bitch. You try to get me back, you wait till you're desperate and on the streets and see if I take you back. Bitch! *Bitch!*"

Icy calmness flowed over me and I took slow breaths. "Richard, you have a real ugly side. Do you know that?" I hung up the phone and it rang again, almost immediately. I put two pillows over it and went to the bathroom. Funny thing was, when I got there, I couldn't pee after all. I couldn't do anything but cry.

The next morning, I packed my things. My stomach growled and not for vending machine foods. Bacon and eggs sounded good. A big glass of orange juice. I took a hot shower. Three days of sitting around had not done my lungs any good but at least there was no sign of infection. I fingered the short ends of my hair. It didn't look too bad. Made me appear older. Independent. The hell with Richard. I wouldn't kill myself over him and his stupid photos. I wasn't the child he thought I was. Richard would see, they'd all see. I'd find a way to walk out of this mess and grow stronger with every little step I took.

After breakfast, I'd give Mason Kennedy a call. If anyone could help me get a name change and new I.D., he'd be the one. Even if he disapproved, he'd do it for Mom's sake. Down the road, I'd find a way to get by. A new name, a new life, a new me. As for Richard and Travis and Mom, they'd have to find their own paths. I was of no use to them now.

It would be six years before I saw any of them again.

Part Two

Chapter Fifteen

Traffic was the usual five o'clock gridlock, stop-and-go all the way. U-Penn students streamed across the road on foot or bike, heading for restaurants and coffee shops on Chestnut Street. End-of-season tourists trudged back to hotels to bathe their tired feet and plan an evening's foray into the Philly club scene. As soon as the light changed, I turned onto the side road just past an art supply shop, and up the driveway of Cornerstone Music.

Inside, Pete worked the console while three guitarists worked on a flamenco-flavored bluesy number in Studio A and an old guy with a goatee added congas and surdos from the drum room. I waved at him through the glass and went into the kitchen where the kids, Jemima and Cody, sat on the floor playing with modeling clay. Pete had left some new arrangements, written in his typical cryptic fashion on dog-eared notebook paper, and I pulled out my guitar to work through them, humming along.

Jenny appeared at the doorway, smiled wanly, and hurried to the sink where she struggled with dry heaves. After a few minutes, she sat down, pale and clammy. "Morning sickness, pah! More like all-day sickness." She re-knotted her long red hair and clamped it in place. "It was the same way with these two. Man, I don't know if I can deal with this much longer. All I want to do is sleep." She leaned back and closed her eyes. "How'd you like to take my place this weekend?" I kept strumming and she opened her eyes and looked at me. "I mean it. You know the routine. Pete'd be okay with it."

"Pete would be okay with what?" His husky voice came from the doorway and Cody and Jemima jumped up and ran to his arms. Pete scooped them up and sat in the big rocking chair, blowing huge raspberries on each of their necks.

"I'm trying to talk Connor into substituting for me this weekend." She leaned toward me as I began to shake my head. "Who else could pick up the slack on such short notice?"

"Oh, Jenny, I don't think I'd be any good. I'd get too nervous." Holy heck. Appear on stage? After working so hard to disappear, wouldn't that be ridiculous? I loved helping Pete with his studio work, playing back-up for other musicians or recording commercials for local businesses, but jeez. Appearing on stage, in public, having a sea of faces looking at me? No way.

Pete set the kids back on the floor and stood up to rub Jenny's shoulders. She stretched and purred. "Yeah, it's probably time. We all knew Jenny couldn't last much longer. This next gig is at GingerPop's. A funky little place, no big deal. I've got back-to-back recording sessions the rest of this

237

week, plus the re-mixing, and I'll be lucky to find a piss break, let alone time to line up somebody else and rehearse."

With both of them looking at me so trustingly, I said I'd think about it. Jenny and the kids left, while Pete and I got to work. The band that had reserved evening hours arrived, and we spent the rest of the night working on their overdubs and solos.

At home, later that night, I sat in my little one-room apartment three flights above the Asian grocery store, thinking about Pete's request. The scent of homemade noodle soup had followed me up the stairs and my dinner—celery, cream cheese, and raisins—didn't hold much appeal. In the morning, I'd turn twenty-five. As with all my birthdays in the past six years, there'd be no celebration. No cake and candles, no gifts, no Hallmark moments. I was okay with that, it was my own decision to keep private, but twenty-five years was a milestone, wasn't it? A time for reflection.

I began my exercises, stripped to panties, t-shirt, and toe shoes. All the furniture in my bare-bones apartment was pushed tight to the wall to make space for a mirror, a wall-mounted *barre* and enough wooden floor to accommodate a *jeté* or two.

As I drew up tall, feeling the stretch through my spine and the expansion of my rib cage, I could almost summon up the scents and sounds of dance class. With my eyes closed, I heard Madame Trohatchev's voice, her querulous manner. *What are you doing, Amanda? What are you supposed to be doing?* Sometimes, I thought, I still didn't know.

I opened my eyes and looked at the mirror. Since quitting the dance, I'd grown taller and heavier. I even had curves. The woman I saw looked strong and capable. I liked that. I liked believing my life was finally my own again, under my control. Between my part-time job at the bookstore and working for Pete, I made decent money and loved what I did. People accepted me as Connor Long, nobody gave me any flak. Whenever someone asked if I was Amanda Long, I lied. "Amanda Long? No, but I'm her cousin, and I don't like to talk about it." I was content with where I was at—didn't want to fly away—but how long could I stay there?

With Tchaikovsky's *Romeo and Juliet* for background, I went through my stretches and *barre* exercises. Every day without fail, my routine helped calm my mind and give me balance, but I was not the dancer I'd been. Strength and control were my forté now, but something had been lost, forfeited. Joy, perhaps. That sense of flight, of freedom. I didn't like to dwell on it.

After the workout, I sat on the edge of the bed and toweled off. Almost midnight, too late to call Mom. I'd wait until tomorrow morning, when she'd be at school, and call to leave my twice-monthly message on her machine. "I'm fine," I always said. "I'm healthy; I've got a job and a place to live. Don't worry about me. Take care, love you." There was really nothing else to say and I didn't want to hear fervent requests to come home. I wasn't ready for that. Not yet. Maybe, not ever. Rubbing my face against the prickly towel, I thought about Pete and Jenny's request.

The whole idea was crazy. I should just say no and have done with it. Miss Invisible, that was me. So why did I still think about it? On the one hand, Pete and Jenny were my friends. He'd not only introduced me to the world of studio music, they'd both made me a part of their family, something I hadn't experienced in a long time. I owed them a return favor. On the other hand, maybe I was being paranoid. Nobody had recognized me in almost two years.

And on the third hand . . . jeez, it would be nice to pit myself against a challenge. Push myself, strive. I stood again, rose on my toes and crossed the room in a series of tiny sideways steps, my arms raised. Performing in public brought out all the sharpness and clarity, gave an edge that mere rehearsal and recording did not. It put your skills on the line.

Maybe I would tell Pete yes, after all. It was only a few nights in a rather obscure bar in the suburbs of Philly, after all. No big deal. Everything would be fine.

The gig turned out to last more than a couple of weekends. Jenny's ongoing nausea led to dehydration and low blood sugar and the doctor ordered her to rest. Pete's mother moved in, taking over like the good Italian mama she was, and shooed the rest of us out us out of her kitchen. Pete and I rehearsed the act a lot and lined up other jobs, including a regular Thursday night gig at a little club off South Street. By mid-October, things were clicking along.

We began to expand, taking jobs outside of Philly, enlarging our base of fans. Well, *his* base of fans. They still remembered his days as lead singer of Tad Paranoid, even though he'd swung in a whole different direction now, musically, to a folksy type of blues. I played lead guitar and sang back-up vocals. When Pete got promotion-minded and ordered a bunch of flyers with our pictures, I felt a little nervous about having my face splashed all over town. The black-and-white photos with our names—PETE TIONESTA with Connor Long—came back from the printers slightly out of focus and I convinced Pete they were better that way; unusual, edgy. He bought it and I doubted anyone would recognize Richard Gessler's little play-toy.

We booked an appearance at a club in Hershey, about a hundred miles from Philadelphia. The locals and Pete's fans would probably be outnumbered by visitors, we'd been warned, antique auto enthusiasts who were in town for a huge car show. Pete thought it'd be fun to do some acoustic versions of old rock 'n' roll car and road tunes by Jan and Dean, Bruce Springsteen, Bob Seger. We borrowed a drum machine to add some punch and even rehearsed a number or two for me to sing solo, so Pete could rest his voice.

"Nervous?" Pete stood in the doorway of the little dressing room backstage, watching me put the final touches on my make-up. "You're not gonna throw up or anything, are you?"

"I'm frosty. Cool as a zucchini." I set the mascara wand down so he wouldn't see my hand shaking. "Any calmer and I'd be catatonic."

"Yeah, right." He fiddled with his shirt cuff a minute. "Connor, listen, you've been doing real good. More than good. I've been able to lean on you, in these gigs and at the studio, and please know I appreciate it. Jenny and I have been talking. You've really come out of your shell." His eyes met mine in the mirror. "We were thinking, maybe you'd like—"

"Five minutes." Glenn, the manager, stuck his head in the door. "Holy crap, Connor, you look like a ghost. Put some color on your face, would ya?" He disappeared again.

"What, you don't like vampires?" Pete called after him. Grinning at me, he added, "Hey, don't worry. You look real good. I mean, you know, you don't look terrible or anything."

"Gee, thanks." I rolled my eyes. "You're very reassuring." Maybe they were right. The heavy black eyeliner and red lipstick did come off as extreme, especially compared with how pale I looked. I brushed on some blusher, adjusted the cuff bracelet of crimson beads and took a deep breath. Show time.

Pete opened the show as he always did with an acoustic version of *Don't Let Me Bother You*, the biggest hit from his bad-boy days. Customers crowded the bar wall to wall, unusual for a first show. They definitely loved it, so we cut back on the quieter songs and played our more lively numbers. *Carnivore, The One and Only, Past Due*. Pete stayed to the front left of the tiny stage, legs spread as though he were balancing on a swaying ship deck, tethered to the guitar mike. I perched on a high stool, fighting the impulse to jump up and improvise a little grapevine jig across the stage. The upbeat music cheered me, matched my mood. Toward the end of the evening, Pete's voice began to give out. He had a cold that wouldn't die and the tenor range of some of the numbers took its toll.

242

During an intermission, he asked me about taking over for a song or two. "Give 'em *I Drove All Night* and give me a break." Pete sucked on a cough drop. "See how it goes and then maybe you could do another one."

Solos were different from duets. I concentrated on the old Cyndi Lauper tune, hard-driving strums on the guitar that brought a recognizing moment of applause from the audience and then a hush as they settled in to listen. As soon as I began the solo vocal, I felt the change. All eyes were on me and suddenly I couldn't look at the audience, couldn't glance out over the sea of faces, the waitresses moving back and forth with drink orders, the couples snuggling in back booths. I closed my eyes, feeling the guitar strings vibrating under my fingers, aware of Pete behind me on drum machine and keyboard. My voice seemed disconnected from me, sexy and urgent, channeling ol' Cyndi as best I could. As I went into the long final carried-out note, I glanced at Pete and saw that he felt it too. That audience was in the palm of my hand; I controlled them and the feeling lifted me about five feet above the stage.

Pete suggested we finish with an old Huey Lewis number, *If This is It*. He harmonized with me on the final stanza. The audience loved it and during the applause afterward, Pete remarked that we should perform that number more often. We clasped hands and swung them in the air like prizefighters after a knock-out, and then I saw Travis.

He stood near the entrance, within a pool of light that glittered off his hair. The same golden hair and the same old reaction from me. My mouth went dry and my stomach plummeted. Pete threw me a glance as I snatched my hand out of his and for a second, I felt dizzy. What was Travis doing there? Pete accepted the audience's demand that we play one last number and hissed at me to wake up. I grabbed my guitar, pulling the strap over my head and jumping on the stool so awkwardly it nearly went over. I forgot Pete had to wait for my opening chords before he could begin singing *Not Now*, and when I did remember, my fingers stumbled and staggered. I kept my eyes lowered, scared to look. Afraid Travis would still be there. Afraid he wouldn't. Pete's shoulders twitched and I realized I was late coming into the chorus. God, I was blowing it.

Somehow we got through the last song and I managed to get offstage without falling. "What the hell happened?" Pete asked, and I shook my head, unable to answer. Travis was nowhere to be seen. I pushed through the throng of people wondering if I'd only dreamed it and then there he stood, and six years collapsed in an instant.

"Hey, Amanda. Good to see you." His voice sounded the same but he seemed different. Older, heavier, more rugged. Something else, too. Little lines at the corners of his eyes, a weariness in his posture. He looked . . . frayed.

"Connor," I told him. "I'm Connor now."

"I know. I saw the flyer." He stuck his hands in his pockets and leaned toward me. "Almost couldn't believe my eyes. Everyone's wondered, for so long, what happened to you. Whether you were okay. What you were doing." He glanced around the bar. "I'd never have dreamt of this."

"I know. Who'da thunk? Lucky break, actually, I'm just filling in for his wife." I couldn't look directly at him, my heart raced, and I felt a ridiculous impulse to rise on my toes and flit away on tiny sideways steps, my arms arching and flexing like the Swan Princess. The crowd began to thin out and I looked around for Pete. He'd expect me to help pack up. I asked Travis if he could stay a while. "We usually go out to eat after a show. I want to talk with you." He nodded and followed me backstage where Pete was unhooking the amps and wrapping them in travel pads. I introduced the men to each other, explaining that Travis was an old friend.

The Waffle House felt like an old friend too; the same layout, the same waitresses in every city. Two people sat at the counter, an old couple sharing french fries, and we three squeezed into a booth back in the corner. Pete took up more than a half seat, so I sat next to Travis. Felt better anyway, only seeing him out of the corner of my eye instead of full-face. I could watch his hands, capable-looking as ever, stirring his coffee, gesturing as he spoke with Pete.

They discovered a shared love of old cars. "That's why I'm here," Travis explained. "I'm restoring a '64 Mustang and came to the car show looking for parts. You wouldn't have heard," he added, turning toward me, "but the hardware store closed down." His eyes darkened and he frowned at his coffee cup. "We really tried—well, never mind. Dad retired. He and Ma moved to Florida. They love it. Sold the house to Sissy and Dave."

"How's Sissy?"

"Bossy as ever and twice as mean." He chuckled. "Don't tell her I said so, you'll have to peel me off the wall."

"And how's . . . how's everyone else?" The waitress brought our food and I welcomed the interruption. It got difficult to breathe. All the questions I wanted to ask, all the things I wanted to know.

"Everyone's fine." Travis waited until Pete had taken a large-mouthed bite of cheeseburger. "Some changes, of course."

"But nothing bad?"

He picked up the salt shaker and rolled it between his fingers. Set it down and picked it up again. "Not bad. Depends on how you look at it."

Pete swallowed and set his burger down. "Am I missing something here? Did you guys rob a bank together or something?"

I could feel a buzzing in my ears. "Nothing so exciting. It's just that I haven't been home in a long time." My stomach felt sealed with hot glue. Nothing would go down. The scent of eggs and cheese made me slightly nauseated.

Pete peered at me and frowned. Turning to Travis, he said, "You're a *friend* of Connor's, right?"

"Absolutely. Only came by to say hello." The two men eyed each other and Pete relaxed slightly. I pushed away my dish and managed a weak smile. Travis nudged me with his elbow. "You all right?"

"Yes." I picked up my tea mug with trembling hands and gulped half of the hot, sweet brew. "I'm not hungry, that's all. Pete, everything's fine. Why don't you go back to the motel?

Trav and I can catch up on gossip and he'll drop me off when we're done." I managed to ask this while keeping my eyes focused on Pete's middle shirt button. He grunted a reluctant acquiescence and we completed the meal in silence.

Once he left, I took his seat so I could face Travis. From the grill off to my left came a sizzling sound and the scent of onions. The cook made some kind of joke to the waitress and she laughed in deep gulps. I wanted to ask so many questions, but couldn't speak. I could only fold my arms tight and try to control my breathing.

Travis accepted a refill on his coffee and took his time adding cream and sweetener. Finally, as I was about to scream, he looked at me and started to talk. "Sissy says you write your mom from time to time. No return address, different postmarks each time—Texas, Kansas, Florida, New Jersey. You leave phone messages on your mom's machine. So obviously you know she still lives in the same house. But you never phone when she's there—or maybe you hang up if she answers, I don't know. And you don't allow Grace any way to reach you."

"I know." Breathe in, breathe out. "Tell me what I don't know."

"Your dad is gone."

"Oh my god, dead?" My hands shot forward, slapping down on the table top with enough impact to make my water glass jump.

"No, no. I'm sorry, I mean gone, as in gone away. Left. Took off." Travis reached out and covered my hands with his. "God, I'm sorry, I didn't mean to scare you." He lost the judgmental look and compassion entered his eyes. "He and what's-her-name, his second wife, they split up. The marriage didn't last long. I think she left him for a younger guy. Anyway, about a year ago, he quit his job and took off."

"Does Mom know where he is?"

"Apparently. But from what Sis says, he's not been back since."

"Jeez. Poor Mom. Everyone seems to disappear from her life in one way or another." I pulled my sweaty hands out from under his. I knew what he thought. Me, too. I had disappeared, too. I was a rotten daughter. I sucked in my stomach and asked, "How is she? How's she holding up? I . . . I think about her a lot. Really. I know you have no reason to believe me, but it's true." My voice started to wobble and I swallowed hard. "Please tell me everything."

Travis sighed and ran a hand over his face. He looked tired, rumpled. He leaned back in his seat, resting one arm along the back of the booth and turning his coffee mug around and around with the other hand. "You know Grace. She's a survivor. Not that it's been easy." He shot me one electric-blue glance. "Things were pretty bad after you left. I think if it hadn't been for Sissy, your mom would have completely fallen apart. Sissy virtually moved in on her, brought the kids over, kept Grace busy. She quit teaching, you know."

"No, I didn't know." Mom loved teaching, how could she quit? "I owe Sissy."

"She didn't do it for you." His words cut to the bone. "She loves Grace like a second mother. More mother to her

248

than our ma is. You know Ma." He leaned forward, folding his arms and resting on his elbows. "Grace is working at a retirement center now. Activities director. She seems to like it."

"Is she . . . seeing anyone? I thought maybe Mason Kennedy."

"Nope. They had some kind of falling out. So far as I know, she doesn't date at all."

I wondered what they'd quarreled about. I had a bad feeling it was me. "So . . . she's okay? I mean, considering. She's all right?"

"Yeah. Which is not to say she wouldn't love to see you. Amanda, why haven't you come home in all these years? For crying out loud, who cares about that other stuff? It was a long time ago."

I didn't have anything to say. Couldn't explain even to myself. For so long, staying hidden was my goal, but I couldn't use that excuse any more. And it went so much deeper than that.

"Can I tell her I've seen you? Will you at least let me do that? You don't know what she'd give to have the assurance that you're really okay, that you're healthy and busy and doing some kind of work you enjoy. And you do enjoy it, don't you? You seemed to have fun up there." He took my hand, chafing it between his own.

A little thrill ran right up my arm. After all this time, he still had the power to slay me. "It's fun. A lot more nerve-wracking than studio work, and harder than most people would believe, but it's fun." I could feel a blush rising and spreading across my cheeks. "What about you? What are you doing now that the store's closed?"

He shrugged, leaning back in his seat again and releasing my hand. "Messing around. Working on cars, doing some renovations at the cottage. Why don't you come home and see for yourself? Your mom would love to have a visit."

I pulled in, shoving my hands into my pockets, huddling deeper into my jacket. "Oh, well, I don't know. I'm awfully busy."

"How long are you going to punish her?" His voice, soft and low, cut right through the noise and clatter of the Waffle House. Why didn't he just pull out a sword and be done with it? "You know she forgave you. Long ago."

"I'm not trying to punish her, or anyone. I simply . . ." I shook my head. There were no words to explain.

"You ever hear from the guy? Gessler? Do you ever see him?"

At the sound of Gessler's name, emotion surged through me like wind through a city street, and anger with it like scraps of paper. I looked up, directly into Travis's eyes. "Is that what this is about? Why didn't you just ask right up front? No. I don't hear from him, I don't see him. He's out of my life. Has been, ever since. You think I'd still. . ." Rage washed over me and I dug in my pocket, threw some money on the table. I was halfway out the door before Travis got to his feet. By the time he caught up with me, I had reached the edge of the parking lot and stood there, looking left and right, trying to figure out what to do.

250

"Amanda, for chrissake. Wait up." Travis grabbed my arm and pulled me to a stop. "I'm sorry. I shouldn't have even suggested—"

"What? That I might still have something going with him? Why not? Why not ask me what you're really wondering? See, this is why I don't want to go back. Everyone judges. Everyone thinks they know all about me." I dashed a hand across my eyes and saw mascara streaks. Great, now I probably looked as repulsive as I felt. Five minutes with someone from home and I was already a wreck. "You think I should go back? Thanks, but no thanks."

A tractor-trailer went by on the highway, blasting cold air at us. I turned away from Travis, stumbling on hard chunks of gravel that seemed to cut through the thin soles of my boots. Travis followed, his steps easily keeping pace with mine. "Of course Mom forgives me. She's a saint. Saint Grace, we all know that. But everyone else, shit. How does anyone forget? And that's what I want to do, forget the whole thing ever happened." Those old bad feelings began to grow inside me. All those feelings I'd pushed down, buried, now rising from the dead. "But how would you know? You've always been blessed. Always did the right thing. Everyone's Golden Boy. You could fall into a septic tank and still come up smelling like roses. You've never—"

Travis took hold of both my arms and shook me. "Stop that," he said, his voice snapping like a flag on a mast. "Stop that shit. I hate it. In the first place, my life has nothing to do with yours. So whether you're right or wrong about me, it doesn't matter. What *does* matter is you and your mom. Talk about unforgiving. You're the one who won't forgive or forget." He let go of me suddenly and we stared at each other, our breath coming hard and steaming in the cold night air. Then his shoulders slumped and his fists relaxed. "Sorry. Looks like I don't have any manners either. Better let me take you to your motel."

We rode in silence. The sound of the motor wasn't enough to drown out my thoughts so I concentrated on the tune that kept running through my head, lines from Pete's final song this evening, *Not Now*. We'd written it together six months ago.

> *I'll laugh at this story some day*
> *Tell it to all my friends*
> *I won't always feel the same way*
> *At some point, this pain will end*
> *But that day, that time is not now*
> *No, that time is not now.*

As we pulled up outside the motel, Travis spoke again. Keeping his eyes directed at the road, he said, "There's one more thing you need to know before you go home, and I hope it won't keep you from going. Your mother has Josh."

"What?"

"Joshua. Your dad's son. When what's-her-name ran off, she left him with your dad and when your dad took off, he left Josh with Grace. She's been raising him ever since."

Chapter Sixteen

I didn't sleep much that night. Just thrashed around in bed, unable to stop thinking about Travis and everything he said. I was angry with him for his question about Richard, angry with myself for being surprised. Why shouldn't he wonder? In his shoes, I'd be wondering too. And what the hell was going on with Mom and Joshua, Dad and Janine? How could Mom raise this kid, this living symbol of Dad's infidelity? Was she some kind of masochistic doormat, torturing herself with good deeds—and at what cost to herself? The questions twisted my guts until I turned on the TV and forced myself to watch old horror films. None of which seemed nearly as horrible as real life.

Pete didn't say much in the morning as we drove back home. We ate fast-food egg muffins and drank coffee from styrofoam cups. Listened to a CD. Now and then, Pete cleared his throat and darted a glance at me, but he waited until we'd hit the outskirts of Philadelphia before he spoke.

"You okay?" When I nodded, he drummed his fingers on the steering wheel and cleared his throat again. "That guy Travis didn't get you upset, did he?"

"No, Pete. I'm okay."

He twiddled his fingers a bit more and shifted in his seat. "If you say so."

I watched the landscape slide by, suburban sprawl low-lighted by strip malls, auto body shops, and subdivisions full of look-alike houses. Traffic streamed along—big rigs, small rigs, SUVs, cars full of commuters with flat, bored faces. Somewhere out there, Travis was on the road too, heading back home to North Carolina with his precious car parts. I wondered what he would tell Mom about seeing me.

"Pete, you were pretty wild in your younger days, right?"

He laughed, a short burst like a dog's yelp. "You could say that."

"I mean, women, drugs, all that, right?"

"Yeah. Back when we were on the charts, anyway." He shook his head and grinned, remembering. "Women. Oh yeah. Women everywhere. Women falling out of the sky. Women inviting us into their homes, their beds. Amazing." Catching sight of my amused smile, he stopped himself and frowned. "Of course, I don't do that anymore. Or the drugs."

"Oh jeez, Pete, I know. I wondered . . . how did you get your head straight? How did you get from there to here?"

He cocked an eyebrow at me as if asking why I'd brought it up. "Didn't have much choice. I was stone broke, babe, down in the gutter. No money, no work, no friends. Burnt out on drugs. I had to straighten up or die. And then Jenny came along." Pete shrugged. "Shoot, it came easy after that."

"Really? Simply by her being there?"

"Okay, maybe not easy. Worthwhile, I guess. Gave me a purpose." A slow smile spread over his face. "She didn't care

254

what an ass I'd been. She loved me for the fascinating, gorgeous guy I am." He laughed again, a rumbling chuckle that filled the van. "There's something seriously wrong with that woman."

We rode the rest of the way in thoughtful silence. Pete dropped me off in front of my apartment. "You feeling better?"

"Yeah."

"You're not gonna be all weepy-eyed and miserable over that guy?"

"No. I told you he's just a friend."

"Right. And I'm Elvis. Viva Las Vegas." He waved and drove off and I wondered suddenly how much of my reluctance to go home had to do with Travis.

I needed to get my head straight, but easier said than done. Travis's comments had stirred up a lot of old pain and, try as I might, it was hard not to knead the bruises a bit. Sleepless nights and frazzled nerves began to take their toll.

For the next couple of months, Pete and I traveled and performed. In ever-widening circles, we played big cities and small ones, college towns and factory towns. Pittsburgh, Wilmington, Trenton, Allentown. Between gigs, I worked at the bookstore preparing for the Christmas onslaught, and collaborated with Pete on three new songs. I kept thinking about going home. Next week or next month, as soon as we were less busy. As soon as my truck heater got fixed. As soon as Jenny had her baby. Then I ran out of excuses because early Christmas morning, Pete phoned.

"Jenny's gone into labor early. We're at the hospital, she's having some problems. Can you come stay with the kids in the waiting room?"

"Sure, but where's your mom?"

"Went back to Jersey yesterday. Dad slipped on some ice and broke his collarbone, would you believe? So come right away, okay?"

I hurried over to Holy Redeemer Hospital and was directed to the maternity ward waiting room. Pete looked white and nervous, pacing the green linoleum with Cody clinging to him and Jemima sitting in a corner holding a picture book. The place was otherwise empty, with ragged copies of *Reader's Digest* and *People* strewn about.

"Go on," I told him. "Go to Jenny. I'll take care of them." He disentangled himself from Cody and left the room, running a nervous hand through his hair. I'd never seen him so shook up. Cody started bawling and I took him in my arms, shushing and murmuring as if I knew what I was doing. His little legs wrapped around my waist like a monkey's, and he plastered himself so hard against me that I began to sweat. I sat down next to Jemima. Her hair hung in fuzzed-up braids and she wore a pajama top with her jeans. They must really have rushed out of the house.

"So," I said uneasily. I wasn't good with kids, never had been. Just wasn't natural with them. "Did Santa come? Did he bring you lots of stuff?"

She nodded up at me, sniffling. "I got a paint easel. We didn't get to open everything. Momma wet her pants." Jemima

256

cuddled up to me, her eyes big and scared-looking. "She had *blood* on her pajamas," she whispered.

"Oh, now, don't worry." I tried prying Cody's arms loose. He just clung tighter, his face buried in my neck and smearing something—either snot or drool, no telling which—into the hair at my nape. "That's nothing, it's from the baby coming. Your mom will be okay." Jemima didn't look like she bought it, and I couldn't blame her. Sounded pretty lame, even to me. "Are you guys hungry?"

They didn't answer, just pressed their hot little bodies even more closely up to my own. I didn't know what else to do so I rocked, patting Cody's back, and put an arm around Jemima. "You guys want to sing? What can we sing?"

Jemima began half-heartedly humming *Jingle Bells*, so I joined her and went through every kids' Christmas song I could think of. *Rudolph, Jingle Bell Rock, Up on the Rooftop.* The clock hands moved like they had lead weights on them, and no updates from Pete. I segued into other kid songs, stuff I barely remembered from my own childhood. Gradually, both Jemima and Cody relaxed, letting go of their death-grips on me and giggling. I was singing *Grandma's Feather Bed*, with much emphasis and exaggeration, when Pete finally showed up. He stood staring at us from the doorway for a minute and wore such a strange expression on his face that I almost reached out to cover the children's eyes. Was Jenny all right?

Then he broke into a big grin and held out his arms. The kids flew to him and he gathered them both up, giving them big smoochy kisses. "She's fine," he said. "Momma's fine, and you have a new baby sister. She's a teeny-weeny—five pounds, five ounces—but not bad for a preemie." He tickled Cody with his beard and they all laughed.

I couldn't believe the relief I felt. "God, you scared me for a minute. You looked so strange, like you were in shock." I stood up, weak-kneed from the tension of the past hours.

"I *was* in shock," he laughed, pulling me into a four-way hug with the children. "You have no idea what a sight you were, clowning for the children. I thought I had the wrong room."

"Oh, hush." I grinned, ducking loose. "Drastic times call for drastic measures. Jenny's really okay?"

"Yeah, she is." A big sincere smile lit him up from head to toe. "She's a trouper. No drugs, no stitches. I swear, the woman is amazing." He laid a huge smacker on top of my noggin. "Okay, who wants to see a baby?"

Jenny looked pretty chipper for having just given birth. Her skin glowed and her hair made a fiery nimbus around her head. The baby lay in the crook of her arm, a little pink cap pulled down low over a mottled red face. "Easy now," Jenny warned as Jemima crept up close to the bed and Cody leaned down from his father's arms. "She's had a hard day and she needs her rest."

The children were suitably awed, looking at the baby with big eyes and open mouths until Cody suddenly squirmed down with a broken-voiced *Momma* and buried his face in Jenny's neck. Jemima crawled on the bed too, and Pete pulled a chair as close as he could, taking the baby so Jenny could hug the kids.

My eyes blurred, I didn't know why. Pete was so proud, so tender to Jenny. Kissing her hair, murmuring in her ear. The children were encouraged to kiss their new sister and the whole family cuddled together in one big ball of joy.

"Isn't she beautiful?" Pete asked me. "We're naming her Natalie. You know, *Buon Natale*, Merry Christmas."

I nodded, my eyes filling ridiculously with tears. I couldn't speak. Jenny smiled blissfully, her children curled up by her side. "Thanks, Connor," she said. "I hope we didn't screw up your Christmas."

"Are you kidding?" My voice wobbled and I had to clear my throat. "This made my day." I leaned down to kiss the baby too. Her rosebud mouth seemed almost too big for her face, crumpled in on itself and her cheek was so soft and sweet. I wanted to hold her, to let her little fingers grip mine and feel her warm weight in my arms.

Instead, I wrapped my jacket around myself and backed off as Pete pried the older kids off the bed and lifted them in his arms. "And now," he said, "you've got some time off. I'm taking my children home so they can open their gifts, and I'm going to feed them happy-face pancakes and orange juice and bacon, and *then*," he added, backing out the door, "I'll bring them over in the afternoon and let them make friends with their sister." He blew a kiss at Jenny and nodded at me. "Merry Christmas, Connor. Thank you. I hope the Big Guy gives you what you truly want. See you in a couple of days."

I drove home through a light snowfall, emotions roiling in my chest. The streets weren't busy—most businesses were closed, although the church parking lots were full. The world seemed quiet, just those big swirling flakes of snow moving in slow motion, spinning against a pale gray sky. I had no special plans for Christmas. I thought I'd sleep in late, read, maybe noodle around on my guitar. Instead, there I was, wide-awake at eleven a.m., with lots of pent-up energy and nothing to do.

Back in my apartment, I threw myself on the bed and pondered. Pete didn't need me for a while. My boss at the bookstore owed me unused vacation days. Maybe it was time.

At this thought, I expected resistance to kick in, the way it always had before. Pure reluctance, an unwillingness to face Mom. I didn't worry she'd reject me; quite the opposite. There'd be no reproaches, nothing but pure forgiveness all the way. Unconditional love, something I so did not deserve. I'd always had love from Mom and I remembered how Sissy would snap at me for taking it for granted. "Do you have any idea what I'd give for that?" she'd demand, usually adding a pinch on my arm. "Your mother's practically perfect. Amazing Grace. Any time you want to trade her for my mom, just say the word."

A million times, over the past six years, I'd thought about going home, or at least phoning Mom, having a conversation. Each time, I got halfway between the thought and the action, and I'd come to a dead stop. Guilt kept me mired in place, my own personal La Brea tar pit. I couldn't move forward, couldn't take a step without sliding deeper into all the remorse and shame that only piled higher as time went by.

But this morning, I couldn't remember all the reasons for not going home. My fears, my worries all seemed insignificant, overrated. Lying there on my bed, my face mashed into the pillow, all I could think about was Jenny looking at her kids, and Cody's one little cry. *Momma.*

Yeah. Maybe it was time to go home.

I threw clothes into my duffel bag, grabbed my guitar and hit the road. In no time, I was barreling down the interstate, silently thanking Dwight D. Eisenhower and the U.S. highway system. The snow had moved northeast, up the coast, and traffic was light.

All the way south, I kept imagining what would happen. Mom's face would light up with a huge smile, her arms would wrap around me, we'd be laughing and crying at the same time. Damned if I didn't nearly start bawling right there on the highway, thinking about it. We'd sweep into that kitchen and Mom'd plunk me down at the table, scurry around to fix something to eat and I'd be able to look around, see all the familiar family mementos, catch up on what she'd been doing. I'd fill her in on my exodus—the expurgated edition, of course. No mention of the scary times or downright terrifying moments of living on the fringe of society, sleeping in my truck at highway rest areas or two-bit campgrounds. I'd make it sound like an adventure; after all, I had seen a good bit of the U.S. I could surprise her with the mention of college classes I'd taken, oddball jobs I'd had. And she could catch me up on what everyone there had been doing. Sissy and Dave, Mr. and Mrs. Pennell, Dad. I'd see for myself that everything was okay, she was still strong and capable and whole, that I hadn't destroyed her by running away.

261

However, once I crossed the state line and entered North Carolina, my stomach clenched like a fist. I was really here, I was doing this thing. Twelve miles after getting off the interstate, there it was. Painter's Creek.

Night had fallen. Main Street was deserted, holiday street-lamp decorations swaying in the wind. Some of the storefronts looked different and it gave me a real pang to see the Pennells' old hardware store sign missing. Almost midnight. What was I thinking? I couldn't drop in on Mom now. She'd probably be asleep. I turned onto Azalea Drive and crept slowly along the road. Cars were parked along either curb and in every driveway. I'd forgotten how narrow the street was. Mom's house looked the same. Tiny white Christmas lights strung in the trees and along the eaves, a blue and silver wreath on the front door. I didn't recognize the car in the driveway but it was a Buick, what Mom always drove. A Christmas tree shone in the front window, but other windows were dark and the porch lights were off.

I couldn't breathe. I allowed the truck to roll right past Mom's house and down the street, past Sissy's place, three doors away. The lights were on in every downstairs room. Sissy had company, probably her whole family. I kept going. To the end of Azalea Drive, left at the corner, back to Main Street. I could be back on the interstate in less than fifteen minutes, at home in Philly by noon, done with the whole emotional whim. Then I thought, don't be a horse's ass.

There was a new motel on the edge of town, near the textile plant. The clerk seemed irritable to be working Christmas night, but at least he wasn't anyone I recognized. I got a room, undressed, and climbed into bed. An old Paul Simon song popped into my head—something about 'slip-sliding away'. The nearer my destination, the more I thought about slip-sliding away.

Morning brought a whitish-gray sky and hints of rain. I dressed and showered, did my make-up and hair, and stopped to take a critical look. This was me. Now. Short spiky hair, black eye-liner, crimson lips. Jeans and black t-shirt, black suede jacket. Not her little girl any more. How would I look to Mom? How would she look to me?

I hurried right past that thought, shoved my stuff into the duffel bag and got back in the truck. Coming down Mom's street, nervousness struck again as though I'd been zapped by a wayward amplifier wire. I pulled into Sissy's drive instead. Only one car sat in the carport; a mini-van, Sissy's mom-mobile. With some difficulty, I unwound my fingers from the steering wheel and got out. The colonial style house had new siding and the big wrap-around porch had been partially screened in since I'd left. I rang the bell, noticing the bright cushions on the porch swing and the handmade fabric wreath hanging from the front door. Sissy and Dave had come up in the world.

The front door opened and I looked down to see a little girl with long blond hair. From behind her a voice wafted out. "Teri? Who's at the door?"

"A lady," Teri called back. Then I heard footsteps on hardwood flooring and Sissy swung the door open wider, staring at me with a wooden spoon in her hand.

"Hi," I said, shifting my purse on my shoulder. "It's me. Amanda."

"Amanda?" Sissy froze a minute and something flickered in the back of her eyes, a moment of hesitation. Then she pushed the screen door open. "Come in! Lord, I never expected—" She hugged me, one-armed, laughing with embarrassment over the batter-dripping spoon. "I can't believe it!"

I hugged her back, awkwardly, our arms at angles to each other, banging elbows. She stepped back to get a good look at me. "You booger!" she cried, smacking my shoulder and then hugging me again. "Come in the kitchen, let me put this spoon down."

She'd been in the middle of making waffles. A burnt smell came from the waffle iron and Sissy jerked the contents out into the sink and unplugged it. "You could have called or something," she said, smoothing back her hair. "Look at me, I'm a mess." Wrapping her pink velour robe more tightly about herself, she added, "You're here, I can't believe it."

A little boy sat at the table, orange juice glass forgotten in his hand. He wore Scooby-Doo pajamas and Sissy introduced him as Gideon, the baby she'd been carrying when I left. Teri, still watching us with big eyes, wore a nightshirt. "I guess it's kinda early," I said, easing down onto the bench seat in the breakfast nook. "Sorry."

"Don't be ridiculous. Does your mom know you're here?" Sissy poured us each a cup of coffee and sat down to face me. "No? Oh man, you *are* a booger. Soon as we have breakfast, you and I will have to go over."

264

"How is she? Travis said—"

"Travis? You've talked with him? Why, that bum. Teri, you and Gideon go play. Yes, I know you haven't eaten. Take a muffin with you. Go on. I'll make waffles another time." She shooed the kids out and sat down again, smoothing her hair back and folding the edges of her robe over her legs. "He never said one word. Ooh, I'll get him. Your mom is fine. Now where the hell have you been all this time?

Sissy looked great. Even without makeup. Her hair was glossy, her skin a clear pink-and-white. She'd lost the extra weight that had dragged her down. Bright and cheerful, the kitchen had been modernized since her parents had lived there. It felt warm and inviting, making me think of Mom's house. "You're doing good, I can tell. How's Dave?"

"He's fine. Had to work today, do you believe that? After the store closed—did Trav tell you about that?—Dave got a job with Tru-Bilt Homes. Production supervisor. And I work part-time at the school as a teacher's aide. But who cares? We're here; it's boring to anyone but us. I want to know about you. How the heck did you and Travis run into each other?"

I explained the meeting in Hershey and told her about Pete and Jenny. Sissy snorted when I mentioned car parts, and I asked, "Isn't that what he's doing now? Restoring cars? I got the impression he had some kind of restoration thing going."

"Yeah. He's got something going all right. A distraction, that's what it is." She got up from the table and opened the refrigerator. "Want some scrambled eggs?"

"What do you mean, a distraction?"

"He's getting over a girl." She cracked eggs into a bowl and began whisking them. "Vanessa. They were going to get married and then she changed her mind and Travis has totally lost it since then. You want some cheese in these?" I shook my head no and she put a frying pan on the stove, sprayed it with non-stick cooking spray, and added a dollop of margarine. "They lived in Charlotte. He did PR for the Carolina Panthers, and next thing you know, she wants to move to Oklahoma City and take up real estate. He goes out there with her, changes jobs and everything. And then she decides she doesn't want to get married after all, but go sell real estate in L.A. So what does he do? Good old Travis, he drives her and her ten-year-old son and all their stuff to California, gets them settled in and bikes back, *bikes* back, with his bad knee and all, over the Rockies like some crazy monk doing penance. He's accomplished zip since then." She finished the eggs, buttered some toast, and set the plates on the table with a flourish. "Want juice?"

"Juice would be good," I whispered, my vocal chords failing me. I swallowed a little coffee and cleared my throat. "When was this?"

"About a year ago. And he's been holed up at that cabin ever since, fiddling around with this and that, no real job. I mean, who'd have thought Travis would take it so hard? He's always bounced back from everything—his knee, losing the scholarship, the store closing. I never liked her anyway. Her kid was great, though. Dustin. So why aren't you eating your eggs? Finish them up and I'll get dressed and we'll go see your

266

Mom." Her eyes ran over me and she said, "Boy, you sure look different. I don't know if I'd have recognized you."

"That's kind of the idea." I explained my name change and the fact that I still remained incognito. "The people where I live now don't know who I am. It's easier, not having to deal with the curiosity."

Sissy nodded, her face blank, unreadable. "Grace will be thrilled to see you."

"I hope."

"Oh, please. You know she will." Sitting down, she leaned her chin on her hand and looked out the window. Our eggs sat on the plates between us, growing cold as I waited for her to speak. We had too many shared years for me not to know she was planning her words. Finally, she crossed her arms and looked at me again. "You know, after you left, there were a lot of people with plenty to say. They couldn't believe you'd do such a thing, get involved with something like that, something so *sordid.*" Her eyes regarded me, flat, impersonal. "Even me. When I really thought about it, my skin crawled."

My ears popped. Literally popped, or it felt that way, hearing these words from Sissy. My fingers felt icy and I wrapped them around the coffee cup for warmth.

"But I could get over that part," she continued. "So could most people, I think. They were ready to forgive, to write it off as spoiled innocence, you know? Blame it all on Gessler. But you'd better be prepared. A lot of people will have a hard time forgiving you for what you've done to your mother, staying away so long." She took a sip of coffee, looking meditatively at me over the rim of the cup, and then carefully settled the cup on its saucer. "Grace has had a hard time. You'll never know how hard. Maybe you shouldn't go home. It'll stir things up all over again. Why do that to her?"

For a second time, my heart stopped. I could feel the chill sweep down my arms and I folded them tightly against my waist. Her eyes met mine and we watched each other for a moment and I'd swear, not a sound existed in the whole world.

Then Sissy broke the spell by standing up and tightening her robe sash. "I'm not saying this to be mean, Amanda. I'm truly not. But I think you should leave. Now, before everyone is up and about. You say it took you six years to make the decision to come home. Well, you know, maybe six years was just too damned long."

Chapter Seventeen

I stared up at her, dumfounded. This sure didn't fit in with my imagined scenario. "You mean come all this way and then just turn around and go back?" She nodded. "Jeez, Sissy." I couldn't think. If this was her reaction, my best friend, what would I get from others?

The warmth that flooded my face at her words ebbed, leaving me chilled and shaken. Of course, no one else's opinion mattered, just Mom's, but would she feel the same way too? I had waited until the timing felt right for me, but maybe it was wrong for her. I swallowed, my mouth dry, but I couldn't reach out and pick up the coffee cup, Sissy's china, with little blue and yellow flowers.

Sissy's china? *Mom's* china. The same pattern. Had Mom given it to her or had she just copied? I looked around the kitchen, noting the bright copper-bottom pans hung on the wall, the print curtains, the hand-painted cabinet knobs. Children's artwork decorated the fridge, a row of antique silver sugar-and-cream sets stood on a shelf. I suddenly understood. "You're jealous."

"I am not."

"You are. You're afraid if I come back, Mom won't need you anymore. Oh hell, Sis, I'm not here to take your place. Couldn't if I wanted to."

"That's right." Sissy grabbed the plate of eggs from in front of me and whisked it off to the sink. She stood with her back to me, smacking the faucet lever and washing my breakfast down the disposal. "I'm a better daughter to her than you are. I stood by, took care of her while you were running all over the country. Dave and the kids love her like she's kin. If I'm protective, it's with good reason." Self-righteousness formed a ridge down her back and I thought of Sissy's mother in one of her trademark tirades. "Why come home now and stir everything up, especially when she's worried already about—"

She paused, holding the plate for a second as though debating whether to throw it, then setting it down gently on the counter. In a different tone of voice, she said, "Besides, what would be the point? You're going right back to Philadelphia anyway, aren't you? Got a whole new life there, right? Why not go for it, get your big fat music career going and forget about everyone here?"

Sissy began filling the sink with soapy water. She peered over her shoulder at me, her face radiating distrust and resentment, and I choked back my excuses. "Tell me first what Mom's so worried about," I said.

"Nothing. Well, nothing important to you." Sissy shrugged and started clearing the table. Neither of us had touched the food. "She's trying to get legal custody of Josh."

"Custody? Good grief. I gathered from Travis that the boy lived with Mom, and I thought that was crazy enough, but *legal custody?*"

"See? This is what I mean. You don't know anything about the dynamics around here. Personally, I think it's a good idea but how would I know, I've only been on the scene every day. I don't have the advantage of a long-distance view like you have. Shoot, you're just like your dad. Zip in, throw everything into a major snarl of confusion, and then zip out again. Why don't you spare us?" Sissy dried her hands on a towel and threw it on the counter.

Just like my dad? I felt like she'd stabbed me with the metal spatula. We glared at each other, and I had opened my mouth to speak when the children burst in on us, arguing over the TV remote control. Sissy grabbed the control and put it on a high shelf. "There. Problem solved. Now y'all go back to the family room before I find you some chores." With a little more bickering and a half-hearted shove, the kids left the room and Sissy turned to me, shrugging. "This is my life."

I got up from my seat and zipped my jacket. Slinging my purse strap over my shoulder, I nodded and took a last sip of coffee. "You're busy. I'll be going."

"Will you?" She came to stand by the doorway, one hand resting on the counter top. "You probably think I'm being a bitch but, really, I'm only saying what's best for your mom."

"Yeah. Whatever." What could I say? My best friend didn't want me around. I went out and sat in my truck for a few minutes, looking at the familiar street, damp under gray sky. Sodden evergreens lowered their branches to the ground, red Christmas bows drooped dispiritedly on lamp posts. A day-after-Christmas letdown seemed to permeate the whole neighborhood. Everything smelled like cold, wet cement.

271

After a minute, I started the engine. Was Sissy right? I knew what it was like to struggle for a sense of peace and I sure didn't want to make Mom upset. Damn. Should I give it a shot? See if either of us had learned anything during our time apart? I *wasn't* like Dad, running from responsibility. Sissy was wrong. And no matter how Sis dressed or decorated her kitchen, she wasn't Mom and she didn't think the same way.

My nerves ratcheted up tighter and tighter and I drummed my fingers on the steering wheel. The crimson polish caught my eye and I thought, well, some things have changed. My fingernails were no longer ragged, bitten to the quick and slightly grubby to boot. I'd changed. Maybe Mom had too. In any case, I'd come this far, it would be foolish to go backwards now. It had taken me six years to build up enough courage to face the consequences of what I'd done. Who knew if I could ever do it again?

A Chevy Blazer was parked at the curb. Maybe it was Dad's? I pulled into the driveway behind Mom's Buick and got out of the truck. My knees didn't want to work. They kept jerking like when I had 'crazy-legs' while dancing, when my muscles would get so over-excited they'd refuse to do my bidding.

I took a deep breath, consciously straightening my shoulders and stretching my spine. It was now or never. I could hear voices inside the house, raised voices, the sound of the doorbell as I pushed it, and then footsteps on the hardwood floor. The front door flew open and there she was. Mom.

We stared at each other for a moment through the glass of the storm door. Her green eyes blazed out against paper-white skin and for a second, it seemed she didn't recognize me. Then, with a gasp, she pushed open the storm door, grabbed my sleeve, and pulled me inside. "Amanda! Thank God you're here!"

She practically shoved me into the living room and I stumbled, my shoulder bag making an immediate nosedive to the floor. Despite being aware there were other people in the room, I couldn't help noticing changes. The walls were jade green with touches of pale yellow and melon, the wall-to-wall carpeting had been removed, all the furniture was different. A Christmas tree stood in front of the bay window, traditionally trimmed in stark contrast to the radically changed décor.

"My daughter's here now and she's not going to let you take him!" Mom stood shoulder-to-shoulder with me, facing off the two individuals who seemed to take up all the space in that small room. With difficulty, I recognized Janine, Dad's ex. She had gained weight, making her seem all puffy, as though someone had filled her with hot air and she was plenty cross about it. She advanced on us, fists clenched, and I threw a protective arm in front of Mom.

"He's *my* son and I want him back! Steve had no right to leave him with you!" Janine's eyes bulged and I wondered where her complacent little Mona Lisa smile had gone. Behind her, a rather beefy man stood with his back to the fireplace. He wore a navy sports coat over a golf shirt and his expression suggested he'd rather be sitting on a stool in front of a cold beer.

"Janine, maybe we should—"

"Shut up, Hank," she snarled, never taking her eyes off Mom. "I can get Steve for desertion. Now pack Josh's stuff and get him dressed or I'll—"

"No!" Mom's hair kept falling in her eyes. "The terms of the custody papers make Steve in charge and if he's seen fit to name me as temporary guardian—"

"Seen fit?" Janine's face got even redder. "*Seen fit?* What makes you think you're so hot as a mother? Given how your own daughter turned out?" Her gaze flickered over at me with contempt. "Oh yeah, some great mother *you* are."

"*I am the god of hell fire!*" I shouted. Everyone's attention turned to me, their faces frozen in astonishment.

"What?" Janine's stupid face sagged and I felt a surge of adrenaline.

"*Eight hundred die in New Delhi mudslide, will you follow them?*" I went blank-faced, half-circling Janine so she backed away. "*Peter, Peter, Pumpkin eater. Had a wife and couldn't keep her,*" I insisted, my voice rising slightly. "Gug-gug-gug-gahh!" I spasmed like a cat with a hairball, and Hank tripped on a footstool, grabbing Janine so she fell backwards, hitting the arm of the sofa with half her butt and nearly landing on the floor. "*Where'd you put the silverware, Florence?*"

I twitched my shoulder up toward my ear a couple of times, blinking rapidly, and loomed over Janine so that she scuttled out from under me like a sand crab. Hank pulled her into the hallway and I followed. "*Stiletto! She's got her sweet stiletto,*" I continued, slamming my feet down on the wood

274

floor and pursuing them as far as the front porch. I finished with a grand jeté. *"Play a little of that old melody!"*

Janine was actually panting, grabbing for her purse and shouting one last epithet at Mom before Hank hauled her down the steps and out to the Blazer. "You don't scare me! I'll be back with my lawyer, and then we'll see."

"Rattlesnakes!" I yelled, hanging and swinging from the porch awning like a monkey in a tree as they drove off. *"Know ye them by the sound they make!"* I turned, leaning against the doorframe, and laughed to myself until I caught sight of Mom's face, her confusion and doubt. "It's okay, I'm not crazy. Are you all right?"

She started to grin, then tears burst their dam and I took her arm, propelling her back into the living room to sit on the couch. "Oh my god, Amanda. They were so—I can't believe you're here!" I pulled her into my arms and rocked back and forth, a wordless hug. "I thought they were going to—"

"It's okay, everything's okay." I snagged my purse from where it'd landed under the coffee table and fished out a tissue. "Where's Josh? Did he hear all this?"

That helped pull her together, gave her a reason to mop her face and push back her hair. "I don't know if he heard it. He was asleep . . ." She nodded her head back toward my old bedroom. I patted her knee and got up to check.

From the hallway, I could see into Mom's room and the bathroom. The total change in appearance hadn't stopped with the living room and I felt disoriented, as though I'd stumbled into a stranger's house. None of our old furniture was there. Nothing familiar. Josh's door had drawings taped to it, things he'd apparently done at school or wanted to save. A magazine photo of a motorcycle, crayon pictures of race cars and speed boats, a Jeff Gordon NASCAR poster.

I eased the door open, noticing first the red-white-and-blue color scheme and the child-sized furnishings, the morning light squeezing in around the edges of white mini-blinds. Josh was in bed, the blankets pulled tight over his shoulders, his back to the door. He lay quite still; too still for me to believe he didn't know I was there. Probably he'd heard everything. Poor kid. I remembered all too well how the sound of arguing could carry in that house. A pair of jeans lay crumpled on the floor with white athletic socks snaking out from the cuffs, and dirty sneakers nearby. He was a long, skinny kid, looked like. Let him maintain his pretense a moment longer, I decided, until Mom was herself again and could speak with him. After all, he didn't know me, and the good guys were difficult to distinguish from the bad guys in this little domestic drama.

I went back into the living room. Mom stood by the couch, her arms folded tightly against her waist. "I didn't even welcome you," she said, opening her arms to me and getting weepy again. "Oh honey, I'm so glad you're home! Are you okay? I always knew you'd come home some day!"

Hugging her, I realized she had grown smaller. Or was I bigger? At any rate, we stood eye-to-eye, two women now and almost the same size. I breathed in her scent—different, not White Linen perfume any more—yet still as sweet and wholesome. Before I could open my mouth to answer her questions, the doorbell rang. Mom jumped and we both glanced at each other before she pushed her hair back and went to answer the door.

"Sissy! Come in, you'll never believe who's here!" Mom hauled her in by one arm. Teri and Gideon pushed their way past, obviously feeling right at home. Mom turned, beaming, to look at me, her arm draped over Sissy's shoulders.

"Hey," I said. "So glad to see you." I gave her a big bear hug while she tried to smile and respond appropriately. Poor Sissy was no actress. Mom turned on the TV to some children's show, told the kids to play quietly until Josh woke up, and asked me if I'd had any breakfast. "Almost," I grinned. Sissy shot me a nervous glance and I took pity on her. "Mostly I'd love some coffee."

We sat in Mom's kitchen, her reborn kitchen with modernized cabinets, new wallpaper, framed photographs of flowers and birds. Mom gave me a cup of decaf with skim milk and artificial sweetener. I looked down at the pathetic thing and muttered *Jeez, what's the point,* but she was busy explaining to Sissy what had happened with Janine.

"And Amanda was wonderful, she chased them off." Mom turned to me, laughing. "What in the world were you doing, shouting that nonsense?"

I shrugged. "Street smarts. Amazing how handy they come in." Pushing aside the ersatz coffee, I asked, "Why did you let her in, in the first place? And where's Dad?"

Mom sluiced back her hair, revealing feathery tufts of gray at the temples. "She said she had a gift for Josh. I should have known better, but I always keep hoping she'll change. Your dad's in Columbia, South Carolina. He's an investment advisor for Glenco. We keep in touch and he sends money for Josh's expenses, but—"

"But he's still a total jerk-face." Sissy's pronouncement drew a shaking of the head from Mom, but she continued. "Grace, you never learn. Janine's never going to change except for the worse. And don't keep making excuses for Steve. He dumped all his responsibilities on you and ran off to have his little midlife crisis. Asshole."

Mom frowned and looked away, but I noticed she didn't make any denials. I reached over and clasped her hand. "What do you want to do now?"

A small noise drew our attention to the dining room doorway. There, caught in a shaft of light from the bay window, stood Joshua. I'd have known it was him at first sight even if I hadn't been aware he was staying with Mom. He looked just like Mark. Standing in the doorway, his hair sticking up, his gaze skittering over to mine, I almost thought he was Mark's ghost. A little prickle went up the back of my neck. He was tall for his age and slim, not such a solid chunk of a kid as Mark had been, but the unmistakable shape of his head and the angle of his brows were so familiar.

Mom squeezed my hand and went over to him. Standing behind him, her hands on his shoulders, she said softly, "Amanda, this is your brother. Josh." Then, squatting to get level with him, she explained, "You remember the pictures in my room of the girl in dance shoes? Here she is. Amanda."

He nodded. His face was solemn, a little sleepy and, even in wrinkled pajamas, he wore a curiously dignified air. He was a person. Not an anonymous kid, or a symbol, or some faceless being I'd tried not to think about over the years, but a real person with long sensitive fingers and intelligent eyes. As he turned to face Mom, I could see his diffidence and awareness that he'd been discussed. She whispered something to him and he nodded again, his body relaxing. Their relationship was something real. Not Mom in her 'good works' mode, but caring deeply about him, despite who he was. Or maybe even because of it.

Whatever lingering jealousy I might have felt melted away. He owned a place in my parents' lives and hearts, but it was neither easy nor secure and my strongest feeling was pity.

"Hi Josh." I sat on the edge of the chair, my hands clasped in my lap. Under Sissy's observant eye, I didn't want to overdo things or scare him off. "We met once before. You were just a baby. It was a long time ago." There was that little notch in his ear, just like Mark's. "Did you have a nice Christmas?"

He nodded again, a man of few words. Mom patted his shoulder. "Why don't you run and get dressed, okay? I'll fix you some cereal." When he was gone, she sighed and gave me a shaky smile. "Not much of a welcome home, I'm afraid. Can you stay? There's so much I want to ask you."

"You better call Steve first," Sissy said, standing up and looping her purse strap over her arm. "Janine's no quitter. She'll be back, with bigger guns next time. I think you and Josh better come over to my place, where you'll be protected. Amanda, if you don't want to get your name in the paper again, maybe you'd better clear out."

"Oh no," Mom wailed. "She's only just got here."

"Sissy's right." I stood too, forcing my voice to stay low. "Janine probably will be back. But I don't think you should run away. It doesn't solve anything, trust me." Sissy raised an eyebrow, which I ignored. "How about if I take Josh somewhere away from this and leave you and Sis to deal with Janine. Call Dad, but also call whichever lawyer drew up the custody papers. Mason Kennedy?" Mom nodded. "Well, call him and make sure of your rights."

I didn't like it. Mom looked shrunken and unsure, all the vitality sapped out of her. Sissy took Mom's hands. "Grace, come on. We can see this through together. I won't leave you. Janine will find a whole mess of trouble if she shows up again. I'll send Teri over to her girlfriend's house and Amanda can take the boys to Travis's for a couple of hours, until we figure out what we're doing. Okay?" Mom nodded and brushed her hand over her eyes.

"Sounds like a plan," I said, patting Mom's arm. Sissy and I looked like a pair of mismatched bookends, eyeing each other over Mom's head. "And don't worry, I'm not taking off anywhere. We'll catch up with each other tonight."

Chapter Eighteen

Josh didn't say much of anything on the way to Travis's place. Neither did I. Fortunately for us, Gideon kept up a running chatter, telling us about his Christmas presents—a new bike, a basketball, X-box games. He'd brought with him a handful of tiny metal cars which he kept running along the arm rest or up and down his blue-jeaned legs. Between us, Josh sat silently, his hands shoved in the pockets of an over-large yellow parka.

I'd had to dig out the spare seatbelts from behind the seat; I wasn't used to having passengers in my truck. In fact, I was beginning to realize I wasn't used to dealing with other people at all, their needs or their problems. Mine had consumed me for so long, it seemed strange to be involved with someone else's troubles.

We almost drove right past Travis's house. If it hadn't been for Gideon shouting and pointing, I'd have missed it completely. Things had changed since my last visit. The cheap aluminum siding had been replaced by brick and cedar shingles. A new addition filled out one side of the cottage, and a new garage stood on the other. Gideon scrambled out of the truck almost before we stopped. Josh followed more slowly, perking up a little when he saw Travis rounding the corner of the garage, a load of firewood balanced on his shoulder,

He looked good. Healthier than when I'd seen him in October, more vibrant. His hair was longer than usual, auburn along the sideburns, sun-bleached to palest blonde on top. Dressed in jeans and boots, flannel shirt and down vest, he looked like something out of a Land's End catalog or maybe the Brawny paper towel guy. His grin widened as he tipped the logs down and sat on his heels to admire the little metal cars and tousle the boys' hair. I got out of the truck and wrapped my leather jacket tightly around myself. Off the lake, the breeze came cold and sharp, ruffling my hair and stealing my breath.

Travis stood slowly and smiled at me, his easy, lazy smile. "Well, hey."

"Hey, Trav." I swallowed hard, feeling like I'd forgotten how. "You doing okay?"

He stooped to pick up the logs and nodded toward the garage. "Come in out of the wind." The boys ran ahead of him to open the door and we stepped into a space of light and warmth. This was a garage? I'd had apartments far less cozy. In one corner, a wood stove radiated heat. In another, an old wooden desk sat under a layer of papers, tools and bits of automobilia. Gideon whispered to Travis and got permission to climb into a low-riding sleek sports car in the first bay. I didn't know anything about cars but it looked like something from the sixties, a little convertible that brought to mind Audrey Hepburn in sunglasses. Gideon got behind the wheel, hunching himself into racing position and making engine noises.

Travis poked the fire a bit and turned to me, dusting off his hands on a rag. "I'm glad you're home. Not quite what you expected, I bet." We glanced at Josh, sitting stiffly next to Gideon, a frown on his face.

"Not exactly."

"I'm glad you're here anyway. Grace'll feel better, having you by her side."

"How bad do you think it's going to be?"

He picked up a wrench and moved over to the second bay. A fifties-era Chevy stood up on blocks, the hood raised and a clamp-on lamp shining down on the engine. Standing where he could keep an eye on the boys, Travis removed a cap to something and I edged a little closer. His sleeves were rolled up and fine gold hairs glinted on his forearms, a light haze over lines and ridges of muscles and tendons. His hands moved with precision and I balled my own fists in my pockets. "Depends on your dad, I think, whether he'll come home and straighten out the mess. Janine can be a real—well, not very nice."

"So why is she coming after Josh then?" I kept my voice low, moving closer to Travis. "Doesn't sound like she really cares about the kid."

Travis replaced the cap and wiped his hands. "Why does anyone do what they do? Beats me." He lowered the hood, wiping his hands one more time. "Hey guys, want to go out on the pier? You can feed the fish. I've got some bread in that bag there."

"This time of year?" I asked. "Will there be any fish?"

"Oh, yeah. The water's pretty warm here from the steam plant and I feed them regularly so they know to come around."

Josh's face lit up. He and Gideon grabbed the bag of stale bread and ran outside, down the path that went around the back of the cottage to the pier. Man, I remembered that path and the morning the reporters showed up. It was the same time of year, too, and the trees were bare, dead leaves thick on the ground. Pine needles littered the path, sticking to my boots as Travis and I followed the boys. The sun came out, teasing us with an illusion of warmth even though a cold wind still blew in off the lake.

Travis got the boys squared away, each with a half dozen slices of bread to throw to the fish. Only a crappie or two to start. Gideon sat on the edge of the pier, kicking his feet and throwing pellets of bread as far as he could. Josh stood a few feet away, solemn in his yellow parka, meticulously tearing the bread into neat squares and dropping them one by one into the dark water below.

"So how long you can stay?" Travis hunched his shoulders against the wind. A stubble of whiskers edged his chin.

"Pete and I have a gig New Year's Eve, and then it's kind of dead for a while. That's okay, Pete planned to take some time off when Jenny had her baby anyway. She just beat the clock, is all. So I probably better head back the 30th." Travis nodded, looking out across the lake. "I'll stay in touch this time." I wanted him to believe me, that this was more than just good intentions. In a moment of bravado, I added,

"Maybe I'll even coerce Mom into visiting me in Pennsylvania."

"Travis, look!" Josh pointed at something in the water. A fish swam near the corner post of the pier, with a hook caught in its mouth. Both boys hung on the weathered railing and I grabbed the backs of their jackets while Travis squatted down to reach the fish. He had to lay full-length on his stomach and I became aware of the strength of his legs, muscled calves straining against faded denim, a flash of skin at his waist as he stretched to grab the thing. He pulled it flapping from the water, the gills shutting and opening, one wide eye gaping at us as the fish fought the assistance Travis offered. The barbed hook still had a foot or two of fishing line fastened to it and I couldn't watch as Travis gently worked it free. He reached back down into the water, rocking the fish back and forth slightly until it seemed to get its bearing. Then, with a flash of its tail, it was gone.

"Good job, Josh. You saved its life." Travis stood and rested his hand on Josh's shoulder. "I wouldn't have seen it if not for you." Josh ducked his head and grinned, the first smile I'd seen him wear. "Well, if the bread's all gone, maybe you guys want to go inside? Play with my cars?" Josh looked at Gideon, they both whooped and began running up to the cottage.

Travis watched them, grinning. Turning to me, he shrugged and said, "I've got a bunch of old Hot Wheels I keep around for the kids."

I stood at the end of the pier, breathing in the cold air and looking at the lake. "It's beautiful here. You're lucky, I love being near the water. You've got a way with kids, too. I never did."

He wrapped the bit of line around the hook and stuffed it into the empty bread bag. "How do you know? You ever been around kids much?"

"Well, no—"

"Every do any babysitting? Work with kids?"

"No, not exactly—"

"Then how do you know?"

"Well, if you're going to get technical about it." I laughed and bopped him on the arm. "Anyway, I see you're still a hero, saving that fish."

"Oh man, don't start with that again!" He laughed, folding the bread bag over and over on itself and putting it in his jacket pocket. "My hero days are over. Me and my bad knee will shuffle off into oblivion, thank you very much."

"Sissy says you're kind of at loose ends now." The words just shot out. "She says you're getting over a girl."

"Sissy has a big mouth." Travis's eyes went dark, like clouds blotting out the sun. He took a step or two along the pier, toward the house. "Besides, that's over."

"Did you really ride your bike all the way back from California? Over the mountains and everything?" The pier was so old, I could feel it sway as we walked, our shadows striding ahead of us. "Why'd you do that?"

Travis gave one short laugh but his expression was rueful and he shook his head. "I was a fool. Thought it'd prove something."

"Did it?"

"Yeah. Proved I'm a damn fool." We got to the foot of the path and Travis picked up a stone, skimming it across the water before he turned to me. "Look, I'm not eating my heart out over her or anything. I finally figured out I can't save anyone. Tried to save the big game; blew out my knee. Tried to save Dad's store; had to sell. Tried to save Vanessa from her situation, but I'm not too bright. It took me a long time to realize she didn't want to be saved. Didn't need to be saved. When I see something going wrong, it seems natural to try to help. Like that fish. But maybe he's too wounded to survive anyway and I've only prolonged the agony. How the hell do I know?"

"You do help. Got me to come home, didn't you? But yeah, eventually, people have to save themselves. Dig their own way out of the pit." Travis's gaze met mine and for the first time, I felt like his equal. Not in strength or honor or, for sure, pure goodness, but at least in experience. "You shouldn't feel responsible for how it all turns out in the end. I think we each choose our own hell."

We looked at each other and our breath steamed in the cold air, soft clouds that intermingled. He reached out and brushed my hair back from my forehead. His hand fell to his side and my lips grew warm. "And then what?" he asked. "Once we've built that hell, then what?"

"I don't know. Some people wallow in it. Me, I'm tryin' to climb back out. Exploring ways and means."

"Let me know if I can help." The words were uttered in all sincerity, and then we both began to smile. "Well, shoot," Travis laughed. "Back-sliding already."

"Oh, lord. I can see we're gonna have a time with you." I took his arm and we climbed the path. We slipped and slid on the wet leaves and I could feel a ridiculously wide grin spreading across my face. "Learn from me, Travis. Embrace your inner idiot. Commit random acts of stupidity. Don't you remember what Mark said? Reee-laxxx. Everything's—"

"—co-pathetic."

An hour later, I stood outside the so-called terminal of Lowrance Field, waiting for Dad to fly in from Columbia. The bitter wind froze my face, snaking under my jacket and chilling me to the marrow. Sissy had called over at Travis's, telling him to pick Dad up and leave me to stay with the boys, but that didn't sit right with me. There were some peculiar vibes going on at Mom's house and I thought I'd better experience them for myself. Travis nodded when I suggested the change of plans. "Sissy's used to calling the shots around there," he said. "But don't get yourself pulled in too deep. You just got home, don't go drowning on me already."

I thought about that all the way to the airport. How involved *did* I want to get? I could barely tread water myself.

Dad arrived in a snappy little two-seater plane, bright blue and white. He jumped out with the agility of a man ten years younger. My god, he looked different. Like a Doberman, thin and taut, his skin deeply tanned, his hair slicked back.

"Surprised by your old man, huh?" he grinned, putting an arm around my shoulders.

"I'll say. Nothing but surprises around here. How long have you been flying?"

288

"About two years. Signing up for those lessons was the best thing I ever did. I jog, too." He patted his flat stomach. "Now, what's Janine been up to?"

I filled him in while we drove back to Mom's house in my pickup. He didn't say what he thought about it, just kept talking all the while about his plane and the places he'd gone. "I love it, Amanda. Flying makes me feel so free, like I finally know what I want from life." He chuckled. "Who'd have thought it'd take me so long to figure it out?"

I kept trying to assimilate all the changes I'd seen in the past few hours. Dad looked great, full of energy and life. Next to him, Mom was a Christmas tree in January; drooping and tired, aware that the glory days were over. It didn't seem fair.

"Maybe I can fly up to Philly some time and visit you. Never been there. And you're in a band now? I'm glad for you. Do you love it? Do you feel like you can't *wait* to get up in the morning, just so you can live your life?"

I swallowed hard. "Yeah, Dad. I do. But I worry it'll all get washed away, that I won't be able to keep that feeling." Jeez. He understood. *Dad*, of all people. "Sometimes I feel like I have to fight every moment, just to hang onto one little corner of the good stuff."

He nodded. "That's right, you do. And there's nothing wrong with that so long as you know what exactly you're fighting for. Having something you love to do makes all the difference." Dad glanced over at me. "Wish I'd known, long ago . . . If you're meant to fly, Amanda, you gotta fly. Someone like your Mom fights to keep her feet rooted in the ground. Don't get me wrong, I respect the hell out of her, but what she needs from life is different from what you or I need. It's understandable, but . . ." He put his arm across the back of the seat and tapped his fingers against my shoulder. "I flew with Mark once. Before I did any piloting. We rode with that guy who used to do aerial photographs of the lake. Of course, you can imagine, your brother . . ." Dad grinned. "He spent the whole trip doing Tweety Bird impersonations and singing *Up in the air, Junior Birdsmen.*"

I had to smile. "God, I miss him."

"Me too. You'll never know how much. How badly I felt about . . . " Our eyes met for an instant before I forced myself to watch the road. "There are a lot of things I would have done differently, if I had a second chance. A lot of thing I *will do* differently, in the future."

Wow, more surprises. How many more changes should I anticipate? I glanced at him out of the corner of my eye. How well did I know Dad after all this time? How well had I ever known him?

As soon as we got to the house, the hassles began. Accusations and counter-accusations. Janine arrived with Hank and her lawyer in tow, Mason Kennedy came over at Mom's request, and Sissy provided acerbic editorial comment.

"Okay, now this whole thing is ridiculous. I have total custody by law."

"Except you're never here! In my book, that's desertion."

"Desertion, ha! When was the last time you even tried to see Josh?"

"Please everyone, can't we sit down and discuss this calmly?" Mom's hands fluttered ineffectively as she urged people into the dining room.

Mason pulled out some papers. "If you'll look right here in Section II, article B. . ." "With all due respect," the other lawyer said, "that agreement could be ruled null and void by your client's actions. I suggest we discuss some compensation."

Dad snorted. "I knew it. Money. That's what this is really all about, isn't it? You can forget about it, I'm not paying her a dime."

"Jerk," Sissy said, *sotto voce.*

Mom tried again to appease the warring parties. "Please, everyone. Let's sit down, I'll make some coffee."

"I don't want coffee! I want justice," la Bitch replied. "Steve's been living it up, having his little fling, and here I am working my ass off as a secretary again. I didn't get one single thing out of that marriage."

"Well, except maybe the kid, and you dumped him off pretty quick." I'd had enough. "Hey! How about if we discuss what this is really about? Josh. Remember him?" Everyone turned to look at me. Janine rolled her eyes and I allowed a little hiss to escape my lips. "Mom's right. We need to sit down. But forget about the coffee. Let's talk about the Josh."

They all glanced uneasily at each other but eventually moved into the dining room. There were only six chairs around the table, so Hank took the kitchen stool in the corner and I remained standing. Mason Kennedy cleared his throat and enumerated the provisions of the custody agreement,

291

concluding with, "Of course, if you wish to discuss further compensation, we can do that. But in view of the fact that Mrs. Long—er, Mrs. *Janine* Long, that is—has not contributed to Joshua's expenses, we'd have every right to expect some kind of equity."

Janine leaned over and whispered in her lawyer's ear. I studied her, looking for some trace of resemblance to Joshua. Her height, maybe. He might eventually have that. Janine's lawyer, a fastidious man with long, narrow white hands, suggested that perhaps Mom was not the best person to be named secondary guardian. "No insult intended, but Grace is already fifty-two years old. Josh is only six. How capable is she going to be as a parent-figure when Josh is, say, sixteen? My client has also pointed out that Ms. Long—Ms. *Grace* Long, that is—has no actual familial ties to Joshua. What my client proposes is either an adherence to the original terms of the custody agreement—that is, the boy should remain in his father's care—or some kind of compensation that would—"

"I don't want *her* to have him!" Janine's face turned a mottled red. "Why should she have everything? This house, all those antiques. Steve gave her everything when they divorced, he never once thought of my needs."

"That's not correct." Mason Kennedy cut through her outburst. "You and Steve split the possessions in your apartment when you divorced. Steve didn't own any of this house by then. Grace purchased his share at the time of *their* divorce."

Mom's hand convulsed on her tissue. I wondered if she was thinking what I was—how could Dad have left her for such a cold-hearted money-grubber?

"Why don't we cut to the chase?" Dad leaned forward, his eyes drilled on Janine. "You want more money. I'm not going to give you any. Subject closed."

She glared back and whispered some more to her lawyer, who said, "In that case, we will begin proceedings to recapture custody."

"Hell with that!" Dad stood, pushing his chair back from the table so precipitously that it fell over with a huge clatter. "I'll take Josh myself. Keep him with me in Columbia. There go all your objections, so you can just kiss my ass and clear out."

Voices rose in such a babble that I wanted to scream and the room suddenly seemed way too full of people.

Janine had her lawyer by the sleeve, whispering furiously into his ear while he nodded and gathered papers. Mom was on her feet, pleading with Dad, Sissy huffed in annoyance and tried to pull her out of the room. Mason Kennedy sat with his hands clasped on his stomach, fingers tapping against each other, his gaze roaming over each person in the room and returning to Mom. She was in tears, urging Dad to return to the table, make some kind of settlement. "I don't care," she kept saying. "*I'll* give her the money, just please don't take Josh." Bile rose in my throat and I pushed my way out of the room, diving out the back door and gulping in great blasts of cold air.

293

How typical. No matter how much change we'd all gone through, things remained the same. Jump on a problem, cover it up, patch it over, but don't give anyone time to *think* about it, don't discuss it, just argue. Jeez, we were a hell of a family. If something didn't work the first time, we kept doing it again and again, even harder, slamming ourselves against rock walls and then complaining about the pain. We made me sick.

Janine and her lawyer, followed by the ever-impassive Hank, stormed out the front door. She bitched all the way down the sidewalk and I could see her mouth still yammering as they drove away. When I went into the house, Dad was preparing to leave as well. I watched as he checked his appearance in the mirror, smoothing back his hair, adjusting the fold of his turtleneck. "Aren't you going to wait and see Josh?" I asked. "I mean, you're planning to disrupt his whole life, don't you think you need to mention it to him?"

"Not yet." He slipped on the bomber jacket and aviator sunglasses. "He gets nervous if there are questions with no answers. Let me set up a few things and then I'll come back and explain it all." We both glanced into the kitchen where Mom's sobs could be heard, and Sissy's murmurings. "I know she's upset, but what can I do? I'll be damned if I pay Janine one cent. Grace *asked* to keep Josh, while I got going in my new job. I thought it might be the best thing for everyone, despite how it looked. Never mind. It didn't work out. But she can visit him any time she wants." His gaze kept straying back to the kitchen door. He slapped his gloves against his palm and said softly, "I can do better, Amanda. I really can. Sorry this has all blown up on the day you finally come home. We've missed you, hon." His eyes met mine and I gulped, not prepared for the sudden turn of conversation. "You didn't let it get to you. You didn't whine or complain, that counts for a lot in my book. When all this other stuff gets cleared away—"

Mason Kennedy walked up and Dad straightened, the hardy explorer once more. "Thanks for coming by, Mason. Hey, can you give me a lift to the airport?"

Mason leveled his gaze at Dad. "Sure. Let Amanda stay here with Grace." Turning to me, he added. "I'd like to speak with you later, if I may."

Dad patted my arm, his eyes suspiciously bright. I felt a little leaky myself and after they left, I went into the kitchen where Sissy had persuaded Mom to take an aspirin and put a cold cloth over her eyes. Mom's face, ravaged with grief, looked like she'd aged a decade in the past few minutes. Sissy sat close to her, arm around her shoulders, and she kept reminding Mom that Janine had tried to cause trouble before. "We always knew this day might come. Better Josh be with Steve than that she-dragon. And don't forget, you still have us. My kids love you like a grandma. You can be with us as much as you want."

Mom nodded, fumbling with the wet cloth. Her fingers shook so bad she couldn't hold onto it and suddenly she balled the thing up and threw it across the room, covering her face with her hands. "But I don't want to be on the edge of someone else's life! Even yours! I can't stand it. Everyone I love leaves me." She burst into sobs—angry, wretched sobs that shook her whole body.

I flew to her side. "Not everyone, Mom. Sissy's here and she's always been here. And I'm here now too."

She threw me off. "You won't stay. I know you won't. You could have come home any time, you could have at least phoned."

"I did!"

"You left messages!" Mom slammed her fist down on the table. "That's not the same. I'm *sick* of messages. You have any idea how many of those damned little cassettes I saved, making sure they didn't get erased, trying to hang onto some tangible evidence that I still had a daughter? If you didn't want to come home, I would have come to you. Don't you know that? But you didn't need me. You were fine. You worked, you went to school—"

Her tear-blotched face rose in anger and I found myself backing up, stuttering. "But-but- how did you know?"

"I went out there! You think I wouldn't find you, if there were a way? I hired a detective. He finally located you working in L.A., cleaning motel rooms and taking classes. I flew there, sure that I was going to help you, carry you home." Mom's anger suddenly dissipated, leaving her like a deflated balloon. "But I didn't. You were doing fine. Getting by. I watched you for a day and a half, sitting in my car with a pair of binoculars. It killed me. You were so young and helpless, I thought. But there you were, taking care of yourself, growing strong. So I turned around and came home. You didn't want me and there was nothing for me to do." She mopped her face with a napkin and sighed, looking out the window.

Sissy stared at her. "You never told me that. When was this?"

"That first Christmas, almost a year after Amanda left. I told you I was going to my mother's." Mom got up slowly from the table. "Maybe Janine is right. Maybe I'm too old for this. Old and useless." She walked away, swaying slightly as though she were drunk or suddenly struck blind, going down the hallway to her room and shutting the door behind her.

Sissy looked at me and sighed. "Well, shit. Now what do we do?"

Chapter Nineteen

Dinner was a subdued affair. Even though Sissy invited us over to eat, Mom didn't feel up to it. Instead, she prepared meatloaf and mashed potatoes while I set the table and told her about some of the classes I'd taken. "Nothing that will end up with a degree, I'm afraid. Just stuff I found interesting—literature and art and history. And during the times I wasn't able to go to school, I spent a lot of time at the public library, studying on my own. Who'd have thunk, eh?"

She nodded, her gaze on the salad she was mixing. In the middle of sprinkling oregano over the lettuce, she said, "I wonder if Steve will realize he needs to register Josh for school."

I took a quick glance into the living room. Josh lay on his stomach, watching cartoons. Leaning toward Mom, I whispered, "I'm sure he'll figure it out. After-school care too. Try to relax. Dad's out of touch, but he's not an idiot."

"I know, I know." Mom pushed her hair back and straightened. "Well, what kind of art classes did you take? Anything on the Impressionists? I love Monet."

During dinner, Josh picked at his food, glancing occasionally at Mom and keeping his thoughts to himself. He was no fool, I could see, and he'd picked up on the tense atmosphere. All my attempts to involve him in conversation ended up with monosyllabic responses.

"Maybe y'all could visit," I told him. "Mom would love the Museum of Art. Monet, Turner, Caspar David Friedrich. Great gift shop. And you'd like the science museum. They actually *want* you to touch everything. Maybe you could come in the spring during school vacation. They have a great baseball team. And horse-racing and—"

"Do they have car races?"

For the first time, he directly addressed me. "I don't know, but I can find out. Or there might be some place nearby—"

"We don't know what will be happening by spring break," Mom said. "Better not get anyone's hopes up." She poked her fork into the slice of meatloaf on her plate, now cold. "Better to take it a day at a time."

"Come on, Mom, let's be more optimistic. Who can tell, there might be changes for the good coming up." I smiled at Josh. "You absolutely have an invitation from me to come visit on your break. After all, you're my brother! Don't you think it's time we got to know each other? If Aunt Grace can't come, then maybe Aunt Sissy and Gideon. I want some company!" He smiled back, shyly, revealing little baby teeth with a couple of gaps and my heart flopped around like a fish on dry land. I could see why Mom didn't want to lose him but she'd have to develop the will to fight.

We got through the evening okay. I taught Josh to play a couple of chords on the guitar. He was so cute, his tongue sticking out the corner of his mouth in an effort to stretch his fingers to touch the correct frets. Mom brooded all evening, curled up in her big chair, watching the fire.

After Josh went to bed, she and I went upstairs. Mark's old bedroom was full of furniture, stuff that Mom had moved out of the lower rooms. "If you don't want them, why don't you sell these things?" I waved a hand at the piled up chairs and dressers, lamps and tables. "Let go of the past. Why shouldn't someone else get pleasure out of them?"

"Because this is the way I want it," Mom snapped. She pulled the cover off the daybed and began stretching a bottom sheet over the mattress. "What do you care? I have my reasons."

I picked up the top sheet and unfurled it over the bed. It wafted sideways and Mom grabbed it, jerking it into place. "Jeez, okay, I'm sorry." I said, bending to tuck in the corners.

"Well, it's my life, let me live it my way. Do I jump on you for your choices?"

Nope. She didn't. "Okay," I said again, softly. "Sorry. I don't know, seems kind of sad to me that this stuff is just sitting here."

"No, I'm sorry." Mom put her hand to her eyes and slumped down on the bed. "I don't know what's the matter with me. I've climbed all over you and that's the last thing I wanted to do. I never meant to say those things, they jumped right out of me. Like this afternoon. I bet it shocked you."

"A bit. But, hey, impressive as hell. You ought to let loose more often." I sat down next to her and put my arm around her waist. "Mom, I'm sorry. It was a terrible thing I did. Not only with Richard, but staying away all these years. I didn't realize—" I paused, taking her hand in mine. "No, that's not true. I didn't take the *time* to realize. Didn't think. Didn't *want* to think. It was easier not to. I kept telling myself that so long as I let you know I was okay, it was enough. But it sure wasn't and I am so sorry."

Mom started to cry again. She kept her head bent down and I held her and rocked back and forth. She felt so fragile in my arms, her bones like matchsticks, barely covered by tissue and skin. How had this happened? How had Mom, Amazing Grace, become this pitiable creature, barely holding together? No wonder Sissy felt disgusted with me—I was to blame.

"Mom, listen to me." I held her firmly, my cheek against her hair. "We're going to get through this problem together. The main question is what's best for Josh. Would he be devastated at having to go live with Dad?"

"No. Not *devastated*." Mom sat up, taking a deep breath and wiping her face with a tattered tissue. "They have a decent relationship. But Steve doesn't realize how hard he can be sometimes, judgmental. And he lives such a crazy life—picking up and taking off at moment's notice. What kind of life is that for Josh? But maybe . . . to be honest, I guess I'm thinking about *me*. I'll miss him so much."

"Well, go visit him. No law says you can't go to Columbia on the weekends. It's not that long a drive." There were solutions to everything if people would think creatively. "And Columbia's an interesting city, you could—"

"Why didn't you ever come home?" Her question, her soft voice caught me by the throat. "I never did understand.

301

Don't you know I'd have welcomed you? Didn't I make it clear that you'd always have my love and forgiveness?"

"I couldn't, Mom. Even now I can't really explain it." I couldn't meet her eyes, that hurt expression. "Here, I'll always be Amanda Long. In Philly, I'm—"

"You're still you. Call yourself Connor, call yourself Tinkerbelle if you want, you're still you. No one escapes their past."

"That's not true!" I lunged to my feet, pacing back and forth. "You say that because you refuse to leave Painter's Creek, but there's a whole huge world out there, Mom. I learned that the first year after I left, when I went from town to town to town, all the way across the country. No one knew my past and no one gave a damn! People judge, all the time. They judge on the basis of what they know, even if it's inaccurate, even if it's false or misconstrued. When I changed my name to Connor, it was like dropping a heavy mask and costume. Not simply the stuff with Richard, but all that stuff I carried before too. That whole Long Family shtick, that pretend-game that everything's all right, everything's fine, when it was just a façade. I was *miserable*, Mom. Don't you remember? *You* were miserable. Mark was dead, Dad was all caught up in a twisted mess, and we couldn't talk about it. You kept trying to pretend I was this daughter you never had—"

"I didn't."

"You did! God, Mom, admit it. For once, admit that our relationship wasn't all rosy. I know you always said you were proud of me, but be honest. I wasn't an easy kid. I didn't like cooking and gardening and all your girly stuff. I was

302

complicated and crabby and not very appreciative. I'm more like Dad, God help me. I have ambitions and—"

"Please stop taking the Lord's name in vain." Mom folded her arms and half-turned from me. "You know how I hate that."

"*God, God, God!* Why shouldn't I say his name? He deserted this family a long time ago! Look, if we're ever going to get anywhere in our relationship, we've got to start by being honest. I don't believe in God and I don't believe in dealing with all the things that should be or might be or ought to be. I deal with what *is*."

"Right. Big talk, coming from a girl who doesn't deal with *who* she is."

We faced each other from across the width of the room. The small bedside lamp threw a halo of light on the floor but left Mom's face in shadow. Everything around us was silent and, with a spasm of regret, I remembered Josh downstairs and wondered if he'd heard us arguing. Was this house always going to be filled with the sound of conflict? My mouth filled with a bitter salty taste and adrenaline seemed to run off me like bathwater.

"Jeez, here we go again. I wish we could talk without fighting. Okay, Mom, you have a point. I suppose it's easier to see what someone else should do, than to see what I should do myself. But it seems like we all keep doing the same thing over and over and then we're surprised when it doesn't turn out any different. Dad jumps into something without thinking it through. You let people walk all over you. Or walk *away* from you. And me? Oh, I'm a real prize. I get to combine all

303

Dad's traits with all yours, and a few little knockout doozies of my own. Wouldn't it be nice if at least one of us learned something along the way?"

Mom bent to smooth the quilt, her face averted. She picked up a small alarm clock, wound it and set the time against her watch. My guitar case stood propped against a chair and Mom touched it lightly before turning to me. Her eyes never quite met mine. "Maybe you're right, but I'm too tired tonight to figure it out." Walking to the head of the stairs, she let her fingers drift against the old desk that had belonged to Grandma Connor.

"Mom, I'm sorry."

She turned and the light caught her face, those wide cheekbones, that fair skin. One corner of her collar stuck up at an angle. I wanted to smooth it down. "I have gotten out of Painter's Creek occasionally, you know. Went to visit your grandparents in Michigan a couple of times." Her voice faltered and she glanced around at the excess furniture piled up in the room. "Your grandpa still drinks a lot." She swallowed, started to say something else, and stopped again. I took a half step toward her but she looked away. "Good night, hon. Sweet dreams."

Long after the household noises died down, I lay awake in bed. Thought about Grandpa and Grandma Connor, tried to imagine Mom visiting them. When I was little, the trips to the blue cinder-block house in Sparta had been exciting. I never knew what Grandpa would pull, like the time he got drunk at the Memorial Day picnic. Something made him angry so he tipped over the picnic table in the back yard. Airborne lemonade, flying potato salad. Grandpa picked up a gob of the stuff and threw it at Mark and for a second, we all stood and stared at him, almost afraid to breathe. Then Mark slowly wiped the potato salad off his shirt, gave Grandpa the evilest grin I ever saw, and threw it right back at him. Grandpa was so stunned and outraged I wasn't sure what would happen. Then he scooped up more potato salad and, with a great whoop, the free-for-all began, no onlookers spared. Mom was mortified and left the yard in tears but I thought it was spectacular, all of us running around, laughing our fool heads off, flinging edibles to the four corners of the yard. My grandparents were a little crazy, maybe, but they were *alive*.

I flopped over in bed and mushed my face to a cool spot on the pillow. Mark had been the turning point of that day, changing a horrible moment into something funny, but we'd lost that ability afterward. Everything became so damned serious, so rigid. I knew about the not-so-colorful side to alcoholism. I'd witnessed the verbal abuse, the chaos, the way Grandpa drank himself into a sodden heap of caustic depression by dinner-time every afternoon. But somehow, after Mark died, we lost our resiliency. We couldn't recover, none of us had the gift of laughter. None of us were Mark.

No, and it hit me all over again that I would never see his face or hear his voice. He wouldn't be there to lighten up a bad moment with some cheesy pun or terrible joke. Oh god, I missed him. His absence in the house made me ache all over. I hated it, hated the big hole he left. How could Mom still believe in a God who would take Mark when we needed him so? Without him, our family was as brittle as old china.

And Mom could lose Josh, too. She could have her heart ripped out all over again because Josh's parents were two fools who used him as a weapon. I heaved myself out of bed and began to pace. There had to be a way to solve the problem. Something none of us had thought of yet. I couldn't bear to think of this family being destroyed again and again and again. This time, somehow, we had to stop and make things work.

"So that's where we left it. Right plunk in the middle of nowhere." I sat on Travis's pier, throwing more bread to the fish. "For three days now, Mom's been all cheery and bright-eyed, anxious to cook me something special, eager to hear about all the places I've been, but avoiding any more serious discussions. I know she's glad I'm home, and trying to please me, but this act she puts on . . . it shuts me out of the process. I don't think she even realizes she's doing it, probably thinks she's being strong, not burdening me. Cripes! I want to help, but I don't know how. This whole custody thing. I have real mixed feelings about it."

"What did you expect? That you'd come home and everything would be fine?" Travis leaned back on his elbows, his face tilted up to the sun. "Doesn't work that way. Grace is struggling. Just be there for her."

"I don't think that's enough. Gahhh." The lake sparkled with a thousand diamonds. I wadded up the empty bag and stared out over the water. "You're so lucky to live here. I love the water. Used to sit on the beach for hours. I'll tell you what, if you ever want to get your problems into perspective, go stare at the ocean for a while. See how every wave erases the one that came before, think about how long that's been going on. Sure makes your own particular hassles seem pretty darned puny."

I stretched out on the old wood boards next to Travis, turning on my side so I could look at him. "I'm frustrated. Mom seems so pitiful. I'm not fully convinced that having custody of Josh is really a good idea for her, but jeez, without him, she might be lost." I thought about that for a minute. What would she do with her time without someone to look after? It was all too easy to remember that cold, bleak feeling of waking up and having no purpose to my day. I didn't want that for Mom. "Mason Kennedy says Janine could still screw things up. His words were 'she has a legal right to be as big a pain in the ass as she wants'. Mom asked if I'd consider being named secondary guardian to Josh, but that won't work. I'm sure Janine would object and bring up all kinds of nastiness, publicity. . ."

"So? It's old news."

"Doesn't take much to be news in Painter's Creek. I don't want to take the risk."

Travis acknowledged that with a nod of his head. After a moment, he rolled over to look at me. "If it could be done without involving the press, would you? I mean, take on guardianship of Josh? That's no small step. I'm kinda surprised you'd even consider it."

"Ha. Surprises me too. I'm not going to be around here much. A visit was all I planned. Getting involved at that level, gads, I don't know. I've been a loner for a long time." A lock of hair fell across Trav's forehead. His face was too close and his eyes kept questioning mine. I couldn't help noticing his lips and wondering how it would feel to kiss them. The thought made me sit up straight and look away. "On the other hand, he *is* my brother. It's not his fault we've screwed up. I've got to think about it some more." I wrapped my arms around my knees and lifted my face to the breeze. "I wish Mom would realize Mason still loves her. He's right there in front of her, but she's too blind to see."

"Yeah," Travis said drily. "I hate when that happens." He sat up and massaged his knee. "Sissy tells me Mason helped you leave North Carolina and your mom hasn't forgiven him for that."

"She wasn't supposed to find out. I practically blackmailed him into helping me get the name change and driver's license and a new social security card. He didn't want to, but I kept pointing out I was going to leave anyway and if he'd help me, I'd stay in touch. He only did it out of concern for Mom. I guess I was pretty ruthless, but I didn't think it would break them up."

"You were trying to survive. And now what?"

"I have to go back to Philly. We've got this New Year's Eve gig. After that, who knows?" I shrugged. "I'm trying to convince Mom to come visit—yeah, I know." Travis had raised an eyebrow. "I might be sorry later. But she's narrowed her world down to such a tiny space, I'd like to see her get interested in other stuff. Hey, maybe you could come too." My face grew warm. "I mean, if you'd like. You know, if you're not too busy."

He nodded. "Yeah. I'd like to. Things are pretty slow this time of year."

"Travis! Travis, look what we found!" Josh yelled from the back porch. Gideon held up a bag of marbles and Travis got to his feet.

"I forgot I had those. Let me see." He jogged up the path and sat on the porch steps. Gideon poured the marbles out into Travis's cupped hands. "Oh yeah, these are good ones. Some of these are my dad's. Real glass. See, these are aggies, these are immies. That's a shooter . . ."

I sat next to Travis and Josh came over to lean against my leg, looking at the marbles. Without shyness, he scooted back on my knee, making a place for himself on my lap and twisting to show me a large red cat's-eye. "Pretty nice," I said. He held it up to the light, squinting through it, and I got a whiff of his hair, a boy-scent composed of fresh air, sunshine, and a little bit of funk. How would he be in a week, uprooted from the life he knew and starting afresh with Dad? Would he like to fly? Could Dad slow down his pace enough to let Josh be a part of his life and not just an incidental bit of flotsam?

I put my arms around his waist and held on. "Don't forget, you're going to come visit me this spring," I murmured into his ear. "Maybe you could even ride on the train, would you like that?"

He nodded. "And do the guitar some more. And see the sharks."

"Yep. Hey, can I have some sugar?"

Josh dutifully puckered up and pecked my cheek. I had to get going, it was a long drive to Philly and Travis kept looking

309

at me in a way that was most unnerving. I gave each of the boys a tortoiseshell guitar pick as a keepsake and got in my truck. "Listen," I told Travis as he stood by my rolled-down window, "thanks again for getting me to come home."

"You'd have done it on your own, sooner or later. Hey, any chance of *me* getting some sugar?" He leaned forward, coming into the shadow of the truck. "We strong silent types need love too."

I grinned, though a blush rose to my hairline. "Haven't noticed you being all that silent, but okay." I aimed for his cheek, but he turned his head slightly and our lips met. Clumsily, off-center. But, oh, so soft and warm. Even as a near-miss, it was everything I'd been imagining. So why did I pull away so quickly, too shy to look in his eyes? "It's only eight hundred miles. To Philly, I mean. If you decide to come. Oh god, shut me up, I'm babbling." Travis nodded, leaning in for another kiss, a more definite kiss, a promise.

"See you soon," he whispered and I drove away. At least, I guess I did, don't really remember. I was halfway through Virginia before the smile wore off my face.

The New Year's Eve gig was supposed to be uneventful. We were hired as background music for a private party at a country club, mostly university people. "Not too loud," the host explained. "These people love to hear themselves talk." He winked and Pete grinned. A perfect opportunity to promote the hell out of Pete's newest songs, the 'quieter, more thoughtful' version of Pete Tionesta. In honor of the holiday, I dressed up more than usual in a black velvet top Jenny had designed, trimmed with bands of jet and sapphire. I wore a short black leather skirt instead of jeans, and took extra care with my hair and make-up. I just hoped they wouldn't be expecting chamber music or something. At one end of the room, the catering staff was already at work on the buffet and we set up our stuff in a sort of alcove at the other.

"Good grief. Look at the trophies." Pete eyed the wall of gleaming laurels, grunting as he lifted an amp off the dolly. "How la-di-da. I don't think we'll see any fistfights or moonings tonight. Can you stand it? Nuthin' but butt-kissing and back-stabbing and a little nice white wine." I laughed, but he was right. During breaks between songs, all I heard were discussions about seminars at Winterthur, who had published what in which quarterly or review, and how to extend sabbatical leaves. Watching the facial expressions alone was as good as a French farce.

Who cared? I felt serene. Whatever happened tonight, it couldn't possibly matter as much as the fact that I had finally begun a reconciliation with Mom and Dad. It was New Year's Eve, and the beginning of a new life for me. Maybe a life that included Travis?

Around eleven, we took a short break and a balding man with wiry eyebrows came up to us. He introduced himself as Gavin Bell, a producer with Tin Roof Music. "Can we talk? I'm really intrigued with what you've been playing here. Very nice. I have to say, very nice indeed. A big difference from your younger days, eh, Pete? I remember Tad Paranoid well." He turned to look me over, appraising me as though I was a new car. "And a lovely accompanist. Your wife?"

311

"No, no, this is Connor Long. Jenny's at home with the kids. Did you say Tin Roof?" Pete looked distinctly rattled. "So what do you think? Any chance Tin Roof would be interested?" Pete's hair stuck up in back and he shoved his hands into his pockets. "I've got a lot more stuff ."

"Oh, we're interested. Very. In fact, I've got someone here—he's not actually with Tin Roof, but he's thinking of investing. A real player. Soon as he saw it was you, he got interested and—"

A sudden surge of party-goers interrupted us. They were obviously feeling no pain, screeching with laughter. So much for not getting rowdy. Pete, excitement mirrored all over his face, suggested talking again after we finished for the night and Mr. Bell okayed that. As the evening continued, the room became more and more crowded and the caterers were kept busy replenishing platters of smoked salmon and paté, shrimp croustades and hazelnut truffles.

At midnight, Pete guided us through the obligatory countdown and subsequent hilarity, then we changed the mood with some slow tunes. Couples paired off and filled the miniscule dance floor. I soloed on a song Pete had written for Jenny, a bittersweet lament with Baroque imagery. Pete eased on through several of his oldies and we finished with *Or Thereabouts*, the newest of his songs and my personal favorite. He stood in front of the mike, swaying slightly, his deep husky voice like smoke and brandy. I perched on the high stool, concentrating on the elaborate fingerings. Halfway into the song, I could sense the revelers quieting down, becoming engaged with the music. I concentrated on my playing, praying

312

that I wouldn't mess up, hoping for a perfect moment. At the end of the song, we received the most enthusiastic applause of the evening, and Pete flashed me a huge smile.

"Thanks," he said to the audience, "that's from my new, hopefully-soon-to-be-produced CD. And thanks to my partner, Connor Long, who wrote the amazing guitar riff."

We began breaking down the set shortly thereafter, packing away instruments and stands, microphones and amplifiers. Gavin Bell came out to the van as we were loading it and suggested we meet him back inside for a few minutes. We finished putting everything away and Pete kept muttering to me, "They're a great label. Bigger than I ever hoped to sign with. Slideboard recorded with them. So did Piper Jones. And Leo Tucciarone."

The caterers had nearly finished clearing up. We snagged a table near the door and Pete grabbed us a couple of bottles of ice water. After a short delay, Mr. Bell sat at the small table with us, gesturing to his friend across the room. I was wrestling with the stubborn bottle top when I heard the friend coming up behind me, his voice familiar—rich and melodious with a trace of southern drawl.

"This is a real pleasure. I told Gavin I had to meet you. Mr. Tionesta, I've been looking forward to this. And Miss Long. *Connor* Long. A very unusual name. How nice to finally meet."

Chapter Twenty

There could not be two men in the world with that voice—the voice from hell. For a split second, I wondered if I could fake it, fool him into believing I was someone else, but in the next moment, Richard seated himself opposite me and I knew the game was up.

Pete reached across to shake hands, but I sat frozen, tightly gripping my bottle of water. Richard had changed little. His hair had more white on top, he'd lost a few pounds, but otherwise he remained the same. As confident and ruthless as ever.

"When we walked in the room, I didn't realize who you were," he said, "just thought the music sounded good. Guess you must have played three or four songs before it began to register." His charm act. Easy-going, affable, selling himself to Pete. "Then something clicked and I took a closer look and I thought, boy, something about that person is so familiar. Looked again, and damned if I wasn't right." His gaze slid over me and our eyes met for a second before he turned to Pete again, smiling. "Tell me about yourself."

I must have been subconsciously twisting the bottle cap, it came off suddenly in my hand and some of the water splashed over onto my arm. Automatically, I held my wrist against my face, hoping the coolness would revive me. I couldn't think, couldn't move. It was all too sudden. How could Richard be there, no warning? He glanced my way once or twice. I felt it, even though I didn't look directly at him. Instead I replaced the bottle cap, concentrating on the blue color, the ridges around the sides. My palms were wet, whether with condensation from the bottle or sweat, I couldn't tell. The men talked, low murmurs that seemed like a foreign language, which I couldn't hear clearly in any case because of the pounding in my ears. Richard was *right there*, not two feet from me, and nobody knew about us. Pete surely hadn't a clue, music was his only world. Gavin Bell seemed oblivious, so I assumed he was unaware as well.

Only Richard and I felt the impact, the quake that went down to bedrock. And he seemed to be enjoying it, getting off on my discomfort.

"So you're making a comeback," he said to Pete. "How old are you now? Forty? Forty-five?"

"Forty-two." Pete glanced at Gavin. "Not too old, I hope. A lot of people out there still remember me. I'm counting on their tastes having grown up, just as mine have."

"Maybe. Of course, they're not the biggest demographic for buying music." Richard's voice became even lower and silkier. "We have to consider the probable return."

"True." Gavin hitched his chair closer to the table. "But at Tin Roof we pride ourselves on promoting alternative artists."

"Yet even they have to make a profit." Richard leaned forward on his elbows, ignoring me, focusing on Pete. "What

315

makes you think you can earn that profit? What do you have to offer? How do we know you won't go back to boozing and drugs? What kind of stability do you have?" He switched gears suddenly and leaned back in his chair, Mr. Geniality. "For example, how long have you two been working together? So many bands break up, implode the minute they taste success. What kind of stability do you have? Will you stay together? Young ladies have been known to run off with no warning."

Blood surged through my veins and I stared at my drink while Pete asked, "Excuse me. What exactly is your connection to Tin Roof Music?"

Richard tilted his chin up and raised his glass. "Financial. Strictly financial. Everyone loves my money. Gavin here will make all the final decisions, but I like to sit in on the process sometimes. I find all the performing arts fascinating. Don't you?"

Gavin leaned forward, jabbing the table with his forefinger. "The thing is, Pete brings a certain fan loyalty with him. I bet a lot of his old Tad Paranoid fans would be interested. So he'd have a base to start. Plus, he's been playing in the area. I remember now seeing the ads, but I didn't realize the music was all new. And we could tie his promotion in with a couple of our other artists—"

"You mean he can hang onto their coattails? Better men who've gone before and all that?" Richard nodded slowly. "That might be possible. I don't know, I'm just a virgin in the music industry, really. Myself, I prefer leading to following."

"Wait a minute. Nobody needs to carry me. My music will sell itself." Pete pushed his chair back from the table.

Gavin grabbed his sleeve. "Of course it will," he said. "And I'd like to talk with you a little bit more. Richard, I don't think you realize—"

"I realize plenty. This has-been is leaning on the talent and good looks of a pretty girl who may or may not stay with him. If she were to leave—"

"Hey, I'm just the back-up player," I said, stung into speaking. "It's Pete and his music you want."

Pete stood, towering over the two men. He took a demo from his pocket and tossed it onto the table. "It's late, I gotta go. You call me if you're interested." He shook hands with Gavin, pointedly ignoring Richard who leered at us, lolling back in his seat, and left. I grabbed my jacket and hurried after him.

Neither of us said anything until we were in the van, driving down the highway, and then Pete rolled down the window to let in a blast of cold air. "Sorry, Connor. I had to get out of there or slug that guy."

I couldn't stop shaking. My shoulders rattled like dice inside my coat. "No need to apologize. He was being a jerk. Gavin's the one who counts, though, and he seemed real interested."

"Yeah, but if this other guy is the money-man, I could be sunk. What the hell was his problem anyway?" Pete shook his head like a spaniel coming out of water and rolled the window back up. We drove another couple of miles and he gave me a sidelong glance. "What's all this about only being the back-up player? Shit, you helped write three of the songs. Jenny and I were counting on you being there if we did a self-produced CD and I'd feel the same if I got a contract. In fact, I was thinking both you and Jenny could sing on some of those numbers. Like what's-their-names did on the *Missouri Slow Dance* CD. That was a great mix of songs and voices. I was picturing something like that, building up a repertoire and getting serious about it next fall, when the baby's older. You aren't thinking of leaving, are you?"

Was I? I couldn't even answer, my voice would have shook too badly. If my involvement would keep Pete from getting the contract, maybe I should leave. In fact, getting out might be the kindest thing I could do. Go home for a while, see if I could help Mom and Josh get straightened out. Or would I only mess things up there too?

Jeez. My brain was blasted. Richard had been sitting right across from me, I'd seen him, heard him, smelled his aftershave. How could I possibly think or make plans?

Pete dropped me off at my apartment and I trudged upstairs, shedding my belongings in a trail from door to bed. My first impulse was to bury myself under the covers, but the nasty feel of hairspray and cosmetics changed my mind. I took a quick shower, scrubbing my scalp with frenzied knuckles, gargling hot water, barely rinsing off before I hopped out of the tub. I savaged myself with the towel and used a corner of it to wipe steam off the mirror.

Without make-up, I looked younger, unformed. Childish. My skin was pale, milky; no trace of tan or freckles, just pure ivory white. Except for the scars on my chest. I traced them, felt the familiar ridge of shiny skin. Even after all this time, the

318

scars were pink, satiny-smooth. Like the pink toe shoes I kept wrapped in tissue, they were perfect reminders of another life, another time. One dime-sized scar for the bullet from Diane Gessler's gun. One for the chest tube that kept me alive.

I smacked my hair down with a brush and jerked on an old t-shirt. No one could see the scars when I was dressed, only I knew they were there. And only I knew about other scars, hidden deep in my psyche. Seeing Richard again—it had been too abrupt. I wasn't prepared. Too many memories were flooding back—the way we'd been, the things we'd done. Richard seduced me with the promise of strength and security, but was that all? Hadn't I also fallen for his sexual dominance? What did that say about me, about what kind of woman I was? I wasn't sure I wanted to find out.

I woke late the next morning with a headache. Hadn't slept, just rolled from one side of the bed to the other, turning over my pillow again and again, trying to relax. Impossible, with Richard's image so fresh in my mind. I'd been such a vulnerable fool back then. He'd danced me right into the corner where he wanted me, my own terrible *danse vertigo*.

Well, that wouldn't happen again. If he came around and tried to start up, he'd find out I was a changed person. Strong. Able to spot bullshit with a single glance. Richard had convinced me he was God at a time when I had no one else to believe in, but I didn't need to lean on him anymore. Or anyone. Security was an illusion anyway, that much I knew. The only real security was a belief in oneself.

I took an aspirin and did my morning stretches. As always, the pull and flex of muscles and tendons revived my self-confidence. It was a new year and I was going to do the right thing. Which, first of all, meant telling Pete and Jenny the truth.

It would be hard. They'd be shocked, maybe. Surprised. At first, they'd have doubts about how it would affect the contract—but hell, if Tin Roof wanted Pete that bad, so would some other music company. They were my friends, they'd understand. And if they didn't?

Oh hell. If they didn't, then I'd probably hit the road again. Life would go on—a little colder perhaps, a little lonelier. Either way, I owed them the truth and I'd have to deal with the consequences. Maybe it was high time, at that.

There weren't many places open on New Year's Day, but I knew of a little diner where I could get scrambled eggs and a cup of coffee. Afterwards, I walked to Pete's, freezing in the wind off the river that howled down the canyon of Market Street. There would be snow soon, I could smell it.

Pete and Jenny were home, enjoying their day off. As soon as I walked in the door, Pete gave me the news that Gavin Bell had called. "He's definitely interested, no matter what that other guy says. Loves the demo. He's playing it for the other partners tomorrow. We could be looking at a contract within the month. I can't believe the speed this is happening!" He threw an arm around my neck and kissed the top of my head. "So no more talk about being just a back-up player, okay? We're all in this thing together now."

Jenny sat on the couch, nursing the baby. Pete dropped down next to them and proceeded with details. As he talked, he kept stroking Jenny's hair, absent-mindedly letting a thick auburn lock slide between his fingers again and again. They looked so happy. Sure of their love for each other, delighted with their children, excited about the offer. I thought it couldn't happen to a nicer couple and wished my secret could have been kept indefinitely. I took a deep breath and perched on a stool, sitting very straight and tall.

"Listen, guys. I have something I need to tell you. It's important. Probably should have told you a long time ago."

The baby finished nursing. Pete put her to his shoulder to burp, murmuring against her fuzzy little head while Jenny buttoned up and made herself decent. I bet neither of them cared a rap for what I was going to say and I couldn't blame them a bit. They had their new baby, a new life right in front of them. What else mattered? Why didn't I just keep everything to myself?

But there was Jenny looking at me, waiting for me to speak. And there was Pete, who'd welcomed me into his family, who'd helped me begin in studio work, who wanted me to be a part of his good fortune. I had to tell them. Nervously, pulling my sleeve ends over my fingers, I began.

"That guy you met last night, Gavin's friend. His name is Richard Gessler. He used to be the president of GBW. You know, the software company. I'm not sure what he does now." Pete smiled and patted the baby's back, his big hand making her tiny pink-pajama'd body seem even smaller. Jenny leaned against him, curling her legs up under her robe. "I don't know if you remember, but a few years ago he was in all the papers because his wife caught him having an affair and she tried to kill him and shot herself." Neither of them showed any sign of comprehension. This was going to be harder than I thought. I began to feel sick—clammy, nauseated, unable to breathe. "Last night, Pete, he was being really nasty to you and the reason was me. I'm the girl he had the affair with. I'm Amanda Long."

The words rang in my ears and there was a flicker in Jenny's eyes.

"Wait a minute, I don't understand." Pete turned to look at Jenny and the baby chose that moment to upchuck all over his shirt. "Oh shit. I shoulda used a towel. Here—" He handed the baby over to Jenny and went to the sink, pulling the wet shirt away from his skin, peeling it off carefully so the puke wouldn't drip on the floor. "Babies always throw up on me. I don't know why the hell that is."

Jenny concentrated on wiping Natalie's face. What she was thinking, I didn't want to know. Pete left the room to change shirts and no one spoke until he returned. I swayed slightly, feeling lightheaded, and had to grab the stool seat with both hands, curling my fingers under the smooth maple. "I always meant to tell you. Guess that sounds lame, but I really did. While I was gone this week—"

"I don't get it. You're that girl? The one—" Pete hushed for a minute when Jenny threw a hand up, but a moment later muttered, "So what? Doesn't matter to me. Hell, after all the crazy stuff I've done . . ."

"Why are you telling us now?" Jenny had always been the most business-like of us all. Trust her to concentrate on the essentials. "I always wondered why you were such a loner."

"Richard might still try to mess up the contract. So I thought I ought to warn you. Besides . . ." I couldn't look at them. I focused on my denim-covered knee. "I went home this past week. I haven't been home in a long time and it made me realize it's time to get over all that stuff. Move on with my life. And here you guys are, making plans. Plans that include me. It's only fair to tell you."

"You didn't expect to see him last night? You didn't know he'd be there?" Jenny rose from the couch and set Natalie in her bassinet. "How much power do you think this man has?"

Pete frowned. "What does that matter? I don't care if he's King Tut, he can't go around expecting to get his way."

"I don't know what he expects. He's capable of anything." I couldn't move off that stool, even though I felt as though a strong wind was going to swirl through the room at any moment, knocking me sideways. "He might lean on Gavin Bell to dump the project or he might do nothing at all. Either way, at some point it could come out publicly who I am. So I think you guys better consider that before asking me to keep working with you. The publicity might not be very nice."

"Tell me about it," Pete muttered, his gaze skittering over the family room. "They've dragged me through enough mud, God knows. Even years after I got sober, they still—"

"Pete! This is not what Connor needs to hear right now."

"Well, shit, it made me mad!" He hushed up, though.

Jenny leaned forward, elbows on her knees, fingers forming a little steeple as she thought. "We'll have to think this through. If it's like you say, and this Gessler guy might cause trouble, then we'd have to back away from the deal. Who needs that kind of aggravation? But even if we find another producer, we'd have to tell the truth. I don't like the idea of deceiving anyone." She threw an apologetic glance at me. "Of course, I understand why you felt you had to keep it a secret. But now—"

"There's another choice." I forced myself to let go of my seat and folded my arms across my waist. "I could drop out of the project. Still work at the studio, maybe, but not appear on the CD. It's Pete they're interested in anyway." Pete started to protest, but it was Jenny I watched. Her face was very calm, no expression, and I wondered what she thought. Amanda Long, that dirty joke, working with her husband. I couldn't stand it anymore. "Look, I have to get going. I promised my mom I'd call and . . . well, you guys have a lot to think about. I'll . . . I'll check back in a day or two."

"Don't be ridiculous, Connor." Pete's voice followed me out the door but I could almost see Jenny holding up a hand, silencing him again. I plunged out into the cold air, where faint swirls of snowflakes were beginning to appear.

My boot heels rang on the pavement, metronome beats that mocked me all the way home. Damn Fool. It was all going to start again. The look in other people's eyes. The speculation, the distaste. In Jenny's eyes, oh god. She'd always been so great, so solid, Pete's right arm. Their home was such a place of warmth, full of light and color, filled to the brim with kids and music and Jenny's artwork. The scent of spaghetti. The warmth of a wood stove. Damn Fool, Damn

Fool. I should never have told. Better to just leave, better to never see them again than to see that look in Jenny's eyes.

I hurried home, head against the wind, sleet stinging my face. My feet were soaked and my jacket shed a shower of ice particles, like broken glass, as I took it off. With a pair of dry socks, a quilt, and some hot tea, I huddled in my rocking chair, trying to figure out what to do next.

The phone rang, with Mom at the other end. "It's so nice to be able to dial your number and speak to you," she said. "You have no idea how good I feel, simply being able to do that."

"Happy New Year. Break any resolutions yet?"

"Well, I've had some real bad thoughts about Janine. Does that count?" She laughed and then grew serious. "Talked to Steve yesterday. He's found a school for Josh, one with a nice after-school program. He's supposed to go over and fill out all the registration forms on Tuesday. Classes start back up on Wednesday."

"That soon? Have you told Josh yet?" Poor little guy. Jeez, that scene would be even more painful that the one I'd gone through with Pete and Jenny.

"Not yet. I dread it. I don't know what I'm going to do with myself . . ." She breathed hard into the phone and I realized she was crying.

I kicked off the quilt and got to my feet. "Come visit me. I mean it. When Josh has gone, come stay with me a while. You could go to all the museums and stuff while I'm at work and then we could explore the city together. It'd be good for you. For both of us." Energy surged through me. I could stay busy with Mom. Helping her, for once, instead of causing pain. And then if Pete and Jenny decided they had to let me go . . . . "It's not a big deal. Get an open-ended ticket, fly up, and stay as long as you like."

"I don't know. I guess I could. Nobody here needs me."

"Well, I do. So don't worry. We'll figure all this out together, okay?" I made her promise to check on airfares and we hung up. Jeez, what a day. I looked around my room, eager for action. Mom would probably be shocked at my bare bones essentials but heck, fixing the place up would give her something to do. I'd need another bed, or maybe I could get a futon and let Mom have my bed. Closet space, what would I do about closet space? And shoot, I'd better get a new shower curtain too. I piled a load of laundry into a basket and threw on my coat again. The laundromat should be open. I could at least get one chore done.

As I bounced down the stairs, my neighbor, old Mrs. Krogalecki, opened the door to her second-floor apartment. "Connor, you got a package. Some guy dropped it off while you were out." She set the large envelope on top of my basket and backed into her apartment, which smelled of cats.

I went out to the truck more slowly. Who would be sending me a package? No return address, my name hand-lettered in black marker. The snow was coming down in earnest and I started the engine running and turned up the heater before I pulled off my gloves and opened the thing.

Photos. A dozen of them, color enlargements. Me, practicing ballet movements before a large mirror. Richard had taken them shortly after we went to New York. I

326

remembered how he coaxed me to dance for him, how proud he'd been of the photographs afterward. I was so *young*. So thin, almost scrawny in my pink leotard. My hair was drawn back in a knot, I wore leg warmers and toe shoes. Old ones, streaked with black rosin marks. Richard had photographed several different poses—classic arabesques from *Swan Lake* and *La Bayadere*. A pirouette straight out of *Firebird*.

In one photo, he caught himself in the act. His reflection appeared in the mirror behind me, smiling as he took the shot while I appeared to be totally focused on what I was doing, involved in the moment.

I couldn't help examining the pictures. They were some kind of trick, Richard had sent them for a purpose, but oh . . . How I had danced! My whole life had been wrapped up in those movements, in the effort required to stay *en pointe*, in perfect alignment, balanced. I had poured my heart and soul into the dance, it was everything to me. And then, when it was gone. . .

No, I wouldn't go there. I tried to shove the photos back into the envelope but they caught on a piece of paper. Fishing that out, I realized it was a note from Richard. Of course.

Where is this girl? I looked for her last night, but she's gone. What happened to you, where is that hunger I used to know? You were so alive.

Richard

I ripped the sheet into tiny pieces. Threw them out the window to mix with the snow. Oh god, what a bastard. Recklessly, I backed out into traffic and tore down the street.

He had found my address, which meant he could be watching me right that minute, gauging my reaction. There wasn't anything obvious in view, no sinister sedan, no rucked-up window shade, but that didn't mean a thing. I drove to the laundromat, threw my stuff into a couple of machines, and sat there on the cheap orange plastic chair, thinking things through. I knew Richard. He never did anything without a motive. What was the point of those photos? Did he want me back? I doubted it. Hell, I was too *old* for him now. What he probably wanted was some kind of revenge, some way of getting me to crawl on my knees so he could kick me down. Well, he could send that idea to the shredder, I wasn't falling for his tricks.

Chapter Twenty-One

Two days later I still hadn't heard back from Pete. My stomach hurt all the time and I couldn't sit still. Even practicing guitar became a form of torment, stirring up thoughts about all I could lose.

My day job at the bookstore didn't give me enough distractions either. With the Christmas rush over, and the flood of returns petering out, I had back-room duty, sorting stock and stripping covers. I hated that chore, ripping covers off paperbacks that hadn't sold, to send them back to the publisher for credit. The rest of the book would get destroyed to save shipping costs and it bugged me that we couldn't just donate the books to someone who'd read them. Taking something that someone had put their hearts into and reducing it to trash really bothered me. What a waste.

It made me think of Mom. All that potential she had, all her dreams and desires bottled up to fit into the shape of good wife and mother. And why? To please others? To help her forget she'd been the drunk's daughter? Such selflessness was laudable, but I wondered if she had any unfulfilled longings left, whether she even allowed herself to think about them.

I didn't want a life full of regrets or what-ifs. Those photos Richard sent had given me an unexpected gift. I didn't want to go back to the past, but they sure opened up thoughts of what I might want for the future.

My boss poked his head in the door and announced I had a visitor. I looked up and Pete walked through the door, filling the space and making the workroom seem much smaller than it had a few minutes before. He wore his big suede rancher's coat and snowflakes clung to his hair and the sheepskin collar. "Tried to phone you, but it didn't go through. Your line dead?" He blew on his fingers and looked around the room. "Cheerful little hole, this is."

I moved a stack of fliers from a folding chair so he could sit. "As far as I know, my phone's okay. Used it a couple of days ago. What's up?" I perched on the corner of the work table, trying to act casual. "How are Jenny and the baby?"

He grinned. "They're good. That kid's a keeper, she already slept six hours last night." Pete sighed and ruffled his hair with one hand. "Listen, Connor, I think I did something stupid." He explained that Gavin Bell had stopped by earlier with an offer. "A bona fide offer! Which is great, but we got to talking and I tried to explain why I wasn't so keen on that Gessler guy and, well, things spilled out."

I rose to my feet. "What do you mean? About me? You told him about me?"

"Uh, yeah." Pete spread his hands and tried to smile at me. At least he had the decency to look embarrassed. "Me and my big mouth. Thing is, he didn't seem too surprised. I think maybe he already knew. The good news is, he's still interested. Said Gessler already told him he didn't care to be involved, but didn't say why. Simply took himself out of the deal. And not in a nasty way either—he's still going to bankroll Tin Roof on some other stuff, so they're cool with everything and Gavin seems real eager to get us on contract."

I sat back down. Man, everything was happening fast. "Well, how do you and Jenny feel about it? Because—"

"Well, you know, it's a whole lot different from what I'd been planning. Tin Roof is a much bigger music house than I'd hoped for, and they'll expect us to do a lot more promotion, but—"

"No, I mean about me. How does Jenny feel about me working with you?"

"Oh hell, Connor, we're fine with that. We don't care what went on in your past. Like I'm lily-white? Forget it." He rose, shoving one hand in his pocket and jingling his car keys. "The thing is, if you're okay with it, Gavin would like to talk to you. He's out there now, in the bookstore."

Oh crap! Didn't anyone believe in giving some warning anymore? We found him over in the sports aisle, perusing a book on basketball trading cards. He smiled when he saw us, shoved the book the wrong way onto the shelf, and held out his hand for me to shake. "Amanda. I mean, Connor. Great to see you again!" Big toothy grin. Eyeballs all a-gleam. "I'm so glad you're going to be signing with us, we think this CD has a lot of potential. Can I talk with you for a sec?"

He still had hold of my hand and pulled me over to a table in the coffee shop area of the store. Pete sat down with us, shucking his jacket and checking out the baked goods case. I made myself sit tall, folded my hands in my lap. I'd do this with a bit of class if it killed me.

331

Gavin glanced around for a waitress, completely missing the fact that the coffee shop was self-service. Half-distracted, he said, "Anyway, I wanted to assure you I had no idea—*no idea*—the other night about your, er, relationship with Richard Gessler. You see, he started working with us about a month ago on some other projects. My wife is on the alumni board at U-Penn and they met at a conference." He looked around again. "Good grief, what does it take to get coffee around here?"

"Tell me this. Did Richard plan that little meeting the other night or was it pure chance?"

He shrugged, his gaze avoiding mine. "No, not chance exactly. The point is, Mr. Gessler won't be involved in any way with the contract. We totally respect your feelings on this." Frowning, he checked his watch and looked around again. "I guess they're not going to—Pete? Could you get me an espresso? I've only got a few minutes."

Pete slipped me a glance and lumbered over to the counter. Gavin leaned forward, putting his hand on mine. "Seriously, we don't want to capitalize on your, er, situation. But there's no denying, sooner or later the truth will come out. People are curious. What we'd like is to plan a couple of interviews, timed to coincide with the release of the CD, and go public then with your story. Trust me," he said, raising one hand as I reared back in my seat, "it's important to control your publicity. I know you've been private so far, but you can't keep that up forever. Not if you're going to appear onstage too."

Pete returned, two large coffee containers in his hands. He set one down in front of Gavin and one in front of me and I curled my fingers around it, fighting for self-control. Pete eased into his chair and I could sense his gaze on me, gauging my reaction. I took a tiny sip of coffee, burning my tongue. All around me, the usual bookstore noises continued, but our little table seemed encapsulated in a vacuum. Each sound magnified until I could practically hear the slosh-slosh of blood chugging through my veins. Carefully, I chose my words. "I have nothing to say about my past, and I never will. So, any interviews should be with Pete, about his music. The best way I know of to control publicity is not to have any. Not about me, anyway."

"Don't you want to tell your side? Set the record straight?" Gavin assumed a hearty we're-all-in-this-together demeanor, slapping the table and leaning back in his chair. "I think it's fascinating. And imagine what good you could do for other young women, warn them against making mistakes."

"No, thanks." I rose and turned to Pete. "You probably need to discuss this with Jenny. If you want to sign with Tin Roof without me, that's fine. I understand. But if I sign, it's as *Connor* Long, and it stays Connor Long. No interviews." I returned to the workroom with all the dignity I could muster and began stripping covers with a vengeance. Three copies of *Lydia's Lament.* Five copies of *The E-mail Murders.* One Monica Lewinsky autobiography—yikes! How did that get there?

I heard a noise behind me and turned to see Pete lurking in the doorway, looking sheepish. "No good, huh?"

"He's a jerk. 'Not capitalize on the situation', my ass. And I don't believe him for one minute about not knowing beforehand."

"Okay, admitted. He's a jerk. But he's not the only producer working for Tin Roof. They're a good house." He sighed and put his hands in his pockets. "No, never mind. You're probably right. I get a little carried away sometimes. Wanted to believe it was me he was drooling over."

All the irritation drained right out of me. "Of course it was. Any producer would be lucky to get you. My notoriety is just icing on the cake." Shit. This wasn't about me. Pete and Jenny's livelihood had to be considered. I slumped in the swivel chair and began rotating slowly. "How did you deal with it, Pete? How'd you get past the bad press?"

He dropped down on an old leather chair that creaked alarmingly under his weight. "Time, kid. After a while, they lost interest. Hell, who cares about an old, fat, sober musician with a wife and three kids?" Sighing, he slapped both his knees and gave me a one-sided grin. "Maybe we're both crazy to open up this can of worms. If they trot out the old drug stuff, Jemimah's of an age to understand. What would I say to her? *Sorry, kid, that was during your dad's Stupid Period.* I suppose you and I could stay like we are, working at the studio, getting by. So why don't we? What makes us push through all this shit when we could be safe and secure in our comfort zone? Damned if I know." Pete stood up and buttoned his coat. "All I know is, the comfort zone'll kill me. It's like being half-dead and a whole hell of a lot scarier than the risks."

334

He headed for the door and I stopped him. "Pete—are you sure Jenny's okay about me? 'Cause I gotta tell you, over the years, I've had a lot more trouble from women than men. They see me as a gold-digger and—"

Pete smiled. "Oh yeah, that reminds me. We both want you to come to dinner tomorrow night. The kids are still talking about singing with you in the hospital. We'll even let you hold our baby. I don't think there's much more I can say."

I worked until ten and drove home. Mrs. Li's shop was about to close and I asked if she'd had any trouble with her phone. "Yes, yes," she nodded, sweeping vigorously so that I had to stand on the threshold of the shared vestibule. "Phone been crap all day. Last night, too. They gonna send somebody tomorrow, like I can wait that long." With a roll of her eyes, she stooped to hold the dust pan. "Good night now. You stay warm, big snow coming."

I backed out of the shop, checked my mailbox, and had just unlocked the inner door leading to the stairs when Mrs. Li's store lights went out and a man opened the outer door. "They're closed," I said, and looked up to see Richard's face.

"Hi, baby," he said and I immediately reached for the grocery store door. It was locked. Mrs. Li always went out the back way.

"Richard. I can't talk right now." As calmly as possible, I pulled my keys out of the lock and held them in my fist.

"Not even for a minute? Did you get the pictures?" His shoulders were still as wide as ever, and he blocked the door, looming over me. He put his hand on my arm and I pulled away. "Did you talk to Gavin Bell?"

"Yes. Yes, but I still can't talk right now. Why don't you phone me tomorrow?" The stairs were accessible behind me but I didn't want to go up, not with Richard able to follow. I tried edging around him toward the outer door, but he didn't move and there wasn't room.

"Why can't we talk now? Aren't you excited about the offer from Tin Roof? I thought you'd be pleased."

"We can talk about it tomorrow. Please, it's been a long day."

"I see you're still a selfish bitch." His voice lost its silky timbre. "I cleared the way for your friend to get his record deal and do I get any thanks? No. Your typical reaction, take it all for granted, don't show any appreciation, not even any recognition that I did something nice for you."

He took a step nearer and I backed away. If I yelled, would anyone hear? The building was old and solid. "Richard, I really don't have time—"

"Time? You made me wait for two hours in the freezing cold once. I could talk about time."

In the small vestibule, the scent of his aftershave was overwhelmingly familiar. I remembered rubbing my face against his, my lips on his freshly-shaven cheek, drinking in his masculine odor, sliding down to nuzzle into the curve of his throat. "Richard, please . . . let it go." I retreated, one foot on the lowest stair step. Behind my back, I held the keys so they poked out between my fingers like pronged brass knuckles.

"You think I want you back? Ha. That's not why I'm here. I only want to return your belongings." He reached into his coat and pulled out a crumpled manila envelope. "A few little mementos you left behind." Tipping the envelope open, he showed me the contents. My braid, coiled like a snake at the bottom. The jeweler's box holding, I presumed, his diamond pendant. Some other small items I vaguely remembered as mine. "Just to let you know, I haven't clung to any illusions. Who needs you? I don't."

Richard shoved the envelope at me but I couldn't take it. I just backed up another step. Our faces were level and he peered at me in the poor light, the crinkles at the corners of his eyes suddenly emphasizing how he'd aged after all. He pushed the envelope against my breast and dropped it, the stiff paper making a sharp cracking noise as it hit the floor. "You think you're so hot," he said, dropping his fist to his side. "Strutting around with that guitar. You'll never be anything but a freak, a sideshow attraction. A no-talent little bitch. There's nothing that sets you above the rest."

His gaze traveled over me, head to toe, taking in my clothes, my hair, my make-up. I backed up another step, feeling for the banister with one hand, taking a tight grip on my shoulder bag with the key-crusted fist. Richard's gaze flickered over to my improvised weapon. The single ceiling bulb shone down on his hair, highlighting the white streak, making the rest shine like a silver cap. Melting snowflakes glistened on his herringboned shoulders. I rose another step and he put his foot on the bottom tread.

Softly, his voice controlled and dispassionate, Richard said, "So who's fucking you now? Hmm? Look at you—black leather, black suede. You look like a dyke. Is that your thing now? You sleep with whatever comes along? You always were a horny bitch, I remember."

"Stop it. Don't talk to me." I put the flat of my hand against his chest and pushed hard. Blinking, he stumbled back into the vestibule. "Don't come around here again or I'll call the police."

He smiled. Actually smiled, rocked back on his heels, put his hands into his pants pockets. "Sure," he said softly. "I'll leave you alone. Physically. But you'll never be rid of me in your mind. I was your first lover, opened your whole world, and I'll be there every time you take a man to bed." He bent forward from the waist, hissing at me. "See, I know you, baby mine. Like nobody else ever will. You needed me, even if you won't admit it. And you still, way down deep in your heart, want to crawl in my lap and be my baby. Don't you. A girl never outgrows the need for her Daddy."

I shut the door in his face and backed up the stairs, never losing eye contact with him through the glass. When I reached the landing, Richard left, whistling as he went out.

By the time I reached my apartment, I was gasping for air, fighting to keep from exploding. Oh god, what a bastard! I flung my keys across the room, ripped off my jacket and fell to my knees, clutching the bedspread. I hated him, hated him. And myself. Oh, that one moment of flashback, seeing myself in his arms, remembering in an instant with such clarity how it had felt to be held by him. I couldn't bear it. A shriek built up

338

in my chest and I screamed into the pillow, a scream that tore my throat and nearly made me black out.

I wanted to beat him up. I wanted to rip his face with my fingernails. Staggering to the door, I put my ear to it and listened, making sure he was gone. I rammed the bolt home and twisted the lock, slamming my hand against the smooth wood of the door.

I wanted to slap his horrible smiling face again and again. At the thought, my fist doubled up and I beat it against the door. Harder and harder. Both fists. I slapped the door, beat my shoulder against it, kicked and pummeled it. Hard choking sounds tore out of my throat, foreign to me. The door vibrated in its frame but remained otherwise unimpressed with my volley of blows.

Hopeless. There was nothing I could ever do to hurt that man and I slid to the floor, burying my face in my arms. He would never know or care about all the pain he caused me. I was only hurting myself.

Slowly, my breathing returned to normal. My fists and shoulder ached, my throat was raw. I crawled into the bathroom, pulling myself up at the sink. The face staring back at me was one unholy mess. Streaked and red, make-up smeared, I looked like the victim in a bad horror film.

Finally, I calmed myself, my little fit over. He'd been a bastard, I'd gotten past the anguish and it was over. Still shaking, I unzipped my jeans and sat on the toilet. My pale blue panties stretched tight between my knees and I looked down to see a damp spot. Oh jeez, no. Didn't want to see that, no. Richard had made me wet.

*

Half an hour later, I lay curled in bed, the sheet pulled tight over me. A shower and some herbal tea helped. I felt calm and sleepy, even floaty as though all my feelings had drained away and there was nothing left to weigh me down. The radio played some nice string quartet music, something by Purcell, and I let my mind drift back to the college classes I'd taken along the way. Eighteenth century British Literature, Folk Music in the early Baroque Era, Art Appreciation 210. I loved those courses, learning how people lived and thought, the things that influenced them, the rich cultural heritage. Studying had been something on which I could concentrate, give my all.

Was I really selfish? Maybe Richard was right. What had I ever done for someone else? I only cared about me, me, me.

I flopped over in bed and tried to calm my mind again. Living on my own, when had I had chance to think about someone else? I tried to be nice to people I met along the way, but after all, I couldn't get too close to them. Couldn't risk their curiosity, their questions. Only in the past two years had I stayed in one place longer than six months. Of course I'd been concerned about myself. I had to be.

But damn, what about the panties? I sure hadn't been turned on by Richard's presence. Was it just the automatic physical reaction to memories? Scents? Jeez, what kind of perverted lowlife was I? No normal woman would react that way.

With an impact like a slap in the face, I remembered the envelope in the vestibule. Just sitting there where anyone could find it. I pulled on a sweater over my t-shirt, yanked on jeans and shoes and opened the door. The lights at the landing were cheap and low wattage, leaving the stairs fairly dark. All the tenants complained about it, but nothing ever changed. I grabbed my broom as a weapon and crept down the stairs. On each floor, two doors led to apartments. All were silent except for Mr. Oldham's. He had probably just gotten in, he worked till midnight and I could hear the TV.

The envelope had fallen against the bottom step, half propped up by the wall, lying in shadow. I grasped it by the corner, using just my finger and thumb. Silly, really, but it felt like I was handling an unexploded bomb. As I straightened, a face pressed up to the glass door. Holy shit! I hollered and jumped back, dropping the envelope

"Amanda, it's me!" Mom rapped on the door. "Let us in! We've been knocking and knocking."

Jesus, Mary and Joseph. I slid the bolt. "What's going on? I thought you weren't flying in until tomorrow. And who's 'we'?"

Mom struggled through the door, carrying a heavy suitcase, an overnight bag and her purse. "I was worried about the snowstorm, afraid my flight would be cancelled, so—" The door opened again and in came Travis, smiling apologetically as he set down two grocery bags and stomped his feet, shaking off snow.

"Good grief! You mean Travis *drove* you?" I started to laugh. "Still being a hero."

341

He leaned close and murmured, "More like random acts of stupidity. We tried to call, but couldn't get an answer."

The door opened again and Sissy stepped in, bearing a large carton with a bouquet of flowers balanced on top of it. "Surprise!" she said, grinning wickedly. "Guess who's coming to dinner."

"We kept trying to call you," Mom repeated when we reached my apartment and she looked around for a place to set things down. With four people crowding in, there wasn't much room. "My goodness, those stairs! Isn't your phone working?"

"Or your doorbell?" Sissy ripped the cellophane off the flowers and plunked them in a pitcher, which she filled with water from my bathroom sink. "How do people get hold of you?"

"Smoke signals, generally." I slid Richard's envelope into a drawer and tried to get Mom to sit in the rocking chair. "What *is* all this stuff?"

"Well, we hadn't eaten yet, and didn't know if you had, so we stopped at this little Chinese place. . . there, Travis, put those on the table." Mom rocked herself right out of the chair and began unloading the carton Sissy had brought in. "We've got wonton soup and egg rolls and some of that pressed duck you love."

Travis eased me into the rocking chair in Mom's place and proceeded to direct efforts to unpack the groceries and set my totally inadequate card table. The whole thing was ludicrous. I didn't have space for all these people and I wasn't hungry anyway. It was after midnight, for crying out loud.

Voicing an opinion seemed a waste of breath, though, so I gave in to the inevitable, folded my legs lotus-style, and watched them scurry around like it was freakin' Thanksgiving dinner. I had to admit, they'd thought of everything. Cold drinks, paper plates, plastic silverware. I had only two folding chairs plus the rocker, so Sissy perched on the edge of the bed. The mattress and box springs sat on the floor, so this seat was way too low, but I took a perverse pleasure in seeing her stuck in that ridiculous position with the table almost up to her chin.

"What a time we had finding your place," Mom said, spooning wor shu opp onto my plate. "And then when you didn't answer, I worried maybe you were out on a thing. You know, a whatchacallit."

"Gig. Not on Mondays. But what about Josh? I thought Dad wouldn't pick him up till tomorrow." Sissy kicked me under the table and Mom shook her head, making an elaborate production over closing the carry-out boxes. Travis explained that Dad had made a sudden change in plans and I got the impression Mom was still getting over it.

"So with the snow predicted, we decided to drive straight up. Dave took our kids over to his mom's house, so I'm free to sightsee with Grace while you're at work." Sissy cat-smiled over a forkful of mandarin beef. "Maybe we can get your doorbell fixed."

"I've got a microwave that's spitting. Want to give that a whirl too? Knock yourself out." I didn't care if my bad temper showed. The whole idea of getting Mom up here was to break her free from the spell of Painter's Creek for a while. Sissy knew that perfectly well.

Later, while Mom and Sissy cleared away the dinner things, Travis walked me down to my truck. The futon I'd rented wouldn't arrive until the next day; I'd have to survive for the night with my old sleeping bag and air mattress. As I dug around in the back of the pick-up, I asked "Why in the world did you let Sissy come? Couldn't you put a stop to that?" I bumped my head on the roof of the bed cover and swore under my breath. Travis chuckled and I heaved the sleeping bag right at him.

"Hey, give me a break! The whole thing was a done deal between the two of them. I didn't know a thing about it until your Mom showed up at Sissy's, her car already packed. I had to talk them into allowing me to come along, didn't want them to get caught in the bad weather. Believe me, I've been punished enough. It took twelve hours to get here and I don't think Sis stopped talking once the whole time." He gave me a hand as I climbed down and watched while I locked the tailgate and rear window. "Besides, maybe if they're busy together, you and I can have some time."

Drawing me closer, Travis tipped his face down to mine. Despite the snowflakes pelting us, I burned to press my body against his. Our lips met, his tongue brushed mine, and suddenly I had to pull back. "What's the matter?" he whispered and I couldn't answer, only shake my head and clutch the bag with the air mattress to my chest. Travis looked at me, frowning. "Did I take too much for granted?"

"No," I gasped. "I'm fine. It's just—Mom and Sissy will be wondering where we are." I turned and fled, unable to completely bury the mental image of Richard's sneer, his leering face beyond Travis's shoulder. Just like he promised, just like he said. I would never be free of his impact on my life.

Sissy and Travis had reservations at a Holiday Inn. They left soon after I returned to the apartment, Travis's face cold and drawn. I tried not to think about it. Busied myself putting clean sheets on the bed for Mom, making room for her things in the bathroom. While she washed up, I inflated the air mattress and set up my sleeping bag. It still retained the stale metallic scent of the truck and I wondered if it would make me dream of old times. Not that I hadn't already experienced enough that day to give me nightmares for a month.

Mom came out of the bathroom in her robe and nightgown, her hair softly brushing against her shoulders, the scent of hand cream preceding her. She always took such care. I never bothered to do any of that stuff, just showered and slept in an old t-shirt, but I liked Mom's meticulous ways. Funny, they used to bother me.

She drew back the blankets and sat on the bed, bending forward to smooth more cream on her feet and pull on a pair of socks. "I'll have to remember to call you Connor. Hope I don't slip up." Removing her robe and setting it aside, Mom slid under the covers and lay on her side, facing me. "I'm glad you kept your middle name. Even if it does sound a bit masculine."

"You think so? I always thought it seemed strong." I rubbed my face against the pillow and realized with a slight sense of horror that I wasn't wearing make-up. Travis had seen me like that. *Gahhh.* Stretching out on my back inside the sleeping bag, I folded my arms under my head. "So Josh is with Dad now, huh?" Mom nodded, her eyelids veiling anything I might have seen. "How'd he take the news?"

The small lamp on my milk-crate nightstand cast a glare onto Mom's face and she reached out to snap it off. Security lights outside threw an orange-ish glow through my window shades as though dawn were approaching. Mom shifted in the bed, the rustling of sheets seeming to echo her sigh. "He was worried about his Wii and his bike. I said he could take them with him. I think he looks on it as a temporary situation. A vacation. He's been back and forth plenty of times, more than people realize, but of course, he's been going to school in Painter's Creek all along. So, he's more apprehensive at the thought of a new classroom than he is about staying at Steve's. I hope Steve can deal with it, be sensitive to Josh's needs."

"Maybe Dad will do better than you think. People can change, you know. Sometimes for the better." We lay in silence for a while and I thought she'd fallen asleep when Mom spoke again.

"You never liked your name, did you? I remember how you fought against being called Mandy. You hit that girl over the head with your lunchbox, remember? And got kicked off the bus for doing it. So I guess you'd prefer Connor anyway, even if there hadn't been a reason for changing it."

I laughed. "Jeez, Mom, I'd forgotten about that ugly lunchbox incident. Well, it was Charity Scruggs. She deserved a good smack. I don't know, Amanda always seemed like a wishy-washy name to me. Vanilla milkshake. Pearl necklace. It just doesn't suit me."

"It's so pretty though." Mom sighed again. "Must be some kind of family curse. Names, I mean. I always hated 'Grace'. It's such a harsh-sounding word."

That made me sit straight up. "Get out of here! Are you kidding?"

"And if I never hear an Amazing Grace joke again, I'll die a happy woman." She shifted position a second time, sending forth a little wave of warmth and sweet scent. "Given a choice, I'd pick the name Elizabeth. So melodic. Elizabeth Taylor, Elizabeth Bennet. Queen Elizabeth."

I flopped over on my belly and smiled in the dark. "Gee, Mom. Maybe you should get it legally changed. Who knows where that might lead you?"

"Oh, hon. I'd still be me. Don't you know that? Just me with a better name."

Chapter Twenty-Two

By next morning, the snowfall had begun in earnest. Mom and Sissy were excited as a couple of kids when they saw three inches on the ground and more falling. I told them about the RiverRink at Penn's Landing and they agreed to meet me at the bookstore at two o'clock.

The walk to work left me cold and a little wet, but I felt exhilarated striding through the snow, leaving my tracks in the pristine white. My footprints would disappear soon, obliterated by later footprints and eventually completely erased by someone's snow-blower, but for the moment, I'd made my mark.

The bookstore seemed too warm and stuffy after the brisk winter air outside, but the morning passed quickly and I hoped Mom and Sissy were having fun. Travis had mentioned plans to visit some car dealer and a restoration shop; he'd meet up with us later. Around noon, I caught a news report on the weather and realized it was a good thing Mom came when she had. There were delays and cancelled flights all along the upper east coast.

The store was nearly empty, so I decided it was a good time to reshuffle the travel section. I sat on a stool arranging copies of *Cooke's London* on the bottom shelf. A customer studied books on the next shelf over and I scooted my stool to the left, reaching for another stack of books. The customer—black dress boots, charcoal trousers wet at the hem—moved to the left as well. I scooted again, he moved again, and finally I looked up.

"Hey, sweetheart," Richard whispered.

I stared up at him, too stunned to move. "What are you doing here?"

"My flight got cancelled." He selected a book off the shelf. *Frommer's Great Britain.* "How's my girl today?"

"You have to get out of here!" I spoke in a hiss, glancing around to check if anyone could see us. "Are you crazy?" I started to rise but he put his hand on my shoulder, pushing me back down, and squatting to be eye-to-eye with me.

"What's wrong with a little chat between friends? I'm curious as to how you've been." The warm light in his eyes disappeared as I pulled away and stood, books pressed to my chest. Richard straightened and shook his head. "Ah, sweetie. There was a time you did anything I said."

"What do you want?" I kept my voice low and held my ground, taking a deep breath and straightening my spine. "What's the matter, you bored? Not enough challenge in the stock market? No buyouts on the table?"

He chuckled and rocked back on his heels, shoving his hands into his pants pockets. "Oh, I've plenty to do. New projects, left and right. I like to tie up loose ends, that's all. I wondered how you're doing." His glance ran up and down. "Last night—well, we both got a little upset. I was jealous, seeing you with that singer."

"We're just friends. I learned my lesson about married men."

Richard smiled. "Good. Now, let's start over. You look pretty trim—do you still dance?"

"You bastard." The pulse began to pound in my ears and I started to shake. I set the books down and growled, "You know that's impossible for me now. Get out of here. I want you gone. You have no right to bother me this way." My voice had begun to rise and I glanced around quickly, aware that a customer or two had looked this way. I folded my arms tight and forced myself to whisper. "My mother is in town; she'll be here any minute. I do not want her to see you. Now get the hell out of here."

"Beg me." The crinkles around his eyes deepened and he leaned slightly forward. "Come on. For old times' sake."

Oh god, I wanted to kill him. I wanted to slap his stupid face until his head spun like a top. I focused on his tie, taking deep breaths to control the shaking in my body. A little buzz in my head warned me of vertigo and I grabbed an edge of the nearest bookshelf. Richard leaned forward and took my arm as I started to sway. I couldn't even shake him off without losing my balance. "No, I don't dance any more, you creep," I whispered. "Is that what you want to hear? But what the hell does it matter? Because either way, I'm getting by without you."

"Okay." His voice was soft, his lips brushing my ear. "I only wanted to know. It must be tough on you."

"I have the music."

"A poor second best." He brushed his thumb against the back of my hand and walked away. I sagged against the bookshelf and dropped to the stool, dizzy and sick. One spurt of tears escaped and I dashed them away, fingers shaking. I made a beeline for the ladies' room and huddled in a cubicle, breathing in and blowing out until the trembling stopped. Each time I saw Richard, my protective armor cracked and revealed its weaknesses. Guilt, self-doubt, shame, grief, *shame*—he knew where my pain lived. There was no question in my mind he intended to destroy me, one way or another. Just for the fun of it

Mom and Sissy arrived, rosy-cheeked, laughing over their adventures.

"You should see Grace skate!" Sissy nudged Mom and grinned. "The woman's a regular Michelle Kwan. I had no idea."

Mom blushed, but her eyes sparkled. "I guess it's like riding a bicycle. You don't forget. When I get back to Painter's Creek, I'll have to take Josh to the skating rink." A little of the glow left her eyes, then she rallied and lifted her chin. "I'm sure I'll get to spend *some* time with him."

"Sounds like a plan to me. Listen, we need to get out of here." I put my arm around Mom's shoulders and tried to steer her toward the door. "The snow's getting worse. Why don't you flag down a cab and I'll be right there. Just got to get my jacket."

"Oh, for pete's sake." Sissy pulled off her gloves and hat. "Twenty minutes won't make any difference. I want some biscotti and a mocha."

She marched over to the counter to place her order. Mom tilted her head, trying to get a good look at my face. "If it's alright with you, hon, I'd like some coffee too. Besides, we've got to wait for Travis. Come sit with us."

Oh, man, I wanted them out of there. What if Richard was still around somewhere, watching from his car? My insides shrank up tight inside my ribs. The damned snow kept falling—silent, unrelenting. It made a lovely white blanket over everything, a colossal cover-up that seemed to make the whole world perfect and pristine, but really causing nothing but trouble. Like the way all my little lies had seemed to smooth things over at the time, but later they melted away to reveal the ugliness beneath. My past had caught up and overtaken me and all I could do was sit in that frigging bookstore, twisting a napkin and humming the same eight bars of *Winter Wonderland* over and over.

Mom and Sissy kept gabbing on about other things they wanted to do; stores to hit, places to see, maybe even take in a show or concert. My smile felt like it was held in place with surgical tape and my spine had become so rigid I could barely nod. Please, let us get out of there without seeing Richard, I thought. And without hearing from Pete. As much as I felt on tenterhooks waiting to hear his decision, I didn't want to chance him spilling the beans about New Year's Eve. I certainly wasn't going to tell them about Richard's subsequent visits, either. The whole thing was a nightmare. I'd try to hang on until they left and then deal with it myself. If the goddamned frigging snow would stop falling.

Travis arrived around the time we were starting to worry. "This weather is something else." He slapped snow off his clothes and loosened his muffler. "They're predicting almost a foot of fresh snow tonight, on top of all that's fallen today. We should probably all hole up and ride it out. Grace says your apartment is freezing. Maybe we should all stay at the hotel. Sissy's room has two double beds."

Aghast at the thought, I snapped, "This isn't North Carolina where they all panic if snow is even hinted at. If Mom wants to stay with Sissy, that's fine. I'm used to the cold. But maybe we *should* get going now. The sooner, the better." I pulled on my coat. "Come on, Mom. If you're going to stay at the hotel, we need to get your things. Sissy, let's go. Now."

"Who died and made you queen?" Sissy narrowed her eyes at me. "Is it okay if I finish my coffee? May I wipe my lips, O Anxious One?" She gathered her stuff with maddening deliberation while I grabbed the trash and shoved it in the bin.

We rode in silence, listening to the newscaster on the radio announcing that the airport had shut down. Amtrak, too. The weather service suggested businesses close early and send people home before the snow got worse. Every grocery store we passed had crowds of people rushing in and staggering out with full shopping carts. Sissy and Mom insisted on stopping at one to pick up a few supplies. Travis and I waited in the car.

"This could be a real blizzard, a super-storm," Travis said. His eyes were shining, he *liked* the idea.

I folded my arms across my chest, glaring away from him toward the view outside my window. "Trust me, it gets old fast. And you'll all be cooped up in the hotel together. With Sissy." We both watched in silence as three young guys on bicycles whipped through the parking lot, two carrying sacks of groceries, and one with a large frozen pizza box under his arm. "I'm sorry, but she's really getting to me."

"She'd probably say the same thing about you." He took off his leather gloves and slapped them against the steering wheel.

"Yeah. But don't you see? The more she helps Mom, the more Mom is convinced she *needs* help, that she can't stand on her own."

The snow seemed to fall harder every second, until it covered the windshield, and only the side windows provided any light. In that pale-gray haze, sounds seemed muffled.

"Apparently, that's a failing in my family," Trav said, his voice clipped. "We like to help people."

"Oh, don't get defensive." I reared back in the seat, unclipping my seatbelt and turning sideways, my back against the door. "It's great that you guys want to help, and I know Mom really needed Sissy. But I'm worried; it's like Mom doesn't trust herself anymore. She doubts every move and man, that's a killer. I know. To survive anything, you have to believe in yourself, and she doesn't." Travis looked at me and suddenly I felt self-conscious. I drew up one leg and picked at the laces on my boot. Keeping my gaze on that, I added, "I know it's hard for her, after getting beat up by so many things in her life, but if I could do one thing, that'd be it. Help her get back some self-confidence. I'd even be willing to get myself named as co-guardian for Josh, if that would help. Problem is, I don't know if it's the right path for her. Maybe she should be moving on. After all, Josh is *Dad's* son, not Mom's. Another problem is I know Janine will fight it. Drag everything up in court. I don't care anymore, but if I look like someone who'd be a bad influence—"

"That's crazy. It's old news."

"Maybe not." Abruptly, and without dramatics, I told him about Richard's re-appearance.

Mom insisted I spend the night at the hotel, too, and considering the possibility of Richard showing up at my apartment again, I agreed. We stopped and got our things and went to the Holiday Inn with Sissy and Travis. Travis had little to say. It was obvious to me that he was mulling things over.

"What did that bastard want?" he'd asked before Mom and Sissy returned to the car.

"To bug me. Give me a hard time." I'd shrugged. "Whatever. I can deal with it."

He hadn't been happy about that. When I insisted he let me handle it, he insisted in return that he was there if I needed him, and then he retreated into silence. I wanted to explain, but didn't know how to make him understand. Turning to him for help would be too easy, a coward's way out. Just as Mom had to stand up for what she wanted, I had to stand up for what I *didn't* want. Long ago, I'd turned to Richard to solve my problems. I wouldn't spend my life repeating old mistakes. This whole thing was my fault and I had to resolve it.

Since then, mostly silence on Travis's part. Sissy seemed to pick up on the vibes and was on the alert, her eyes bright, and her voice damn-near nonstop. We played card games. Rummy, Hearts, Bullshit. Meanwhile the TV kept blaring more bad news about the storm. My mind kept going over my problems again and again—Richard, Pete and the contract, Mom and Josh, Travis. It was easy for me to say Mom needed self-confidence, but a lot harder to accept that my own lack of courage kept me mired in conflict. If I could only decide what to do!

Mom and I didn't have a moment alone until late in the evening, when the party broke up. Travis didn't even look at me when we said good-night for the evening and only nodded at Mom. She eyed me, clearly aware that something was amiss, and we watched him walk away to his room. So many unspoken things, too many spoken ones.

We sat on the beds and Sissy decided to take a shower. Once she was in the bathroom, with the water running, Mom said, "What's wrong between you and Travis? I thought you two liked each other."

"We did. Do. I don't know." I moved to the armchair, my knees drawn up. "What's the point? I'm no good at relationships, and hell, we hardly know each other. We've been thrown together at moments of crisis, and that's about it. I swear to God, Mom, why even try? Why risk getting all crazy about him, if it's only going to end in disaster?"

"You want to be alone all your life? That's no way to live."

"Look who's talking!" She flushed and I had a momentary wish to bite back the words. Then, in a rush, I added, "Mason Kennedy has been on the sidelines for you all this time and you won't give him a chance. Maybe it's a case of like mother, like daughter. Ever think of that? Maybe this is the one area where we're alike."

"Maybe. I hope not. Loneliness is a pretty high price to pay for peace."

Mom busied herself rearranging her clothes and I just sat in the chair, watching snow blow past my window.

Loneliness, hmm. Wasn't all it was cracked up to be. Yes, I was free from the angst of most relationships. No conflicts of interest, no having to compromise, no giving up in order to get.

But also no one to talk to, no one to care about, no one to even notice whether I walked in the door. My mind went back to Pete, to his conversation with Tin Roof. What had they discussed? If it was either/or, play by their rules or don't play at all, could I live with that? Doing an interview, talking about my relationship with Richard—oh man, everything within me rebelled at the thought. I couldn't do it. What the hell would I say anyway? I was stupid, a fool, I was a sick kid who didn't know what she was getting into? Oh, that was no good. Whiney, poor-me shit. And a lie.

Maybe that was the worst part, knowing I had known better, that I always knew it was wrong, that he was married. Yet I did it anyway. How could I not cringe at that? Recognizing I'd gone into it willingly. I'd had so many chances to make the right decision, and each time, I chose wrong. How could I forgive myself for all that came after?

The next morning, awake early and restless, I decided to go for a walk. I bundled up quietly and headed out before anyone else even moved. The snow had continued to fall during the night. An unbroken expanse left landmarks obliterated. I could barely tell where the sidewalk ended and the street began. I knew of a coffee shop a block away and I cut a path through knee-high snow, seemingly the only person out and about in the whole city.

We didn't get snow like that at home in North Carolina. Ice storms, yes, when everything became glazed with a quarter inch or more of clear magic and the whole outdoors looked like some kind of fairy wonderland. Snow, however, arrived much more rarely, and usually only a few scant inches. Once, when I was fifteen, we'd had a real winter storm and school closed. Mark and I tracked up every lawn in the neighborhood. We rode a large sheet of cardboard down the backyard slope until we'd worn a wide divot in the grass. We made snowmen. Well, I made snowmen. Mark made snow dogs. Snow turkeys. Snow boobs with colored handkerchiefs for a bikini top. "Look, it's Kimmie Howard," he said. "Hooters of ice and a heart to match."

It made me smile, remembering. Later that day, he and Dad had gone up to Boone for the skiing. They'd come back the next day, laughing and full of that weird male insult-your-best-friend thing I've never understood, shooting zingers at each other and seemingly bonding more with each put-down. There *had* been some good times for them.

I thought about Dad and Josh. Could they work things out? Become a father-and-son team? Was Dad too selfish? Would he be willing to compromise on what he wanted in order to provide what Josh needed? Would Josh suffer for it if he stayed with Dad? And then, back to back, the same questions about myself, if I did step in to be Josh's guardian. I remembered the old Dustin Hoffman movie, where he got custody of his son despite being completely unprepared. Mom and I cried gobs of tears over that movie. But he stepped up in the end and became a good father. Could my dad do that? Maybe it was time to forgive him and give them both a chance.

And, oh, damn it. Maybe it was time to forgive myself, too.

Too cold to think any more, I went back to the hotel. Sissy still slept, but Mom had gotten up and dressed. "You forgot your cell phone," she said. "You're a popular girl. You've had two calls while you were gone. Pete says he needs to talk to you. And that producer phoned. Gavin Bell. His number's on the pad."

Gavin Bell? Probably wanted to lean on me some more about doing interviews. I picked up the cell phone. Might as well get the worst part over first. Mom excused herself and went into the bathroom, kindly offering me some privacy.

He picked up on the first ring. "Mr. Bell? It's me. Connor Long."

"Hello, Amanda." Oh no. That familiar voice, southern honey dripping off the comb. "I figured this was the only way to get you to call back," Richard said. "We need to talk."

A little adrenaline zap went through my veins and I rose on the balls of my feet. Bouncing slightly, I took a deep breath and found my voice. "Interesting you should say that. I think so too."

Chapter Twenty-Three

Louie's Diner on Market Street was known for its salmon patty sandwiches, locally brewed beer and disdain for pretension. Tourists rarely noticed it, tucked away down an alley with only a small sign above the door. I parked my truck in back, followed the narrow shoveled path to the entrance. Ordinarily, office workers and U-Penn faculty crowded the place, but this day only a handful of customers sat in the high-backed booths. This worked against my plans a bit, but I hoped the lousy lighting would still allow Richard and me to pass unnoticed.

I fiddled with the cuffs of my white oxford shirt, thinking of Mom's worried frown as she watched me get ready to go. "Shouldn't you call Pete back first?" she asked. "See what he has to say before you talk to this Mr. Bell?"

I hadn't answered, just continued with my stark makeup—pale foundation, black eyeliner, crimson lipstick. I spiked my hair and wore my heaviest leather jacket and highest-heeled boots, and looped a red scarf around my throat for courage. "Everything will be fine," I told her. "This won't take long."

And I sure didn't intend to let it take long. This was it, one final meeting with Richard and I would move on. Time to be free, get him out of my life.

He loomed over me suddenly, arriving during the couple of moments I'd let my attention wander from the restaurant door. A big stone wall, that's what he looked like in a gray overcoat with wide square shoulders. Richard dropped down onto the seat opposite mine, pulling off his leather gloves, unbuttoning his coat to reveal a burgundy turtleneck sweater as silky as his manner. "Thanks for coming," he said. "I appreciate it."

"What do you want, Richard?"

His head lowered and he peered upward at me, his eyes amused. "I came to apologize. Believe it or not." Slapping his gloves together, he beckoned to a waiter. "Coffee, black." Raising one eyebrow at me, he added, "Tea? Ginger ale?"

"Tea."

The waiter nodded and disappeared. Richard shoved his gloves into his coat pocket and eased himself to a more comfortable position. Smiling, he said, "You know, I didn't even recognize you at first. That night at the party, New Year's Eve. Didn't expect to see you, of course, but something . . . you turned your head or something . . . all at once, I knew it was you. Even with that short hair." His gaze traveled over me and I sat up straighter, pulling the edges of my jacket together. "I thought I'd forgotten all about you."

The waiter returned with a tray. Two heavy white mugs, a bowl with packages of sugar, sweetener and fake cream, a small metal pot of hot water with a tea bag soaking in it. I was aware of Richard watching me as I went through the ritual of preparing a cup of tea and my fingers shook a little.

"So. You've grown up. I'm sorry I missed it." His voice was very soft, melodious. *Insidious*, I thought. How did I never recognize that? Even more quietly, he added, "Sorry about a lot of things."

I wanted to say, *Don't*. Don't be like that, don't be gentle and kind. It's bullshit. "Richard..."

"Daddy."

"*Richard*." Our eyes met, challenged. "Don't start that up"

"I understand Pete's signing without you." A glaze of satisfaction went over his face.

Air filled my lungs and I blew it out, almost a whistle. After a moment I said, "I'm not surprised. It's a good deal for him. And he's got his family to think of, his dreams."

"What about your dreams?" Richard's hand slid across the table toward mine and I pulled back "You used to have such dreams, wonderful dreams. Are they gone? Have you buried them, like you've buried all your fire? Is it all tamped down inside you, waiting to explode? I think it is. I think you're just *this far* from igniting and—"

"Don't talk like that."

The waiter came over, asking if we wanted to order and Richard said we weren't ready, to give us some time.

I needed some time, that was sure. Time to recoup, to pull my scattered senses back together. If I was ever to resolve this thing, the time was now. I couldn't allow Richard's taunts to drive me away, I'd forever be haunted by all the things I hadn't said.

Sitting bolt upright in my seat, my hands pressed together in my lap, I took a deep breath. Reminded myself to sit tall and clear my mind, all those pre-performance methods I'd learned in the *corps de ballet*. From behind me, in the kitchen, I could hear the clash of pots, sizzle of grease. A man's voice called out something in Portuguese, another man answered in English. Every time someone walked in or out of the restaurant, a blast of cold air and bright sunlight hit the room and the scent of steak with onions made my stomach rumble. "I have something to say."

Richard watched me, his eyes alert, discerning. "Go ahead."

Now that the moment had come, I wasn't sure. Everything I'd thought about saying seemed too little, too late, too lame, but he waited for me to speak. "Okay, this is it." I took another deep breath. "Thank you."

"What?"

I hurried on, almost tripping over my words. "Seeing you again, all this stuff. It's made me think. Despite what a mistake our relationship was—and you *know* it was a mistake—I do have some things to be grateful for. I was lost back then. Didn't know where to go or what I wanted. Didn't know how to go after things. And, if nothing else, you did teach me about fighting for what I want. There's a price, there's always a price, but if I decide I'm willing to pay it, then at least I know something now about being decisive. A lot of people never learn that. They're scared to fight. They keep their dreams bottled up and suffer for it in the end. So I'm glad you taught me to fight. It was a lesson worth learning."

364

I hadn't been able to look at him while I spoke. Kept my eyes focused on the stupid napkin I was shredding to bits, but as I finished, my gaze rose to his face. His expression seemed compassionate and I forced myself to push the napkin aside and lace my fingers together. "This is the last time we're going to see each other and I'd like it if we could part as—well, maybe not friends—but at least, not as enemies." I leaned forward on my elbows, pushing the tea away. "Can we do that? Can we just part and say *I wish you well* and leave each other alone after that?"

The light went out of his eyes and he suddenly looked old to me. His body relaxed, shoulders slumping, and I had a momentary remembrance of crawling onto his lap, resting my head against that wide expanse of chest. He'd been such a refuge once. Not now—my feelings were clear on this subject—but once.

"What will you do?" he asked. "If Pete's going to be moving on, so to speak?"

"I might go home for a while. That's one thing I don't know for sure yet. But I'll decide soon."

One corner of his mouth tugged into a smile and I found myself smiling back at him, sharing the joke. Oh, what had made me want him so badly? I came like a puppy under his hand, wanting that pat on the head, needing his approval. Yes, he knew what he was doing all along. Yes, he manipulated me, lied, propelled me every little step I took to his way of thinking. But I couldn't erase the knowledge that I'd wanted it. His seduction had been sweet. Even at that moment, there in the diner, part of me wanted to smooth away the lines in his forehead, to kiss his freshly-shaven cheek, to believe in what *could have been.* So much tenderness had been mixed in with everything else, and I missed that. Man, I missed it. The warmth and giving, the two becoming one. Sleeping all night in the arms of the man I loved. As bad as Richard had been for me, he had also taught me the sweetness of physical love. I might never have it again, might never trust any man enough to open up. Might not trust myself. "What about you?" I asked softly. "Are you headed back to New York?"

"Soon as the weather lets me." He ran a thumb around the rim of his cup. "Things are pretty good now. Both my daughters have come to work for me. I've got grandkids." His eyes lit up. "You should see them, two boys and a girl. The best part of my life."

His gaze met mine. Those familiar eyes, so dark and brown, those little crinkles at the corners. I felt drawn, like a sleepwalker, like Aurora to the spindle. No wonder his daughters had accepted him back into their lives. He'd been mesmerizing them since their births. "The one thing I really do regret," he said, his voice quavering slightly, "is that you gave up your dance career, that you felt you had to. I hate it for you."

My heart seemed to rattle in my chest and my face burned. I had a vision of the long gray tunnel I'd traveled. Not dancing, just torturing myself with the pale facsimile thereof. I'd accepted that long ago, even chose the penance I wanted to pay for Diana Gessler's death, but oh! how I ached. My hand automatically covered my eyes as I mumbled, "It's okay. And I do have the music, that's something."

366

"But not enough. It's a whole different language, isn't it? Don't you ever get tired of it? Don't you ever miss your mother tongue?"

I couldn't speak, could only stare at the table top, my cup of tea going cold. He reached out and took my hand. "Come with me, Amanda," he whispered. "We could still be happy. We're alike, you and I, full of hunger. . ."

I pulled my hand loose. "You never change."

"Why should I?" He leaned forward, speaking softly. "Stay with me. I'm not married any more. You're not a kid. It isn't too late. We could go to Europe, you could still dance"

Digging around in the bottom of my purse, I found a couple of dollar bills to throw on the table. As I did so, I remembered the small paper-wrapped package in my pocket.

"No. Not even for the ballet. There are some prices I'm not willing to pay." I stood and looped my purse strap over my shoulder, handing him the box containing the diamond pendant. "This belongs to you. Good-bye, Richard. I do wish you well." Holding out my hand, I thought it's done. Over. Somehow not quite satisfying but . . .

He ignored my gesture. "So you're just going to run off home to Mama, are you? Be a quitter, give up your dreams? I guess you're not so grown up as I thought." With both hands flat, palm-down on the table, he stared at me, his expression sharp, his eyes unreadable.

"She needs my help right now, and I owe her, big time. What do you know about it? What do you care?"

He threw some money on the table and eased his bulk out of the booth. Leaning toward me, he whispered, "I don't."

He turned and left, leaving me rattled in his draft, in the smack of cold air that whipped around him as he opened the door.

The impact was everything he intended. I backed up a step and sat abruptly on a corner of the booth bench. Wow. So much for a peaceful ending, but it was my own fault. I should have remembered, should have known he'd turn on me, snarling, as he had before. His stupid diamond pendant was still on the table and I resisted the impulse to hurl it across the room. Instead, I shoved it into my pocket and charged across the restaurant, pushing the door open with a stiff-armed attack that made the other customers jump. What was that line from the Rolling Stones song? Something about not being able to get what you want, but instead getting what you need. A good cold wake-up call, maybe. I couldn't, *shouldn't* romanticize him, and allow myself to believe he could change. Some people could, but not Richard. I slip-slid down the alley and rounded the corner to the parking lot.

"Lies. All of it lies, wasn't it." Richard's breath warmed my ear as he suddenly came up from behind. I dropped the damn keys and had to fish them out of a puddle of mud and ice before I could straighten and face him. His face was dark with anger and I remembered the day he spanked me. "You never loved me. It was all an act, wasn't it? God, I was a fool! I fell for your line, the poor little baby. *Oh Richard, my folks are divorcing. Oh Richard, my brother is dead. Oh poor me, I'm just a lonely little ragdoll.*" His voice rose in a falsetto, then dropped again. "When I think about all I gave up for you. Sacrificed for you. Damn it, I cared!"

I reeled back, feet churning in the snow, reaching for the truck. Richard pursued me, his face pressing toward mine. My hand skittered along the side of the pick-up, trying to grab something, to hold on, but only met the cold metal seam of sidewall and bedcover. Snow stung my face as I glanced around the parking lot. "I cared about you too," I insisted, "but it's over, *finis*!" There was no one in sight, just Richard coming after me step by step and I continued to back away, around the tailgate. "We've both been scarred by this, but don't make it any worse. For god's sake, Richard." I found something, the rear window latch, and curled my fingers over its cold, wet surface.

"I was your Daddy. Your *Daddy*." He grabbed my other wrist, shaking me. "You can't just walk away from that, no matter how hard you try." Flecks of spit gathered in the corners of his mouth and his face became almost purple with anger. "I gave you everything and you threw it back in my face. You goddamned cunt!" He hit me, slamming his gloved palm across the side of my head, above my ear. I nearly fell but his other hand, dragging on my wrist, pulled me upright. "I'll ruin you. I've still got pictures, other pictures, ones the papers never got. I'll destroy you, ruin any plans you might have—"

He aimed again and I ducked, twisting under his hand, breaking loose from his grip. I staggered back toward the driver's-side door, turning my ankle and going down on one knee. His blow reverberated in my brain as his words seared my consciousness. More pictures? Other pictures? That bastard. If he thought he could still control me . . . he rushed at me and I rose to meet him full up on my toes, shoulders back, chin raised. "No!" I said. "*Enough.*"

Richard froze. He stopped in mid-stride, his hand raised, and I could feel his energy, the phantom slap. It rushed over me like a blast of cold air, dissipated, and was gone. His gaze wavered and he let his hand drop to his side.

"I don't care," he said. "You asked for it." He began to weave on his feet, fingers shaking as he buttoned his coat and smoothed back his hair. "You're a pathetic little bitch and you'll never amount to anything. I know. I know you better than anyone else does, than any of your so-called friends."

Maybe he was right. Maybe I'd never do anything important in the world's eyes. Like that mattered. I swung the truck door open and climbed up into the seat. "You might know me better than anyone, Richard, but you don't understand me at all."

He grabbed the door edge, holding it open. "You think I'm a bastard, don't you? You think this mess was all my fault. Well, fuck you. I don't think so. I don't think I did anything wrong."

"That's where we differ then. Because I *know* I did."

I pulled out of the parking lot. Calm. Clear-headed, as though my mind had been snow-blasted clean. I couldn't see Richard in my rearview mirror, but I imagined him growing smaller and smaller, his face red with rage, his mouth bellowing obscenities. His figure kept dwindling down until it was nothing but a speck, blown away in a swirl of snow and then gone. Outta my life.

Funny, but I had thought he was gone long ago, buried under my mounds of guilt, silenced by time and distance. All those lonely days on the beaches in South Carolina, Florida, the Gulf Coast, I had grieved him out of my system, mourned the loss of my one experience with love—as twisted as it had been. I'd hardened my heart, I *thought*. Maybe all I'd really done was crystallize the pain, turn it to ice.

All I knew was it felt like my heart was melting now. Growing soft, making my chest feel warm and full, overflowing the narrow little cavity where it had hidden for so long. They didn't matter anymore, all those boundaries I'd set for myself. Whatever happened in the days ahead, somehow I'd handle it. My past didn't have to control my future, my life belonged to *me*.

At that thought, I pulled off the road into a grocery store parking lot and cut the motor. All around me, people were going about their business, getting back into the stream of things, recovering from the snow storm. Everything was going to be fine. I smiled at the thought of how astonished Mom would have been if she knew. I used to get so irritated whenever she said that, but now I saw it was true. Everything would be fine, because we'd *make* it that way. In the long run, we'd all survive—me, Mom, all of us. I wanted to phone her and say, hey, I get it at last. Guess I'm just a slow learner. It's all right, everything's okay. *We are going to be just fine.*

I ran my fingers up the curve of the steering wheel and rested my forehead on them. This was what it was about then, having faith, daring to hope. Believing in the possibility of change. I just hadn't known. I'd been too wrapped up in my own guilt and shame to see the new possibilities that life held, if I could just have the courage to see things through from one day until the next.

Tears slid down my cheeks but I brushed them away and restarted the engine. A Hispanic woman with two children hanging on her coat paused to jerk a shopping cart loose from the rack. I rolled down my window and called out, "Here, catch!" Her eyes opened wide as I tossed the small velvet box in the air and her hands automatically came up to receive it. Without another word, I backed out of my parking space and left.

Some decisions felt really good.

Chapter Twenty-Four

Amazing what a few good tears can do for the psyche. I mopped my face, ran a comb through my hair, put on fresh lipstick. First things first, I thought. Time to talk with Pete.

I phoned ahead. He didn't come to the phone himself but Jenny said to drive on over, he'd been at the studio but was on his way home. I could hear the baby crying in the background. "Sorry to be a problem," I said.

"It's no problem," Jenny replied, sounding exasperated. "Don't be so quick to assume what people are thinking." I hung up feeling apprehensive. Just because one set of problems was over, didn't mean a new set wasn't about to blossom.

Jenny smiled when she opened the door, holding the baby over one shoulder and motioning me into the kitchen. A pot of tea steeped on the counter and she offered me a cup. "Don't look so nervous," she chided me. "You're not the only one with a complicated past." She turned and pushed down on the waistband of her jeans. Just above her left buttock was a tattoo. I'd never seen it before—a curlicue of linked hearts and daggers and the legend, *Benny's Bitch*. She hitched her pants back up and shrugged. "We're all among the walking wounded, hon."

Pete arrived just then and I didn't have a chance to do more than give a grateful smile to Jen before she shooed the kids out of the family room, and left Pete and me alone to talk

He had a sheaf of papers in his hands and a pair of reading glasses sliding down his nose. We sat at the big table, kitty-corner from each other, and I warmed my hands on the mug of steaming tea.

"This is the deal," he said, frowning at the papers, avoiding my glance. "Tin Roof would like to sign us as a duo—"

"You mean you haven't already signed? Someone said you had."

Pete's eyebrows screwed up even higher. "No, I haven't signed anything yet. Who've you been talking to?" When I didn't answer, he continued. "Like I said, we're a duo. Lead guitar, co-songwriter—you're not just back-up. They're prepared to do a major marketing job on the CD. Tour. Promoting. All that jazz. They'll want to get started right away and you know, they mean it about controlling the publicity. Which means interviews, and they'll open it up about who you are." He put the papers down and leaned on his elbows, looking at me directly. No hint of a smile on his face. "It's their right, Connor. You gotta see it that way. They'd be putting a helluva lotta money into this thing, making a real commitment, and it's only fair to cooperate. You would retain some control over the situation—that is, you choose what you say. They're not going to script it for you, but they do want to know ahead of time what it will be." He paused a moment, gauging my reaction but I gave him none. "Anyhow, that's Plan A."

He took a deep breath, shuffled the papers some, cleared his throat. "There's also a Plan B. If you decide you can't deal with Plan A, then Tin Roof still wants to sign me as a solo artist." I felt tears start at the back of my eyes and I blinked a couple of times, forcing them down. "I want this, Connor," Pete whispered. "I want it so bad. Makes me feel like shit."

"No, it shouldn't."

"Well, it does." His gaze held mine. "This might be my last chance. How can I throw it away? They want me, they're a good label. How many times does an opportunity like this come along? Hell, even if their excitement is a little less, getting me by myself. Let's face it, I'm not so purty as I used to be." He managed a weak grin. "In some ways, the deal is even a little better. Not moneywise, but at least they'd gear back a bit, give me more time before they start recording. I'd have a chance to get things organized at the studio, be able to help Jenny with the baby, get my ass in gear. And you'd still be credited with the songwriting—we'd hold the copyrights. You'd get a share of the publishing money, they can't have any say over that. But the downside is, you can't perform on the CD and you can't even play in a back-up band with me on the road. It's all or nothing with them."

Pete leaned back in his chair, running a hand through his hair and giving me a rueful look. "Can't say I'd enjoy breaking in a new partner. You and me, we get along. Some of those other monkeys out there, man, they'd break your heart. Good musicians, maybe, but assholes. I respect whatever decision

375

you feel you gotta make, but damn, I hope you'll consider signing. I feel like we're just getting started. We could be great." He drummed his fingers on the table and added, "You don't owe that joker any loyalty, you know. And sooner or later, if you want to stay in the music business, someone will find out about your past. Why worry about it? People forgive and forget."

"Do they?" I thought about it a minute. "Maybe they forgive. Sometimes. But they never truly forget. Even if they think kindly of you, they don't forget." I struggled to explain myself. "It's like this woman I knew at home. Anne Carricker. A friend of Mom's. Her little girl died of leukemia. Now, everyone in town knew about this and so they all treated Anne like she was made of glass. Trying to be compassionate, I guess, but they're also making the assumption that she *needed* to be treated with care. Maybe she'd rather they just forget about it. Let her get on with her life, not remind her of her tragedy every time they speak in those gentle tones. Because *they* don't forget, *she* can't forget. I don't even know if she wants to, but—oh, I'm not saying it well." I shook my head, helpless. "I'm just saying, even if people don't *want* to remember, they do. They can't help it."

"So? So what if they remember? Don't you think people admire this woman even more when they realize she survived that tragedy? And even if they don't—Shoot, life is a big enough challenge just dealing with the things I *can* control, let alone the ones I can't."

I looked at his familiar rumpled face and thought about all the good times we'd had. Working together, laughing, getting so involved in some song we were trying out. I loved the creative end of it—exploring riffs, tweaking lyrics, just jamming on a caffeine-fueled high, in love with the music. Performing had never been my favorite aspect. The solos I'd sung, the moments of holding the audience in my hand—for me, they weren't worth the sense of peace and security that I got from staying in the background. Just as in dance, I was happiest in the *corps de ballet*, not the solo part. Belonging to something, that's what mattered most. And Pete still wanted me to belong.

His eyes were on me, watching, waiting for my decision. I couldn't say yes to Plan A. Forcing myself to sit through some stupid interview, talking about Richard, no. I couldn't do that. Profit off that experience? No way. It felt wrong from every angle, and not even good for the music. So much for Plan A. As for Plan B, the thought made me ill. Give up everything I'd worked for, say good-bye to Pete, lose two dear friends. I wouldn't kid myself. If I walked away from this, it'd be over. Pete and Jenny would be too busy to have time for me other than a moment snatched here or there. I'd be back in the cold once again and Pete would be stuck finding a new partner, going through labor pains at a time when he needed complications the least.

Plan A or Plan B? One choice seemed as bad as the other and I wondered, did it always have to be this way? Could I make a decision that was the best one for me *and* for my friends? Was that ever possible?

It hit me. Hot damn, I *was* a slow learner. Like falling dominoes, it all fell into place. Or out of place. Whatever, big

Stonehenge-size dominoes were falling, *blam, blam, blam*, and I almost laughed as they hit the ground. The idea seemed nearly too big to grasp but, oh man, what a freakin' deal it could be.

"I can't agree to the interviews, Pete. I won't have Richard Gessler's name tied to our music, the very idea is gross. And I don't want to give up what we have either." I smiled and placed my hand over his. "So Plan A and Plan B are out the window. But you know what? I've just had a thought about Plan C."

The snowstorm ended at last. Within a day, the plows had cleared at least one lane in each direction on most major roads, and the day after that, Mom decided it was time to go home. "There's so much to do," she said, giving me a hug as we waited for Sissy and Travis in front of their hotel. "I'm supposed to talk with Mason and meet with your Dad. Oh, a million details. And I've made a decision too. I'm going to volunteer with the Color Guard again. See how it feels, get involved a bit. You made me realize I've been wrapping myself in a little cocoon, staying in limbo until the situation with Josh cleared up. Trying not to feel anything too deeply." She smiled and brushed my hair back from my forehead. "I don't want to desert my little old ladies at the retirement center, but maybe it's time to get involved at the high school again. The Color Guard is getting into the competition season and, Lord knows, they always need some volunteers. It'll be fun. Keep me busy."

"Not too busy, I hope. Remember, I'm coming down for a visit soon. And we'll go to visit Josh together." We hugged and turned to watch Sissy and Travis maneuver their luggage through the lobby door. Sissy's luggage mostly, a matched trio in green brocade. Travis had only one battered-looking leather bag, but Sissy traveled in style. "Think you got enough stuff there, Sis?" I asked, nodding my head at the numerous shopping bags.

"Nope. Couldn't get that spa tub in my suitcase. I sure hate leaving that behind." She grinned and raised one eyebrow. "You just gonna stand there and watch?"

I moved forward to help load the trunk but Travis waved me off. "Better let me figure this out myself," he said. "Some of Sissy's bags have breakable items."

She nodded. "I got one of those snow globes with the city skyline. Thought I'd let the kids see Philadelpia the way I did. And I found the cutest little outfit for Teri." She opened one bag and began pulling out a frilly something in green, inviting Mom to get a closer look. They moved a few steps away and Sissy made an awful grimace at me over her shoulder, indicating I should go talk with Travis. Good old Sissy, she'd have made a great stage manager or maybe a Mother Superior, if only she'd been Catholic.

It didn't look promising. Travis had that stiff-backed thing going, like he got when he and Sissy bickered over something. I watched him swing the suitcases into the open trunk, arranging things with precision so nothing would shift during the drive. Sissy's precious snow globe was packed with care and the mountain of luggage dwindled rapidly.

I stepped closer. "Listen, Trav, I wanted to thank you. For bringing Mom and, well, everything. You've been great."

He glanced at me over his shoulder and reached for another bag. "I didn't do anything special."

"I want to thank you for that, too." He turned then, a rueful smile on his face and I tentatively smiled back. "You didn't play hero this time. Thanks. I needed to deal with it myself." Although Pete had nearly blown his top when I informed everyone about my final meeting with Richard, Travis remained silent, just nodding as I told my tale. "I'll be coming home in a few weeks. To see Josh. And get things started."

"Good. That's good." He stowed the final item and glanced over at Sissy and Mom, now studying with apparent absorption the display in a travel agent's window.

"Um, there's something else," I added with my usual lack of eloquence. "I'm sorry I've been . . . kinda standoffish. It's just that—"

"That's okay. I crowded you. I'm sorry."

"No, *I'm* sorry." We both had to laugh. "Jeez. We're getting awful good at this apologizing stuff." I rose up on my toes, feeling the flex in my calf muscles, and rocked back on my heels again. Took a deep breath. "This has been a hell of a two weeks, you know? Ever since Christmas . . . and I'm feeling really, oh, bombarded. So much coming at me, so many things to decide. I can't decide about us right now."

"That's okay."

"No, it's not." I tried to find the words to say what I meant. "You and I .... We do mean something to each other. I know that, but exactly what, I'm not sure. I mean, jeez, I haven't even been very nice to you."

380

He grinned. "I know. I'm beginning to get peeved."

"Don't laugh! I'm trying to have a serious moment here!" In spite of my words, I couldn't help smiling too, but we both sobered as I continued. "I don't even have a clue about what problems you might have. Never asked. That's not right between friends, is it? Who do you go to for help? Where do you turn when things are bad? I wonder about that."

Travis looked away and cleared his throat. When he finally glanced back at me, I said "I don't want to repeat old mistakes and go rushing into something too quickly. I'm . . . I'm not sure if there's any hope for us. I come with a lot of baggage."

His gaze met mine, then he looked over at the neatly-packed open trunk and a little twitch appeared at the corner of his mouth. "That's okay. I'm not scared of baggage." Travis eased the trunk lid down and shoved the keys in his pocket. "So what do you want to do?"

"I thought maybe when I come home, we could get together. You know, casually." I suddenly felt embarrassed. "Go out on a date or something."

"A date?" He grinned. "You mean like bowling? Miniature golf?"

I laughed and swatted him on the arm. "Well? I never dated much. Seems like it would be a good place to start."

Travis caught my hand in his. "Okay," he said, his face growing serious. "When you come home, I'll ask you for a date."

I nodded, too wrought up to speak. Sissy and Mom appeared miraculously at my side, chattering loudly about travel routes and gas stations and the best place to get a meal. "No McDonalds," Sissy brayed. "Or Kentucky Fried Chickens either. I want real food, darn it. One of those truck stops with the never-empty coffee pots and waitresses named Mabel and chocolate cream pies." She made an awkward lunge at me, half-hug, half-wrestling takedown hold. "Come home soon," she whispered. "You booger."

I hugged her back. "I will. And thanks for everything." Then I had a hug for Mom and a quick, shy kiss on the cheek for Travis. Sissy winked and I had to look away. Some moments are just too much to stand. They drove off, waving, and I watched as the car disappeared into traffic. Next to the hotel entrance, a bright red cardinal perched on a hawthorn branch, pecking at berries. I looked at the blackened gunk of snow piled up on the curb and realized how fast the city was recovering. Pretty soon, it would back to normal. This would be the storm by which every other snow storm would be measured. It would be the benchmark, the record-breaker, the big, big news until some other winter storm came in and blew the hell out of all the old statistics and then this one would be forgotten. But not by me.

Spring came so quickly that year, my winter sweaters were still drying on the line. On Easter weekend, I flew down to North Carolina and on Sunday, after church services were over, we gathered in Mom's back yard to have a cook-out. I watched Josh playing softball with Sissy's kids, all of them screaming with laughter when the neighbor's dog ran off with the paper plate that was first base.

Mason Kennedy watched with me, leaning back in his lawn chair, lacing his fingers together across his flat stomach. "You ready for Tuesday?" he asked, flicking at a ladybug crawling up his trouser leg.

"I guess. Not sure *how* to be ready, since I don't want to use canned answers." I folded my legs lotus-style, soaking in warmth from the old quilt spread in the sun. "Nervous, of course."

"Don't be. This is just a preliminary hearing and the judge is Merrill Young. He's one of the good guys. Make a point of mentioning how you've worked to improve yourself, taken classes, all that. Don't dwell on the homeless period."

"I was never homeless, Mason," I said, glancing from him to Mom, her eyes bright with laughter over something Sissy had said. "Just temporarily too foolish to go there." He nodded, his own expression softening as he looked at Mom.

The mouth-watering scent of grilled chicken, sweet Vidalia onions and red peppers lifted on the breeze. Sissy and Mom bickered good-humoredly over the best way to place the shishkebob skewers on the grill. Dad pitched to Gideon while Sissy's husband, Dave, played catcher, and Josh stood on the old dishtowel that substituted for first base. He swayed from side to side, ready to head for second and Teri crouched at third, pounding her fist into her glove and calling *batter-batter-batter*. Travis stood in the outfield, near the crepe myrtle. There was no denying it—the sun gleamed on his hair and I still felt that old zing. Next week we planned to take his boat out for the first test-drive of the season.

I could feel my hair frizzing as the humidity rose, going into tiny little corkscrews at my temples and nape. "It's bizarre to be back here," I said to Mason, shaking my head at the wonder of it all.

"But good, I hope. After all, you'll be seeing a lot more of this place, as your plans go ahead."

"That's bizarre, too. Having plans." I wrapped my arms around my knees, and looked sideways at Mason. "It's so ironic, after all this time vowing never to speak about Richard Gessler and here I am, preparing to open up in court."

"It's for a good purpose. Josh needs that security, knowing that if anything happens to Steve, you'll be there to serve as guardian. And through you, he'll also have access to your Mom. I take my hat off to both of you."

We watched as Gideon swung his bat. The ball flew into the air and Gideon took off for first base while Teri headed home. Travis moved in slow-motion, as though he was underwater, and Josh made it safely to third base.

"Word is leaking out," I commented. "Mom's received calls. The Charlotte Observer. Channel Nine News. I know it's supposed to be a closed court session, but . . ." I pushed the thought away. "Gil Benningham from the Painter's Creek Chronicle wants an exclusive."

"Tell Gil to take a flying leap. No, better yet, let me tell him. He was part of that wolf pack years ago, yapping at your heels." Mason straightened his legs as Mom called us to eat, unfolding like a carpenter's ruler. I joined Sissy at the picnic table and long wooden benches set out in the afternoon sun. She waved away a gnat intent on dive-bombing the potato salad and pointed out seats to the kids as Mom brought over a plate stacked with cornbread. Josh teased Teri with one of the helium balloons that made the centerpiece. Already summer freckles were popping out on his nose and sun-bleached streaks shone in his hair. We held hands and bowed our heads as Mom said grace. Ice clinked in the tea pitcher and daffodils did the Wave over by the fence.

In June, Pete would fly to New York to begin the recording process. I would run the studio as his new business partner and, thanks to Travis's marketing suggestions, we had a full schedule. Jenny would record with him, exactly as it always should have been, and I'd keep things going while they were on the road. In between gigs, we'd still be able to work together on songwriting. By initiating this suit, I'd be outing myself, but I hoped to limit my statements to the courtroom. The right to refuse any public interviews was mine. And if the papers picked up on the guardianship case, better for the focus to be on that than on Pete's music.

However the court case went, I was committed. To Pete, to Josh, to my family. My stomach tightened each time I thought about the hearing, but I had made up my mind to go ahead. There were no guarantees that I'd win, but heck, there were no guarantees in anything. This was the right thing to do. Josh was my brother and that was that.

Mom finished the blessing with a final "We thank You for this beautiful day," and we began passing plates, serving food. I helped myself to salad and passed the bowl to Travis, who passed it to Dad, who handed it on to Mason. On and on, around the table.

"Hey everybody, guess this." Josh stood up, waving his corn-on-the-cob by one plastic holder. Mom's hands came up, ready to catch it if the cob went flying loose. Josh grinned, displaying his snaggly new front teeth. "What did the coke machine say to the wrinkled old dollar bill?" Before anyone could answer, he took a deep breath and shouted out, "You don't make any sense! Get it? The dollar bill doesn't make any *cents!*" He giggled, overcome with his own wit, and I couldn't help thinking what a changed boy he was. Earlier in the day, he'd about talked my ear off, describing with elaborate gestures the visit he'd made with Dad to an airfield.

Travis raised an eyebrow. "Why does this seem so familiar?" he asked under cover of the dutiful laughter produced by everyone else. "Sounds ominously like a Mark-joke to me."

"No, this actually made sense. Or rather, cents." I grinned. "Then again, there might be something in the DNA . . ."

"Hey, I never told a Mark-joke in my life," my dad said in an aggrieved tone of voice. He glanced across the table at Mom and winked.

"That's what you think," she laughed. "And don't look at me, I'm completely in the clear on this one."

Josh climbed up on the bench, the better to address his audience. By this point, we were all regarding him with a sense of fatalism. "I got another one," he crowed. "Even better. What's all that green yucky stuff on the cafeteria lunch tray? Give up?" He couldn't wait to tell us the punch line. "Some say it's spinach, but it's not. Get it? It's *snot*." He nearly fell down laughing. "Oh," he sighed, "I crack myself up."

Travis nudged my knee with his and I snorted, trying to cover up with a napkin. It was too much, it really was. My heart took off like a little bird, flying up over the backyard in a surge of joy. Whatever the next day brought, this day was worth having. I'd remember that.

"Gideon, look at you, you're covered in barbecue sauce! Were you raised in a barn? Where are the napkins?" Nobody responded to Sissy's questions. They were all too busy talking themselves.

"I need more lemonade."

"I got another joke, listen to this. What did the pickle fork say to the other pickle fork?"

"Hey, that's my glass you're drinking out of."

"Who's hogging all the potato salad?"

"Jeez, you buy 'em shoes, you send 'em to school, and for what? For what, I ask?"

"I *said*, what did the pickle fork say—"

"Mom, Teri took my brownie!"

I pushed my worries about the interview and its aftermath into a cubbyhole at the back of my mind. Tuesday would have to take care of itself. I was happy to be right where I was—in this place, with these people—and despite any evidence to the contrary, I really believed that nothing could hold me down.

Acknowledgements

* * *

A big thank you to:
My children – Joanna, Kate, Rebecca and Dan – who've supported my writing habit all these years, to my sisters – Lori, Debra, Kim, Jacki and Linda – who never laughed at my aspirations, to Michael Mendershausen, who exchanged critiques with me as I tried to make this book as professional as possible. May his novel, A Night Devoid of Stars, live long and prosper! I also thank my long-time writing teacher and mentor, Barbara Kidd Lawing. Her Monday-afternoon classes gave me courage. And again, I particularly thank my husband, Matt, who encouraged me to think outside the box. His constant support is a major blessing in my life.

Carolyn Steele Agosta is the author of over 35 internationally-published short stories and three novels. She graduated from the University of North Carolina at Charlotte and lives with her husband in North Carolina. Her website is www.carolynagosta.com.

Look for more books from Carolyn Steele Agosta soon.

Cover Art by Alina Solovyova-Vincent (front) and Diane39 (back).